Something Very Like Murder

Something Very Like Murder

Frank Kuppner

Polygon
Edinburgh

First published by
Polygon
22 George Square
Edinburgh

Set in 11 on 12.5 Goudy
Printed and bound in Great Britain by Short Run Press Ltd, Exeter.

A CIP record is available.

ISBN 0 7486 6181 6

The Publisher acknowledges subsidy from

THE SCOTTISH ARTS COUNCIL

towards the publication of this volume.

I will take every last one of these clouds home with me.
I will keep them in a safe place until someone calls for them.
What would be the point of it if it went on for ever?
There would be no mornings, if morning did not pass.

M & L

T his is the last full day of my mother's 72nd year of life. Seventy-two years does not seem to me to be a remarkably long life. And five months ago she was still alive. Only just, perhaps; but still alive. This time last year, although she was ill, it did not genuinely occur to us that this might be the last birthday she would live through. But it was. It turned out all the same that it was.

Nearly two months ago, there arrived—though exactly where it arrived it might be difficult to say—my father's 81st birthday. He lived through that. He is still alive. The seats she used to sit in are still in this house—in fact, I am standing beside one just at this moment (the back of my left thigh from time to time leans gently against it)—but already there are headstones marking the two graves just past hers, of people who died in this small town over a month later than she did. Those stones have appeared in the last few days and the place no longer seems as private as once it was. It no longer seems so appropriate a resting-place for her.

However, this existence here, one's own little existence, such as it is, continues. At least, I take it that that's what's happening. One tries not to be dogmatic. Some years ago I wrote a book, *A Very Quiet Street*, (published 1989) which mixed discussion of a famous Glasgow murder of 1908 (usually known as the Oscar Slater Case) with a little autobiography, excusable since I had been born and had grown up into adult immaturity very near to the locus of the crime. I was, needless to say, rather hurt by how little the previous commentators on these scandalous occurrences had made of this obviously quite staggering coincidence. But such is life. Or whatever it is.

While I was writing this book, I met someone who was research-ing the same case for a successful English literary student of crime; someone who was prepared to investigate, to pry things out. Someone unlike me, in other words. This book has not yet ap-peared, as far as I know. Of course, I might just have missed it. But a few weeks ago—actually, just over three weeks ago (on the 22nd of July)—I discovered quite by chance in a secondhand bookshop a recent study by this author concerning the celebrated Scottish criminologist, William Roughead. It had come out two years previously, and from a Scottish publisher at that but I had not had even a suspicion of its existence until then. I bought it at one-third of its original price, which much pleased me. But had it been any dearer at all, I would probably have had to let it go to someone else. It was, I believe, while researching Roughead for this very book that its author had had his attention caught by the Slater case (which he would certainly have already heard of) and was intrigued by its numerous and particular possibilities.

This book then contains two thick files of material which the author thought it wiser not to try to work into the main text proper. One of these is a sequence of brief accounts of murder cases—in-cluding the Slater case. (The person murdered in that case was an old woman called Marion Gilchrist.) But it was another which caught my eye this time—one I had not heard of before. It had taken place precisely in the ten-minutes-across area which lay between my childhood home in West Princes Street, and the spot where my father's first shop was situated—the first shop he owned—at the eastern end of North Woodside Road, southern side. (He only ever had one small shop, but there were three locations in all.) The district has more or less vanished, radically restructured some twenty or so years ago. But by then we had moved away.

One or two people, perhaps even three, have asked me in an interested way whether I thought I might ever write another book around a real-life murder, but I had always assumed that I wouldn't. It seemed to me to be grossly unlikely that I would ever find another such process which involved me as the Slater case had done. And yet, entirely to my surprise, this obscure story which I had never heard of, and which I so casually discovered, had the same sort of effect on me.

What, then, is it about? Well, in brief, it concerns a young man of twenty or so, whose mother had died a few months previously, and who was spending his life alone with his father, as far as domestic arrangements went, having taken over the housekeeping chores. His mother had died at the beginning of the year (1929), and, towards the end of the year (November 4th), the father was discovered lying on the floor of their small, definitely not affluent (excuse me: I have just had to go through to another room, to ask my sister, who is usually in Aberdeen, 'What is a word for "well-off", sounding like "effluent"?'—for my brain refused to work properly for a moment) kitchen; lying, I repeat, on the floor of his small kitchen, with his head bashed in, and his blood splattered all over the place. As the priest says, you neither know the minute nor the hour.

The sole discussion of the case that I as yet know of is William Roughead's own article, 'The Edge of Circumstance', in the June 1930 issue of the *Juridical Review*, a Scots Law quarterly. This I promptly photocopied in Glasgow University Library a couple of days after discovering the book. I may discover more about the case, I suppose, but I think I ought to make it clear that I don't particularly intend moving heaven and earth with the effort. At the moment, my plan is merely to embroider Roughead's account, regularly straying into areas of personal reminiscence and the discussion of other famous (or not) cases which come to mind for one reason or another. Indeed, so unhealthily pronounced is my bias for imaginative investigation over practical investigation that I am not entirely sure where it is I should go to if I did want to find out what else, if anything, there is to know about the primary facts, either of the case itself or of the principals involved. I suspect that this is the sort of thing that other people pay researchers to do.

(6.30–14th August)

I t is a matter of delightfully simple arithmetic that on my mother's 39th birthday, 15th August 1960, I was only nine years old. Obviously, hordes of the things I remember must have happened in that year, but I don't think I can specifically link anything to it. Even recalling the fact that I went from primary to secondary school in August 1962, and working back from that, seems to do nothing to help. My second-last classroom? My third-last classroom? Which were they? (Though I presume they are still there, in a building less than five minutes walk away from the room where I have lived for almost twenty years. Every morning—well, most mornings—I hear the same bell ring again, and more or less different children playing and shouting. As to who might have lived there while I was playing and shouting . . . .)

So my head, like almost everyone else's, is full of unsorted memories. I do recall, at the start of 1961, visiting my granny's house in Buccleuch Street, fairly nearby, and lifting up a newspaper in order to demonstrate to the amazed adults that, in some scripts at least, the year 1961 read the same upside down as right way up. I think I had lately seen someone point this out on television, and it struck me as being of mighty importance. I don't remember anyone mentioning the 6th of June 1966 (6.6.66) though someone doubtless must have done. We were still in West Princes Street then. But I do remember the new landlord's agent, in my present room, commenting on the impending 7.7.77. I am still there, and he is still the landlord's agent. Sixteen years back. As 1961 was sixteen years back from then. But of 1960, nothing—unless, perhaps, it was that moment of someone alerting me to the great truth about the number of the year next coming up. I dare say I bought my parents horrible little presents for their birthdays and I dare say (I certainly hope so) that each was moved by it. But that was just as full a year as any other—domestic crises, domestic joys, domestic hopes. Dad, turned forty-eight, carrying on the endless struggle. In fact, since it was a leap year, it was slightly fuller than most others, no doubt.

My mother was always of a remote, inaccessible age to us then; one that we ourselves would obviously never reach. Yet now, here I am, well over three years older than she was on that day. What was it like when I was thirty-nine? Last of the years before the Great Divide, when one turns forty. Not that I've noticed the slightest difference. 1990. A *Very Quiet Street* had come out the year before. Both my parents had read the book—particularly unusual for my Dad, who read very little beyond the newspapers. It was early in 1990 that I seriously re-engaged with classical antiquity, largely ignored since my teens. Diogenes Laertius, bought in February. And in May, at a sort of party in a friend's house, I talked to a couple of actual, living Greeks—one from Athens; and one, if you don't mind, from Arcadia. Then we all walked together to St George's Road. The famous words, *Et In Arcadia Ego*, I too am in Arcadia, were of course exchanged. But *Et In St George's Road* I once was too, and when it was the *real* St George's Road.

And it was on that very day, as some memoranda allowed me to work out, on the evening of which I was talking to Greeks in Glasgow, that my mother in Largs spotted a few most unwelcome drops of blood on her underwear, and that was the start of it. A sequence of almost unbroken troubles, which led to her death not quite three years later. Not that she told me until some weeks afterwards, having no wish to alarm me unduly. It was only a day or two before she was to be admitted to hospital that she rang me up. 'I thought I was going to see out my time without needing any operations,' she said, without making a fuss; 'but there it is.' All this, however, has rather crept up on me, and I think I ought perhaps to double back to my original idea.

All I really wished to do was to refer to an event which happened on her 39th birthday, in 1960, the 15th of August—which is the Feast of the Assumption of the Blessed Virgin Mary in the liturgical calendar. This assumption was once taken literally; but now that it is generally held to be impossible, it is usually interpreted as being only a symbol—though of what is not entirely clear. Her name was Mary too, but she had only four children. Enough, certainly; but most probably fewer than the number produced by the earlier one, the legendary virgin. (Five or six are named in the Bible, I think. One of them became quite astonishingly famous, all things considered.)

So, twelve days ago, in Edinburgh, in (where else?) a second-hand bookshop, I chanced upon a couple of very interesting volumes which I just finished reading three or four hours ago. (I read them in tandem.) They were collections of brief descriptions of real-life murders—nearly 400 of them in all—arranged chronologically, in terms of days of the year. A double diary of death, no less. Curiously enough, the Willox murder, the one I intend to discuss, is not included.

But among those which are is one from August 15th 1960 that I had never heard of before. Now: where did I put the book? Excuse me. Hmm. Beneath that blue and white shirt on the chair in the nearer back corner of the room. Let me see. I read about this one for the first time only today—just before noon, I think. My father is in bed, ill, (he has a heart condition), and it wasn't until the afternoon that I was left entirely to my own devices for a while. I realize that this may not interest you. But if it doesn't, then I think you really ought to try to be a bit more sensitive in future.

Anyway, on that day, in Wolverhampton, an English town renowned for its sheer physical beauty, a forty-eight year-old woman called Margaret Brindley was found, battered to death, in a house where she was living with another man, having left her husband some time before. She had been beaten to death by yet another man who lived in the same house. My source says that he did this with a shoe (which sounds barely possible to me) after being insulted when he asked her to repay some money which she owed him. One presumes there must have been a bit more to it than this; although, even so, one finds oneself rather wondering just what sort of insult it might have been, to draw down such a ferocious response on the maker of it.

Now, this murdered woman had a daughter, also called Margaret Brindley. (Which name, I have to say, is curiously like that of Margaret Bradley, my Aunty Peggy, who died in September 1990, when I was thirty-nine. She is buried in Largs, now fairly near to my mother, who had put a gravestone up for her. The inscription on this runs: 'In Loving Memory of my Sister, Margaret Maxwell Bradley, 1912–1990.' That is all. No mention of who the person is, whose sister this was. Both had cancer. Peggy never married.)

At nineteen, this younger Margaret Brindley had met up with a Turkish Cypriot charmer who had persuaded her, doubtless through friendly words, to take to the streets. However, after a few months, she became pregnant, which seems to have lethally low-ered her worth in the eyes of her admirer. So he battered her with a metal bar until her face was unrecognisable. Thus we have a case of both mother and daughter being violently killed in quite sepa-rate incidents. In fact, now that I look at it closely, the daughter was murdered some eight months or so before the mother, who presumably had still not come to terms with the loss.

Both men were given a life sentence, although capital punish-ment was then still an available sanction (1958/59). The extenu-ating circumstances are, to say the least, not immediately obvious. Both men may well still be alive. The one who killed the daughter would not yet be even sixty. I can't pretend it comforts me much to think that they might still be out there. But, be that as it may, through the wall the clock in the living-room strikes nine in the evening. I am sure that fine, reliable old clock was bought at some point in the 1950s. From a shop called the Royal Stores, I can remember Mum more than once telling me. I can't remember a time when we didn't have it in West Princes Street. A rough calculation suggests that it must by now have struck over two million separate sounds.

(9.01–14th August)

erhaps it was even striking when either (or both) of those murders was committed. If we go forward another three years, and about 200,000 boings of that clock, to my mother's own 42nd birthday (15 August 1963) we stumble upon what is perhaps an even more remarkable case. On that day—another inexpensive present, perhaps; another group circling round her singing, 'Happy Birthday to You'; another absence of memory—a sixty-four-year-old recluse was discovered, lying dead in his farm, near a Cornish village which seems to have been named after a Roman Emperor. He showed multiple injuries: a shattered skull, gashed throat, fractured jaw, and much besides. The place had been ransacked and looted, but a very considerable sum had been missed, and still lay there, undisturbed.

The two murderers were found with relative ease: a pair of young men, one of whom claimed that the other had gone berserk, and that the killing had been in no way part of his own plan. The other, according to his counsel, sounds to have been suffering from pretty well classic schizophrenic symptoms. Both were found guilty, and both were hanged—their offence being apparently of a different order of gravity from merely murdering a pregnant woman whom one had turned to prostitution, or from beating a middle-aged woman to death with a shoe because she had made an insulting remark. I have to confess I don't quite see this myself.

Already, there has been a worrying amount of battering to death in this work. But what gives that particular case its interest is the history of the victim. A deserter in the First World War, he had been sheltered by his family for thirty-nine years (it had to be thirty-nine years!), given out as dead, ever more dead; until at last an amnesty was declared, and he was able to crawl out hesitant and blinking into the light. Nine years earlier, he had actually taken part in the move to a new house, hiding beneath a pile of clothing in a cart. So; this is possible too, is it? To live for nearly four adult decades, wholly unknown except to very close family? What would have happened if the parents had died earlier, and left him hiding alone? He left various large sums buried on the farm, with keys to their locations in a diary written in Esperanto. But of course. The two murderers managed to find £4. This reminds me of a celebrated American case, but I have probably already strayed too far from my intended ambit.

(10.49–14th August)

So, going back to my original case, there is a crucial date to keep in mind: 23rd of January 1929, when a woman surnamed Willox, living at 79 Grove Street (a tenement building in a rather poor district of the city) died. I don't think even her first name is given in Roughead's account. Nor is her age. Since, in November, when the father is killed, he is fifty-five (*or is he?*), and the son is twenty (he appears to be an only son), we may, I think, assume that the dead woman was in her early fifties.

She seems to have been ill for some time before she died. Is that all that is known? Is it even known for certain? You might think a little more would have been said about her. I expect that, even in Grove Street itself, in 1928 or 1929, there were quite a few people who had died of natural causes without seeing their fiftieth birthday. Presumably one of the many lethal, debilitating ailments which carried off so many in the slums or the poor districts carried off her too. I expect some office somewhere must still have the salient facts. It looks as if she married fairly late, had one child (*no, not quite*), and either couldn't, or wouldn't, produce any more.

Incidentally, eighteen years earlier, on 23rd January 1911 (which was seventeen months before my father was subjected to the huge initial shock and insult of being born in West Prussia), there occurred in New York the strange murder of a popular author of the time. This was David Graham Phillips, whose last work was among the bestsellers of that day. Alas, a rich thirty year-old Philadelphian neurotic somehow formed the idea that one of the less attractive figures in *The Fashionable Adventures of Joshua Craig* had been based on his adored sister. So what, even if it had, but this was pure fantasy on his part. Nonetheless, this inspired personage travelled to Manhattan and confronted the unlucky author as he was leaving his apartment. Thus does one come across one's public. Instantly, without words being exchanged, he shot Phillips five times. He then turned the gun on himself, with a peculiarly carefree (and accurate) cry of 'Here I go!' And indeed, he shot himself once and went. Phillips, however, lingered for several hours, before succumbing; having made the memorable remark, 'I can fight one bullet, but not five'. On learning what had happened, the assailant's parents explained what had been going on. Presumably they had heard their son voice his dark suspicions, too obviously absurd to be seriously responded to. Whether the news of why he had been killed reached the poor author before he died, I do not know. I suppose not. As an explanation, it is not an obvious improvement on ignorance. Does one want to know such things under such circumstances? Does it help? Is it an eventuality we should spend much time in contemplating? How shall we ever know? But, however ridiculous the motives are, the bullets they fire can be fatal. Knowledge is power, but a bullet-proof vest has its uses too.

I remember I happened to be visiting my parents' house here in Largs for a few days, when the news broke that Rajiv Gandhi, the Prime Minister of India, had been assassinated. Someone, they said, had presented him with a bouquet of flowers, and the concealed bomb was then detonated. Mum remarked, as far as I can remember, that it must have been a horrible way to die. I replied to her, 'but surely he would have known nothing about it. He would not even have known for sure that he was being assassinated or even that he was dying. He might just have heard the start of an explosion, a loud sound, but that would be all.' She thought about this for a second and then said, with a wry smile, something like, 'It's a strange business, isn't it?'

Actually, he may have known even less, for I recall reading later that the bomb was simply detonated as he passed nearby, and that the story about a primed bouquet was only an imaginative early surmise. I'm not sure. But during the last few weeks of her life (she had a spreading, inoperable cancer, although the immediate cause of death was heart failure), my mother more than once would break a silence to say to me, sitting nearby, 'It's strange, isn't it?' And I replied, 'It certainly is,' or, 'Yes, Mum, it's strange'. We were extremely close at those moments. Though not only at those moments.

(7.18–15th August)

T hus, in January 1929, a family occupying a very small flat, consisting of a room and kitchen, with a minuscule lobby and a w.c. all to themselves (a progressive touch), on the upper floor of 79 Grove Street, Glasgow—each floor containing three such flats, plus a fourth which boasts an extra room—is deprived of a crucial member. At this time the son is still in work, with a yacht-outfitting firm—rather a rarefied line of business, I would have thought—and earning sixteen shillings a week. Not a princely sum even then, but at the height of the Depression every contribution must have helped.

He is described (by Roughead for one) as being slim, young-looking for his age (born 15th May 1909—a tiny bump when Marion Gilchrist was murdered and still a foetus when Oscar Slater was sentenced to hang, May the 6th), well educated and 'exceptionally intelligent for his years and station'. From a later personal encounter, Roughead also terms him 'a well-spoken, pleasant-mannered lad, of a rather effeminate type'. Clearly, whatever his manners might have been, he is not your stereotypical hard man from the mean streets. Indeed, I do find myself wondering just how much weight to give to the distinctive phrase 'of a rather effeminate type'. I suspect it might well have needed something fairly striking to elicit such mild distaste from Roughead.

A week after his mother's death—which, however long it might have been in coming, must still have brought about a huge up-heaval in domestic atmosphere and circumstance—the son, it seems, freely gave up his job in order to, in effect, look after the diminished home. His father's pay was 50/3, fifty and a quarter shillings, per week. Just over two and a half pounds sterling. He also received a war pension of half a crown—2/6—two and a tanner—12½ new pence. (I grew up with the old money. Real money, in other words. Indeed, it occurs to me even as I write that I must have been about the same age as he was then when the bizarre and unconvincing new coinage came in.) Thus, with the loss of the son's sixteen bob, quite a sizeable bit of the domestic income seems to have been voluntarily given up. This is odd. Though I am assuming that the son would not have kept, or would not have been allowed to keep, very much of his own pay for himself.

Perhaps the father could as soon have started speaking fluent Japanese, as have known how to clean a toilet or cook a meal. Perhaps he knew how to, but felt it was beneath his dignity. Or perhaps he felt that being out at work pretty well all day and every day was enough for any one man. (*It's too much for one man* was *something my own father used to say, according to my sister.*) But it's still a little surprising just how smoothly all this seems to have devolved upon the son—who presumably, for his part, had to learn all of it, or most of it, for himself.

My own father over-extended himself and his already compro-mised heart last Monday, probably while trying to solve a minor problem with the washing-machine. Inactivity is alien to him, and he has a hard time listening to advice. It is now the following Monday afternoon and we are fairly imminently expecting the arrival of a sort of itinerant cardiac specialist who is in the area today. My father's doctor has arranged that he should look in here to see what's what. While catering recently to the patient's re-quests, I myself tried my hand for the first time at making an omelette for him last Tuesday; and then scrambled eggs for the first time last Saturday, the day when I also started to write this, as it happens. He seems to love the scrambled eggs. Myself, I am rather taken with the omelettes. I find that I am simply having to learn how to do numerous little household tasks for the first time. When I'm on my own I don't bother but he is too used to it to be willing to do without. I even started making his porridge a few mornings ago. This is not just a question of male laziness; for many women it is an important matter to have complete control of their own territory, is it not ?

To go back to the story, one does rather notice that no other woman even seems to look in from time to time to see how they might be getting on. This suggests, particularly for that era, a severe degree of social isolation. But I must abandon these trivial matters for a moment, to point out that a minute or two ago I was using an air-freshener, with the attractive name of *Alpine*, and it struck me forcibly that it was the very one I had bought during the last weeks of Mum's life, now already half a year behind us. She died exactly five months ago today. She said more than once that she liked the scent. There are flowers lying at present in the bedroom that I mean to take up and put on her grave this afternoon. It is a fine, warm, sunny day, as yesterday was.

I also thought of how in my last book so far, not a very good one, I had mentioned hearing her voice on a malfunctioning phone—I could hear her, but she could not hear me—and how I had keenly felt that I would not be able to do this for much longer. But that was over three years before her death. Indeed, all that stuff was written when, insofar as one thought of it in the least, one effort-lessly assumed that she would still be within direct reach for many years to come. Certainly, that she would outlive Dad: after all, not only do women live longer than men, it being a man's world, but Dad had also been given over nine years of a start.

Let us return. The father in this case seems to have been a native of Aberdeen, who, in his early twenties, did a bunk from the Silver City, leaving unpaid debts behind him. Apparently, so complete was the break with his native turf that even his family did not know what had become of him until they read about his death. This is extremely bizarre: to learn of a missing son, or brother, or cousin, or whatever, only as you also learn that someone has murdered him. And then to learn one has an unknown grandson, or nephew, or something like a nephew, or whatever, just as he is being charged with the murder of his father. Well, there must have been certain sporadic outbreaks of excitement at some spots in Aberdeen on those nights. Thus are separate communities linked.

Bearing in mind this history of the father, and the earlier given history of the hiding deserter who had learned Esperanto—unless we somehow assume that people with dark personal secrets are uniquely likely to be murdered, we have here surely a glimpse of how numerous must be those people who have a stupendous secret right at the core of existence—and one, I suppose, which is most often never discovered, or never broadcast, since the majority of the possessors of them (I think we may safely assume) manage to escape being battered to death. However, as better people than me have said: it's a strange business, isn't it?

(15th August)

Actually, my younger sister, who will be here in Largs until Wednesday, arrived on Friday from Aberdeen, where she has lived and worked for a few years now. I have visited her abode twice, for a fortnight or so each time. The first was in October last year, when my mother was still alive. My mother was by then clearly ill, and she had just persevered with great fortitude through a grim course of treatment that was itself highly debilitating. ('Well, no one can say I haven't tried everything.') But even then we would not have dreamed that she would die so soon.

In fact, Mum actually encouraged me to go off on this holiday of a sort by offering to pay my fare. Which she did. (My sister, as I remember, was visiting Switzerland, where she used to work.) I explored the town from Don to Dee; wrote a book review of Doris Lessing's autobiography (not one of the world's comic masterpieces) and tried to finalize the text of a work I was completing at the time, a series of aphorisms and sundry great thoughts called *Tartan Wisdom*. In this I succeeded, though not a line of it has yet managed to get itself published—not even for free. But enough of these triumphs.

It is literally the case that, as a footslogging tourist, I fulfilled all my targets but one. The one route I still had in mind, to help give me a complete view of the inner city, involved going down Constitution Street and getting back to King Street by following the natural long curve of the road into Urquhart Street, skirting round the location of the City Hospital. This was the sole intended itinerary that I had still not carried out when I left. For the rest, I had gone as far north as to cross the Brig of Balgownie; south far enough to cross the Bridge of Dee; west to King's Gate, I suppose; and east to Footdee. And all that with a dodgy right knee too. So, let's hear no more about that rank amateur, Mungo Park.

Indeed, I well remember phoning my mother from a public callbox near Kelvinbridge Underground Station—within sight of the domicile of one of the leading suspects in the Slater case; the phone where I live takes incoming calls only—to tell her that I had gone to the doctor with my troublesome knee, as she had strongly advised me to. The doctor had had it x-rayed, which greatly impressed me and the verdict was the wonderfully grandiloquent, 'early degenerative osteo-arthritis'. She gave such a gasp when she heard this. Genuine sorrow and sympathy for her poor beset offspring. When was this? Early 1991, I suppose. May or June, perhaps. I had to rush to assure her that the present pain was virtually nil and that all it meant was that things might very slowly get worse over the course of a very long time. After all, I said to her, you can't really expect to get to forty without having the first signs of things that will eventually go slightly wrong.

I returned to Aberdeen in June. On my very first day there, not long after seeing my sister off at the station (she was now going to New England), I walked along the westerly part of Urquhart Street. I was struck by the strength of the architecture—honest, rugged tenements; obviously not the financial heart of the city, but a decent enough place to live in, I would have thought. And it even occurred to me to reflect while there (the same thing occurs to me all over the place in Edinburgh) that, well, I could easily have passed some of my life here, and it would surely, to say the least, have turned out no worse. And later, near the end of my stay, I carried out the entire walk that I had, as it were, left over from my previous visit; learning belatedly that Constitution Street is a rather odd but by no means uninteresting thoroughfare. Which brings us almost to the point.

Some few days or so after I had arrived back in Glasgow, I bought the book about Roughead earlier referred to. Among the cases described in it was one, only one, from Aberdeen: the Helen Priestly/Jeannie Donald case. The broad outlines were not unknown to me. An eight year-old girl (Helen Priestly) had gone missing one lunchtime, during her midday break from school. In the early hours of the next morning, her body was discovered lying in a sack, in a sort of recess on the ground floor of the public space of the tenement where she lived. There were signs indicating likely sexual assault.

It transpired that one of the ground floor neighbours (Jeannie Donald) had had occasional dust-ups with the child. What actually happened is still not fully clear, for Donald never, to my knowledge, publicly admitted anything. Clearly, she did kill the girl, but almost certainly as the result of a horrible series of mishaps, possibly fuelled by intense irritability and a violent bad temper. Or there may even have been something more to it, I suppose. Most commentators surmise that the pair just happened to meet in the close-mouth, that the child cheeked her again and the adult flew off the handle; or that the adult saw the child leaving, lay in wait against her return, and leapt out at her in a way that terrified or shocked her. Perhaps the adult even caught the child by the throat—a fairly extreme measure, unless pure accident—and the child, who had some sort of thymus condition which led to her instantly blacking out when her throat was constricted, fell senseless to the ground.

Even so, it would be a rare panic which led one instantly to suppose that she was dead; and perhaps something worse than that would lead one to think of attempting to disguise this—particularly in the way actually chosen. The adult carried the girl off into her own house—they were at its very door—and sought to engineer safety for herself by taking up her household scissors and disfiguring the child's genitalia to suggest sexual assault. This shows a deeply worrying presence of mind. If only she had had less of it!

What happened next? The pain of the assault brought the child back to consciousness. Or at least, she cried out. But some sort of final boundary had been passed, and the adult, unsure what bad dream she was now in, killed her by suffocation. Could she perhaps have returned the child, mysteriously alive but suffering from inexcusable wounds, and politely explained what had happened? What sort of altered state is this? You retaliate against a child, and it dies! It dies. Then it wakens up again because you are inflicting gross injuries upon it. If you had just legged it up to her house for help straight away, things would have been all right; more or less all right; five minutes back. And here is her dead body with your own hands on it! Two steps sideways from normal life, and you are deep in something too horrible even for Dante.

This happened on 20th April 1934, at 61 Urquhart Road. I must have walked unconcernedly past the venue that day, decades afterwards, perhaps even on the same side of the street. Just as so many others must have done before and since. All these principals were, I trust, already in their places, leading ordinary lives, at the time of the Grove Street murder, just over four years earlier. Perhaps the child had already begun to try to needle her neighbour. After all, what can go wrong? It is what children in thousands do to their neighbours. And, for all I know, Robert Willox senior might himself even have come from Urquhart Road. But that's enough on this one.

(12.48–16th August)

Since we have thus wandered onto the woeful topic of murdered children, this too. I remember how, not long after Mum died, a very young child was abducted from a shopping centre in Liverpool, by two other, not very much older boys; after his mother had let him stray from sight for a few seconds. Apparently, it was not the first time that this pair had tried to do such a thing. There were blurry images of the trio, caught at hazard by video security installations, as the two led the third past. They later killed the child. They were quickly apprehended, which given the mounting state of public hysteria, was probably just as well. Their arrival for the start of legal proceedings produced some very ugly and unruly scenes on the streets outside, which might have looked to some to be fuelled by urges which lay too close for comfort to the urges which the demonstrators were presumably protesting against. It was not just shock and sorrow that was on display here. I remember thinking that perhaps it was not an unalloyed disaster for my mother to be safe and out of a world in which such things were going on.

There was a riot of talk in the media about the decline of moral values, in the wake of this one crime, and the increasing, unprecedented brutalization of our society. For myself, I thought that the extent and intensity of these outcries and inquests were to some degree self-refuting; for if things really had gotten so bad, then how could so many people possibly care so much about a single murdered child? The protests themselves showed that certain moral values were still well in place.

As I was over by the sideboard, checking what age Slater was when he died—the only available book, as I already knew, did not give the precise date—I clumsily knocked over onto the floor a packet of *Bisodol* tablets, 'for Rapid Indigestion Relief'. They were Mum's. They must have been in this room for quite a while, from long before her death. By then there had ceased to be much point in taking indigestion tablets.

I must mention this too. I have just got back from my father's room, where I went in response to the tinkling of the little ornamental glass bell we gave him to summon assistance with, should he need it. It might take too long to try to explain what it was all about. Basically, did that slamming car door which he had just heard signal the expected arrival of the heart specialist who should be here any time to see him. (No; it didn't.) (I remember standing at this very window here on the morning after my mother's death, and watching a neighbour from across the road climb nonchalantly into a car parked directly opposite and routinely drive away.)

It was exactly that absurdly fragile little bell, bought years ago, I suppose, for sheer decoration, which latterly, so recently, had often been rung by my mother. It was so strange, so gripping, to suddenly hear it again; rung by her husband of more than forty years, who, though a decade the older, seemed once again to be fairly lively. I first ever responded (to that bell) at about 4 o'clock one morning. She was grateful that at last someone had managed to hear it, for she needed to be helped to the bathroom. Sometimes, later, you could not be sure whether she really had rung, or whether, as occasionally happened, you had just imagined the sound. She would be sitting perfectly still, as if asleep. You would stand by the door, watching, to see if she would purposefully move again or not. Then she would look up, see you, say 'Oh, good', and smile in welcome.

That very first time, as I was dressing into decency as swiftly as possible, I could hear her try to summon help with her voice. I had just risen from the bed. By then she was not able to utter much in the way of a shout. So, I heard that still living voice saying something. Something curiously difficult to recapture with adequate exactness. Something like, 'Am I not going to be able to . . .', or 'Am I going to have to . . .'; but not said querulously. There was still, very clearly, a sort of resigned humour in it; of the absurdity of these predicaments, despite all the pain.

(Now is surely the right moment for me to take those flowers up.)

Actually, I washed the dishes first. A van from Aberdeen passed me when I was on the main road. Further on, a squashed but still living wasp was lying convulsed on the pavement. In accordance with my western Buddhist beliefs, I stepped on it heavily. Another living object removed from the universe. Every little helps. Perhaps it has re-emerged somewhere else by now, as an Indian peasant, or a koala bear. Another wasp was crawling over one of the bunches of flowers we put on the grave yesterday. At least, I have to suppose it was a different wasp.

There are so many gross tragedies to be inferred from the gravestones even in this quiet cemetery. This time, I noticed that a stone near to where Auntie Peggy's remains lie had been added to. Formerly it commemorated only a teenage girl who had died in an accident aged eighteen, just before Christmas a couple of years ago. Nearly our own last normal Christmas. Now it also records the fact that the body of the mother lies there. She was sixty-two. It is hard not to believe that the first death somehow helped to bring about the second.

My mother, who died a few days before this other one, had had two sisters. One, Molly, died at the age of five, before my mother was yet anywhere. The other, Margaret, died at the age of seventy-eight, two and a half years before my mother. She had been rather eager to be taken to the glorious afterlife for quite a while. 'In Memory of My Beloved Sister', or 'In Loving Memory of My Sister'? I forget which. I suspect the second is indeed right. But now the body of that unique 'My' itself lies in the same cemetery, a few dozen paces distant. Sometimes I get a worryingly clear image of all those boxes which lie in the space between. Let me hurry back to some unfinished business.

(9.07–16th August)

On the day of Willox's 39th birthday, whatever he might or might not have been doing, a child of just under four years of age was discovered to be missing from a ground-floor children's ward of a hospital in Blackburn, Lancashire. Some may prefer to improve on the funny old universe by skipping what follows. There was a search, and a couple of hours later her dead body was found nearby, still in the hospital grounds. She had been raped. She had then been murdered, by being held by one leg while her head was dashed against a wall. It happened in the earliest hours of the very morning on which she was due to be discharged. (She had had a bout of pneumonia.) There were still five other children in the ward; but whatever it was they had seen, if anything, they were entirely unable to help, for the murdered girl had been the only one of them who was yet able to talk. Do we remember things from before we are able to speak? I would imagine not; but I may be wrong. In this case, one rather hopes not.

I would not like to have to try to summon up a worse possible murder than this. Footsteps were observed on the floor, consistent with a man having taken his shoes off, and having walked about silently in his socks. Cautiously and deliberately done, in other words. He had come in, inspected the cots, and then gone back to the first one, nearest to the door. There, as the marks indicated, he stood for some moments, doubtless having his own thoughts. In the total absence of a more promising resource, other physical marks were next called into play. The police, believing that the killer was probably a local man, decided to try to fingerprint every single adult male between the ages of fourteen and ninety who lived in that town at the time.

One does rather start at the thought of many octogenarians being thus brought in on the first sweep. After all, if a ninety year-old could do it, so presumably could a ninety-one year-old. And a thirteen year-old would surely be distinctly more realistic a suspect than either. However, perhaps they would have been next. One has to begin somewhere, I suppose. Actually, they began with the Mayor, who was the first to volunteer. Fortunately for all concerned, he was cleared. And then, some time after the 46,000th candidate had in his turn been tested and passed, they reached with appalling suddenness and certainty the fingerprints they were looking for. Number 46253. There can hardly have been anyone left. No doubt he had small choice, but it is a little odd that he did not do anything rather than submit to such an inevitably damning process.

He was a twenty-two year-old former guardsman. He confessed, saying that he had had a few drinks (which can get you off many things) and that he had beaten her head against the wall to stop her crying. He was hanged on November 19th 1948—which, for all I know to the contrary, may have been the very day when my parents married. Certainly it was round about then. He was also suspected of having murdered an eleven year-old boy in Farnworth, Lancs., earlier that same year; but that case was never satisfactorily resolved.

My uncle Stephen had settled in Lancashire by then, as a Salesian priest, near Bolton, at Farnworth. There were difficulties, but by and large he and my mother were very close. In one of my two or three favourite photographs of her, which were given to me after her death, she looks quite staggeringly like him—far more so than I had ever thought of her as being during their lifetimes.

He died in 1986, aged sixty-seven. Mum was in Aberdeen at the time, visiting her daughter. It was clearly one of the saddest days of her life. He had a heart condition. I am told that he had just played a shot on a golf course. Then something happened; he called out his wife's name (he was no longer in the priesthood by then), and he fell to the ground, more or less beyond everything at once. I had always assumed, without giving it any thought, that he would be vaguely off there in the middle distance of my life for ever. I mean, even today he would only have been seventy-four, when my father is still alive and eighty-one. His widow still rings this house fairly often. Of all my relatives he was perhaps the one with whom I most felt a close kinship of interest. I admired him and liked to be with him, and, I have to say, I doubt whether he was even for a single second of his entire life aware of this.

(9.49–16th August)

A closer reading of my source, not before time, informs me that the mother's maiden name was Swift, and that she too was a Margaret. They married in 1908. Something rather depends on the actual date of the marriage—for the son was born, as we already know, in mid-May 1909. The father was wounded at Mons in 1914. (But it seems he still served out the War.) He kept very much to himself—to such an extent that his next-door neighbour of ten years' standing (the one who had the three-room house, classically referred to as a 'two room and kitchen'), one William Watt, who worked for the same firm of shipbuilders in Partick, had never, even under such hugely favourable circumstances, progressed at all beyond exchanging the most superficial civilities with Willox snr. A man, then, who presumably had no friends, to add to his no functioning relatives, and who now had no wife either. And even this, such as it is, would be pretty well gone and forgotten beyond all hope of recovery, but for the fact that he failed in the way he did to die an ordinary death.

When the son was arrested on the day after the killing, he was found to be in possession of various pawn-tickets, and also of a message, obviously the text of a telegram, for a Mrs William E. Dreyer, of South Seventh Street, Newark, New Jersey, USA. ('79

Grove Street, Glasgow, 5/11/29. Father met with an accident last night and died. Will send details later. ROBERT WILLOX, JUNR.') This is the only person of whom any such transaction is noted, so it must presumably have been someone close. Perhaps a sister of the mother? It is noteworthy that, on the night of the murder, Bertie, still at liberty, went to stay with 'an òld friend, Mrs. Smith, 5 Canal Street'. This street, which has now also virtually disappeared, is quite a decent little walk away. 'A constable took him to that address and explained the situation to the lady, with whom he stayed the night.'

From which one deduces that there was no likelier candidate for the honour—and also that this candidate was not particularly close to the Willoxes; unless I am reading too much into the distinctly awkward, formal sound of all this. There appears to have been no available relative; no neighbour whom it would have been the simplest thing to ask. What a night that must have been! In a (one assumes) strange room; in a strange bed; in a very strange situation indeed. Does one lie there contemplating that one is even able to carry out one's plans? Not merely is one's father murdered; but there you are lying there almost as the very body that killed him. And what of the old lady (for some reason I automatically see her as an old lady) in bed next door? A very fluttery, unsleeping business altogether.

But off they eventually drifted to sleep anyway, I suppose; in the, I suppose, demolished house; with all their innumerable possibly not-too-well-off but at least unmurdered neighbours on every side. A gothic complex of motorways now separates the point once occupied by the building in which some of the father's bloodstains still lay that night—actually, I suspect the body itself was still there that night—and the points where his surviving and never so greatly doubted son, and the practically helpful if unhelpfully named Mrs Smith, lay in possibly troubled slumber.

(11.10–16th August)

T alk of this troubled sleep reminds me of a couple, merely another unseen couple, who were sleeping peace-fully one morning in a flat on an upper floor of the rue de Rochechouart in Paris. No. 76 this time. Their fairly banal idyll was disturbed by a knock at the door—ostensibly of a man who had come to discuss the sale of a car, following an advert in the papers. They asked him to return later—or the man of the house did at any rate. But he said he had come rather a long way, and he insisted on the need for some sort of immediate discussion. So the gent—small, bearded, bald, fifty-year-old—left the warm, reassuring side of his loyal young woman, and walked over to open the door ever so little. Why pass up a good deal, just because of the time of the morning? At which point two men rudely pushed past them, and forced their intrusive way into this peaceful little haven of tried and tested mutual love and respect.

Pulling out guns, they ordered the terrified woman to—but no. They were police officers, and thus was the dreadful serial killer Landru arrested. He had murdered at least ten women, inveigling them down one at a time (one of them brought a son with her) to a secluded villa in the country and routinely killing them there for whatever it was that their worldly possessions amounted to. It was usually extremely little. Some think that, basically, this was the only reliable way he could find of supporting his dependent family.

The woman in bed with him was not family as such. She had also been picked up by the expert, but some years ago now; and the idea of realizing her cash value had apparently never occurred to him, in this single, exceptional instance. She did also genuinely love him; but that in itself was not enough for safety, as other women had already discovered. Or perhaps they were sent unconscious so quickly that they never discovered it. Needless to say, she had absolutely no idea of what it was that her beloved engineer got up to in his spare time. Nothing very unusual in that. In fact, one rather doubts if she was *ever* able to grasp it. It was not done with understanding in mind. She survived him for another half-century. Eventually she killed herself, to escape an ever-worsening spinal condition. Her final note began, 'I still love him'. There was of course absolutely no need for her to say who it was that this 'him' referred to. So: that too is possible here—powerful enduring love, real love, for someone who had cold-bloodedly staked out and murdered various wholly innocent women, almost as a career.

Another thing she had had to come to terms with was that, during all the time that she knew him, whenever Landru (his real name, and she first heard it when the police thus addressed him!), whenever he was not as it were at work, he was (if not with her) probably spending his time with his wife and four children, whom he diligently supported, and who apparently didn't suspect a thing either. There is no guidebook anywhere to tell you how you ought to deal with such unimaginable things. She had cooked numerous warm, affectionate meals herself over a stove in a country house in Gambais. And now she learned that Landru had burned some of the remains of various no longer useful female bodies in that very same stove; on either side of the ordinary, chatty meals. What is the proper way to assimilate such information into your own swaying, continuing life? Nothing obviously suggests itself. Nothing suggests itself obliquely either. Love, especially first love, is renowned for having its difficulties but all this is surely from another planet entirely.

Except that it isn't. But it is the couple lying in bed, on just one more morning, in ordinary surroundings, with the police waiting outside unknown to them, for the moment when it is light enough for them to be able to effect a legal entrance, that is almost the least believable thing of it all. Five seconds before the knock on the door, what thoughts are in his head, or in her head? Two more heads just beside each other. Not the same thoughts, I think we may safely assume.

And, while we are on the subject, with this peculiarly compatible pair at rest, not to mention the two Willoxes with their nine-year-old infant, and the millions on the roads between their cities, we shall also invoke a figure who presumably had a harder time sleeping than most of them. It was learned from an intercepted letter that, a couple of days later than the arrest, a woman called Nina was to meet Landru, or whatever name she called him by, by arrangement, at the Gare St Lazare. She was then to travel with him down to his country villa, and there begin a blissful new mode of life. Presumably she read the papers. What an illumination! She was never traced. Enlightened perhaps, more than she had ever wished to be, she would have doubtless viewed in a different light any anger or irritation or even grief which she might have felt at her solicitous admirer's non-appearance the day or two before, while she waited and waited and hoped. I take it she also thought long and hard over the significance of the fact that Landru habitually went on these shared trips to the rented villa by train, having bought two tickets—one of them a single, the other a return. No point in throwing hard-earned cash away. The human capacity to think ahead; to control the future. So, off she went and joined a nunnery; or had ten children by somebody else, and her grandchildren chatter away in various offices at this very moment.

Landru operated in Paris, like any honest citizen, and he made no attempt to disguise his staggeringly memorable appearance. One's first response to seeing photographs of him—perhaps after fear; or the sudden realization that all those absurd stories about his powers as a hypnotist might well have had some basis in fact—is that, short of actually wearing a placard saying 'I am a mass murderer: please arrest me at once', he could hardly have looked more like a killer if he had tried to. Presumably he walked past gendarmes on a daily basis, even when he was being actively looked for. Was he invisible too, or what? But this is no doubt naïve, and I suppose the police had enough to do, particularly in war-time, without having to go looking for trouble. After all, by the end there must have been dozens of people—victims' relatives and so forth—

who were extremely eager to remake his acquaintance; and still he took to the streets of Paris for month after month with bizarre impunity. Even at the wheel of his van he must have been an unforgettable sight. When he was eventually spotted he was in the rue de Rivoli—one of the busiest streets in Paris. And even then it required luck considerably above the odds for his trail to be picked up again after he had eluded the first observer. But it occurs to me that I am actually writing a book about someone else.

(11.32–17th August)

P erhaps a little straightforward narrative would not go amiss now. At about 9.20 in the evening of Monday, 4th November 1929—exactly a year before the death of the principal in the Alice Thomas case, a fascinating Cornish affair which I don't have time to talk about just at the moment—the occupants of the third floor flats at 79 Grove Street, in or near the Cowcaddens district of Glasgow, just north of New City Road, heard loud cries from the landing outside, and the sound of someone feverishly banging or kicking at doors. All three flats threw out a concealed inhabitant to discover what was going on. What was going on was a bravura display of histrionics by young Bertie Willox—who, with his extremely reticent father, made up the usual full quota nowadays of the fourth flat on the landing. (Four doors per landing was normally a sign of poverty. Three was more usual. And most usual of all, I think—but perhaps only because such were the arrangements in West Princes Street—was a mere two; us to the left, and slightly less real people to the right.)

He appeared to be in great distress, and kept on crying: 'Look! Look! Look!' as he pointed to the open door of his own home. So, eventually, they looked. I don't know quite how an innocent man would be likely to react under such circumstances, and I trust I will never be given the chance of finding out for myself, but I must say that this sounds a convincing enough effort to me. From the landing outside, they were able to see, in the gaslight, the body of the father lying on the floor. His feet were clearly in the small hallway, but he stretched off into the kitchen, his arms extended, his head lying in a pool of blood. His legs were slightly drawn up. No one could bring themselves to actually enter the house. (Well: would you?) Nor do I know the dynamics of how a body which had just been full-bloodedly beaten on the head falls to the ground. Do the arms get extended? Perhaps it's a reflex defence mechanism, but I can't help thinking he might well land on top of at least one of them.

'The boy' was advised to run for help to the nearest police-station, which he did. This sounds a bit clueless—but one can easily imagine how, in all the bafflement, it was the first or the most urgent thing that anyone suggested to him. It also rather indicates the shortage of telephones in the building. So, off he ran, thinking his thoughts, leaving a knot of presumably highly uncomfortable people there on the uppermost landing, to observe his father's corpse from a discreet distance—arriving at 9.30 at the Northern Police Office in an excited and exhausted state. I don't quite know yet where this building will have been. Perhaps Stewart Street, to the east; or Maryhill Road, to the west. However, he himself seems to have known well enough where it was.

(1.55–17th August)

At half nine of a Monday night, amid all the domestic disputes, drunken breaches of the peace, car thefts and so on, this apparently rather soft youth enters a police station, and gasps out to a not easily impressed man in uniform at the counter: 'Send an ambulance—send an ambulance—my father is bleeding!' Asked, not unnaturally, why, what's the matter with your father, he produces the impressively oblique reply, 'My mother died some time ago'. If he did indeed do the killing himself, which I suppose he did, this is a very intelligent piece of flimflam. Perhaps, 'my mother died not long ago' would have put any sympathetic listener even more off guard. Nor would it have been a lie.

He then fainted. Do healthy young twenty year-old males faint? In the Cowcaddens? On reviving, he said that the injuries were to the head; and that his father could not have done it himself. This too sounds either very plausible or beautifully judged. It may even threaten to be almost too clever for his own good. After all, no one had mentioned such a bizarre possibility (*as far as I knew—which wasn't very far, it seems*) and it was hard to see why it should have sprung unbidden to mind. Two constables accompanied him home.

On the way back 'he appeared to swoon a wee bit', whatever that means. Perhaps he leant against a wall or two with impressive pathos. He told his quiet companions that his father must have fainted and fallen against the iron bed-couch, hitting his head, 'because the blood was coming from the head'. Perhaps some inherited fainting tendency among the male Willoxes is being lightly sketched out here. He added that he and his father had had their supper, their main evening meal; and that he himself had also washed the dishes and set the table again, to be ready for the next morning's breakfast. This last remark is not as innocent as it sounds. However, at least one household in Grove Street had utterly finished with such ordinary breakfasts. And doubtless numerous of those remaining took a good deal of time to settle back into something approaching normality.

(2.35–17th August)

13

Back at the house however, the table seems to be set for a meal which has not been consumed. The cutlery is clean; a piece of boiled beef lies untouched on its plate and upon the gas range there remains a pot of soup, full almost to the top. Curious. To all external view, it might appear that supper had very obviously not even been started.

Eventually a detective arrives (Inspector Cooke). He asks the youth when it was that he last saw his father alive. Answer: about 6.30, when he had left him alone in the house. 'I tried to comfort him as he was still excited.' (Not 'upset', notice. 'Excited'.) 'And I laid my hand on his shoulder, and said, "Now, son, try and control yourself. Were you and your father on good terms, or has there been any trouble?" ' It is fairly obvious what is in this detective's mind, even at this early stage.

Bertie replies, 'Yes, he is a good father,'—which does not quite answer the two-part question he has just been asked—and then he slips from the chair onto the floor in a swoon, before the inspector could prevent him. Restored, he was taken to the house next door, where a Mrs Mackenzie lived. Whether he continued to fall off the chairs there too does not seem to be in the available record. Is this someone doing his best to behave as he thinks a person in deep shock *would* behave? At 10.30, a Detective Inspector Stewart arrived, the man henceforth in charge of the case. He too had an interview with the son, which centred particularly on what was it he had been doing between 6 o'clock, when the father arrived home, and 9.30, when the corpse was discovered. Then, the police being in possession of the *locus delicti*, Willox, as before mentioned, duly went off to Canal Street, at the more Venetian end of Cowcaddens.

He does not seem to have stayed there for longer than necessary. It was deponed that at 7 o'clock the next morning he was in Haddow's shop, evidently a general store very near to his own domicile. He had bought cigarettes there the previous evening, at about 6.25—according to Isabella McKinney, the shop assistant. He seemed normal enough then; but in the morning he was (she thought) 'very flurried and upset-looking'. There is no mention of his buying anything this time round. (*There is, up ahead.*) However, Miss McKinney said she put to him the following, which Roughead calls 'the pertinent question': 'Are you sure, Bertie, you didn't do it?' ('Pertinent'? Does he mean, 'impertinent'? I should think 'astonishing' was the least it deserved.)

This is a fascinating exchange. According to her, his reply was, 'Oh no. My father has been good to me'—which seems an extraordinarily restrained way of responding to the suggestion that you have just battered your father to death. What are we to make of the fact that she felt able even to voice such a doubt? That it somehow was not a wholly unexpected or implausible event? If not, why not? (As one of my maths teachers used to say time and time again to us in the early 60s. 'Does the angle ABD equal the angle BDF, and if not, why not?' We always took this as a strong hint that the answer must be 'No'. All that remained was for us to stumble upon some sufficiently plausible reason.)

He then added that she would see it all in the papers, that he had been through a terrible ordeal and that he had made one slip. Roughead italicizes this last remark, and adds: 'It would be instructive to learn the nature of this indiscretion.' This suggestion (which he in effect repeats later on) strikes me as being on the face of it rather absurd. As if Willox were saying he had made a slip in his perpetration of the deed! In which case the remark would be as good as a confession. (Incidentally, if it had been such a slip that was at issue, the likeliest candidate would obviously be the fact that he failed to clear away the uneaten food, the continuing presence of which contradicted his story.)

What I take him to be saying is that he made an error in his interviews with the police force the previous day, and that at some point or other this would have to be rectified. The very next sentence, 'He said something about vengeance—"I will have my revenge on whoever did it!" '—although probably the phoniest thing he has yet come out with—clearly shows that he is not saying he made a mistake when carrying out the killing himself. But the question remains: why did the shop assistant think that he might have done it? And within about twelve hours of the deed too! One might have thought that that would be the last thing they would think of—and even so only with the greatest reluctance.

(3.57–17th August)

14

At 11 o'clock that morning, Bertie Willox was met by a reporter on the staff of the Glasgow paper, the *Weekly News*. It was arranged to interview him and take his photograph later on. (Some time before 4 p.m., when he was back in the police station.) He gave a photo of his father to the man, who rejoiced in the name of J.R.M. Christie. When all this happened, and when Roughead's account was written—in 1930—it would have seemed in no way of moment that this name was incredibly close to that of J.R.H. Christie. This man, at that time a comparatively minor deviant in his early thirties—would eventually be hanged in 1953 (dear God—I was already alive then!) for the murder of several women, including his wife. His motive was sexual: he liked to have sex with their fresh corpses. Such conduct apparently stimulated his fading potency. I think even nowadays it is generally permissible to term this a perversion—be the term never so judgemental.

Less than four years before he was hanged, of course, Christie (J.R.H., not J.R.M.) was the main prosecution witness at the trial of a lodger or sub-tenant of his, one Timothy Evans, for the murder of Evans' wife and child. Almost entirely as a result of Christie's evidence, Evans was convicted and hanged. The judge, I seem to recall—it is a long time since I read about the case, and it will be even longer before I read about it again—specifically went out of his way to point to the trustworthiness of the witness, a special constable during the late war, and so forth. That Christie himself had nothing to do with these deaths is vanishingly improbable; and the widespread view is that he was the killer, and most likely the sole killer. It certainly makes for a very convincing explanation of events.

In one of the classic Glasgow cases, the McLachlan affair of 1862, something of the same thing happened. Here the prosecution's chief witness—virtually their only witness—a pious elderly reprobate called James Fleming, whose testimony led to the conviction of the accused (Jessie McLachlan), was almost certainly himself the guilty party. But at least McLachlan got off lightly. Her death sentence was commuted to life imprisonment, and she was let out after a mere ten years. True, she was probably wholly innocent; but it doesn't do to expect too much from the legal process.

Since the locus of this crime is in Sauchiehall Street—it's still there—on the way to the Art Galleries and Kelvin Hall, we may, I think, be confident that both Robert Willoxes passed it at some time or other. Indeed, walking back from Partick to Cowcaddens could lend itself fairly directly to this route, along the western half of Sauchiehall Street. But so what. A more puzzling point is worrying me. If you lived next door to someone who works at a reasonably distant location, and you worked there too, the most obvious conclusion to draw would be either that two friends or colleagues had gone to some trouble to secure neighbouring accommodation—or (perhaps more likely) that one neighbour had managed to get the other a job at the place where he himself already worked.

Yet we are told that although Watt and Willox were literally next-door neighbours on one side of the third floor of a tenement, and although they worked in the same place, nonetheless in ten years they had not progressed even to having one reasonably close conversation. Did the concern they worked for somehow locate them there? Hardly. In which case, was it all merely a coincidence?

Well, in a complex universe there must be coincidences, and universes don't come much more complex than this one. To what degree is it either less probable or more probable than the likelihood that a lodger and tenant each murdered his own wife?

Alas, for technical reasons, I am unable to list the correct answers at the back of this book.

(4.44–17th August)

15

I suppose I shall have to seek out the relevant copy of the *Weekly News* some time or other. For these transactions with the press, Willox was paid £3 in notes. (60 shillings. More, notice, than his erstwhile father's weekly wage of 50/3.) Two were Bank of England oncers; and the third a Treasury note. He then went to his regular hairdresser in Grove Street, one Thomas Duff, where he had a haircut, a shampoo, and a shave; no doubt wishing to look his best for the forthcoming photographer.

According to Roughead, 'he remarked that his father had been murdered the night before, and that he had last seen him alive at 6.30.' This sounds bizarrely casual. 'Oh, by the way, my father was murdered last night.' 'Really, sir? How tragic. Care for anything for the weekend?' And why tell the hairdresser—did he perhaps ask?—so precisely what the time was when last he saw his father alive? On leaving, he gave him a tip of sixpence, 'the only occasion on which, though a regular customer, he had ever been so generous'.

What was this? The start of a new life as Man About Town? A sweetener, that his useful hints might not prove to fall on deaf ears? I don't know. But the results of all this pampering can still be inspected in the resulting photographic portrait, for Roughead includes it at the start of his essay. It doesn't reveal much, particularly on a photocopy. A slightly petulant-looking youth whose face is certainly not pinched with famine. I suspect he might well be good-looking, so I have just gone through to the sitting-room to ask my sister how she would describe this photo-copied face. After a pause, she said, 'A bit arrogant'.

'Is it someone you would trust?'

'Definitely not.'

I think that is probably fair enough. But I dare say the father more or less trusted him.

(6.30–17th August)

16

On the Tuesday, Willox likewise called twice at the Police Office, by arrangement. Inspector Stewart told him there were certain errors in his previous statement. Willox apologized, and declared himself quite prepared to correct any that might be pointed out to him. (Which I dare say he was.) Then, having this time been cautioned, he made another statement.

Accordingly: on the previous day, his father had left for work at the usual time. (4.45 in the morning!) He came home, as usual, at 6 p.m. (13¼ hours! At the very least, Bertie had a huge part of each day entirely to himself.)

'I had his tea ready for him when he came home; or rather his dinner, of soup, rice pudding, and a drink of milk.' I don't quite understand this. Presumably Willox is suggesting that his father had consumed the rice pudding and the milk—and perhaps that he chose not to have any soup. Or maybe the level of the soup in the pot was nonetheless low enough for it to be arguable that some of it had been taken after all. But what of the boiled beef that was there? What was that: a conversation piece? Perhaps it has just been missed out of the list, from its correct position between the soup and the sweet? After more than 12 hours at work, one might suppose a man would not turn his nose up at a decent bit of boiled beef. And yet, of course, the beef indeed *was* untouched. Bertie looks to have got himself into a tidy little mess here.

'When father came in that night he took off his coat and cap and hung them on the peg in the lobby.' Beneath these he seems to have been wearing, if I read this correctly, some sort of military uniform. In 1906—after, among other things, seeing service in South Africa—he went into the reserve, joining the Corps of Commissionaires in Glasgow. (*Two quite distinct events. Such stupidity is painful. A mere crossing the room to the dictionary helps clarify all this late on.*) Since he was fifty-five, it may even be that the free suit (if such it was) was one of his reasons for staying with them.

Then, or so I gather, they had dinner and 'immediately after dinner father said to me: "How much do I owe Daly?" I replied: "I think over £2".' (Dennis Daly, salesman with the Household Supplies Company, said that when Mrs Willox died in January she was £4 in their debt"—from the trial. Over a week's wages; a tidy sum. For food, I presume.)

'Father replied: "Well, you'll better pay him and Mrs Duffy tonight and get them off the map".' The colloquialism of the 'off the map' is a nice touch. I'm not so sure about the unusual formality of 'father'. Is that how he habitually addressed his father in real life?

Thereafter, by his own account, the son washed the dishes and prepared to go out. His father, he said, gave him £3-3-6 for Mrs Duffy (£3.17½), and £3 for Daly: six single one pound notes, half a crown, and a shilling. When he left the house between 6.30 and 6.45 (note this 6.45, coming straight from the horse's mouth), his father had sat down and was cleaning the buttons on his tunic. By the defence's version of events, he was just about to be struck down by an unknown assailant soon after his son had left the house bearing all his money with him. Which is not physically impossible, of course. Not as such.

I find myself wondering whether the idea of getting £3 from the journalist came from the journalist himself or from Willox. Anyway, this Mrs Duffy, who was the agent for a firm of credit drapers, was something more than a mere commercial supplier, having been a friend of the late Mrs Willox, and having known Bertie from his childhood. This came out in evidence at the trial. She testified that, in January 1929, Bertie had borrowed a pound from her 'for Dada' in order to 'get a doctor for Mother'. A fortnight later he returned, not with the borrowed pound, but with a memorial card for his late mother. In March or April he brought some six shillings towards the reduction of the debt. In September, he enquired of her whether she had received 'the 15 shillings which was sent to her from Rothesay'.

Not surprisingly, she hadn't. 15 plus 6 equals 21, a guinea, not a pound; but we'll let that pass. I take it that they had at least managed to get away for a holiday, doon the watter. It is, to say the least, a little odd that he waited until he was out of town, before entrusting a fair amount of money to the vagaries of the public post. After all, he might have waited for another week or two until he was back in Glasgow before doing it. Or he could have repaid his debt before he left. I presume that even Mrs Duffy was not so trusting as to credit him with quite so spectral a repayment.

Oddly enough for someone apparently so recently in funds, he soon thereafter proposed to Mrs Duffy that she give him £2.10s, to let him get his father's medals back out of the pawnshop before they were forfeited. Whether father himself knew where his medals were we may take leave to doubt. This she, rather surprisingly, agreed to. And that was the last she saw of her dead friend's vexing offspring until 7 o'clock on the night of the murder; when he called to repay the debt in full. Three pound notes; a half-crown; a shilling. In other words, the £2.10s for the medals, plus a further 13/6. I assume that this 13/6 is the missing Rothesay 15/- in a new and slightly reduced guise, but that is sheer supposition. She, no doubt heartened by this perhaps slightly overdue display of honesty by Margaret's sprog, gave him over a sixpence, 'to himself'. From whom it next went to the hairdresser, as like as not. But off he vanished into the extremely wet and traffic-laden night anyway.

17

Daly, the other creditor, testified that Willox arrived at his house in 91 Hopehill Road, Maryhill, at 7.15, and paid off his debt in full, which rather sounds as if he had gone on there from Mrs Duffy's at 532 St George's Road. However, in his statement, Willox depones to having done these visits in the opposite order.

The debt was £2-14-11. Willox first took out his money and sought to pay it exact; then, finding that he lacked the requisite denominations, he asked Daly whether he could change a fiver. Daly assented. He was able to identify the particular fiver in court, for there was a name and address written on its back. He had this note delivered to the police the day after he received it, having heard in the interim of the murder. Incidentally, all the relevant witnesses, including Daly, agreed that there was nothing in the least out of the ordinary about Willox's demeanour that evening.

But where did this fiver come from? Did anyone remember it, for instance, from the cashier's department at Willox senior's place of work? Willox junior had explicitly told the police that his father had given him six single notes (plus odds) to pay the debts. (I confess that I am rather at a loss to understand why Willox didn't just say right off that his father had given him a fiver. What could this have lost? Was it somehow meant in theory to be left for the imaginary assailant to steal? Did it perhaps sound unreasonable to send someone out with a fiver, a very large sum in those days, to pay off such debts? Lest the payee might well not have had enough on hand to return the correct change? I don't quite see this).

Willox told the police that he knew nothing of what money his father might have had. That, on paying anything out, he was always secretive about it, turning away so as not to be watched. (A search of the body produced 2½d: twopence halfpenny.) Asked whether he had at present any money of his own, Willox replied: 'I do not possess any money myself. I have at present 2/11, which is the remainder of the £3' (note: *not* the fiver) 'which I got to pay Mr Daly. I got 5/1d change from Mr Daly,' (£2-14-11 + £0-5-1 = £3—ah, a clear breath of air wafting in from my glorious schooldays), 'and I have spent 2/2d today for food and cigarettes.' So, children: how much money does that mean that Robert Willox Junior *should* have left? Now, you should know that because he has already told you.

Asked to produce such money as he had, he did indeed turn out two shillings and eleven pence. Inspector Stewart, however, noticed a small leather wallet protruding from his waistcoat pocket, and 'on an inspiration', he cavalierly took it out and examined it. This was careless of Willox, to say the least. Perhaps it simply never occurred to him that a policeman might just reach out and lift things as the spirit took him. This wallet contained three Treasury £1 notes, one National Bank of Scotland £1 note, and four pawn tickets. ('It suddenly dawned on me that *this* might be the criminal.')

If so, Inspector Stewart seems to have been a rather trusting soul—for the circumstances positively cry out that Willox junior must be at least a very likely suspect; and, as we have seen, it did not take long for his colleague, Inspector Cooke, to entertain the same thought within minutes of arriving at the scene of the crime. Willox junior denied the fiver, and was detained on suspicion. Daly was summoned, and he duly repeated his statement that a fiver did indeed change hands. Willox again denied it, and this led to his being charged with having assaulted and killed his father, and having stolen £8 from the house. (The £3 to Mrs Duffy, plus the £5 to Daly, I assume.) His response, 'I have nothing to say meantime'—sounds rather tame for an innocent man accused of patricide. And as it turned out, he had nothing very much to say later either, for he chose not to take the witness-stand during his trial.

(10.31–17th August)

18

T his carelessness with the wallet was all the more remiss of him in view of a similar incident which had occurred the day before. For as yet we have not recounted in full detail what Willox did after leaving his father for the last time.

It appears that, almost as soon as he had reached the street, he happened to meet (purely by chance) his 'pal', James Turner, aged nineteen, a friend since schooldays. What was he doing? Hanging about in the rain? They then went to Sinclair's Billiard Rooms, at St George's Cross. (Very close by. It is where St George's Road, New City Road, Great Western Road, and Maryhill Road all met, in a five-way intersection. St George's Road to north and south; New City Road, to the east; Great Western Road, appropriately enough, to the west; and Maryhill Road, off to the north-west, between the first and last previous. These were all major roads. If you just missed the traffic-lights at St George's Cross, and the feeling was that you usually did, you had a long wait for your next experience, I can tell you. I who often ran for a school-bound bus of a morning, already rather threatened by the prospect of being late, spent many an anguished moment, sitting tense by an upstairs window, willing the lights to change.)

The billiard-hall manager, another man called Duff (Angus

Duff—to add to Thomas Duff the hairdresser, and Margaret Duffy), said that Bertie used to play there *nearly every night*. Did he ever talk to his father at all, one wonders? He paid for the game that night: ninepence. (A florin offered; 1/3d returned.) If the father only gave him something between 2/6 and 4/6 per week (30–54 old pence; 12½–22½ new pence), then this already suggests that a certain amount of financial stringency is a likely outcome for young Bertie. All which time he was breezily carrying over £8 in his pocket; perhaps more money than he had ever had before in his life. Taking rather a risk, one might have thought. Departing the hall, he then and only then set about his necessary errands. But I am running ahead again.

Nevertheless, let me digress sufficiently to say that I am sure that there were still in my day the opaque windows of a billiards hall dustily and mysteriously fronting St George's Cross along the wideish gushet (the building still stands, vastly refurbished) between Great Western Road and Maryhill Road. But this may merely be, I suppose, a trick of memory. All the same, it would surely have been the perfect site for such a place.

When Turner met Willox, at somewhere about 6.30, the latter was coming out of Haddow's shop bearing a packet of cigarettes. (Isabel McKinney, who worked there, put the time at 6.25.) This is certainly a very convincing way of suggesting that things are all as per usual. Was Dada really already lying dead or dying up three flights of stairs? The pair of buddies then went into a shop owned by Eugene Meehan, who lived in the flat below the Willoxes. In return for displaying a cinema bill, listing the coming attractions, Meehan's sometimes had free tickets for the pictures—which evidently he was willing to pass on at times to his upstairs neighbour. But there were none there that night. (Which, given that there were still the errands to do, and that he had arranged to be at another friend's house at 7.30, as shall appear, was probably just as well.)

Meehan put the time at 6.30. His assistant, Margaret Maguire, put it at 6.35. (Good Irish names, both. As will be seen to satiety people vary in their estimates of time—not least, of course, because watches and clocks run slow, run fast, or are wrongly set.) Meehan left the shop after them, caught the pair up, and asked them if they were going to the cinema anyway. Turner replied, no, they had no money.

It all gets a bit more fankled now. A certain Felix Carey, who knew both lads, met them outside a barber shop, still in Grove Street at (he says) 6.40. (This, presumably, is Duff's shop.) He made a joke to Bertie about the Margaret Maguire above mentioned. One assumes some typical piece of juvenile rudery. Now, Carey, it seems, had also met the pair when they had been in the shop in question (Meehan's) just lately; and, while he was there (or so I understand the passage) Turner had asked him whether he could change a £1 note for him. He was unable to; but he did see the money, a green £1 note. Turner, however, denied that any such incident had occurred.

Something seems to be happening here that I can't quite make out. Is Carey simply mistaken? Is he deliberately making it up? Is Turner up to something? Is he trying to deny the existence of the pound note for the same reason that he was trying to divest himself of it for the more discreet equivalent in loose change at the time? Something is going on here. Might Willox even have given Turner the pound?

Well, what might not have happened? He might have found it in the street, or even have nicked it from his own father. He might even have lifted it from Bertie, I suppose.

Enough of this frenzied fantasizing. Willox and Turner then went on to the Billiards Hall (6.35 to 7.05), and on to the two messages thereafter. According to Willox, Turner was still with him, but Turner denied this. Actually, he denied being at Mrs Duffy's, so probably this was indeed the later of the two visits. There seems to be no mention of whether either creditor saw or deduced that Willox was alone or accompanied.

According to Willox's statement to Inspector Stewart, after the second call the pair of them walked down from 532 to 490 St George's Road, where they parted company, Willox going in to visit a friend by prior arrangement, and Turner going on home. I can't really see why Willox would want to *invent* this extended companionship. What difference would it make? I get the sense, with Turner, of someone just trying his best to de-involve himself from something which he was in some way part of, but which he wishes to have absolutely nothing to do with.

No; I've mulled it over for a while, but I can still get nowhere. Perhaps he was only saying, leave me out of this—some friend *you* are. Perhaps they had discussed depriving the old man of his cash;

or even of his life. Mere riotous speculation. I just don't know; I am tired; I have had a long day. Dad will go into hospital tomorrow for observation and tests. It is getting on for midnight. I am now away to my weary and innocent bed.

(11.40–17th August)

Alas, none of this wandering around seems to have taken anyone through West Princes Street. It's almost as if they are deliberately avoiding it. But there are a couple of tiny echoes of the Slater case here all the same. Oscar Slater lived in St George's Road, for a brief but crucial few weeks of his life—albeit at No. 69, which is practically at the other end of the street from these other, extremely northerly addresses. And I am pretty sure that Mary Barrowman, whom I take to be the fantasizing teenager who was in very large part the cause of his unjust incarceration, also lived in Hopehill Road. I must check this. (No; only the echo of an echo. She lived in Seamore Street, almost facing Hopehill Road across Maryhill Road. (But North Woodside Road crosses Maryhill Road between them.))

Of course, by 1929, twenty years on, other people will have been inhabiting those houses. Presumably innocently. But the neighbour in that case, Arthur Montague Adams—the man past whom the probable murderer calmly walked, out of the door of the old lady's flat—he was still there in the same place in West Princes Street, where he lived on until the early 1940s. Though never quite the same again, I rather think.

Anyway, whether Willox parted from his friend at 490 St

George's Road, or arrived there alone, what he did next is clear enough. He went up 'to visit his friend Alfonso Jacovelli, with whom he spent the evening, and who, when he left later, accompanied him part of the way home'. This was not the only appearance that Jacovelli had made in Willox's most memorable day. And one wonders why he didn't pass the traumatic Monday night at the house of this friend. But perhaps there was simply not enough room.

However, this Jacovelli, aged twenty-one, already married (Bertie had actually been his Best Man), living in rented rooms, might have seemed to be the better bet for such an honour. At the trial he said he had known the accused intimately for eight years, and was often at his home. (Perhaps they met at school. Bertie must have had more opportunity than most for acquiring schoolfriends, for, before going off to work at fourteen, he had attended no fewer than four of them—two of which were Protestant and two Catholic. (No agnostic schools, obviously.) He seems, officially, to have been Roman Catholic.)

He said that Bertie had been unemployed since his mother's death (ten months before: already he must have been becoming virtually unemployable, a risk that no employer would wish or need to take); and that he was always complaining about being short of money. Not the least telling remark made at the trial by any means. Jacovelli claimed that he had given him 'numerous' small loans; and said that Willox was in the habit of taking clothing and other articles of the house to the pawnbrokers.

Jacovelli further said that on the day of the murder, he had gone up to visit Willox in his house between 1 and 2 o'clock. He had invited Willox to come and spend the evening at his place, at 7.30. The table, he noticed, was even then set for a meal. There were two plates, with a small piece of pudding on them; some cold meat waiting on the coal-bunker (waiting to be cooked, presumably; if not, where did it go to? And where did the boiled beef come from), and there was a pot on the gas cooker. (For the soup, I take it.) Bertie also 'remarked that he was hard up'. But no loan seems to have been forthcoming this time.

So, it would seem to be the case that the table was virtually already set for the later meal at six. Not for the first time one begins to wonder exactly what it was that Bertie did all day. (Or perhaps just all *that* day. Perhaps he wanted to have everything in place well beforehand that Monday.) It was a tiny house and one not rich in contents—so, how did he normally occupy himself until 6 o'clock, when the father returned home? He must at the very least have had a fair amount of free time on his hands. (Jacovelli appears to have been something of a free spirit too.) What did he do between two, when Jacovelli had left, and six, when his father got back from work? Rehearse? Ponder? After all, visiting the pawn-shop is not a full-time job. Certainly he seems to have had plenty of space for dreaming in, if he wished to use it.

Be that as it may, Bertie did indeed arrive at Jacovelli's house punctually, at 7.30. 'He said he would not stay long, as he was tired and wanted to get to bed. He was quite cheery; some moments he was quiet.' I'll bet he was. 'Witness had seen him so before. They amused themselves with a gramophone; and Jacovelli, noticing a small leather case sticking out of his guest's waistcoat pocket "made a grab for it" in fun, but was "prevented" by Bertie.' There seems to have been something almost irresistibly provoking about the appearance of this knicknack. Jacovelli, be it noted, evidently married the Invisible Woman. Perhaps she was keeping herself busy elsewhere.

Jacovelli accompanied his friend for most of the way home, to the corner of Grove Street and Scotia Street, at 9.30. I assume he was later grateful that he left it at that. Perhaps Bertie did not encourage him to continue. Willox, he said, was at that time wearing his brown trousers, with his black jacket and vest (i.e. waistcoat). He had two suits. In the afternoon he had been wearing his brown suit entire, which is rather interesting. So far as Jacovelli knew, the Willoxes were on good terms with each other.

To have retained composure under these circumstances be-speaks a very uncommon character indeed. (Or it argues for his innocence.) Even so, once Jacovelli turned and left him, Willox must have had very considerable forebodings as to what must be about to happen next. Another climb up the stairs past the ordinary doors; one after the other, yet again. And then what? Something intolerable was surely awaiting him, and he knew that; and he knew he had to go through with it while simultaneously trying to work out on the spot how any reasonable and innocent being would have been acting right now. So: on he goes up the stairs, perhaps a bit more cautiously than usual. Just one more returning figure in that street, and not even drunk. As in so many streets, and on just another perfectly ordinary evening.

(2.57–18th August)

20

But there is still a minor discrepancy to be attended to. In his statement to Inspector Stewart, Willox said that, before going on up to his house, he first looked into Meehan's shop again—it was on the opposite side of the street—and spoke to the girl there. It seems he bought nothing. (One notices with some surprise that the shop was still open at 9.30 p.m. Such was not generally the case in my young day. The arrival of Asian-owned shops with longer hours struck us as being something quite new.) The girl smiled but made no reply. (Made no reply to what? Wouldn't absolutely no reply not be a bit odd?) In her own evidence, however, the young woman (Maguire) explicitly denied that such an incident had occurred. Had she just forgotten it? If not, why invent the incident? Did he feel the need to have as many witnesses as possible to his whereabouts that evening? Or to only that part of the evening? My understanding is that Jacovelli is the sole witness as to his whereabouts between, at the latest, 7.30, and about 9.30 (or 9.20; or whenever it was he alarmed the neighbours). There are interesting wisps of something or other here. After all, he appears to have never been more than few minutes distant from 79 Grove Street during the whole evening. Did he intend to look in at the shop, but forgot? Might he even have gone back at some intermediate point? No; sheer weightless speculation. One could hardly count, in such a street, on not being seen by someone. And yet, as a matter of fact, although a battalion seem to have observed him leaving, no one testifies to having seen him when he was on his way back.

However, spectacularly, at least one other person had come to the Willox door between 6.30 and 9.30. Of course, on the defence view, the murderer must presumably have done so too; but no one has ever suggested that Hector Kennedy was the murderer. (Erm: not to my knowledge.) In fact, one doesn't quite know who he was. He turned up in the role of canvasser for a forthcoming municipal election in which his father was a candidate. Voting is on Tuesday. One assumes he impartially knocked at every door in that tenement. And others beyond, no doubt. At 8.30 he knocked at Willox's door. There was no reply; which is just as well. Through the partition, a step or two away, a dead body was lying. He wrote on his card, 'Not in'. I dare say he was a few steps away from all sorts of thing that evening. Not in. Well, not literally correct; but correct enough.

(3.40–18th August)

21

So: he opened the door, discovered the body (presumably where he had left it; what a shock for him, if a corpse had not been there to greet him!) (what if the canvasser had peeped through the letterbox?)—and ran about thumping doors and shouting, 'Look! Look!' Hmm. For some reason this no longer seems quite so convincing an act as it did before. No screams of, 'Oh no!', or 'Dad! Dad!' or 'Help! Help!' Nothing like that. Only 'Look! Look!', after the first witnesses appeared. No rehearsals possible for this, obviously you had to get it right first time. And what, really, is the likelihood that some untraced and unobserved maniac had arrived, had done the deed to a man who seems to have known just about nobody, and had departed silently and with equal unobtrusiveness?

While I am pondering the plausibility of all this, I may as well add the last two details from his second statement to the police which I think ought to be given. One: that it was his father's practice, on entering the house, to leave the key dangling from his pocket-chain until he had hung up his coat and cap in the lobby— when he would put them into his pocket. And two: that Bertie did not know who set the table up as it was when he returned later that night; probably his father, whose nightly custom was to lay it for breakfast next morning. Which is to say, he claimed that it was not he, Bertie, who had done it. I take it nobody is suggesting that the murderer broke in, slew the father, set the table, then departed well satisfied with his work.

I may as well also add the piece of information from Roughead's general introduction that, on the 12th of December 1927 (two years previously) one James McKay (and there are very many of that name still about) was tried in Glasgow for the murder of his mother, 'whom, having killed with a hatchet, he dismembered, and cast the residue into the Clyde. He was found guilty and executed'. I had never heard of this case before. Had it achieved greater notoriety, it might well have permanently altered our view of the river. Meanwhile, last night, a man was charged with frenziedly stabbing to death a part-time model on Wimbledon Common just over a year ago. The woman was stabbed forty-nine times. She had been out walking her dog. Her two year-old son was found clinging to her body, and begging his Mummy to get up again. Already speaking. They have been showing videos of her on television and the images are so extraordinarily recent and alive that it seems very nearly inconceivable that what will happen to the laughing woman moving about in our gaze did indeed, really and truly, happen. But it did happen all the same. Earlier today, I went to hospital with my father, keeping him company in the ambulance. He'll be kept in for a couple of days, for observation. Poor old Dad.

(7.27–18th August)

22

T hus, Dada Willox arrives home for the last time at 6 pm, suspecting nothing amiss. Just one more return to base. By now he is perhaps even somewhat used to the new routine, and the fact that his wife henceforward must be permanently absent. Curiously, his neighbour, Florence Watt, was then at her own door (which virtually made up a right angle with Willox's) and she therefore saw him. No words were exchanged, it seems. She had known him for ten years, but he was a very reserved man. Her own husband came home soon afterwards. Was that why she was waiting at the open door? Such devotion. If not, it's hard to know *what* she was doing. Admiring the landing, perhaps? Constitutional nosiness?

Now, when the body was discovered, it was still (so I gather) wearing the complete commissionaire's uniform. This suggests that, unless Willox senior had the amiable habit of wandering about in full uniform in the privacy of his own home, he had simply not yet had the time to remove his jacket. Two newspapers (morning and evening, I suppose) were found to be still in his coat, as were his spectacles; so, unless he had already exhausted them (in which case why bother to bring them home?) he had not yet got to the stage of sitting down and having a read of his papers. My own understanding is that he was most probably struck down just after he had entered and removed his coat; before he had quite reached the kitchen, which he was about to go into. But, whatever the details, no one as far as I'm aware testified to hearing any sounds of an assault taking place—though, rather obviously, such a thing must indeed have happened. No one heard anything alarming when the body landed on the floor. Whatever went on, it went on effectively in a soundproof room.

However, there was one strange leakage of auditory information. We stay with Mrs Watt for a little. Some time about 6.30, on her testimony, a man named Harrington called to see her husband. She let him in, then went to the w.c. for a couple of minutes; whether to relieve her excitement or to keep discreetly out of the way. 'While there, she heard in their house the "angry voices" of Willox and his son.' (Her w.c. was directly adjacent to the kitchen door through the wall.) 'She thought the father was chastising the boy, by which she explained she meant "going for him". She heard the father say: "You won't get a penny from me!" On returning to the kitchen she told her husband that "they were cross again". He remarked: "Never heed them". She had heard other altercations between father and son on the preceding Friday and Saturday.'

By the time Florence re-emerged, Harrington seems to have left. Mr Watt said he stayed for only three minutes (what was he doing? nobody ever says), and that he departed about 6.45. Harrington himself testified to having arrived about 6.37. But what are we to make of all this? It is also on evidence that by 6.35 Bertie was at the Billiards Hall (6.35–7.05). I suppose it could be that she had actually repaired to the lavatory just after she had seen Willox senior return home—perhaps precisely in order to hear as well as possible any resulting altercation; but if that were the case she would surely have heard rather more than she had bargained for. Also, was her husband home yet, and in the kitchen? Notice that she seems to have repeated verbatim only a single remark—presumably the one uttered with the greatest intensity, whenever or wherever it was. She could not even report what Bertie had said, to provoke such a furious outburst.

All rather airy, but this evidence does suggest the (hardly surprising) conclusion that Bertie and his father were of late getting into troubled waters. And there does seem to be a considerable confusion in her testimony, whether by accident or design. Could she possibly know more than she's telling, but be reluctant to say things which might tend to lead Bertie towards the rope? Might it not even have been something Bertie was doing that led her to listen at her door earlier? Mere hunches. She does not seem to have testified how she and Bertie got on together. (I mean, would *you* admit: 'Oh yes. And then I heard young Bertie bludgeoning his father's skull in'? Of course, if she had heard something extremely suspicious, she would surely have said or done something something fairly urgent about it. Yet it may be that she heard something that did not seem too bad at the time; which in retrospect suddenly became highly worrying. Or, of course, absolutely nothing of the kind.)

She and her husband both deponed to the uproar at 9.20 or so; as did Mr Dale, another neighbour. By the way, according to Roughead, Willox's reputation 'was that of an amiable, quiet lad, who had no bad companions, was given neither to drink, gambling, nor going about with girls, and surprisingly in these times,'—i.e. in those times—'he did not dance'. His leisure was occupied in walking about with his pals, playing billiards (nearly every night!), and going to the pictures—which had recently had sound added to them. Insufficient sound, however, seems to have been available in his everyday existence.

23

About an hour after Bertie Willox climbed thoughtfully up the stairway towards whatever was awaiting him, a casualty surgeon called Dr Campbell was in the house, inspecting the body of the dead father. At midnight, the Professor of Forensic Medicine at Glasgow University was also there—the celebrated John Glaister. Had they ever been in Grove Street before? I don't know. Perhaps they had. Perhaps one of them had been there the previous day. Who knows these things now? (One thing we do know, however, is that Glaister also gave evidence at the Slater trial, over twenty years before.)

Glaister found that rigor mortis, which he would have expected to set in about five or six hours after death, was not yet present; the body was still quite flexible. (At 10 o'clock, the corpse's hand had been 'cold to the touch' of Inspector Cooke.) He believed that the flexibility and the noticeably low degree of coagulation of the blood indicated that the body, though unconscious, had continued alive for some time after the fatal attack.

However, there seems to be a certain lack of detail as to just what this attack consisted of. We learn that Professor Glaister thought that the first blow was struck from behind, 'probably on the back of the head'—but we do not learn how many blows followed it. 'Professor Sydney Smith,' (for the defence—from New Zealand—father of a well-known poet—I've read his book—was never at the scene of this crime himself), 'favoured a frontal attack, producing the single wound between the eyebrows.' Does this mean, as I take it to mean, that there were various other wounds, but that all of them were elsewhere?

And yet the extent of the bloodstaining is eloquent enough. Stewart counted 100 spots of blood on the skirting and near wall of the kitchen. Glaister found twenty-nine bloodstains, due to forcible bespattering, upon the kitchen door alone. There was blood all over the place, suggesting a frenzied and sustained attack, which must surely have stained the assailant too. 'There were marks of blood—spots and splashes—upon the lobby walls, the uprights of the kitchen doorway, the outside of that door itself—which was opened back to the wall and against which the body lay; and on the skirting and walls of the kitchen, on both sides backwards of the body; while towards the table and the fireplace in front the blood had flowed out upon the floor, forming a large pool.'

One of the most eloquent stains (*Eloquent Stains*—a good title for a slim volume of challenging verse; no doubt already used) lay on top of the wooden table surface. Although a white tablecloth covered it, the cloth itself bore no corresponding mark—strongly suggesting that the blood had dried before a cloth was put over it and the table was set. This sounds distinctly incriminating; but one remembers that Jacovelli testified that the table was already set before 2 o'clock. What had happened in between? Was Jacovelli lying, or misremembering, or what? Had the table been cleared, then relaid? Was this bloodstain perhaps just another one of those things?

24

The Yale lock of the outer door was intact. In the kitchen there were three chairs (one each, including absent friends), a table, a bed, and a bed-couch. One of the chairs was overturned and the corner of the tablecloth nearest to the dead man's head was 'slightly pulled down, but not so as to disarrange the dishes'. Boiled beef, broth, sugar bowl, cups and marmalade— the latter rather suggesting breakfast. 'There was no sign of any rice pudding', says Roughead in italics. (Willox had told Stewart that he had given his father some rice pudding that night.) All the table utensils were clean; the beef was uncut; the broth pot full to within 1¼″ (3 cm) of the top. And here Roughead adds what to me is one of the most surprising sentences in the entire work. 'The remaining room of the house was unfurnished.'

Well, it was November. Perhaps they could not afford to heat both rooms. Might they even have been avoiding the other room because the mother died in there? Pure speculation. But what a strange limitation to set to an already extremely limited living-space. The second room was about the same size as the kitchen, but without a bed recess.

When Stewart asked Willox that first night whether or not there might be any likely weapon in the house, he had artlessly(?)

been directed to a heavy hammer, used for breaking lumps of coal. (It was apparently the property of the shipbuilders where his father worked, and where Bertie himself had been an apprentice engineer.) This was found in a cupboard in the kitchen. Of course, if this really *was* the murder weapon, then this single fact is itself almost conclusive against Bertie. It is, to say the least, antecedently much more probable that Bertie was waiting for his father with hammer ready in hand, than that some person or persons absolutely unknown came in, jouked around Dada, managed to locate the hammer, battered him to death with it, then thoughtfully cleaned, and even *replaced*, the implement. A rather far-fetched scenario, you might think.

For the weapon—very curiously so, considering its supposed day-to-day purpose—was indeed fairly clean, quite dry, and wholly free of coal-dust. This last fact clearly calls for some sort of explanation. None appears to have been recorded. Another thought-provoking find was a pair of Bertie's shoes, very wet, leaning against or reposing on the cross bars below the table. (By 9.20 Bertie's feet were clad in boots.)

When were they put there? Before he left the house circa 6.30, one must assume. So: how did they get wet? Did Bertie perhaps wade through a stream some time between Jacovelli's leaving the house around 2 o'clock, and himself leaving around 6.30? Or had they recently been given a damn good scrubbing, then put to dry there, in the discreetest, most overlookable position possible? (By tomorrow, they would presumably have adequately recovered.) After all, what piece of apparel would be most at risk from a pool of blood on the floor?

(10.31–18th August)

25

A search of the clothing on the body produced from the tunic pocket some Army papers; and from other pockets 2½d, a pencil, knife, and scissors.' Scissors *and* a knife seem to be a slightly threatening conjunction. 'A bunch of keys, attached to the deceased's trouser button by a chain lay on the floor behind the body.' We are told that there were no lockfast places anywhere in the house; so, presumably, apart from the front door key, all the others must somehow be connected with his work.

'The linings of *both* trouser pockets were bloodstained, "showing" in the opinion of Professor Glaister, "that a hand with blood on it had been thrust into each of them".' Of course, if Dada had so recently made over the equivalent of two weeks' wages to his son, then this attempted theft was almost too badly timed to be true.

'The inspector Stewart, in the course of his observations, found that the fire was out, though the grate was still warm,' continues Roughead. 'The sink presented to his skilled eye nothing suspicious. A damp towel, hanging hard by upon a nail, and a dishcloth folded up but very wet' ('very wet': just like the shoes) 'on the side of the sink, seemed to him equally innocuous.' A footnote remarks that none of these were subsequently sent off to Professor Glaister for closer examination later, and were therefore never tested for blood. 'If the hammer produced were in fact the weapon used in the crime, it must surely have been washed and dried at that sink; and it is strange that the authorities did not extend their researches to the waste-pipe, which, on that assumption, might have been expected to yield traces of blood.'

This is indeed rather a classic oversight. But it is how such things get done in the normal run of things, I suppose, away from the showpiece centres of excellence. It indicates how the police did not at first pay much attention to the possibility that young Willox himself had done it. All the same, they presumably had control of the location for the whole of the period between the night of the murder and the trial. And if they did think that the hammer was the murder weapon (which was, I think, the official prosecution view), then how else did they suppose it got to be so unsullied?

A loose leaf from a scribbling tablet on the dresser (the dresser? what dresser? This is the first mention of it. What might be coming next? A grand piano?) contained a memo of the messages to be bought that day. 'Monday.—Bone, vegetables, ¼ stone potatoes, 1½ pints milk, ½ dozen eggs, 1 lb. of b.b.' The last being interpreted as meaning, boiled beef. This may perhaps have needed half an hour to collect, but not much more; and perhaps not even that. Fairly basic, but no one was starving. No bread, I notice.

This keenly reminds me that I still possess a modest collection of similar notes given to me by my mother during her last weeks. In fact, now that I look, I discover that I actually have three here with me, in the small plastic Royal Bank coin-bag which I use as a container for cards and so forth. 'Potatoes/tomatoes/rolls/buns' runs one; a terse list which will have been orally supplemented by an 'and anything else you like'. And a more substantial effort on some other day, running: '3 pieces haddock. tomatoes pota-toes/fruit, ¼lb gammon ¼ corned beef/¼ roast beef/4 hard rolls/soft rolls/ (a gap, then) buns.' One for the supermarket, obviously. The fish—to be bought separately, from the fish-shop further down Main Street—will have been for her husband and two sons, I suppose. Latterly there was very little, bar tea and porridge, that she was able to keep down. She writes in a very distinctive hand, tiny, tiny letters.

The third one is actually a note. 'Remember to collect Maria. 3-15.' I'll describe what happened. On the 25th of January this year, as I was still wondering whether to go across to Edinburgh for some literary function or other vaguely to do with Burns, or to take up a very recent invitation for a quiet little meal with a couple of friends, my mind was made up for me by an unexpected phone-call from my father in Largs. He wanted me to come down and help out a week or so earlier than we had previously arranged. Which is to say, right now—as it was then. Mum was going into hospital that day for some sort of routine inspection.

In fact, so worrying was Mum's condition that they decided to keep her in. When I saw her on Friday, four days later, so marked was the deterioration from the previous day that my elder sister and I, who had confidently expected we would be taking her back home on our next visit, realized with terrible suddenness that she might well die within a matter of hours. The staff thought so too. That evening was probably the worst of them all; worse than any which came later. She looked so ravaged. It seemed impossible that this could be Mum, who had always been so reassuring; so reluctant to upset anyone.

And yet there was such spirit there still, as if refusing to be too much impressed by mere cancer. 'Ah well,' she said as we prepared to leave, 'I'll just sleep it out'. Her thought was still of the possibilities of getting better. As she spoke she gave a smile which had enough of her old smile in it to be loveable and enough of something quite new to be terrifying. And if spirit and willingness had been enough, if she had had the slightest real chance at whatever odds against what was, however, a merciless, unstoppable disease, she would have recovered too. Even so, incredibly enough, she did rally yet again; and the very next day she *was* brought back from hospital, to my amazement, to another six weeks of life.

On one of the very last nights of her life, while I was sitting by her bed in the small room where she died, she was uttering broken remarks, like someone trying to escape from a bad dream. At times these were very difficult to make out or interpret. But at one point she just said the three words, '*to get better*'. She said them with force, such eagerness, such warmth of voice. I would have given almost anything to have been able to respond to that loved voice in some way that could have helped her do what she so much wanted to do. But in what way? All I could do was sit there watching her, or try to talk to her, hoping that the love was not as useless as it felt, and that my presence was some sort of comfort or help to her.

How did I get here? When I arrived on that Monday afternoon, I noticed that this small piece of paper was propped against the clock. Yes, the same clock that continues to boing on, months afterwards, getting caught up even in this work. It was a note for my father, to remind him to take the car up to the school at 3.15, to collect his granddaughter. Otherwise he might well have forgotten this untypical arrangement. In the middle of what might fairly be called the more than average tribulations of her own, she was still thinking of other people, and was still alert to their problems. I picked the piece of paper up later on, and appropriated it; for I felt it would have been a great pity had it been thrown away. Which goes some way to explaining what I've been doing for the last two or three minutes.

My father will be in hospital right now, perhaps sleeping. (The same old clock has just struck a single beat, for the half-hour after midnight.) They will continue observing him tomorrow, to check up on an arrhythmie in his heart which has developed since last they recorded it. Less than a fortnight ago he was still driving his car (the Sunday before last was, I think, the last time—'Your father wouldn't walk the length of himsel'' Mum used to say), but I very much doubt whether he will ever be driving it again. Which suddenly reminds me of something else—but I'll wait until tomorrow before I write it down. If I remember. I'll have to go into Glasgow tomorrow, on the morning train; to sort a few things out on what is in effect a day off, while Dad is still in hospital.

Which I did, as far as I could. And now a quite different evening is getting itself involved with golden clouds. Not quite the same clouds, obviously. I think I must have been going, as far as I can make out, to write about Mum's driving. If it wasn't that, I don't know what it was. On one more afternoon somewhere in the sixties, when I as an unsure teenager had got back from school to West Princes Street, through full and complex traffic which, of course, I cannot remember anything about—Mum suddenly announced that she had passed her driving test at the first attempt. We had known she was learning to drive, needless to say; but she had told no one in advance about the impending test, not wishing to put pressure on herself, and, I dare say, not wanting to have to put up with endless tiresome teasing if she failed.

I shrugged the information off with adolescent indifference, because I simply didn't believe her. I assumed it was some sort of obscure joke, and no one was going to put one over on me. However, when from the continuing conversation I finally realized that she was serious; she had really sat the test and had really passed, I did congratulate her and say, well done. I told her I had thought she had just been kidding. Apparently, she had not been much affected by my utter lack of enthusiasm previously. 'I thought it was just you,' she said. Well, I suppose it was.

(8.35–19th August)

26

Also found on that first night in the house were two passbooks (between Willox senior and The Household Supplies Company; and between him and Messrs Gunn, grocers); and two collecting books for the insurance policies which both Robert Willoxes had with the Hearts of Oak Assurance Company. Mrs Willox had been insured there too. When she died, her husband had received £49.1.0—which, whatever their feelings, must have been a significant addition to their resources. Where did it disappear to, one wonders? All gone on the burial? It was the duty of the son to tend ensuing everyday financial transactions; and it seems that he indulged in sharpish practice regarding all of them—as shall later appear.

Willox's trial lasted five days, and was held at Glasgow High Court, from December 16–20. (Thus, it opened exactly six weeks after the killing.) However, at an earlier, pleading diet ten days before, there was shown the intention of lodging a special defence—that of insanity. As the relevant experts reported in a manner unfavourable to such a plea though, this projected defence was dropped. At the trial proper only the formal plea of Not Guilty was advanced.

I can't help thinking that when his agents stated their contention that Willox was probably insane, they were as good as admitting that it was he who had done the killing. Or were they favouring the view that his insanity was, as it were, something of a bonus—and that, in addition to not having performed these nefarious actions, he was also not responsible for his other (innocent) actions anyway? But this would be a little too baroque. One thinks of the old joke: m'lud, my client wasn't there. And even if he was there, he didn't do it. And even if he did it, he was out of his mind at the time.

To my gratified surprise, I discover that 16 December 1931, exactly two years after the start of Bertie's trial, was also a very important day in a rather famous London case; where the degree of surprise at the failure to advance along a certain obvious line might seem to some to be infinitely higher than any surprise there might be that Bertie's insanity plea never got off the ground. Tortuous linkage indeed; but since I had intended to include a brief discussion of this case somewhere, I may as well do so here, I suppose.

There are some similarities with the Helen Priestley affair, in Aberdeen. On that day was found the body of Vera Page, an eleven-year-old girl who had been sexually assaulted and strangled. A cord had been tied loosely round her neck, perhaps to make the small corpse more manoeuverable. There was soot and coal-dust on her face and clothing and candle-grease on her coat. The by and large dry state of her body suggested that it had been hidden indoors. The scene of the crime was probably a disused coal-cellar, which a complete stranger could hardly have known about. Most strikingly, a finger-stall, which smelled strongly of ammonia, was found in the crook of the dead girl's right arm. Obviously, it was not hers, whosesoever it was.

This dreadful crime was never solved. No one was brought to trial for it. It is, in short, an unfathomable mystery. True, there was a suspect, but the evidence against him was as wispy as a spider's web. He lived locally, owned a few candles, and, for some reason, he had pyjama cord in his pocket when he was picked up by the police. He worked as a launderer, which requires ammonia, and he had recently been wearing a finger-stall, to protect a sore finger from that unforgiving substance. Curiously enough, when taken in for questioning, he very obviously still had a sore finger, although he was not wearing a protection of any sort on it. However, no real clues came to light with regard to this one, and so the whole thing remains a study in utter bafflement.

I fear I have no choice but to stop writing for a bit now; so I can watch a television programme which a newspaper I have just looked at describes as, 'the refreshing story of two miners' wives who met and fell in love during the 1984 miners' strike'. Well, people are free to do what they like within reason, of course, but—refreshing? Perhaps that is how the miners themselves responded when they found out. 'Er: my wife has just run off with your wife.' 'Has she really? How refreshing!' And so on.

Perhaps, on second thoughts, I'll just read a bit more about some murders. Learn while you're still young, that's the least exhausting strategy.

(11.01–19th August)

27

After having a bath last night, I forgot to reopen the bathroom curtains. I suppose I forgot I had bothered to draw them. An interested queue of observers was, on balance, probably not forming outside. As I usually close all the other curtains at night, before retiring to my preferred abode up in the loft, it meant that this morning I had to open the curtains in every single room in the house. (Dad usually opens his own, of course, but at present he is still in the hospital.) The living room at the back; the kitchen (which has a blind); the small back room; the bathroom; and the two rooms at the front, which include Dad's bedroom, which once was Mum and Dad's bedroom. Thus do labels change. I am in the other front room at the moment. I need not tell you what I am doing there, I hope. And I was just wondering whether or not my mother had ever been called upon to do that—to open all the curtains in the house—in the nigh on two decades that she lived here. Who may I ask this of? And now, if you'll excuse me, I have to nip out and buy some eggs.

Which I did. I wonder how often she did that herself, whether with or without your permission. Another of these mail-shot brochures arrived for her this morning, though she died months ago. This time from a gardening firm. It offered Mrs Kuppner (in large, tempting letters for her non-existent eyes) three chances to win up to £32,500! 'So, do act quickly!' By now all this becomes nearly as amusingly hopeless as it is painful. If she could still act, be it never so slowly, my dear unknown Dutchmen, some of us would very happily settle for that. However, as things stand, I'm afraid you'll just have to give away all that spare money of yours to someone else. Still, it was a nice thought, and thank you very much for it.

During the last few weeks of her life she was somewhat troubled by such unwanted and unsought catalogues. She would wash herself in the morning, very slowly, from a basin, still wanting to be a normal person; then she would brush her teeth, with such deliberate actions, determined to do properly anything she could still do, even though at times there could be unwelcome side-effects from this. Then she would look at the mail, to see if anything interesting had arrived. Alas, this was rarely the case. Although it would be asking much of any communication, to expect it to be anywhere near equal in significance to those circumstances. A few private letters from various Gods might just about do it, I suppose.

Frequently it was only such catalogues to which she would respond with attractively unchanged cynicism. 'More of this bloody rubbish. I wish they would stop sending them.' But Mum, I fear, had always had something of a shrewd eye for a postal bargain; and the downside of this was that her name had got caught on many mailing lists. I remember the anger I used to feel—it was only fleeting, but it was real anger—that she should at times only have such generalized rubbish to contemplate, to be given her in the morning, another astonishing morning of life, when she so obviously deserved something so much more valuable. She would try, with such intense concentration, to open the package—giving up only if the sealing were too ludicrously or exhaustingly complex, for she still wanted to do it all for herself—then she would closely inspect the contents for a few moments with obvious and increasing lack of enthusiasm; before carefully putting them away to the side, in a neat pile that would be easy to remove, usually with some remark like, always the same old rubbish. My very dear Sirs, I was sorry to hear that your firm was burned to the ground, but, frankly, my own view is that it was no more than you deserved.

However, even this exaggeration is perhaps somewhat ungrateful. At times one of the clothing firms would send a big seasonal catalogue, and she would happily inspect it, leafing through it for quite a while, life returning almost to normal, her terrible illness almost slipping away, as she looked out for something that was clearly good value, and would perhaps suit her granddaughter, or Dad, or a daughter, or perhaps even herself. What else can I possibly say? Such is life. Such is love too. I vaguely remember intending to work in some sort of reference to a murder here, but more important things seem to have driven it utterly out of mind. Good.

(1.09–20th August)

28

Curiously enough, it is only now that I have managed to twig the fact that both the Slater case and the Willox one feature isolated murders in which an older figure is beaten about the head with vast effusion of blood, almost certainly in both instances by a financially-driven younger male relative. In both homicides, blood flies all over the place, and there is some speculation as to how the murderer could avoid—or how he dealt with—being covered by the victim's gore.

In each incident it was presumably necessary to finish the victim off for good right away—since the failure to do so would probably lead to a subsequent identification being made by the survivor, with potentially lethal results. Which is to say, it was not simply a question of getting an awkward customer off your back while a robbery was carried out. And since it is not easy for a hitherto non-murdering member of the community to know just what will be enough to effect the purpose, they will as like as not find themselves erring on the side of blood-lust, and striking again and again, long after death has become the certain result of their assault. Furthermore, I am reliably informed that one of the main reasons why blood covers such great distances during assault with a blunt instrument is to be found in what happens when an already bleeding wound is struck again. This produces an effect somewhat like—but only somewhat—striking a puddle with the flat of your hand.

While we are here, I may as well mention that there seems to have been, as far as I can see, absolutely nothing done in the way of fingerprinting in the Willox business. Perhaps there was nothing worth fingerprinting—but how could one know that in advance? I suppose it may have been done as a matter of routine, and not have been thought worth alluding to so far—after all, whose fingerprints could they possibly discover?—but still, the complete silence on the subject is noteworthy.

The principle of the uniqueness of the individual fingerprint was known by some people several decades before, but the first ever case decided on fingerprinting evidence in the UK was that of the Stratton brothers, who battered an old shop-owner to death in pursuance of a theft, in March 1905. The Marion Gilchrist murder in West Princes Street occurred in December 1908. It would surely have been a simple enough process, a) to take Slater's prints and see whether they were also to be found at the scene of the crime (which they wouldn't be, of course—perhaps a rather serious consideration), and b) to examine the wreckage for signs of intrusive fingerprints on certain crucial props. But, apparently, absolutely none of this was ever done. Roughead even claimed to possess a photograph which showed a chair—the legs of which were probably the murder weapon—which had a hand clearly impressed in blood at the top of it! I don't know of anyone else who has also claimed to have seen this picture—which presumably made its way into Roughead's possession from a police source. But there must have been sufficient adequate marks all over the place anyway.

(3.19–20th August)

A little light and late research uncovers the fact that, in the Stratton affaire, a single print of a right thumb was involved. That single, indiscreet mark more than anything else had a pair of brothers hanged. They had killed the old man's wife too, in cold blood. They were wearing masks at the time. The shop-owner, Mr

Thomas Farrow—his wife was called Ann—was not killed instantly. In fact, he was even able to get back to his feet after the
departure of the assailants. He went to the door of the shop, and
stood there for a few moments, covered in blood, looking out
dazedly into the street. A young girl saw him as he did so, but she
didn't realize enough to know that this was an utterly extraordinary
sight, and one that she should tell others about without further
delay. He then went back into the shop and, from some confused
and too late motive of self-preservation, locked the door behind
him. Then, I assume, he lay down and died. His wife did not die
for another three or (by another account) four days.

T here were actually four charges levelled against Willox at his trial; the fourth being that of assault, theft and murder by him against his father. The first concerned false entries and forged receipts by him regarding the Household Supplies Company passbook, which he then represented to his father as being genuine. The second was the same, but with regard to D.A. Gunn, Ltd; Willox having forged 'Paid with thanks. 2/9/29. J.M.' The third referred to two forged entries, representing fictitious payments to the Hearts Of Oak Assurance Company. It is significant that Willox was unanimously found guilty of all these charges, which in effect provide the background for a fuller understanding of the fourth, the capital charge. Of course, they don't in themselves prove his guilt. But they do rather set you thinking.

(6.33–20th August)

W e were with Bertie and his doctored books.
'He had, as appears,' says Roughead, 'pilfered the housekeeping
money and made false entries in the passbooks to conceal the fact
from his father; but from time to time he did make small efforts to
reduce the deficit.'
One particularly interesting fact emerges. When the rep from
Gunn called on him, as usual, on a Monday, on the 28th October,
Bertie specifically asked him not to call at the house on the 4th of
November, the next Monday (and the day of the murder, of course).
He said that he himself would call at the firm's premises on Wednesday the 6th, and make the requisite payment then. What does this
mean? Is it merely accident that, by this means, Willox has seen to
it that the rep will not call at the house on the day of the crime?
(One would very much like to know at what time of day it was that
this rep habitually called. If it was at 6 o'clock or after then there
would be good reason for a meticulous planner to wish to postpone
this visit.) (Of course, this postponement need not indicate that
Willox genuinely intended to pay up on the Wednesday. After all,
in the maelstrom of events—particularly if his father had been
robbed of the house's kitty too—he could hardly be expected to pay
much attention to such trivial details as that would then be.)

This raises the general question of forward planning. If Bertie did it then it is extremely likely that he put a good deal of thought into it beforehand. It is most improbable that on the spur of the moment, one evening when his father returned home as usual, he suddenly flipped his lid, took out the hammer, and battered in the head of his beloved Dada. If he had, then the whole thing would quickly have gone public in noise, hysteria, and ill-considered continuation or flight. There is considerable evidence to the contrary. The prompt reappearance on the streets, with witnesses to his presence there sedulously cultivated; the coherence of his tale to the investigating officers, one or two blips notwithstanding; the very efficiency with which he carried out the enterprise, cleaned what needed to be cleaned, and got off the premises. This hint to the rep is rather suggestive too; as is the smoothness with which he went through the optimum routine (establish an alibi, pay off the debts) on the night of the murder.

No. Wherever and however the idea was first planted (perhaps from newspaper reports of the Philip Yale Drew case, which involved a murder in Reading on June 22 that year; perhaps even from one of the films he enthusiastically patronized), it must have taken a certain amount of time for him to bring it to fruition. It was, in short, a premeditated murder—and who knows for how many days the taciturn Aberdonian was sharing an enclosed space with, and even sleeping very near to, his sole remaining close family member, and one who was wondering, more than anything else, how best he might put an end to his life. This hint suggests that, with a week to go, the final plan was already largely decided upon.

(8.20–20th August)

31

I't's astonishing. A couple of minutes after finishing the previous section, I picked up a sheet of paper to carry on about Bertie's lesser crimes, and had just written down the number 31 and paused for thought, when there was a repeated ring at the doorbell. It was the sister of May, the woman who lived in the house next door. Evidently her elder sister. She asked to talk to Dad, but Dad was on the phone, in his bedroom. (He got back from hospital a bit over three hours ago, looking comparatively well.) So she said she would just tell me. It was to say that May had died in hospital at 9 o'clock that morning.

I was staggered. I hadn't even known she was ill. I remember talking to her more than once during Mum's last illness, and just after her death—and her genuine sorrow was very obvious and affecting. I mentioned some of this to her sister, and she said, yes, she knew that; and May had told her that 'she missed her terribly'. Apparently, she had had a heart problem and an underactive thyroid. I had assumed it would just be some kid or other trying to collect for a charity, or something like that.

'I always felt that she was somehow there for me, if I needed someone to talk to,' she said to me just after Mum's death. In early 1991, well under three years ago, the two of them were sitting together in the living-room—she had just arrived on an impromptu social call—the sort of thing which, to be honest, my mother sometimes resented—when I looked in to say goodbye to Mum, because I was just then going back to Glasgow after a visit. It must have been a Friday. The rain was pouring down. I had injured my knee again, helping them to shift furniture—Dad had recently had a mildish heart attack, and had to be somehow prevented from doing things—and so, uniquely, I had had to call for a taxi to take me to the station. I said 'Goodbye' to Mum, and the pair of them responded together. Two women sitting in a room talking to each other. My father will have been in the bedroom as usual, I suppose.

'I've got arthritis in my knee', explained her sister, as she made her way with difficulty back down the few steps by the front door. I don't even know her name, although I did gather that she lives in Houston. Houston, Renfrewshire, of course; not Houston, Texas. I dare say that that is how I myself am eventually going to have to take such obstacles, in a couple of decades, if I survive. It has taken me thirteen minutes so far to write this, in my very own, rather inefficient, shorthand. I can still hear, off in the distance, that Dad is talking on the phone even yet. Therefore he still does not know this. But you do. Isn't that astonishing. I wonder who it is he is talking to. Perhaps you know that as well?

The sister also told me that she had informed the other neighbour, Billy, of the death. This is two houses away from us. Yet, I have no idea who this man is or what he looks like. Of course, I may have seen him. Nor, I suspect, does Dad—who certainly must have seen him, I would imagine. I don't remember that Mum ever mentioned the guy either—but what can I decide now of what she may or may not have known, that for some reason or other was not passed on to us? Fifteen minutes plus. I think he has stopped talking.

(8.42–20th August)

32

Ah well. Back to work. The sheets of paper, the photocopies, remain there unaffected. Or so one hopes. Mr Henry Cox, the agent of the Hearts Of Oak Assurance Company, said that he collected the monthly premiums in person at the payer's home, usually seeing the younger Willox. The last time payment had been made was the 7th of September. On the 7th of October, he received nothing, being told that the Willoxes had spent too much on their autumn holiday. The trip to Rothesay, evidently. Only if they were more than two months in arrears and a statutory notice of required payment had been given (which itself allowed 28 further days of grace to pay in) would the policies lapse. Therefore the Willoxes' policies were still in force.

The premiums were 6/4d a month: 5/- for the father's, 1/4 for the son's. This is getting on for a full day's wages of the elder Willox, and it easily exceeds the maximum weekly allowance (4/6) that he ever gave to his son. (If the son is to be believed on this; he is the sole source of such information.) The sum payable on the death of the father was £48.15.0—six bob less than the £49.1.0 paid out on Mrs Willox's policy. And, obviously, this could only go to the son, who, presumably, could never have had so much money in his life before. I suspect that the knowledge of this had some bearing on events.

The next detail is a little troublesome. On October the 7th, it seems, Cox was told that the next payment (a double payment) would be made on November the 4th, exactly four weeks in the future. But evidently he was routinely given to calling on the Saturday previous to such dates (September 7 was a Saturday), and he duly turned up on Saturday the 2nd of November, already looking for the double payment. Willox senior was not at home—which is equivalent to saying, he was at work. (One wonders how he used to pass his time on a Sunday. Or indeed, how *they* did. Did they go to church, for instance?) Willox junior said that his father had not left the money, as he had thought it was not due until November the 11th (i.e. the Monday after next). I assume that, as a matter of course, Willox snr would often leave the money out on the Saturday—perhaps even on the Friday evening, if that is when he himself was paid (or was he paid on Monday?)—ready for Cox to pick it up on the Monday. Perhaps Cox was very eager to get these arrears cleared up as quickly as possible. Anyway, it was arranged that Cox should come back on the Monday after all.

Clearly, by this stage, Bertie was up to his armpits in it. Various sums entrusted to him had been illicitly spent. Indeed, one ponders whether Bertie may not have had fairly conclusive plans for his father over the weekend. Obviously, these payments would have to be made soon enough or the policies would lapse, and such a malign eventuality would certainly be communicated to the father. After all, they were *his* policies. This looks to be clear evidence of financial trouble several weeks before the fatal event.

One thing that is obvious is that Willox jnr just did not have the necessary cash to hand, even though his father must have handed it over to him. The financial situation was tightening by the minute. A pawnbroker, Alexander McLeod, testified that *since September* (the last time an insurance payment had been made), Bertie had hocked his mother's rings (!) (an interesting plural—so much for sentiment), his father's War Medals, trousers, shirts, sheets, etc. (Whatever that 'etc' might be—presumably just about whatever else there was in the house that was not on open display and which Willox thought he could get some money on.) Clearly, this mode of financing his lifestyle was very near the point of exhaustion. *None* of these things had been redeemed. So, the £2.10.0 which he borrowed from Mrs Duffy in order to redeem his father's medals must, one assumes, have been put to another purpose entirely;

unless, of course, they were redeemed and subsequently put back into hock. But I must now break off, to fix my own father his lunch.

Where was I? With regard to the orgy of pawning, Bertie's friend, James Turner, said in the witness box that 'he did not want his father to find out'—this is Bertie, of course—a remark which merely makes explicit what one had already rather taken for granted. The pawnbroker himself testified that on the very day of the murder, November the 4th, Bertie called between 1 and 2 p.m. and sought to pledge a pair of shoes. But that, as they were worn out, this offer was declined. Clearly, he was by now at rock bottom.

Actually there is a difficulty about this pair of shoes too—which Roughead says are the very pair later found, wet, resting on the cross bar below the kitchen table. I take it that Willox was already wearing his boots when he set out to try to raise money on his worn shoes, and that he kept them on all day. (It is in the evidence that he was wearing boots in the evening. It is unlikely that he had yet another pair of shoes—for, apart from general considerations of poverty, if he had had another pair he would probably have tried to hock them too.) So why were these shoes wet? Why, if not because they had got blood on them—whether they were being worn at the time, or were indiscreetly nearby—and had to be washed clean thereafter?

But this occurred to me only as I was actually writing. The difficulty I actually meant to refer to is a completely different one. And, in fact, now that I examine the source more clearly, I find that the supposed difficulty dissolves. Jacovelli testified to going up to see Willox 'between 1 and 2'—exactly the time when Bertie was trying to pawn his shoes. I take it it was only a few minutes' walk to the pawnbroker's and back. I took Jacovelli to have claimed that he had been with Bertie from 1 till 2—but, on closer inspection, it seems as if the claim is merely that at some time between 1 and 2 he called up to see him, and invited him to come round to his place at 7.30. Surely Bertie could so easily have been out when he called. Would he have waited at the door? However, he was there—whether before or after the visit to the pawnshop. And who knows but that the very fact of having this half-alibi now waiting for him at 7.30 may itself have played some part in convincing him that it could well be done today.

(1.51–21st August)

33

This is odd. Picking up the story of Mr Cox the insurance man from where we left off: as requested, he did return on Monday, but at 1 o'clock! Evidently the busiest hour of the day. Bertie suavely lied that his father was 'just away'. In fact, he had left for work at the usual time of 4.45 a.m. Deftly deflecting the subject onto the prospect of likely future gain, Bertie added that Willox senior had actually wanted to see Mr Cox (who evidently had little idea of the hours that the father worked) regarding 'an endowment'. A very professional lie indeed. So Cox said he would come back that same night. This was unlooked-for enthusiasm. (Or, perhaps, growing distrust.) Boldly improvising, Bertie said that that would not do, because his father would then be 'going to the doctor'. (What? At night? For the whole evening?) So Cox agreed to return on the Tuesday evening instead; and finally went off, leaving Bertie to his thoughts—which were presumably increasingly hysterical ones.

I presume it was after he had managed to get rid of the adhesive insurance agent that Bertie, near the end of his tether, hared off to the pawnbroker's to see whether by some miracle he might be able to raise cash on his last resource, a pair of worn old shoes. He failed. Arrived back, wondering what on earth he could do to escape the inevitable showdown on the following night, when Cox and his father would disastrously compare notes, he was visited by Jacovelli. Thus he was offered, not a full alibi (but how could he possibly have one of those, if he was going to do it?), but a useful element of one. Get out quickly, behave normally, Bob's your uncle. After Jacovelli left, Bertie probably then set his mind to making the necessary preparations, and trying to anticipate whatever it was that might yet be required. Of course, all this may actually be some way wide of the mark.

Nevertheless, Bertie's inventions were just about to catch up with him anyway. Since his father would be able to inspect the passbooks, and presumably did, Bertie had had to forge entries in the relevant spaces, stating that payments had indeed been made on October 7 and November 4. Otherwise Dada would want to know just what was going on. One wonders when exactly this second fake initialling ('H.C.') was done. Obviously not *after* the murder. But clearly Willox could never present these books to Cox again; even had he later made the payments which were due. Cox would then have seen the forgeries there, already in place. It is actually hard to see any convincing way out of this one, short perhaps of destroying the books by some plausible means, whatever *that* might amount to. Come to that, it might have been no worse for Willox not to have left the books there in the house for the police to find. Perhaps he vaguely thought he would still have time to remove them later; or, perhaps, in the rush of events, it simply never occurred to him how incriminating they would turn out to be.

I suspect the main thing was, overwhelmingly, the need to prevent the father from finding all this out. Evidently, to Willox, the thought of killing the old fellow seemed to present far fewer difficulties. Bear in mind the temperamental differences, perhaps exacerbated by the absence of the mother, no longer there to keep the peace and smooth things over (Willox snr seems to have had temperamental differences with everybody); add to that the horrible self-centred callousness particularly possible in young adulthood; and the intolerable nature of the debacle which was pressing ever nearer; and I suppose one is already quite a good way along the road to grasping why these events happened.

Thus, the chances of this having been a crime of passion, something done in the heat of the moment, without malice aforethought, are precisely nil. It was a murder planned with all possible care, in order to extricate a young man from a bad jam—or, if he could not hope to be extricated entirely, then at least to save him from the worst of it. The shock waves would have to take care of whatever remained. I take it that, if you are going to kill your father, you will probably prefer not first of all to engage him in conversation, then leap at him with a hammer in a lull during remarks about football or the price of meat. The likeliest possibility will surely be to wait till he comes home, many hours after you have last seen him, and then attack him at once, as soon as the body returns, before anything like personal contact has been distressfully re-established. But I am glad to say I am no expert on these points.

I presume he might wait in the unoccupied room. The father would hang up his things, as per usual, then turn to go into the kitchen and the waiting meal. Willox would emerge behind him, and fell him with his first blow. If he had thought of the risk of bloodstains—and I imagine he would have done—then he would possibly be wearing the least amount that he felt he could reasonably get away with. Most of the stuff he might have protected his clothes with was already in the pawn, after all. There is also to be recalled the fact that, later in the day, he was wearing the trousers from his other suit, the black one, with the brown jacket. Why he didn't just change his suit entirely I can't quite work out. The brown trousers were found by Glaister to have faint traces of mammalian blood; but the garment had been rubbed with a wet cloth. One wonders why. There were also such stains on the brown waistcoat. With regard to the possibility of the shoes having been rendered wet by the rain (and how I wish I could say that just as easily in classical Greek), it is noteworthy that, although it rained later, on Professor Glaister's account of things, the boots of the deceased were entirely dry. So the shoes were most unlikely to have been made wet before 6 o'clock.

The linings of *both* trouser pockets were bloodstained, says Roughead, 'showing', in the opinion of Professor Glaister, 'that a hand with blood on it had been thrust into each of them'. So he did the deed, got hold of the money instantly (in the famous little wallet, one supposes—which would keep any blood off the notes), and only then, or so I assume, went over to the sink at the window and cleaned up himself, the hammer, and whatever else claimed his attention. Where is there the slightest indication that anyone else was involved? Fortunately no one else arrived at the door during that crucial twenty minutes or so. (What if the canvasser, for instance, had chosen just such a moment to call at! I mean, these people tend to have inconvenience down to a fine art. That would be the knocking at the gate in *Macbeth* all over again.) And if anyone, across the surmised back green, had happened to glance out and see a youth at a window, washing something, or even washing something off an item of clothing, why should that in any way be suspicious or memorable?

(3.38–21st August)

34

I think from Mrs Watt's evidence (lurking in the bathroom, overhearing the angry riposte of 'You won't get a penny from me'), we could assume that on that weekend Willox was still genuinely attempting to wring some necessary cash from the old man; in which case, presumably he was not yet committed to the notion of getting him out of the way permanently. But Flo has clearly got something seriously wrong; and it may well have been a previous weekend, a previous visit by Harrington, a previous anything, or voices from heaven come to that. From the sound of it, I don't think she is deliberately trying to help Bertie get off the hook. But at the very least she seems to bespeak a certain lack of the idyllic life between father and son.

I see I got things slightly wrong earlier. Wonders will never cease. Jacovelli testified that when he left Bertie, circa 9.20 on the Monday evening, Bertie was wearing his brown trousers, with his black jacket and waistcoat/vest. (The police agreed. He was wearing a rainproof coat over them; and also a cap.) Whereas, in the afternoon, he had had on his brown suit entire. So it was in fact only the trousers that had *not* been changed. Or (of course) if he had changed out of them, he had later changed back into them. Would Willox not have realized the strong tactical advantage of appearing in the the evening in precisely the clothes that he had already been wearing earlier on?

It is worth noting that, according to Roughead, 'the boy always maintained that they,'—the brown jacket and 'vest'—'were hung by him *behind the kitchen door.*' If the corpse of the father was, in effect, pinning the open door back against the kitchen wall, then it is rather obvious why Willox, particularly if he had by now finished clearing up and was looking for his street clothes, would have had some difficulty in rescuing them from where they were. (Mind you, the police said that they were actually found that night hanging against the door of the empty room. Might he perhaps have put them there for safekeeping, then, in the confusion, have forgotten this—and have assumed that they were out of reach behind the kitchen door, in their usual spot? Or even have looked there, fail to find them, forget what the arrangement was, and have been forced to make do with what came immediately to hand?) (Or not?)

35

According to Glaister and Dr Anderson, the dead man's stomach was entirely devoid of food—suggesting that he had eaten nothing recently, and certainly not a full meal. I take this as read. The hammer had been washed, but apparently (and understandably) in something of a hurry; and in its various nooks and crannies there yet lurked some traces of mammalian blood.

And that is pretty well that, as far as the background to the case is concerned. The only other thing, perhaps, is a very significant silence. Which is to say, Willox himself elected, or was persuaded, not to go into the witness box. To me this is not neutral: that one should fail to take the opportunity of explaining to the best of one's ability just how it comes about, and how wrongly, that one is being tried on a horrendous charge which one is definitely not guilty of.

There are those who think that, more than anything else, a trial should be about trying to get at the truth of the matter—rather than providing us with a sort of debating competition. That those who are centrally involved should all therefore be under the statutory necessity of revealing what they know about it, where this could be of value in clarifying a case. And whatever the accused may or may not be, he is pretty clearly central. This prerogative—of deciding, in effect, not to take part—is not legally allowed to anyone else, whatever their interest in the matter. What is the justification for it? That no one should be compelled to testify against himself? But if he is guilty, why not? And if he is not guilty, then all the more important, surely, to find out his side of things to the full.

Of course, as in practically any complex issue, there are arguments pro and con. But, as things stand, it is quite clear to me at any rate that the weight of the argument supports the contention that the accused should have no more right to keep what he knows about it to himself than anyone else does. However, I may yet learn things that will convince me otherwise, I suppose. Have no fear: I shall certainly keep you informed if I do, and with a mass of detail at that. It would quite possibly do more harm than good to change this one detail, and leave the rest of our adversarial system of justice intact. I should know: I've thought about it for at least ten minutes.

(4.57–21st August)

36

T he learned judge, the Honourable Lord Hunter, made in conclusion what looks to have been a fairly sane and balanced speech in summation to the jury. Among various astute points lay the question as to why, given that the passbook of the Household Supplies Company purported (thanks to Willox's forgeries) to be fully paid up, why then would the father give Bertie a very considerable sum of money to go and pay off the invisible balance remaining? A good question. He further remarked, doubt-less with a certain weariness, that there were *always* discrepancies when a number of people were speaking as to times. (*Always?* I might have thought an alert lawyer could have appealed for mis-direction on this one. There must surely be cases on which all the witnesses agree as to timing—and the lifeline thrown out by Florence Watt's testimony, whether deliberately or not, is just about the only card which the defence has in its possession.)

He also observed, inter alia, that the accused seemed to have spent much of his time in billiard rooms—not the remark of a friend— and that if the father had been assailed by some enemy or maniac who had called at the door, he would have been most unlikely to fall into the position that he did fall into, lying as he did mainly inside the kitchen. The jury left at 3.15 p.m.; and returned at 5.05 p.m., finding Willox guilty, unanimously, on the lesser charges, and guilty by a majority (9–6, apparently; the 6 being for Not Proven, I take it) on the capital charge. They also recommended him to mercy on account of his youth. (After all, he had only murdered his father in cold blood to cover up his thefts from him.)

Hunter sentenced Willox to death—at which Willox again collapsed ('into the arms of one of the police constables beside him'). He was carried off downstairs ('unconscious') by half a dozen policemen.

There was an appeal—in the course of which the Lord Advocate, replying for the Crown, said that the care that the jury took over reaching its decision could be seen from the very fact that it had taken them over two hours to do so. Therefore, either the timings from Roughead given above are slightly out (3.15 p.m.; 5.05 p.m.—1 hr 50 minutes), or the Lord Advocate's Office is having trouble with some very elementary arithmetic. Of course, had the jury hurtled back with a verdict after ten minutes, this would have shown their certainty rather than their carelessness—unless, granted, their vote had still been no more decisive than 9–6.

The appeal judges negatived it, the Lord Justice-General concluding that, 'it must therefore stand; although His Lordship felt bound to add that if the verdict had been one of "Not Proven" he would certainly not have said it was unreasonable either'. Lords Blackburn and Morison concurred.

One does rather notice that no one seems to have mentioned just how they might have responded to a Not Guilty verdict. I take it that this is no mere oversight. Of course, such a verdict would not have been appealed, for even the most bizarre Not Guilty verdict is sacrosanct—but then, neither would a Not Proven have been appealed. And where Guilty and Not Proven are both not unreasonable, but Not Guilty is completely out of sight, what assumption does this lead to, on entirely general grounds, concerning the actual guilt of the accused? Roughead himself seemed rather nervous of the given verdict, and explicitly stated that 'my vote would have been Not Proven'. It all depends on where the horizon between reasonable and unreasonable doubt lies, I suppose. If only there were the slightest indication that anyone else was involved.

Willox was due to hang on the 4th of February. On the 23rd of

January, he heard that his sentence had been commuted to penal servitude for life. So; not quite the end of his problems. The father's estate was valued at £57—£48 of it on the insurance policy which the son had such difficulty in handing over his payments for.

(5.37–21st August)

With which I conclude my scrutiny of Roughead's article. What next? Perhaps I ought to try to find out more about this case elsewhere. Unfortunately, it will be several days before I can leave Dad, and return to Glasgow to pursue any such matters in the libraries there. It is now Saturday 21 August. I'll probably not leave here until the 30th. Rather than waste time, then, I suppose the logical thing to do would be to indulge langorously in my own reminiscences, such as they are, about the area of the city where the crime took place; and perhaps also maunder on about various other crimes which are either relevant or merely of interest. But who knows what the particular future may or may not bring?

(6.54.)

37

Since writing the previous, which I finished. under three hours ago (*the main body of it, that is*), I have discovered a doing which had some striking similarities (and dissimilarities) with the Willox case. It tends to suggest that young Bertie was a rather fortunate chap to get his death sentence repealed. To be brutally honest, I discovered it only a few minutes ago in a book I am reading, a sort of murder guide to London, which I bought last Thursday, when I was in Glasgow.

I don't know London terribly well, but I have once or twice walked pleasantly lost through Pimlico, reassured that though I was none too much in control of where I was headed, the river and the more familiar areas that enclosed the district would prevent me from coming to any great mischief. I am fairly certain I must have been in Tachbrook Street. I seem to remember even seeing the street sign.

It was there, the year before Bertie's awfully big adventure, that an army bandsman called William Holmyard went visiting his grandfather—who had an identical name (compare the two Robert Willoxes)—to ask his advice on getting a job. To which highly reasonable endeavour the irascible elderly gent remarkably responded, by cursing the offspring of his absent son's loins, and going for him with a chair. Can this really be all that happened? I can only give the facts as I find them. The elder Holmyard was by no means the weaker of the two, and the bandsman urgently felt the need to defend himself—which he did by hitting his assailant over the head with a pair of tongs. The respected elder later died in hospital.

Compare this to Willox. A single blow, unpremeditated, accidentally fatal, against a man who himself started the affray, if the facts are as reported; as opposed to repeated blows, unprovoked, deliberately fatal, against an unarmed, unsuspecting man. Yet, the perpetrator of the *second* assault is shown mercy, and the perpetrator of the first is hanged. Evidently not a phenomenon which marches neatly in step with logic.

(8.53–21st August)

38

I t is a matter of some irritation to me that, try as I may, I can never quite summon up from memory a picture of me definitely going through Grove Street. We left West Princes Street in 1967, by which time it was already clear that massive alterations in the area were on their way—but Grove Street (and certainly the line of that street) will almost certainly still have been there at that period.

The directest way from West Princes Street to my father's first shop, opened in the early 1960s on the south corner of the east end of North Woodside Road, looking out at Garscube Road as it anglèd past to the north-west towards its meeting with the top of St George's Road.

I remember this route very well: the curiously shallow terrace (now gone) opposite Glenfarg Street (still there); the impressive width of Windsor Terrace (totally altered), which had some sort of veterinary establishment in it, I seem to recall—but a road which, in its older form, I don't think I ever actually entered; the curving exterior stairways to the upper storey in North Woodside Road itself, somewhere between the top ends of St Peter's Street, Balnain Street, Braid Street.

The last two of these were shorter, and ended up southwards in

Grove Street; St Peter's Street made a T-junction with the start of Grove Street, and then ran on for a further block, to finish at the main road, New City Road. Turn right from there and you're at Bayne and Duckett's shoe shop, which was where my mother always used to take us when such purchases were again necessary. ('Is that shoe too tight, Francis? No: *you* tell *us*. After all, you're the one who's going to have to wear it.') Strangely, there was only one road which linked St Peter's Street to its parallel neighbour St George's Road: this was the rather insignificant Gladstone Street, south even from Grove Street, and disproportionately near to New City Road. This one to some extent survives even yet.

Grove Street had a distinct north-east tilt to it. It was curiously uncut-through. Balnain Street to the north, first of all. Then, a little later, Scotia Street to the south (but not quite parallel to Balnain Street). Then, a bit further on, Braid Street to the north. And then, independently, Abercorn Street, to the south, with a slight dog-leg in it. Then there was a fairly long uninterrupted conclusion leading up to Garscube Road. (The Willoxes lived between Scotia and Abercorn Streets, much nearer to the former.)

Indeed, for such a group of almost entirely simple, straight streets, this was a remarkably involved cluster. Scotia Street extended for a brief distance north *and* south of New City Road. It was, I think, in Scotia Street that William Burrell—not yet *Sir* William—of Burrell Collection fame, was born. Southwards it ended at Shamrock Street, of which I have innumerable memories. A dead-end to the west (Gayfield Street, which I never entered, and which is no longer anywhere) was its only southern tributary. To the north, however, it threw off a sort of southern neighbour to Grove Street, called Burnside Street; and this one, between Scotia Street and Abercorn Street, itself also threw off a little street southwards, which was one small unbroken block north of New City Road, and another one south of it. This was Rosehall Street. One of our downstairs neighbours in West Princes Street I think owned a sweetshop at the southwest corner of Rosehall Street, at Shamrock Street. As children we were much intrigued by this. I rather think we supposed she was the only neighbour of ours who had unfortunately been obliged to work for a living. But what a wonderful job, all the same!

For the sake of completeness, I may as well add that Crossburn Street ran east from Braid Street to Garscube Road, and was long enough for a small street (Northburn Street) to run north from its middle up into North Woodside Road. Northburn Street was thus the first street that one crossed, when one left the shop on the straightforward pedestrian route home—though usually when one left the shop it was in Dad's van, and that van took him just about everywhere in the city. And thus I have named (I think) every thoroughfare in the non-golden near-rhomboid of St George's Road, North Woodside Road, Garscube Road and New City Road. I am not quite sure why. Some of the names remain, and perhaps about 10% of the reality.

(3.48–22nd August)

39

I have one bafflingly precise memory of Abercorn Street. My father was driving his van northwards up it, and I was with him. Who else was with him, if anyone, I do not know. I assume that we must merely have been heading back to the shop after some errand or other—though why we should have been going via Abercorn Street, rather than one of the main roads, escapes me. Perhaps we had a customer to call on. Perhaps it was the most convenient way from our last stop. Perhaps there was some diversion necessary, I don't know. Nor do I know why I should recall this one moment. Perhaps because it was an unusual route? But I associate it with nothing. With no further details. I merely have this very precise recollection, for a few seconds of my life—of our lives—of being in that particular street, in a place now utterly transformed into the completely different lines of a new motorway system. I'm not complaining. It's just that a little more explanation would not have gone amiss, I suppose.

Likewise, I recall once arriving in what my old map tells me is Braid Street, walking or running to Dad's shop—hurrying, anyway—and seeing to my astonishment that, since last I had been there (evidently a long time before), there had been created a completely open square of empty ground, where before there had always been a block of buildings. Thus I discovered the demolition of what I take to be the block bounded by Braid Street, Crossburn Street, Northburn Street (any burn there must have been built over long before), and North Woodside Road. Off they had gone, with their hundred thousand histories.

I must have been going to the shop by what I thought was absolutely the quickest route, beginning to escape the timorousness of boyhood, and the fear of straying from the most familiar paths. So I assume I came from New City Road, up Scotia Street, along Grove Street for a small reach (extremely close to No. 79), then Braid Street—but, of course, I can now remember none of this earlier passage. I certainly can't remember leaving the familial home in West Princes Street—just one of many thousands of such occasions. There it is, the nearest I can get: a moment of my life when I must just have left Grove Street behind me, less than a minute previously. So, if some famous catastrophe should turn out to have happened in Braid Street, well then: I can remember being right there.

And of St Peter's Street I have a particularly treasured memory. This was considerably later, circa 1970 I suppose; by which time we lived far up Maryhill Road, in Barra Street, and I was a university student—a time magical for me in most things, apart from my dealings with the academics, tremendously gifted though they all were. It was probably a Friday. Mum would drive most of the way into town, park the car in any reasonably central space, ideally gratis, and we would walk to Marks and Spencer's. I would carry the bags for her back to wherever it was the car was parked. I accompanied her comparatively rarely, but this nonetheless did happen several times over the course of that period.

I remember how, on one occasion, we slammed the doors of what I seem to recall was an Austin Cambridge, and we walked down off the sidestreet onto New City Road. There was already massive reconstruction going on in the area, which may be why she had had to park at such a hefty distance from her intended goal. Or perhaps there were other things to be done too. Virtually none of the former buildings were still standing. She will have said something like, 'My, they've certainly changed everything around here, haven't they?'; and I looked up at a nearby roadsign which we were walking by together. It said, St Peter's Street. (As I write this, I remember a sign in a first-floor window, containing the word 'Chiropodist'. This had certainly been here or hereabouts at this corner earlier on, and perhaps the building containing it yet stood, though I doubt it.) This is different from the previous cases, because I know why I am remembering this one. Which is to say, I understand why it should be worth remembering.

I want to say some more about this; about simple happiness or whatever it is. I remember too some moments from what must have been my first year and a half as a student. Everything seemed possible. Everything except that, quarter of a century later, I would still be a writer on the breadline, hacking stuff out on an ancient typewriter in a bedsit somewhere. Such, as they say, is life. I remember how once I was sitting (actually, on a desk) by an upper window in Barra Street; and Mum, who had come back from just such a shopping expedition alone, came into the room, said something ('Here you are,' or 'These are for you'), threw over a large packet of salted peanuts that she bought for me, grimaced when I caught them and thanked her, and left. I can even recall what book I was reading: a Pelican paperback of Isaac Deutscher's biography of Stalin. Everything glorious was just beginning. I did not even realize that the author was, at best, not a particularly wise man. Such bonuses were fairly routine. Usually it was either peanuts or a small blue box containing three walnut whips—such as are placed temptingly at the check-out counters, to beguile the shopper as she waits for her turn to pay and leave.

But eventually this ceased, and more than two decades passed. The day after—no. Two days after she died, my sisters and I went to another Marks and Spencer's, this time in Ayr, to buy sandwiches for those who would come back to the house (this house) after the funeral. As we stood at the check-out, I saw small blue boxes of these things, still looking exactly the same, and on impulse I bought one. I didn't eat any of them myself. As I recall, I let my niece eat two of them, and my younger sister the third. The empty box must still be there somewhere back in my room in Glasgow. Obviously, it had never occurred to me to try to keep any of the earlier ones. Why should it have done? Usually the wisest thing is just to leave happiness alone.

How extremely fortunate you are, that I did not die yesterday. And for innumerable other things, no doubt. But if I had thus sadly expired, you would never have learned of this, if you have indeed learned of it. I shall do you the honour of supposing that you will agree that this would have been your loss. Rash, perhaps; but let us be rash, for once at least.

(6.58–22nd August)

I am rather struck by how bizarre it is to mingle personal reminiscences of one's recently deceased mother, with the discussion of a stark local patricide. But there we are: it is bizarre. Some less favourable memories now. I recall that I was once running up Garscube Road towards the shop, from the direction of my secondary school—and, perhaps more relevantly, also from Cowcaddens underground station, a memorable little topographical subtlety then at the foot of a steep cobbled lane where it joined Cowcaddens Street. (This was Cambridge Lane—also entirely gone, somewhere beneath a multilane road system. A phrase which I seem to have used before. Bertie, by the way, was actually born at 122 Cambridge Street, the curving road at the top of this lane. That he too knew this place goes without saying. Perhaps he knew it in no other form.)

I remember this keenly, because at some point very near the eastern extremity of Grove Street—I had not yet got clear of the park of some sort which lay over to my right—a youth wholly unknown to me leaned out as I went running past, and spat a considerable amount of his sputum with perhaps practised accuracy right into my face. Being no fool, I did not so much as slow down a single step. When I reached the shop, where (rather unusually)

both my parents were, the consensus was that the sight of the
Catholic uniform must have moved this sad cretin to assert proudly
his adherence to an alternative strand of the Christian religion,
with its fine tradition of freedom from Rome rule and indepen-
dency of mind. Moving testimony indeed, if things were so, to the
validity of religion as a social glue. So much for Garscube Road,
which is now but a shadow even of that shadowy former self. Except
that I have more than once dreamt (I have no idea why) that I was
living there; and in one instance I was deliriously, Parisianly happy,
one floor up a tenement, on the left just before you reached North
Woodside Road, heading south. Rarely have I known a more
impressive example of the potential for insane joy in dreams.

This reminded me that once—it must have been a couple of
years earlier—I was running eastwards along West Princes Street,
I think going back from school at lunchtime (one of the reasons
why I spent so much time running is that it was utterly normal for
me to spend the busfare or tramfare which I had been given, buying
sweets with it at a convenient shop and travelling on foot under
some pressure of time). We practically never went by public
transport, unless we were just too late or the weather was intoler-
ably vicious. Once I, or we—myself and my older sister—emerged
from a sweetshop in Great Western Road pretty well diagonally
opposite the George Gilbert Scott church; and saw to our horror
the unmistakable form of Dad's dull grey van stopped at the
traffic-lights, on the other side of the road, but facing us. We must
have been returning to school for the afternoon. Dad would have
been going home for his midday meal, which was later than ours
by varying degrees. The next few hours were full of a ridiculous
anguish for us, before we headed back home at four o'clock. What
if Dad had seen us, and wondered what we were doing there? We
should have been on a bus or a tram somewhere. Surely we would
get into considerable trouble? But, as it happened, nothing ever
developed from this. Presumably he simply hadn't taken in just two
more schoolchildren across a busy road. That corner is still there,
and opposite those lights, one floor up, is where my first dentist
used to do his inept work. At one time he took out no fewer than
four of my healthy teeth at one go, apparently believing that the
space would be vitally needed for other teeth in the near future.
One of the spaces was indeed needed. The other three caverns
remain in my mouth, a permanent memorial to his blithe incom-

petence. It was a horrible experience, and left me distraught. Mum helped me along the road, and put me to bed, and sat beside the bed for much of the time. I spent hours spitting blood into a basin. Recently there have been two appalling murderers, one called Neilson and another Nilsson. This orthodontic wizard, it pleases me to recall, was similarly named. He moved years ago; and I don't know whether or not there was a public telephone kiosk below his windows, just in the sidestreet, even then. But it was from one of that pair of boxes, whenever they arrived, that I phoned my mother (who was here in Largs) less than a year ago, to find out how the latest developments were going. 'I'm afraid it's rather bad news,' she said. And, for the first time, knowing that she would underplay anything if she could, I had the sudden chilled realisation that things were not, somehow, heading for the inevitable cure that I had vaguely supposed would surely round this off. (I mean, she was my Mum; of course she was going to be cured.) For the first time my nervous system caught sight of the fact that she was dying. I quickly put it to the back of my mind. This was less than a year ago. But I did not mean to say this. I meant only to say that Mum did not discover this habitual financial chicanery of ours until well over a decade afterwards. Whatever that means. Until long after that period of our lives was over. (Nor had she known, as we discovered years after, that we had more than once broken a neighbour's window—quite unintentionally—while playing a ballgame. It was all news to her. She laughed and said, 'I thought my children were perfect'. This, be it noted, cannot be the literal truth.)

Sorry about that. Anyway, there I was running eastwards in my primary school uniform, when, on the south side of West Princes Street more or less opposite Carrington Street (where there is now a mosque, to add further to the immense spiritual riches of this city), when a boy who was walking past in the other direction, having evidently just finished eating chips, with some force pushed the greasy wrapping into my face, covering my glasses with not terribly helpful or translucent fat. Whether he too was rendering homage to a proud religious tradition, or was just a mundane thug, I, alas, do not know. We did not discuss the point.

And one last incident broadly of this type; far more recent, and refreshingly free of the least taint of bigotry. A few weeks after Mum had died, I had gone to visit her grave one beautiful Sunday evening; and I was walking back along the main road (it being the only available route) while an almost unbroken stream of cars took the day trippers back to their own homes from their stay on the coast. Where the pavement widens, just past a small public park, as I was rather caught up in my own thoughts, for what was in fact the second time in my life I was hit by a raw egg which had been thrown from a passing car. What a lark! It was from the back seat, I think, of a car full of young people enjoying themselves, bless them. As an intervention it was not a particularly helpful one.

It struck my left knee rather forcibly—fortunately, not the one with the osteo-arthritis creeping through it (as far as I am aware; if that is what osteo-arthritis does)—and then fell onto my shoe, where it made a wonderful mess for what had hitherto been so neat and contained an object. As soon as I realized what had happened, which took a couple of seconds, I turned and looked round; but, of course, I could not even be sure which car it had come from, and I could not have done anything about it even if I had been sure. They were already far away, perhaps exulting in this triumph of resplendent, chthonic West of Scotland wit. But I was trying at least to raise some doubt in the minds of any who were watching me, for I assume they did have minds, as to whether I might somehow have been able to identify their car. In which case I might possibly be able to take the matter further. Had they only hit me in the nobler parts, which I suppose is what they were hoping to do (not to worry: practice makes perfect), then I dare say their joy would have been complete. As for the degree of personal bravery needed to throw things at a pedestrian out of a speeding car, well, comment would be superfluous. It must take a certain amount of skill, I suppose.

This happened months ago. The resultant stains on the pavement despite subsequent storms and stresses, proved astonishingly durable. (Since they fell just beside a permanent manhole cover type of feature, they were very easy to relocate.) In fact, the last traces were still discernible a few days ago, when I was last passing there and remembered to look out for them. It is another beautiful evening, by the way. That impressive setting sun is doubtless also shining on the manhole cover even as I speak. Well, technically I am silent, I suppose. The grave must be sunlit too at the moment.

(7.42–22nd August)

41

Quite by chance, just before the clock in the living- room next door struck eight in the evening, I discovered another couple of minor but intriguing coincidences. The case of the two William Holmyards, that I wrote about yesterday, took place essentially in Tachbrook Street, Pimlico. I now discover in my browsing that that is precisely where Dr Smethurst retired to, at the end of a highly vexatious sequence of events. I grow ever more convinced, perhaps after the self-deluding manner of eye-witnesses, that this too is a street I have walked down thinking, well, life could be rather pleasant for me here.

I am also pretty certain that, when I stayed in Chelsea for a couple of days just over four years ago, one of the roads that I managed to reach in the course of my peregrinations was Finborough Road; which seems to hold the record, as far as I'm aware, for proximity of quite separate murders. At No. 13 occurred the murder of a prostitute in the rather well-known Ronald True case, a very bizarre matter involving a homicidal lunatic; while twenty-four years later and two doors away (at No. 17, in 1946) an elderly widowed engineer and conman beat a woman to death in blatantly damning circumstances. And what, one wonders, went on at No. 15, in between? In many ways that is the most interesting building of the three.

But, as for Smethurst, he got his medical degree (in the 1820s) from the University of Erlangen, Bavaria. As it happens, my younger sister (who went back to Aberdeen four days ago) is at this very moment applying for a job at the University of Erlangen. Smethurst looks very likely to have poisoned his mistress. However, there were technical inadequacies in the evidence; so that, eventually, after having been found guilty and sentenced to death, he was released after an enquiry, and granted a pardon. He then applied for—and, of course, got—the substantial estate which the possibly poisoned woman had willed to him, very shortly before her death. During her final illness, in fact.

I think it may reasonably be said that the bare bones of the case at least do not speak loud in favour of his innocence. And what of her next of kin (she was in her early forties when she died), who otherwise stood to inherit, or who stood to inherit under the previous will? What, one wonders, were their views of the good doctor? (Who did at least suffer for his actual bigamy, it seems. One year in jail. A very shrewd investment, by the sound of it.) (*Actually, on October 20, my first morning back in Glasgow after a fortnight in Aberdeen, I finished reading a fine book called* Hanged In Error, *which I had brought back from that city. The final chapter persuasively argues that Smethurst did not kill her.*)

(8.36–22nd August)

42

I may not have quite as much time for this as I had hoped. Yesterday, Dad told me that if the weather was fine, it would be good if I could repaint the painted parts at the front of the house, which do rather need it done. He also mentioned a couple of hedges—one of them disconcertingly long and high— which need trimming. And, since—

To continue. He has just come into the room, asking me if I'll be able to hold out till Wednesday (it's now Monday) without getting any more money, since that's when he'll get his pension. Of course, I am using my own money anyway, such as it is, a lot of the time. He also asked me if, while I am out, I would look into the only shop in this town that sells German bread, of which he is fond, to see if it has any rye bread left. I am pretty sure it won't have, but obviously I'll have to look and see, even if it does rather spoil the preferred route. And he also asked me, as a sort of envoy, to go into the Post Office and buy two stamps at 28 pence, two at 24 pence, and one at 18 pence; for which he gave me a pound coin. How fortunate for him that his son has so little to do with his time. (*This is obviously not quite the epic of self-sacrifice that I seem to have thought it was at the time. I keep this cruel and depressing passage in because my desire to be taken*

for a honest man evidently outweighs my desire to be taken for a saint.)
    I told him that it was all right; that I hadn't planned to buy much today anyway. This was *before* the additional requests, I should say. I can't help wondering quite how genuine the original enquiry might have been. What if I had said: actually, Dad, I'm right down to rock bottom financially myself. It's rather a worrying trend. I think I preferred it when he used to hand me a tenner and say, See how long you can make that last for—which, whatever it might have meant, did not mean, come racing to me for more the moment this has gone. But enough of this small-minded complaining. (I think I may fairly claim that neither of us is quite at our best in the morning.) Anyway, I first have to check that the washing-machine is functioning OK before I go out and get the messages. Quite what I'll do if it isn't, I'm not sure. I could always run away to sea, I suppose. It's near enough, at least.

(9.36am–23rd August)

43

T he shop in North Woodside Road itself, if I may be forgiven for harping on such matters, I remember most as a sort of vaguely oppressive presence in the topography of my youth. It was rarely that anything striking happened there. Just like life. Most often, one would simply be hanging around, waiting for Dad to finish his unending work and take you home—or finish work and then set off on his calls round the customers' houses. As he developed intermittent back trouble, he was frequently under some difficulty in carrying the heavy old tv sets to and from the van. And sometimes the customers lived at the very top of tenements (as we did—it was a popular location), or it was impossible to park the van very near to the house in question; or whatever. Things could go wrong in a wide variety of ways.

Since there was no alternative to helping out like this, I did it; but I must say there were times when, in my charged and imperceptive adolescent way, I rather resented it as a gross and unmerited imposition on my own valuable time. I mean: why did it always have to be me? All the more so as my father's ability or willingness to enter imaginatively into the vagaries of the psyche of his bored son, or make due allowance for these, seemed, I have to say, to be virtually nil. Often he would disappear into a house, some problem would crop up, and he might be forced to spend an inordinate length of time desperately chasing a solution to it (sometimes I would eventually be called back in to take the set away again; or he might even suddenly appear with it himself—perhaps, as I now suspect, sparing me the experience of an ugly domestic argument) while I was left there, sitting in the van, rather like a target, and time dragged on and on. That what he was actually doing was working all the hours of the day to keep his family alive never really occurred to me. One took this wholly for granted. It was what fathers did.

Some of the streets I was thus left in were not exactly places in which one would have chosen to linger. With those early, unreliable valve sets, it frequently happened that they would go temperamental when returned to the customer's house, and could not at first be got to work properly, however well-behaved they had been back in the shop. I take my Dad's expertise for granted. He was a whizz with tools and gadgets generally. He still spends an hour or two most days pottering about in his shed with a lifetime's collection of gizmos.

However, sometimes he did give up, eventually, when faced with some particularly unrelenting brute that refused to reform itself however one might tempt it. He would do his best to patch it up by any available means into the semblance of normal, decent life; and his aim would then be, to take it back to the customer's house, switch on the cleaned-up, newly returned set, shrug off any grateful applause (most unlikely), get paid for the trouble it had caused him, and then hurry back out to the van and make his getaway before any trouble had begun to redevelop. You could easily waste what amounted to *days* on a malfunctioning tv; especially if the owner—as he so often did—had first tried to fix it himself before calling you in, by which time you would have a plurality of interacting faults to sort out. And no one was *ever* going to pay you for bringing back a set that still didn't work—no matter how much time, energy and material you had run through in the attempt to repair it; or how hopeless had been its condition when you took it away. If it still didn't work, it meant you had done nothing. If you wanted to get paid, you had to return either a healthy specimen or a very deceptive invalid. If it proved to be an utterly hopeless case, the set was returned with apologetic solemnity, and you were doing well enough if you got back out of the house without being insulted for your incompetence, or for wasting the good burgher's time. They were invariably desperate to have a functioning tv set back again.

But, whatever view one might take about these complex moral problems, there can be no question but that he worked long and hard. How I grew to hate remarks like, 'I'll just fix this one, and then we can go,' when I arrived at the shop, perhaps after school, expecting us to be leaving at once. I would mope around in an environment not overburdened with pleasing distractions, and Dad would often completely lose track of time, caught up in the problem-solving part of his work, in a game which he was absolutely determined to win. How unhelpful my wholly unsympathetic, hint-dropping accompaniment must have been to him then. The question of practical necessity passed me by entirely. Was there really so little to do? There was a huge cellar, but it was not easy to get into (usually the trapdoor, in the back of the shop where Dad always was, was hopelessly blocked by accumulated jumble); and it was so basic a space, so gloomy, filthy, irregularly floored, that it was good for only a very occasional foray.

I remember once sitting in the van, waiting for Dad to finish locking up and securing the shutters, those now never to be seen again shutters, before he drove off. As he came round the front of the van and was about to get in through the driver's door, he was hailed by an approaching gent, evidently a potential customer. This man then tried to negotiate a visit to some house, I dare say his own, *at once*; in order to repair a troublesome tv set. I mean, that's what we were there for too, wasn't it?

Since Dad had enough on his hands for the evening already, he asked him, perfectly pleasantly, to look in tomorrow if he wanted. At this, the potential customer, who looked rather like a rotund, jovial, twinkling-eyed Irish peasant gone septic, began to make threats—one of them being (here he gestured towards the shop), that if Dad didn't come round at once, 'I'll bust yer gemme'. Obviously a baron of the Glasgow underworld. Or an avid Cagney fan, rendering an *hommage* to his mentor. Quite why that should seem to anyone to be an appropriate response to a perfectly reasonable request to wait until tomorrow I am still not entirely sure. Perhaps his sense of self-worth would brook no rebuff, however trivial. Perhaps there was a programme due on that evening which he desperately wanted to see. Perhaps he was drunk. Dad just said something along the lines of refusing to respond to threats, got into the van, and drove off. Needless to say, there were no repercussions. On reflection, I very much doubt if the guy was pissed. I would imagine he probably behaved like that all the time. Not unless he woke up one morning and suddenly found that he was two feet taller.

Looking back on it, I suppose that the way that Dad made so little of this incident when it happened must rather suggest that he was pretty well inured to this sort of thing.

(1.36–23rd August)

44

I hope now is a good moment for revisiting earlier territory; when I was considering the UK record for two quite distinct murders happening right next to each other. It turns out that the last two women to have been hanged in England both committed murder, and, from what I gather, seem just about to have done it in the same street in Hampstead. The second of these was Ruth Ellis, star of stage, screen and song; but the earlier one sounds an even more interesting case—a family affair like Bertie's (if you can remember who *he* was), but, as it were, even more so.

The two brief accounts of the case that I have to hand contain noticeable discrepancies. According to one, just before midnight on the 29th of July 1954 (and I was somehow living through these minutes, making significant noises I suppose), a Hampstead neighbour walking his dog saw a middle-aged woman trying to burn a near-naked tailor's dummy in a backyard, using newspaper for that purpose. Odd, certainly; but none of his or her business. Alternatively, he or she was reading at an upstairs window; when he noticed much the same thing happening, with a dumpy figure passing in and out of the house, tending the flames.

The middle-aged woman was Mrs Styllou Christofi: a Greek Cypriot peasant, whose son, Stavros, worked as a waiter in a West

End restaurant. He had lived in England for twelve years, married a German woman (Hella), and now had two (or three) children. His mother had joined him about a year before. She was of a rather violent and jealous disposition. She disliked England, could not get the hang of the language (the usual means of communication between the spouses would be English, I take it), criticized the children's upbringing, quarrelled with the wife, and so forth. All fairly common so far, I suppose.

But in fact the tailor's dummy—and what other assumption could one reasonably make but that that was what it was?—was actually the corpse of the wife. The mother-in-law had struck her over the head with an ash-plate (presumably something like the heavy metal rack that we used to build up the coal fire on), and then strangled her. She was now doing her best, her extremely naïve best, to doctor the evidence. Hella had arranged to take the children on holiday to Germany, and had made it very clear that she expected Mummy to be back in Cyprus by the time they returned.

Eventually deeming that things were nicely under control, she ran out into the Hampstead street and persuaded a passer-by that there was a fire in her kitchen, and that children were in danger. Or, possibly about 1 am, she spoke to a couple in a car near Hampstead Station, saying, 'Fire burning! Children sleeping!' When the police arrive (was Stavros still at work?—apparently the wife had a job too, in a 'fashion shop'), they noticed that the wife's body, wherever it was by now, was charred and smelled of paraffin. Also, her wedding-ring, it turned out, was now in her mother-in-law's bedroom.

She was condemned to death, and hanged, after much grumbling in the death cell that her son had not visited her. Poor Stavros! What a homecoming that must have been. That your wife should have been killed—and by your own mother! Oedipus was more fortunate. Are you supposed to treat the rest of your life as a normal thing after that? (It is noteworthy that the husband makes no direct appearance whatever in either account of the case.)

I would imagine that saner people than her have been adjudged to be mad. But there is more. When she was twenty, she had been tried in Cyprus for murdering her *own* mother-in-law, after the latter had died by having a burning torch rammed down her throat. Obviously a woman who favoured directer means than poison; and whom it would be as well to keep on the right side of. I have never before heard of such a barely thinkable method of murder. What? Forcing a burning log into an old lady's mouth—obviously it could only be done by huge physical effort from someone who had completely lost sight of the human capacity for feeling pain. Also, it is not easy to deduce in the abstract likely reasons for the younger woman's having been acquitted here. I mean, presumably no one thought it was a case of suicide? If this is not the act of a maniac, then one rather wonders how maniacs might be supposed to behave. (And what, one wonders rather nervously, might she not have been getting up to in the intervening years?)

(6.12–23rd August)

45

New City Road was a vibrantly busy thorough-
fare—the one closest to the Willox abode where main roads were
concerned, and one which they presumably visited or passed
through on practically every day of their lives. I go through it rarely
nowadays, but when I do the experience produces in me a feeling
of mild but genuine disturbance. Seeing the present travesty, with
the vast motorway that passes above it, and remembering how
vibrant it once was, one's sadness is, I think not entirely devoid of
panic. Not merely because such vitality can come and go, is all too
obviously no guarantee of permanence—but because one realizes
in a general way that any particular drab or unpromising street may,
for all one knows to the contrary, be the mere relic of a former,
more glorious existence; which the present passer-through is by
now hopelessly excluded from. After all, who, coming here now
for the first time, would begin to guess how busy, how indispensable
to the locals, how apparently quite undowithoutable New City
Road once was?

I remember how—this would be in the early 1960s—the bus
which brought me and a schoolfriend who lived nearby back from
our secondary school one afternoon somewhere about half past
four, stopped outside Woolworth's (at the corner with Steven

Street—in Bertie's time there seems to have been a church there) and we got off it as normal. Then there was the most appalling crashing sound. It is still not quite clear to me what happened. But a large pane of glass, having fallen I know not whence, lay in shards a few paces behind us, opposite the front doors of that now vanished store. Had it not happened, I would have forgotten all about that afternoon too. Had it happened slightly differently, I might not have been here to remember it.

At one time, my elder sister, when still a schoolgirl got a job in Woolworth's on Saturdays. I and a few friends went over there in the middle of the afternoon in order to spy on her; to see how she was doing, and generally luxuriate in the strange feeling of being related to, or even just known to, a Woolies' shop assistant. We did so; but, to our vast chagrin, we were rather publicly shown the door by some promenading saleslady, and we slunk out, mortified. We felt we had been proclaimed to be potential shoplifters, which was certainly not the undercover mission on which were truly engaged. However, since we of course had not the least intention of actually *buying* anything, I suppose the instincts of our per-secutrix were accurate enough. I seem to remember that my sister watched our ignominious departure, and had a woundingly gleeful laugh at the sight.

I don't know how long Woolworths had been there; although I doubt whether our patricidal hero ever had the opportunity of visiting it. For us, of course, it had crystallized on the spot about five seconds before we first discovered it. And at least one object actually bought there (by me) is still in this house. It is a (very) cheap ornamental calendar, a permanent calendar, with spaces for the month, date and day of the week to be turned sequentially into place by means of simple keys at the back. There is also a mournful picture of a collie on the front. It was something I bought for the birthday of my Auntie Peggy, in, I suppose, the very early sixties.

She kept it. It was still in her house when she died, in 1990. We then brought it up here, for sentimental reasons, and I myself turned the little dial from SUN to MON and from 22 to 23 this very morning. Someone has been doing precisely that, I would suppose, almost every morning for the last thirty years—and the exceptions will probably have been rather seriously anomalous mornings: absences or illnesses. I suppose if I were to shift it personally every day for the next two decades, I would be approaching her own tally of such manipulations.

And that clock, also in the living-room next door, which I heard strike nine a couple of minutes ago (it is slightly fast), which, indeed I think I could touch with one hand while touching the calendar with the other, where it at present stands, on top of the television—(I have just returned from carrying out the experiment; and, somewhat to my delight, I found it was just impossible, literally by 1 or 2 millimetres, well under an inch)—that too was a fairly local purchase, bought five minutes or so away at the Royal Stores (I've mentioned them before, haven't I?), in St George's Road, southern corner with West Graham Street (one south from Shamrock Street—all quite gone). Mum often remarked on how much service they had got out of it ('It's a Smith clock. Aye, we've had our money's worth from that'), and it was, it seems, bought in the 1950s some time. I can't remember a period when it was not in the house in West Princes Street. And still it continues to go, in a town on the coast, an hour's journey away. 9.12, by my watch. (A present from my parents, from Germany.) An ordinary evening. Fewer people here than one would like to be here, but the clock ticks on all the same.

46

M y mother had a great appetite for crime fiction for as long as I knew her. Over the course of her life she must have read quite a good few thousand of those books. Apart from anything else, she read extraordinarily quickly. Her preference was for the old-fashioned kind: well-plotted; intriguing developments and dénouements; the reader given a fair chance of working it out for himself. Mere gore, or chaos, or delicate modern studies in the psyche of the abnormal mind she could not be bothered with at all. Why go looking for trouble and upset? It was the crossword puzzle aspect of it that appealed to her—a sort of puzzle containing imaginary but interesting human beings.

Latterly, whenever I went down to Largs to visit her, I would always bring her a few old crime paperbacks which I kept an eye open for in my regular dredgings of secondhand book-shops. She was still reading them until quite near her death, when illness and medication made it too difficult for her to bring the required attention to bear on matters. We had a little bookcase full of them, in her bedroom. But one day I arrived here, some months after her death, to discover that Dad had given almost all of them away to charity shops, including the ones I had specifically said I wanted to keep. However, I managed to save a few of them in the nick of time before his final visit; to add to another few that I had already put aside in a safe place as being of especial value to me.

Among the ones I had already rescued was a discussion of the Ratcliffe Highway Murders of 1811 (*The Maul And The Pear Tree*)—most unusually a factual crime book—which is one of a group I had given to her towards the end of the year before last, when part of my Christmas present to her was a pile of new or new-seeming books. I'll probably come back to this one.

But it was the same Royal Stores from which the clock had been bought years before (I'm afraid it's true that it struck eleven less than a minute ago) that she more than once in the early 60s sent me out to to buy her another paperback. She would hand me half a crown (by that era one could hardly hope to find much for less, and the 3/6s were beginning to take over), try to warn me of the sort of thing she didn't want, and off I would go down the three flights of stairs and into the five minutes walk-run.

I was actually deeply ashamed at the thought of being seen in the street carrying a book like that, which might well have a cheap-looking, garish cover to add to its infra dig contents. Certainly I had at least my fair share of adolescent priggishness. Once I picked out what I thought looked to be a likely, comparatively restrained candidate—and I balanced the half-crown on top of it, and handed it out to the girl behind the counter, whoever she was. (Mum was taking a very long shot indeed, sending me out on something like this. At least it does show she did have enough leisure to be at a loose end from time to time. I must also have been ashamed of being seen to buy such a downmarket object in the actual shop.)

What I wanted here was for the girl, whoever she was, to take up both the coin and the book; to put the offending object in a paper bag, and hand it back to me. I would then be able to carry it home with my head held comparatively high. But the girl thought I was just being flirtatious. She gave me a lovely smile, and, with exaggerated delicacy, she lifted the coin off the book and took it to the till. This rather baffled me. I had hardly started to think in terms of eliciting any positive sort of personal awareness from a female. I don't suppose she could somehow have been sending me up, could she?

It was also there, whatever the truth of that, that I bought my first-ever full-sized chess set. Actually, it's the only such chess set

I've ever bought. It is on the low rack beneath the coffee table three paces away from where I am now, and partly within sight. That was a huge enthusiasm of mine for a brief but intense while. It is a rather terrible, uneven set: the white knights, for instance, have crude faces of widely different thicknesses. It looks a bit like what you might expect from a blind or blind-drunk convict. It occurs to me that Mum lived and died without ever learning how to play that game; though these very pieces were in her house for well over a quarter of a century.

All that side of St George's Road has disappeared, several continuous blocks. More roads have been made out of it. But I suppose I should be grateful for having been allowed to see any of it. I remember, a few years back, being at an exhibition which showed what I seem vaguely to recall as the City Architect's great plan for Glasgow, drawn up just after the Second World War. It quite literally involved the complete destruction of the centre of the city—I mean this 'quite literally' quite literally: its total annihilation—and the building of a huge grid of relentlessly intersecting roads in its place. Since I had never heard of this before, and have never heard of it since, I still sometimes imagine that I had only imagined it. (This trick seems to be catching.) Had the plan been carried out, my memories would indeed have been radically different—had there been a me here at all to have them. Would there have been? I can't quite work that out.

(11.31–23rd August)

47

I went up to the cemetery this morning, to see if the headstone had been raised, but it still wasn't there yet. Alas, I met no angels, whether communicative or otherwise. I stood there for a while in the bright sunlight, and then went over to the back corner, where my aunt lies buried. It was a beautiful morning, and the site of the cemetery is also a beautiful one: on a treey slope overlooking the Firth, with various near islands visible—the largest, highest and most majestic being Arran, with its magnificent, almost Alpine peaks. Alas, there was also a murder done just over a century ago near the top of the highest of those peaks, when a holidaying Glaswegian killed an English tourist for money—but I don't want to waste any time on that one.

Once, when I was travelling in the train, where it swung north just after Kilwinning, I happened to look up from my reading, and quite with out warning I found myself faced with a dazzlingly clear view of Arran, seeming nearer than ever it had been, peaks and valleys perfectly discernible. (Quite often one cannot see it at all for mist; for weeks it may have a purely theoretical presence.) That must have been just one more time that I was travelling back to Largs, to my parents' house, such as happened very very often—over a hundred times, I suppose—and always with a sense of underlying happiness which I did not even need to name or think of or do anything of my own to help create. Merely being on that train and knowing where I was headed for were enough for it.

I can even remember what I was reading when I looked up. It was one of those small, olive-green volumes of Chekhov short stories, translated, often correctly, by Constance Garnett. They are, in their own way, odd enough almost to pass for the original work of a curiously word-blind genius; but at least they are roughly of the same vintage as Chekhov himself, and I have developed such a fondness for them that I buy them routinely whenever I see any in stock. They are all secondhand, of course—at *least*. One of the set of thirteen continues to elude me, though I have two or three copies of most others. As it happens I was reading another of just that set in the small room that Mum died in, while keeping a watch on her as she slept, on some of the last few nights of her life. It just happened to be so; I don't read them all the time, by any means.

Or perhaps there was a link after all. Be that as it may. There is something very calming and consoling about standing at my aunt's gravestone, right in the corner of the cemetery; with my mother's grave now also visible not too far away, more or less directly ahead. Auntie Peggy's headstone says, 'In Memory of My Beloved Sister', then the name, and her dates. It does not say who the 'My' is. How keenly I remember my mother talking to the gravediggers at the burial in 1990—there had been a farcical mix-up earlier on—then coming back up the slope to rejoin us. She looked somehow so vulnerable and so permanent at the same time. But less than three years later, I was again walking along that same path again, leaving that same place, in a differently constituted crowd that was in so many ways not the same.

I noticed today, as I walked out down the main pathway, another stone, from the 1940s, which I must have passed unknowingly again and again, which also had precisely that 'In Memory of My Beloved Sister', and a name, and a date, but no additional information. The woman's name, I recall, was Sidney. Presumably that 'my' died long ago. The date was early 1947, I remember. Mum and Dad had recently met (I suppose—it would be rather optimistic to expect a clear answer from him about that), but had not yet married. I learned where it was they got married, from my mother, shortly before she died, in one of the talks we had then. It had been at a small side altar of Saint Aloysius' Church in Garnethill,

Glasgow—where the whole family had often placed themselves when at Sunday mass. So that was one of the reasons why we habitually chose that spot, was it? On not one of the times I had been there had I had the least idea of that. What else did I miss, I wonder? And what else, I wonder, am I still missing?

(1.47–24th August)

48

Whether Mum ever even heard of Bertie Willox I do not know. But she would have been just turned eight when the killing happened, and living quite locally—in fact, I think she was then living in Argyll Street, just opposite Kelvingrove Art Gallery—and, though this must have been almost a half hour's walk away, it has only just occurred to me that Willox snr might well have passed the windows of her tenement on the tram daily, or whatever, as he made his way to and from his work. She might well even have seen him, I suppose. We must all have seen all sorts of people without knowing it. Of course, at the earlier hour, as they slipped past, she would most usually have been sleeping. But not necessarily so. And she may well have heard her mother and father talking about it, for they were no doubt not silent all those years.

I seem to remember my Mum and my Aunt Peggy discussing the heir to the throne—it will have been some time in the 1970s (before his engagement to the Lady Diana Spencer, as we sticklers for protocol used habitually to refer to her)—and Mum at one point said to her sister something along the lines of, 'But you don't think he'll ever marry, do you? You think he's a Jenny Willox'. I can't answer for the utter veracity of the last remark, but it definitely was something similar. The allusion was, I believe, to hermaphrodit-ism. (*'Jenny Wullock: a hermaphrodite; a sexually-deformed male; an effeminate man.' The Concise Scots Dictionary.*) They then spent some time discussing the term they had just used, whatever it was. I really must get one of my research assistants to try to find out about this.

I do certainly remember arriving back at my bedsit in Wilton Street one evening; and finding, to my utter horror, that a large, crass, decorated poster had been put up on the outside of the always visible inner main door to the street; wishing good luck to the blissful couple (Prince Charles and Lady Di) from all the subjects at that address. It would certainly have caught their eye had they ever happened to be passing. One was fair mortified. I mean, there was always a side door one could exit by, but one could enter only through this one. It must have been put up there by the elderly couple who inhabited Room 3. The husband died not long after-wards, about 1983 I suppose—and that must have been cancer too. After he had disappeared for a while, I was once rather alarmed to see an unknown bald man tinkering about the hallway as if he had a right to be there. It was only some time subsequently that I was able to work out who it must have been. His copious, curly, flaxen hair had hitherto been a major feature of his strikingly distin-guished head, and he had somehow become generally shrunken and gnarled. Mum went through chemotherapy too; but though she had been worried about humiliating side-effects, she actually kept enough of her hair for it not to be too distressing. Then it thickened again into a very expensive-looking salt and pepper combination. And as for her skin! Near the end of her life it seemed to be getting younger and younger.

Then, after months of extremely unpleasant chemotherapy, she was put onto radiotherapy for a while; until, as far as I can gather, her case was quietly given up as inoperable, ever-spreading and quite hopeless. But it was never put to her quite so starkly, and nothing could ever quite quench her basic optimism, or her sense that life surely couldn't really want to leave her company so unilaterally when she was so perfectly content, for her own part, to keep things going. She would quite happily have put up with all this and more, to be cured (to get better); and she actually quite liked taking her pills and so forth, for these were good things and could possibly help her. She was not desperate to live at any cost, or particularly scared at the thought of dying; but she did feel that in some way she had a lot of life still left in her, if only that way could be found, and that she was not finished yet.

In 1953, during her pregnancy with her third child (I am her second) she had been very ill indeed (with hyperemesis, I think it's called—in that era it was usually lethal to pregnant women), and she was not expected to survive. She sometimes told us of how, when she was lying in bed in hospital, wholly motionless and apparently beyond sensation, she heard two doctors discussing her case with each other, and one of them said that she clearly would not survive the night. She could remember hearing this and thinking, in wholly invisible defiance, 'No. You're wrong. I *am* going to pull through this.' Since we knew that in fact she *had* survived, we were less impressed by this than we should have been.

So, she liked life and was in no hurry to depart—unlike, say, her sister, Margaret, who had pretty well been waiting to die and be taken to the arms of the Lord from her mid-sixties. She too had cancer. But hers was less aggressive, more reasonable, more amenable to treatment; and her body obviously had great inherited powers of resistance, because it had to do all its resisting, as it were, on its own. The controlling mind would quite willingly have surrendered at any point. When, after several years, infection began to flare up again in what remained of her treated breast, she ignored it, hoping that she might just die before anything might require to be done about it once more. I vividly remember how, one Tuesday, I arrived yet again back down at the house in Largs for another brief stay, to find the whole place in disarray and turmoil. An hour or so before, Auntie Peggy had decided that, alas, the new growth (by now huge and livid) could no longer be ignored, and had called in my mother and my elder sister for help and comfort. Eventually she got her wish, wasting away to nothing in a hospital bed, her rosary tied to the metal bar at its head. The last time I saw her, she said 'Water' in an almost inaudible voice, and I held out some water for her to sip at with great difficulty. I still do not know whether she recognized me or not.

Yet Peggy survived to be seventy-eight, not particularly wanting to. Mum wanted to survive, but somehow, bafflingly, just couldn't. Not even these ultimate wishes are, it seems, respected. It was this enduring sense of her never even having been given a fair chance, a surely perfectly reasonable possibility of getting better, that could be so saddening. We always felt that, had she only been given a fair chance of surviving, no more than what so many of these other people around us had been given, she would have taken it. She would have done it; she would have pulled through. Everything was there, ready and willing, just waiting for the order to progress to come through. But, day after day, something seemed to be keeping it back. There was just too much wrong with her in a crucial part of her physical organization. Or, to be honest, in more than one: for, though I did not know it, she had also long ago had had some heart trouble, and it was actually heart failure which finally stopped her breathing—and it did it gently, while the cancer was still some way short of its last and cruellest stages, as if her heart was itself her own wisest and best doctor.

So one reaches out for consolation to things like—well, seventy is still the generally accepted boundary, after which anything more comes in the nature of a bonus. Or she could have died literally forty years earlier, and what sort of a vast loss would that not have been? Obviously I would not have remembered even a single thing about her, despite the fact that it was her body that produced this life. Which is the sort of thing that happens too, of course.

(4.26–24th August)

49

It struck me just an hour or two ago that the only two books I can remember giving to my mother in recent years—apart from thrillers—were both about crime and both contained the words 'Pear Tree' in their titles. Actually, now that I have written that, I suspect it is not quite accurate. Certainly, one of the books was *The Maul and the Pear Tree*, about the appalling Ratcliffe Highway murders of 1811, when two families of (I think) seven people in all were killed with staggering brutality by murderous thieves. But the other, I rather suspect, may actually be called *The Day They Shook The Apple Tree*. But what does it matter? It's all fruit anyway. I can only vaguely recall this second one. Was it not about some squabble over an inheritance, during which a vast fortune was frittered away? Something like that.

I had found it in one of the cheapest areas of a secondhand book-shop off Otago Street, and I brought it down with me while I was on a visit. I remember much enjoying it, and telling my mother I thought she might like to read it. The stuff I usually read was rarely her sort of thing. So I gave her it to read early one afternoon, and in the evening she told me she had finished it. I was astonished. She got through these things incredibly quickly. It should still be up there in the loft, where I sleep. I must try to search the book out when I go to bed tonight.

I don't know of any other murders which involve someone called Willox—though I dare say there must be one or two of them, not to say one or two thousand, among the dramatis personae somewhere. However, the man who was held to be guilty of the Ratcliffe Highway murders (he died in prison, evidently a suicide, while still under preliminary investigation) was, if not a Willox, or even a Willocks, at least a Williams; John Williams. He features in the long postscript to De Quincey's classic essay *On Murder Considered As One of the Fine Arts*, which I seem to remember as being an entertaining display of the atrophy of normal human feeling. It is a tale which much alarmed and chilled many—whether in its pure form, or when recycled by some hack or other.

The most impressive thing about reading this book (by P.D. James and Thomas Critchley) is to see the ease with which an inspection of the original reports shows just how hugely compromised this classic and much-repeated view of the crime actually is. These make it obvious that it was, to say the least, far from clear what Williams had to do with it at all—and extremely clear that one other person (a native of Danzig, known as William Ablass) was in it up to the neck and beyond. All people do is endlessly recycle the conventional report, the already established story, at third, fourth, fifth, and sixth hand—perhaps much as I am just doing with Willow. (*What a charming typing error. First I'd realized of the similarity.*) And one mistake gets copied; and copies get copied; until it is next to impossible to expunge it from the record, for people somehow assume that it has all been convincingly enough decided, and it is all now cut and dry.

Williams claimed to be Scottish, but the more popular view is that he was Irish. Some indeed thought that his real name was Murphy. As far as I could make out, the greater likelihood is that he was indeed Irish; and that John Williams was his real name. It's usually a Welsh name, of course. There is actually at least one other quite well-known business featuring a John Williams: a case in Eastbourne, Sussex, where a professional burglar caught lurking on the roof of the porch of a house belonging, it seems, to a Hungarian countess, shot dead a policeman who told him to come down. This man too may have been Scottish, for he was (so I learn) the son of a Scottish clergyman (a minister, one supposes). Also, his real name was George Mackay. His girlfriend had his child while he was awaiting execution; and it seems that, on the day before he died, he pressed a piece of prison bread into the uncomprehending mite's hand and said, 'Now nobody can ever say that your father has never given you anything'.

At the time, my own father was actually slightly older than this other child—nearly sixteen weeks old; causing, I hope, a joy not quite so equivocal on a distant farm in Westpreussen, a district which no longer exists. Of his own father in turn I have never heard him speak more than a word. And that word was not a particularly friendly one.

(8.23–24th August)

50

However, the Williams case that I was particularly moved by has the great advantage of featuring a gent whose first name was Frank. Or so I thought. But having written that, when I duly unearthed the *True Crime Diary* and managed to find the right page, I discovered that somehow the man's name had changed to *Ted* Williams while my back was turned. What an astonishing, eery example of the paranormal occurrence! Could I get the Society for Psychical Research interested in this, I wonder? Probably not—even though I *know for a fact* that it happened. Ah well. Life is so unfair.

It's an Australian case from 1924, and it concerns Edward Williams, a poor music teacher living in Sydney. His wife has been in a lunatic asylum for the last two years. He is staying in a single room in what I take to be his brother-in-law's house; along with his three daughters, the youngest of whom is 5½, three years older than my mother. Since Williams himself is fifty-two, he was evidently a comparatively late starter—though, obviously, a very capable one. However, his brother-in-law has little respect for him, and suggests to him that he will very soon have to send off his girls to an institution, as they are now getting to be just a bit too old to sleep in the same room as their father. This is February the 4th.

Earlier that day, his sister-in-law had told him she would no longer be able to look after the children for him while he went out to give music lessons. Perhaps some sort of ultimatum was being laid before him.

On the day after this, Williams is returning after a Mass, that fascinating if somewhat adulterated relic of the ancient classical mystery religions, when he meets a crossing-sweeper called Tonkin, and, most unusually, offers to buy him a drink. In the ensuing conversation, Williams says he is about to take his three daughters to Brisbane—named after a lad from these parts—where he is to take up a position as a choirmaster. A likely story. He offers Tonkin his furniture, to pay off a debt between them, and a deal is struck. Tonkin gives him enough money to take the family to Brisbane— the crossing-sweeping business is evidently booming—and later on he makes his way to Williams lodgings with a hand-cart, meaning to take away the furniture.

But when he arrives, it turns out that this is the first the sister-in-law has heard of it. She rushes upstairs to Edward's room, to see what all this is about. She finds out sooner than she might wish to. Williams is not there. The daughters are lying in bed together, stone dead, with their throats cut. Williams, it is generally agreed, had always doted on his children.

After a few days spent on the run, having rather noticeably not killed himself too, he gave himself up and made a confession. He said he had been frightened for his daughters' futures. With good reason, it would seem. 'I knew what I was doing. I was doing it for the best, because I loved them.' At the trial he went into more detail. 'I saw if my girls went to an institution they would be separated. They would not be able to sit at the same table together, and when they came out they would be tools for the first smooth-tongued person who came along. I know—and you know, gentlemen (!)—that the majority of prostitutes are the women who were raised in public institutions such as my girls would have been sent to had I been agreeable. I saw it all, and saw beyond it.' So, rather than take this frightful risk, he took a blade to three small throats, one after the other.

This language sounds to me to be closer to that of sexual possessiveness or obsession than to love. To murder your daughter because she was just about to become a prostitute would be one thing—and utterly appalling at that, however frequent it may be in strict religious circles; but to kill three girls under the age of six because they might conceivably become the tools of some smooth-tongued male far off in the future, shows a mind so brooding and obsessed that I cannot deny it occurs to me to wonder just what might or might not have actually been going on in that room. Not to mention the question of why the absent wife—who clearly must be rather younger than him—should have lost her mental balance. But I know absolutely nothing specific about all this. Did something else lie behind the brother-in-law's contempt; not to mention his suggestion that it was time for father and children to be separated? Perhaps; perhaps not. But there is also the fact to be borne in mind that Williams, to say the least, did not give himself up at once, and gave a rather good imitation of someone attempting to flee justice. All the same, we should note his claim that he wished to see that his children had been buried first, before he gave himself up. Such tender-heartedness is to be welcomed, I suppose. But was there any likelihood that they would *not* be buried? Perhaps he meant, he wanted to see the ceremony for himself. It is all very strange.

Killing children is a distinctly dubious way of showing your love for them. There are, after all, so many other, safer ways in which you can do it. But perhaps he genuinely was to some degree off in a side-world of his own. I remember there was a case in England not long ago when a Muslim's teenage daughter told him she had converted to the Jehovah's Witnesses, and he killed her. I can't remember whether that was done because he loved her too. I seem to recall it was more like ranting outrage at the shame she had thereby brought on the family. The idea that converting from Islam is more shameful than murdering your daughter is, however, probably one that few non-Muslims and Eurocentrics would agree with. Of course, many Muslims would disagree with it too—though sometimes, of course, one has to be discreet with one's opinions in case one's co-religionists might take it into their heads to murder you for them. (In the last few days, righteous religiously motivated gentlemen, with a great religion of love behind them, have been particularly active with automatic weaponry in Algeria and Egypt.)

As for Ted Williams, he was executed anyway. The Minister of Justice for New South Wales, Thomas John Ley, refused to be swayed by the numerous appeals, and from the little I know of the case I can't much say I blame him. However, twenty-two years later, something very similar happened to this same T.J. Ley, now retired and living in England. He had grown enamoured of a widow in her sixties—which is rather nice, but, alas, he had done so to such an extent that a huge, jealous rage possessed him. He had managed to convince himself of the bizarre notion that a barman who happened to have lodged in the same domicile as the object of his (Ley's) passion, had had sexual intercourse with her. It preyed on his mind. He suspected one or two other youthful rivals as well. At length, Ley had the barman decoyed to his own address in Kensington. Here, aided by a pair of confederates, he had him trussed up and strangled for an old man's fantasy. But it was a real corpse which was then dumped in a chalk-pit.

Thus did the ex-Minister of Justice find himself also being tried for murder; and he too was found guilty. This time, however, there was a commutation of the death sentence. He died three or four months later, in prison, from a stroke. I suppose that the other 'In Memory of My Beloved Sister' in Largs Cemetery must have died at some point between the trial and the convicted man's death. But this may be a month or two out either way, I dare say. And how probable is it, I find myself wondering, that this was actually Ley's first crime of any significant sort? Did this fairly huge character defect suddenly come leaping into existence out of nothing, or from some immediate and catastrophic physiological change? Well; it's just possible, I suppose. Most things are.

(11.26–24th August)

51

It's only this morning that I now remember that, yesterday, as I was writing the previous section, at one point I wandered off to try to find a recent newspaper which contained more information about yet another case that I thought was highly relevant. I didn't find it and when I got back to the writing, I somehow forgot all about it, eager as I was to talk about Thomas Ley. And I remember something else. I have yet to go and rotate the dials one place forward on the collie calendar in the next room. Excuse me one moment, will you? Thank you.

And I also now remember that, yesterday afternoon, I suddenly realized that this rather peculiar linkage of crime and memories of my mother might not be quite so weird as I had thought. After all, my mother did love crime novels; whereas I doubt whether my father has ever read such a book, fact or fiction, in his entire life. Mind you, he did read *A Very Quiet Street*. So, even if it isn't a characteristic I inherited from her, it is something we pretty well have in common. None of the rest share this trait, as far as I know.

Oh, yes—before I forget again. What I was looking for yesterday was some discussion of a similar case in Pakistan. A couple of teenagers had run away together from a small town, for romantic reasons. Evidently they thought they loved each other, but the parents had other ideas. So they decamped. As I recall it, they were only sixteen or seventeen years of age. Anyway, they were encouraged to return to their native lieu by reassurances that everything could still be reasonably and amicably discussed. So back they went. By this time, I think, they had married—without parental consent.

And what then happened was that some elder or other, seeing that they had brought such intolerable shame on the community, killed the pair of them. I think he beheaded them, promises or no promises. So that was the social shame expiated. Well, obviously. Everything tickety-boo now, according to the fine old customs. No further room for complaint. Even so, the case blew up into a public scandal, fanned by some of those who obviously felt that these magnificent ancient traditions were no longer quite in keeping with the needs of any desirable kind of modern society. Odd, the views some people have. I get the impression that these modernists are, however, distinctly in the minority.

(9.24am–25th August)

52

All this talk of Asia, great ancient traditions, and bloodshed, recalls another case from April 1968—when I, but a seventeen-year-old, was waiting to go to university in the autumn. Much good it did me—although I do remember that the trees were nice that year. Of course, we had tensions in our own family, but never anything quite like this. It again concerns a father, a Sikh this time, living in England, and the daughter he loved: 'his favourite child', in the by now slightly alarming phrase.

Once again there is the strikingly *King Lear*-like detail of three daughters. The eldest, who lived away from home, had been back for a few days, and she was alone with her father, while the mother was out and the two younger daughters were at school. Since the father was only thirty-nine, which I now realize to mean, only a mere stripling, she herself was probably still under twenty. Anyway, the father, alone with the daughter, apparently had a bitter argument over a married man living in India. The daughter had had an abortion the previous year; a huge disgrace, I imagine. And she had let her father know that she was in love with a man who was already married. She wanted him, it seems, either to divorce or kill (!) his wife, so that he could marry her. This would, rather obviously, set up strains within what seems to have been a peculiarly volatile family, to say the least.

The daughter now told her father that she had taken poison, and had written a letter blaming him for her impending death. Whereat the man, who was still in his pyjamas, lost his temper and struck her twice with a hammer. A degree of disorientation is one thing—but this? Possibly he just happened to be carrying a hammer in the pocket of his pyjama jacket but it is rather more likely that he had to go off somewhere and fetch it. And then he hit his daughter with it, twice. To call this 'losing his temper' is, I think, to put something of a favourable gloss on it.

'Having done so,' says Bland, 'he dressed quickly and went out, returning to the house half an hour later with a high-tensile hacksaw which he had just bought for the purpose of dismembering his daughter's body.' One or two necessary purchases. I must say, if this is panic, it's a very well-controlled panic. One wonders what sort of chit-chat he had with the shopkeeper. 'Well, sir; of course it all depends on what you want to use it for.' 'Oh, just to dismember my eldest daughter. Yes, this one looks fine. She's been a bit troublesome lately. You know how they are.' 'Ah yes; girls, eh? Still—they grow out of it, don't they?' Or the equivalent.

Then he took the high-tensile saw, and started to cut at his favourite child's neck. She was still alive. (Shades of Helen Priestly, in Aberdeen.) She automatically reached up to grasp the saw, and cut her thumb in the process. And to make the whole thing even more astonishing: a later examination of the contents of her stomach showed that she had indeed already swallowed a potentially fatal dose of phenobarbitone, though this had not yet been fatally absorbed into the system. Thus the father, who had presumably realized that the daughter's words were no empty gesture, rather than (say) ringing urgently for an ambulance at once in contempt of any sequel, must have killed a girl whom he knew was already dying anyway. In which case, it seems unlikely to have been done in anything very like the well-known outburst of blinding rage. It looks to me as if what he was actually trying to do was, to make sure that the real story of the death didn't come out, by taking control and disposing of the corpse in his own way. It looks to me more like wounded self-pride than anything much like love.

So he cut off her head; cut through her waist; and severed her legs at the knees. Earlier that morning he had had three daughters. He dismembered her in a large plastic bag and poured the blood down the plug-hole of the bath. No doubt she had touched that often enough before. Does this not sound terribly expert? As if thought out in advance? Where did this plastic sack come from? A dazzling inspiration of the moment? Love shows itself in many ways, no doubt; but multiple dismemberment inside a plastic bag is one form of it which has hitherto understandably eluded the rhapsodists. I very much suspect that the father had been giving a great deal of thought to the question of how to get out of what he thought was a vast, appalling mess as cleanly as possible. All the same, surely some possibilities really ought not even to occur to one.

Routine police diligence solved the case—even though the head was left in a bag by a road in Essex; the upper part of her body went to Wolverhampton by train, in a suitcase; and the lower part, also in a suitcase, was thrown into a river. Bland says that this was an attempt to comply with an old Sikh custom—'that of dismembering one who had disgraced the family and sending parts of the body on trains going in different directions'. This old Sikh custom seems to have found favour with quite a number of murderers. But if it specifically requires trains for its implementation, not only can it not really be as old as all that, but the rail freight in that area must be particularly spectacular, I would think.

(12.13–25th August)

53

If I may intrude a note of linguistic philosophy here, I have just realized that if Crippen, that curiously famous murderer, had been called Kruppen, then his name and mine would have been perfect anagrams of each other. A terrifying thought, eh? The same would hold true of *anybody* called Kruppen, of course. The mind reels. 'Pet', a charming English term, is also the French for 'fart'; and 'Fahrt' is famously the German for 'journey'. So, it must always be possible that the words or names dearest to us in fact signify some gross, unforgiveable obscenity in another language. I shall be talking about Bela Kiss in a moment—even though the Hungarians don't pronounce it in the English manner (curiously, they prefer the Hungarian manner), and even though, like the Chinese, they give the surnames first: thus, Kiss Bela. And quite the most innocuous little words turn out to be lethal in Turkish, or Hindi, or whatever. I remember Mum telling us how intrigued Dad was when first he heard her used the word 'mist'—a somewhat romantic term in Scotland, whereas in German it means 'dung'. A brief moment preserved from their earlier lives together, before we children came along. Apparently he asked her to repeat it. Also, I completely forgot to check out that other book, called something like *The Day They Shook The Apple Tree*.

I think I have mentioned my mother's favourite brother before—Stephen; the one who died on a golf course, of a heart attack. I suspect I have also mentioned that, in one of the photographs of my Mum which I most love, standing in the back garden of this very house (the front of which I painted this afternoon, not that she will ever know that), beside my younger sister, she resembles him to a quite astonishing extent—far more so than I had ever realized during life. She looks stunningly like him. That is something else I seem to have missed.

It turns out, however, that there is a known murderer of the same name as my uncle, one Stephen Bradley. This is a grim Australian case involving the abduction and murder of a child. The killer was found when police discovered spores on the corpse of the young boy, coming from two distinct types of cypress tree which were very rarely situated near each other. They went round examining local gardens, apparently; and were fortunate enough to arrive at the right one. So: even your trees can testify against you.

Anyway, Stephen Bradley was not in fact the criminal's real name. He was a Hungarian called Istvan something or other. This is the second Hungarian who has been on the scene recently, and it called to mind the only indigenous Hungarian murders that I know anything about: the near unbelievable story of Bela Kiss. Years back, I stumbled upon a fairly dreadful old hardback about crimes and criminals, many of them continental; and I read it with some interest, even though the literary style was abysmal, and the whole thing was obviously deeply unreliable.

This told of a fiend in human form, who preyed on women in the red-light district of Budapest, enticing them to his central apartment, where he gave them drugged drinks, strangled them, and then took possession of whatever he thought they yet had to offer. He also owned a dacha. In this, which was tended by a simple peasant woman (amazingly, the book contained a syndicated press photo of her, and another of Kiss himself, very poor in resolution, but looking like a sort of cross between Bismarck and Falstaff), there was a locked room which no one could enter. Hence the article's title of 'The Hungarian Bluebeard'—though whether the fact evoked the story or the story was used as a source of fact is a moot point. (*Actually*, The Hungarian Bluebeard *is the caption of his photograph. The title of the chapter itself is 'The Secret of the Locked Room'. The book, I find, bought on the 18th April 1989 for 50 pence—I'd thought I'd got it years earlier—was, and is,* Guilty Or Not Guilty?, *by Guy Russell. Mum still had a good year to go before the start of it all. A full year.*)

Anyway, someone looked in through the keyhole and saw in this locked room a row of huge vats. Kiss told him they contained petrol. During the First World War, Kiss was called up. He was added to long lines of ordinary people. Attacking other, similar lines. A huge petrol shortage developed, among other things. Kiss' neighbour remembered the vats. So, they were duly and officially broken open. In each of them was found the dead body of a naked woman, preserved in spirit.

Periodically, he disposed of female corpses in the surrounding areas, releasing the vats for fresh victims. All those women, probably unknown to each other, lined up side by side, in a room abandoned for many months, and which to the innocent observer would always have appeared to be empty. So many brains all wired up to master that extremely unusual language. I cannot quite shake off the absurd feeling that the very fact they could communicate in that arcane tongue ought itself to have been enough to make it impossible for anyone to kill them. He spoke to them too. Other women came forward thereafter; telling of near misses, of a stranger trying to mesmerize them, centering on the image of a man in a private flat moving towards them with a crazed, lustful, bloodcurdling expression, his hands extended. (How anyone escaped this also escapes me.)

And then, the astonishing dénouement: the revelation that Kiss had actually died in the War, fighting, for all I know with genuine conviction, on behalf of Austro-Hungary. That he had fallen unknown in battle, and his corpse could not even be dug up to be execrated—which would always have been something, I suppose. There was no known individual burying place. Who knows?—perhaps as he lay dying the thought of what he had left behind him in and around his villa in Cinkota crossed his mind. Perhaps not. His comrades-in-arms by and large will have left loved ones behind them: disobedient children, pets, photographs, hopes for the future, wives. And what did he leave? Dozens of as yet untraced corpses, probably dear to someone, several of them in a line of airtight barrels. That he died not only unpunished or unapprehended, but in fact wholly unsuspected, even by those who were risking life and death beside him, somehow meant that the whole thing had a horrible but undeniable air of a black boulevard farce about it—even though the bodies had been real ones. More even than Landru, who was killing Parisian women halfway across the continent at roughly the same time. I don't suppose the same evening could once have found them similarly busy? But if not them, then who? One begins to understand those ancient religions which seemed to suppose that in some aspects the world was actually a vast, complicated practical joke, played by some unspeakably malevolent deity for reasons which it was inherently beyond us to comprehend. You understand what I am talking about, don't you? If not, it rather puzzles me as to why you might still be here. If indeed you are.

(4.48–25th August)

54

However there is another version of the Bela Kiss story, in Bland—one that sounds entirely different, and far more reliable. These are the bones of it. (*What an expression to use!*) A house and adjoining workshop, in Cinkota, get sold by public auction, by order of the district court, to raise money for unpaid taxes on the property. The owner's whereabouts are wholly unknown. Another Istvan, Istvan Molnar (another Molnar), buys the ensemble.

A week or so after Molnar and his family have moved in, they discover seven large tin barrels behind sheets of corrugated iron in the workshop. They are sealed and impressively heavy. Oho! Let's see what we've got here. An unlooked-for bonus. They are soon opened.

The women discovered thus are all between thirty and fifty years old. They have been strangled, over the course of two or three years. There is nothing to identify any of them—or the former owner; an elusive gent who had left nothing of personal import behind him. All he had left behind, evidently, were the seven female corpses. However, determined work by a Budapest detective unearthed the fact that the man had put adverts in the newspapers (just like Landru), looking for a soulmate. A signature was found.

The name was false (of course) but a copy of it was published in the papers anyway, since it was the only clue they had. And, incredibly, someone came forward to say she recognized the writing. It was a domestic servant called Rosa. She said it was the handwriting of her former lover, Bela Kiss, who had been called up at the start of the war. (Which suggests that he was still a young man. And that his writing was distinctive. For some reason, it seems oddly ill-fitting that someone who did what he did could not somehow manage to avoid call-up papers.) She produced a postcard from him. It was in and by the same hand. ('Missing you'? 'Wish you were here'?)

More information was eventually prised out, and a photograph was even procured. The man it showed turned out to be a frequent, easily recognizable visitor to Budapest's red-light district. He seemed to have an insatiable need for prostitutes; an expensive habit which he financed by seducing unyoung women, especially servants, and 'coaxing them into parting with their savings'. They had then outlived their usefulness to him. At least twelve bodies were found in all.

The detective, one Geza Bialokurszky, tried for years to get onto the trail of Kiss, but no further sighting of him seems ever to have eventuated. Bialokurszky became convinced that Kiss had died in captivity after being taken in battle, perhaps wounded. On the other hand, who knows what rearrangements the disruptions of war and the consequent breakdown and resetting of empires might not have made possible? Innumerable are the cases of people turning out not to be dead after all.

Still, he *has* to be dead by now, one way or the other. Hmm. I see that the Boston Strangler was forty-two, my present age, when he was stabbed to death in prison, seven years after having been put there. This is sometimes taken to show that some crimes are not acceptable to fellow prisoners—who, one cannot help thinking, ought not to be able to kill their colleagues whether they find their crimes 'acceptable' or not. But I rather suspect that this was simply a case of wanting to be the hard bastard who killed the Boston Strangler. I dare say I may be wrong in this too.

(6.23–25th August)

55

Well, I have at last unearthed that book; and I find that it is in fact called *The Day They Shook The Plum Tree*. Still; a fruit's a fruit. Unless it's a tomato. At least I didn't try *The Day They Shook The Bo Tree*. It's about the growth and dissipation of one of the great American fortunes. It came out in paperback form in October 1966—when we were still all living in West Princes Street—price five shillings. When I bought it secondhand in the late 80s, it cost 25 new pence—by now no longer quite so new; but the exact equivalent of 5/- anyway. Such is their so-called progress. However, as I don't remember any murders in it, that is enough about that.

Oh no it's not. It's nearly 250 not particularly reader-friendly pages—so Mum must have read it at an amazing lick. I see now that I marked at the back when I read it myself that two details are especially poignant. The young son of the richest woman in America (Ned, son of Hetty Green—such quiet names for ultra-millionaires) had to have a leg amputated below the knee, quite possibly because his mother had been so slow to have it properly treated. So his right leg was buried in the family plot, and the rest, the remains, the remainder of him joined it there forty-seven years later. (Re-united in the grave; a fairly common Romantic *topos*.)

Whereas her daughter, Sylvia Green, employed a hard-working labourer (among others) at one of her estates—to whom she talked on precisely two occasions in thirty-four years. Firstly, docking him an hour's pay for being late for his work. Second, to ask him to keep his seven year-old daughter (possibly not yet born when the previous prodigy occurred) off the premises, thank you very much. Had I not marked these passages, I would have had no recollection of reading them. I shall obviously have to go through this book again. It's about 'the eccentricities of the unimaginably rich'—and I do so want to be warned of the dangers in good time. I dread the thought of sudden wealth, and being unable to cope with it.

I also had a vague recollection of another Hungarian murder— but when I eventually managed to run a report to ground, it transpired that, though both the principals were indeed Hungarian (i.e. the killer and the killed), the crime itself took place in the USA. But, since I went to all the trouble of finding it; and since it is, to say the least, highly unusual (thank God), here follows a word or two on the matter. It occurred on the 28th of August 1962. (When, as a matter of fact, I had just begun secondary school. It could have been that very day, for all I know. Right at the end of last year, when I was actually on my way back home, five minutes from my room, returning after spending a few days with my parents at Christmas, with both of them, which will never happen again—I glimpsed my last primary school-teacher, Mrs Ward, perfectly recognisable, walking along Great Western Road just past Montague Street, looking distinctly puzzled.) Dr Geza de Kaplany was thirty-six, and his wife was twenty. They had been married for five weeks. Not much in this book, perhaps, is particularly pleasant; but what follows, I should warn you, is particularly ghastly.

So: this is what follows. One day, very loud music was heard coming from the newly married doctor's apartment in San Jose, California. But even this was not loud enough to drown out a horrible wailing sound from a woman in hugely urgent distress. Alarmed residents called the police. When they arrived, they knocked at the door, entered—and discovered that the doctor was busy soaking his wife with acid. With acid in pure form. (I am of course not suggesting that, had he used some more diluted sort of agent, it would all be so much more forgiveable or understandable.) By the time they got her to hospital, she was over half-covered in third-degree burns, which were particularly severe in the specifically sexual areas. The pupils of her eyes had vanished. Even many of those who thought they were totally inured to exhibitions of human injury and suffering, found out they were wrong about this.

As to what this personage might have thought he was doing—he said at the time that he wanted to deprive her of her beauty to warn her against adultery. So that's that. There you have the reason. Much as one might blind a son to 'warn' him against looking at disgusting pictures. A note found on a medical prescription form at the scene of the crime read: 'If you want to live—do not shout; do what I tell you; or else you will die.' What is this? (And in what language?) Did he imagine that being covered in acid left you with a *choice* of whether to cry out or not? What, if anything, did he seriously expect to happen next? Was it, perhaps, to be hidden from the neighbours? Was it not just a particularly vicious and callous murder, which would leave a body to be disposed of in due time? He had on hand, in a neat leather case, bottles of sulphuric, hydrochloric, and nitric acid. And if the music started before the screaming, then some sort of outcry had clearly been anticipated. Also, these acids had presumably been deliberately brought into the house from outside. If so, for what other purpose than for the horrific one they were actually used for?

The wife died at last, thirty-six days later, after agonising suffering. This seems to have been the longer half of their marriage. At the trial for their murder, Kaplany was at first calm; but he broke down when forced to acknowledge photographs of what he had done. In the implacable forensic evenness of the courtroom, images of atrocities committed in (I surmise) states of overwhelming passion must be doubly revolting, and impossible to duck out of or shy away from. He changed his plea from Guilty But Insane, to Guilty, saying, 'I am a doctor. I loved her. If I did this—and I must have done this—then I'm guilty.' The first and last sentences there sound accurate enough. Evidence was led to suggest that Kaplany's love for his wife had been rejected.

Oh well. Fair enough. She rejected my love so, naturally, I poured three types of acid on her. Or perhaps it was only one. It wouldn't surprise me to discover he was carrying out an experiment. If this is what love does, one shudders to think what maniacal possessiveness might try to do. Rather oddly, after a marriage of thirty-five days, and a torment of thirty-six (during which, of course, they were still a married couple), the trial itself also lasted thirty-five days. This sounds an excessive length of time to the untrained. Thirty-five days? To decide what? He was found guilty and was sentenced to life imprisonment—presumably being adjudged of unsound mind; for I think capital punishment was still in place, and I doubt whether I have ever read anything so wholly devoid of other mitigating factors. Certainly not on the facts that I have to go on.

These say that, a mere thirteen years later, he was released on parole. He then went to work in Taiwan as a missionary! It is not clear what the Taiwanese might have done, to deserve having someone who had killed his wife by means of acid come and put them on the right track with imaginative stories from the various ancient Helleno-Semitic narrative traditions; but such, apparently, is life. For instance, it seems very strange to me that I am able to date this horrendous crime exactly to the first year of my existence as a pupil in Duke Street, Glasgow; in a building which (as I learned roughly two decades later) was designed by that very fine architect, J.J. Burnet; directly opposite what we were told (but hardly believed) had once been the site of the North Prison, Duke Street.

I can remember well numerous incidents from this time. But none of them, I think, is more vivid than that moment just before four o'clock, when we were due to go off homewards for the day (me to West Princes Street; they to some sadder simulacrum of a golden domicile) after a few weeks there—when it suddenly occurred to me that this very strange feeling of having entered into a world of accelerated days, days not nearly so long as the previous days of play and primary school, must be something irreversible and permanent. I suppose before that I had always assumed that, when I finally got used to this newer dispensation of things, it would all slow back down again. But I didn't ever notice that it did.

I also remember another moment exactly so I may as well add it here. It won't upset the delicate fabric of my narrative. Let's hope not anyway. I was walking along the top floor of a double-decker bus, just about to descend the stairs, to get off at the stop opposite the school, on yet another morning. I would suppose that must have been the most convenient stop for the prison, had it not been demolished, as far as I recall the details, just before the Second World War. So, who knows where the most convenient stop might not be for it nowadays? I wonder if my mother ever saw that building. I don't know; and I don't know how I can ever find that out now. She saw the *school* often enough, of course. Proudly she took me along for my interview with the Headmaster, before I was accepted. Actually, now I think about it, that was in another building, but even so she saw the school often enough. And she was probably as apprehensive as she was proud. But should I not really have done better than this? So much is too late now.

Anyway, just at that moment, on the bus, I finally ('Eureka!') twigged what the teacher (a very clearly mentally unstable Irish Marist Brother) who had been introducing us to the French language—just what he had been going on and on about at great length over the last day or two, in his largely futile attempts to get us to understand that there was a very important difference in sound between the vowel of (for instance) *vous* and the vowel of *vu*. By the time I had reached the street, to turn left and cross over the road, I perfectly understood the point he had been making. Of course, this is always a very important moment in anyone's life. And do you know what? I have never forgotten it since. And they say the age of chivalry is 11½.

(1.32–26th August)

56

So, while we languished there, morning after morning, afternoon after afternoon, in that architecturally intriguing school, we little thought of all those others who, under distinctly severer circumstances, had languished across that very road outside, on the other side of a war. And of so much else, of course. Presumably this was where our Bertie was kept, after getting his reprieve, until whatever it was that happened to him next did indeed happen to him next. The other case I know of with Duke Street connections is that of Susan Newell—who was in fact hanged there.

This is an even more depressing case than Bertie's. Newell was a thirty-year-old woman with an eight-year-old daughter by a former marriage. She lived in Coatbridge, a town between Glasgow and Airdrie. (My mother was born in Airdrie. Her parents lived there for some fifteen months in all; though they spent pretty well the rest of their adulthood in Glasgow. Mum was brought to Glasgow at under a year old; and, until they left for Largs when she was fifty-four, she too spent her whole life there. When I asked her about it not long before she died, she said she had never been back to her birthplace. It obviously meant absolutely nothing to her.)

Newell and her husband often quarrelled. There had been a bad falling-out the previous day; and on the day in question she had just been given notice to quit by her landlady. A paper-boy, John Johnston, aged thirteen, came round to the house in his attempt to sell some evening papers, and Newell got him easily enough to come into her room. I could now talk of the Dr Johnston who attended my mother off and on during her last illness, if I wished. Newell's husband was at work in Glasgow. Her daughter was playing in the street outside the house. Doubtless, in that June 1922, the Bradleys were doing something similar in Airdrie. Or, if not there, then in Glasgow. Or, for all I know, it was the day of the flitting. There is no one I can effortlessly turn to and ask these things now.

It is possible that something just snapped. Or that, stoney-broke and desperate, Newell's single thought was that the boy must have some money on his person, and it would be better than nothing. I suppose he must have done; some normal, everyday amount. So she strangled him for it. For that or for something else. When the daughter came back into the room not long afterwards, she saw the dead boy lying stretched out on the otherwise usual bed. Trustingly, she helped her Mum to put the small corpse in a bag of some sort.

Whether Mr Newell turned up that night I can't quite work out. He was in Coatbridge at 10.30, at his sister's—he worked in Glasgow from noon till 9 p.m.—and he then went round to the police to complain about his wife assaulting him. I take it that he stayed the night at his sister's; and that his complaints were about Mrs Newell's general past behaviour—rather than anything specifically done that night to keep him, say, from discovering the body. That she was not behaving normally may, I think, be taken as read.

The next morning, mother and child set off together, to dispose of the corpse; which they took out on a hand-cart, covered by a bedrug. Of course, they had no transport of their own; and presumably they were ready for a walk of several hours. But a lorry-driver stopped and offered them a lift. They went into the centre of Glasgow. The woman got rather excited, and said she would rather continue on foot. As they manoeuvred the cart back down off the lorry—it must have been lying untended behind them, open to the elements, seemingly a normal contribution to the traffic—it was upset. But the driver noticed nothing specifically wrong—though the whole thing perhaps struck him as puzzling.

Eventually, after much trundling about, they left the bundle in a courtyard, and turned to make good their escape. The woman was immediately arrested. When the cart had been upset, another woman, who had been looking, as one does, out of her kitchen window, saw a head, and then a foot, protruding from the bundle. Evidently the onlooker sometimes sees more than any participant. What a reward, for just glancing out of a window to keep your eye on what might be happening! Something to talk about forever! Losing no time, she told her sister, and the pair of them hurried out and started following the woman, the girl, and the cart. A police-man was soon persuaded to add himself to this odd and variously committed female quartet. As she turned to leave, he arrested her.

She claimed her husband had done it, and they were both brought to trial but the guilt was evidently shown to be hers alone. She was sentenced to death. The jury appended a unanimous recommendation for mercy—but, even so, she was not reprieved. So, within a couple of minutes and four decades of the old school, she was hanged—without the least display of fear, apparently. What was she expecting? She even refused to have the white cap put over her face; so, presumably, for the last couple of seconds, she must have seen a few ordinary things which she had never seen before.

(4.21–26th August)

57

T he Newell affair has definite similarities to the Pearcey/Hogg case, a famous scandal of Victorian times. This culminated in a twenty-four-year-old woman pushing a pram around London for several miles and hours in 1890. She deposited the body of an adult female in one place, and a baby female in another. Both of these were called Phoebe Hogg. The crucial thing here was what she felt for the dead woman's husband—who in one version is called Frank Hogg, and in another, Thomas. But I don't really want to make anything out of this one too, or there'll be no end of it. I recall it was only very recently that someone was charged with the murder of various schoolgirls, one of whom was also surnamed Hogg. Her smiling picture had been looking down at one every so often from post offices and libraries and so forth for years. Quite literally for years. Perhaps for a longer period than that of her whole brief life. Has he come to trial yet? I can't recall even that.

I suppose I ought to have said earlier that the school I went to opposite the no longer existing prison was contiguous to the site of the original Glasgow University—which is also no longer in existence. It was knocked down, all past fame and glory notwithstanding, in or around 1870, and the space was made over to a railway station and goods yard. How many other European cities can claim as much? No point in getting too sentimental about the past. And now the goods yard has gone too—but, alas, the University still shows no sign of returning.

Newell was also the name—more or less; the spelling may not have been exactly that—of a family which lived for a while directly beneath us in the tenement in West Princes Street. I remember a son and a daughter; the second about my age (this would be before I was ten, I suppose), and the first a couple of years younger. This latter was the only boy that I ever fought with on anything like a regular basis. Every so often, our differences of opinion would escalate into kiddie-winkie violence—and since I was taller, older and stronger, it was always him that ended up running, crying, from the scene of our fearful but invariably bloodless mayhem.

But one day we were all playing a game which I think is called Grandmother's Footsteps. A few of us had to stand more or less in line, surreptitiously advancing towards a wall, motionless whenever the 'it' at the wall looked round (for those who were seen to move had to go back to the start)—when suddenly this daughter from downstairs, entirely against the run of play, stepped over and kissed me delicately on the cheek. She made some fairly besotted remark as well, but I can't for the life of me remember what it was. As for me, I don't think I reacted in any way whatever; as far as I was concerned, it was just one more of the unfathomably absurd things that girls got up to. I may even have assumed she was just trying to embarrass me.

Indeed, perhaps she was—though I doubt it. I prefer to see it as testimony to the warmth of her susceptible little heart. And, by God, it would need to have been susceptible to have seen anything worth swooning over in the more or less textbook little prig that I was then and thereafter. I dare say that more than one child older now than we were then has at this very moment a perfect right to call her Mother. Though perhaps they're in a huff—or indeed, perhaps they're in bed (night night, dears), for it's after 10 o'clock—and so, as it happens, are not actually conversing with her. I wonder what the father does. Surely not a journalist?

For a while, the neighbours across our landing were the Marr family. There was only one child, a short-necked, baw-faced, likeable son called John. He had a very easy-going, friendly temperament, and I was genuinely fond of him. I think they left before we did. (Other people are at the present moment, nearly three decades later, *still* in those rooms. Have they never heard of hubris? My mind can still hardly take proper hold of this fact.) (*And still can't—19.11.93. Now that I remember, Mum once told me that someone, as she heard, had killed himself by jumping out one of the back windows. Which one? I asked—trying to establish the likely veracity of the story, and always curious about details. What does it matter which one? asked Dad with something of a laugh—from which I deduce that all three of us were in a room together.*) I remember the mother coming into our kitchen after someone else had answered the door to her, and telling my mother that they had been allotted a house in a New Town; and did Mum know where Glenrothes actually was. I think Mum said, 'It's in Fife, isn't it?'—and if she did she was right.

Long years afterwards—we were here in Largs: well over a decade, perhaps nearer two, since last we saw them—Mum suddenly asked me whether or not I knew that that little John Marr who we used to play football with had actually died not long after he moved away from West Princes Street. I was flabbergasted. Lively little John? True, he had always had this dreadful hacking cough, which could at times be genuinely alarming in its intensity; but it had never for a moment occurred to me that he was not in here for much the same stretch of time as we surely must be ourselves.

Marr was the name of the family that was wiped out in the first of the two Ratcliffe Highway horrors. The son was three months old; his throat was cut too. Out of the world again without even having learned that he was in it. I have just looked up a biographical dictionary of murderers which has been in my possession, I blush to admit, for some years—I very nearly threw it out a while back; but retrieved it, rather fortunately as it now turns out, at the last minute—to see whether anyone called Marr figures in that. They don't. None of them. But there is Martha Marek, an Austrian *femme fatale*, who poisoned various people—including her former husband, Emil. This was ungrateful as well as homicidal; because, earlier on, in pursuit of an insurance fraud, Emil had agreed to let his beloved wife hack away at one of his legs, of which he had only two, in hopes of a substantial Loss of Limb payout. The leg had to be lost; it was amputated later just below the knee. However, the angles were all wrong, and there were signs of three distinct cuts having been made; so the story of a dreadful accident was not believed, and the insurance company simply refused payment. So he lost his leg for nothing. And, a few years later, he lost the rest too—certainly nothing like Ned Green, the millionaire, who was forty-seven years in catching up with his severed limb.

Martha Marek was executed on December the 6th (1938—Hitler had reintroduced capital punishment into Austria after the Anschluss, which is a point to ponder in itself). The first Ratcliffe Highway murders were on December the 7th (1811), so the facts just refuse to play the game. But there was another Mar—(indeed, another Mar—Mar—) who was intimately involved with death and murder on December the 6th. To wit Marius Martin, a nightwatchman at the Cafe Royal in London, just at the end of its days of greatest repute (1894), the era of Oscar Wilde before the fall.

This man, 'a sour busybody who brought about the dismissal of several fellow-employees by reporting them if he saw them carrying anything out of the building' (according to another Martin—Martin Fido), was found lying dead, just within the side entry, having been shot in the face twice. It was not a break-in. Evidently, someone had been hiding in the Gents. Neither the murderer nor his motivation was ever discovered—though one does find oneself rather brooding over that 'several fellow-employees'. Not a popular man, evidently. I can't believe that poor old Oscar hasn't mentioned this somewhere or other. I trust he had an alibi himself. Probably off helping to educate some social unfortunates that very night. How like the man.

(10.50–26th August)

58

I went up to the cemetery again this morning, but the stone still wasn't there. Another thing. Late last evening, I was looking through some of a series of cheapo but fairly interesting books evidently designed to be sold immediately at remainder-bookshops. They are all about crimes and mysteries and scandals, and appear to be written by Colin Wilson and his family. I bought them when I was last in Aberdeen. I find that one of them also mentions the Kaplany affair. I hadn't read that bit before. So, if you avoided it earlier, prepare to avoid it again.

But it does make you realize just how dependent a dedicated non-investigative researcher like me is on the veracity of his secondary sources. People like me quote from secondhand accounts, and any errors get preserved and further disseminated. But Wilson reports or repeats things that neither of my other versions has. That the wife was a beauty queen with whom he fell violently in love. That he was or became impotent. That he convinced himself (shades of Ley) that all the other men in the apartment were pursuing her, and that she was encouraging them. So he buys a record-player and starts to play it very loud.

The appalling crime, however, is much the same. Except that the tormented woman has been tied hands and feet to the bedposts—nicked all over the body with a razor—and had three types of acid poured into the cuts. Her face, genitals and breasts are particularly mutilated. When Kaplany opens the door, he is wearing only bloodstained underpants and rubber gloves—a crazy enough act even in itself.

In this version, Hajna de Kaplany dies twenty-four hours later—with her mother praying by her bedside that she will not survive. What sort of survival would be possible after that? And Kaplany is released after eleven years, before he is even officially eligible for parole, and smuggled out of the country into Taiwan—to work there as a cardiac specialist, a position for which he is actually unqualified! This sounds so ridiculous to me that it may even, I suppose, be true. But surely not.

(11.14 am–27th August)

(*20th November. Astonishingly, a few weeks ago I happened to notice in the local paper a snippet of information which said that a man in Dundee had just been arrested on a charge of killing his mother some days before—by pouring acid on her. I have never seen this even alluded to again. Did I merely dream it? (No.) I felt almost as if I had had a hand in causing it. What, one wonders, has he been reading recently? Or was the news deliberately underplayed? But doubtless his trial will have to come up sooner or later.*)

59

Rather a lot seems to be happening in my own patch in Glasgow, which I should be returning to in three or four days' time. Someone has just robbed a bank at the foot of Belmont Street. I have never been there in my entire life (though I know Auntie Peggy used to be a customer for a while); but I do usually send off my packages and so forth from the Post Office to the right at the bottom of Belmont Street—the bank is just to the left—and this was itself the scene of a robbery yesterday. The man ran round a very familiar corner, was sprayed by dye from the cash-box as he sought to open it, dropped the meddlesome booty, and fled. It's presumably the same guy in each case. Perhaps one of my neighbours. At least I myself have a pretty tough alibi to crack. But perhaps skilful cross-examination would be able to pry open significant gaps in it. Now: what else did I want to say?

Ah, yes. More collisions of data. It was on the 10th of October 1923 that Susan Newell was hanged opposite my not yet former school. Forty-five years before, to the day (1878), a policeman, having spotted a man behaving suspiciously in a garden in Blackhall, London, closed with him—and, after a furious struggle in which three shots were fired, one of them injuring him (for the assailant was perfectly willing to add another killing to his tally),

he (all unknown to himself) had been instrumental in apprehend-
ing Charles Peace, perhaps the most wanted man in England, the
'Paganini of Crime'. (He could pick out some tunes on a violin—
often during genteel or religious soirées in his deeply respectable
house. The real Paganini of crime was probably Richard Wagner.)
Peace too had had a serious leg injury in his youth, but had
compensated for it so well that he was wondrously agile—all the
more unexpected given the astonishing debility of his facial appearance. He was hanged the following year, aged forty-seven. A
surviving photograph suggests a wizened and unhealthy seventy
year-old. He had one of the most spectacularly inappropriate
surnames of all time.

Twenty-six years on, to the day (i.e. 1949), a Jewish couple in
Middlesex were murdered by their twenty-three year-old son-in-
law, who had followed them home from the maternity hospital
where they had just visited their four-day-old grandson. He (surnamed Goodman) was hanged the following January—so the little
lad may actually have seen all the three of them together, father,
grandfather, grandmother; but he would obviously never again be
aware of any of them. He'll still be alive, I take it. He'd only be a
month older than my older sister—whom I saw walk past the
window earlier this afternoon, about an hour and a half ago,
bringing her daughter back from school. From which I deduced:
one, that she was not well-placed to be able to pay us a visit, and,
two, that her car has still not been fixed, promises from the garage
notwithstanding. I also take it that he must know this part of his
family history by now, hellish though it must be to have to live
with it. How *do* you ever tell someone something like that? And
yet, it must get done, I suppose.

The murder weapon here was the base of a heavy, old-fashioned
tv aerial. I remember them well. Dad must have handled thousands
of them in his career. Never to any such effect, I hasten to
add—though to suppose that absolutely none of them were ever
used for purposes of household assault would be asking rather a lot,
I think. And only now do I realize that I have made a fatuous and
elementary mistake; that Goodman was the name of the victims,
not of the murderer, who was their son-*in-law*. Still, the small step
from Goodman to Glatman keeps us within the fairly confined area
of tv-related killings, though it shifts from the name of the victims
in one to that of the murderer in the other.

Harvey Murray Glatman opened a tv repair shop in Los Angeles in 1951. My father started work for a firm in that line about the same time (it's the year of my birth)—but their subsequent paths, I am glad to say, diverged very considerably. Glatman used to bind, rape, photograph and strangle young women—I don't say that was the invariable sequence—until (again, through a newspaper advertisement) he met Victim No. 4. In this case, as he was making what are called 'advances' to her, there was a struggle inside his car. Even though the gun went off and injured the girl in the leg (a comparatively rare example of a genuine unintended gunshot in the chronicles of murder, which are full of 'accidental' shots), she somehow got control of the weapon, and kept it trained on her attacker until a mobile police patrol showed up. What sort of wait must *that* have been, I ask myself—and for how long? Meanwhile, I take it, various cars passed by, some of them not noticing the bizarre sight that was freely available to them, and others noticing, marvelling (or wincing), and speeding on, while the man facing the gun would never be out there with them again.

(5.44–27th August)

60

I have a brief list of a few things requiring to be done now, but I am not quite sure what is the best order in which to treat them. There is also another woman called Newell who figures largely in a quite interesting case, but I just don't think I can be bothered going through it at length. (*And yet another Newell case is in the headlines at this very moment.*) (*Or perhaps, to be more accurate, the moment just before this.*) But yet another Williams (*hmm*) got himself involved in a case with some intriguing involutions.

There is nothing very intriguing about the crime itself: one man (Williams, Joseph) who was in serious financial difficulties had been drinking with a retired garage proprietor whom he had known for some forty years (Walter Dinnivan), shortly before the latter was found battered to death. There were many clues all pointing the same way. But the jury, for reasons known only to themselves, acquitted him.

A few hours later, Williams told a well-known crime reporter: 'The jury were wrong. I did it, so now I claim to be the second John Lee of Babbacombe, the man they couldn't hang.' (This is October 1939, just after the start of the Second World War. Perhaps the jury had other things on its mind.) Very early the next morning, he sought the same man out again, clearly in an extremely fraught state, saying, 'I have got to tell someone. The jury were wrong. It was me.'

However, even if this was true—and it almost certainly was; although perhaps, since the case was never solved, there must always be an element of doubt remaining, I dare say—there was absolutely nothing whatever that could now be done about it under the standing legal system. Indeed, even if the most screamingly unanswerable evidence were to come to light after a trial was over, showing that the acquitted was in fact guilty of the crime for which he had previously been tried, there is (as I understand it) nothing whatever that may legally be done about it now. After all, who could otherwise be sure that they wouldn't simply be tried and tried and tried again for the same crime (of course, there could be statutory restrictions on number, and time limits or periods of grace), perhaps from motives of personal vendetta, or sheer incompetence, or whatever. Nonetheless, a legal system which under some circumstances precludes the undoubtedly guilty from being found guilty is not a perfect one. Of course, no human system is perfect, and some flaws always have to be tolerated in order to avoid being faced with worse ones; but the tone of many of the memoirs of retired legal gents which I have read seems to be very much the same; one that would be more fitted to keepers of the Holy Grail—and the awareness that what they are involved in is a more human enterprise altogether could with advantage be somewhat more widely spread. As the Bishop said to the—oops, no, wait a minute.

There does of course exist a facility for reconsidering the outcome of a trial where a guilty verdict has been returned. Indeed, so valuable is the facility that in weighty matters, provided the purse can stand the strain, recourse is had to it pretty well automatically. Common sense does rather suggest that, whatever the internal logic of the system may favour, it is unlikely that all the extremely odd verdicts lie pointing the same way. And one may at least imagine a system in which there were three verdicts (as there are in Scotland at the moment), where what one might call the middle verdict (the Not Proven) functioned as a Not Guilty, except that it left open the possibility of re-prosecution—whether only once, or not for five years, or only once in the next ten years, or once thereafter, or only on years divisible by thirteen, or anything else more likely to make for equity and justice—subject to an acceptable case having been made out to the relevant constituted authorities. That should cut out the errors, no problem.

All of which is, I dare say, only the rambling of an ignorant outsider. There are doubtless enough difficulties in the law already, without our needing to go inventing more. But I must say that at times it does seem to me almost as if the great names among defence lawyers in the English legal tradition (of course the phenomenon is not confined to England—but it's what most of the books I read tend to deal with), those who knew just what points to confuse, what buttons to press, and how best to 'sway a jury', practically made a career out of bringing about miscarriages of justice. I suspect that nearly all, for instance, of Marshall Hall's greatest forensic triumphs (acquittals like Fahmy, Barney, the Green Bicycle Case, the Lawrence case, the Camden Town murder, and so forth) were virtuoso performances in getting the guilty person off the hook. He seemed to specialize in defending people whose guns were forever going off by accident as they tried to kill themselves (add Marie Hermann and Jeannie Baxter to some of the above list—while subtracting Mrs Barney, who on checking I discover to have been a parallel such triumph for Patrick Hastings), invariably hitting the person they were with to lethal effect. Talk about evidence of pattern!

After all, what else do people usually mean by the phrase, 'a good defence lawyer'? Mainly, that if there is the slightest possible loophole somewhere in a case (and what case is devoid of all weaknesses—particularly in the face of an imaginative investigator?), then this one will know how to exploit it to the hilt? But ought not a trial to be about finding out what actually happened, and then responding adequately to what has been discovered; rather than prancing up and down in front of a bemused audience, dazzling them with conman's rhetoric, and pulling endless rabbits (or, it might be better to say, endlessly pulling rabbits) out of a hat? (Rather as I've just been doing, perhaps. But, setting aside the distasteful verbal flourishes, just what exactly does 'swaying a jury' actually amount to?)

(11.55–27th August)

61

P erhaps we do tend to overlook the extent to which any trial—even a trial for murder—does not follow protocols lowered from Heaven on tablets of stone. They are all at the mercy of more or less arbitrary decisions (whether good or bad), which vary from one system to another, concerning what is allowable as evidence, or permissible as practice, and so forth. Other states and systems draw their lines in different places. The really worrying thing is when you get people who are part of one system, talking as if they evidently believe that all differences between their own and other systems are inevitably to the other's or the others' disadvantage.

The ruling, for instance, that the prosecution may seek to attack the accused's character only if his good character is itself part of the defence, or if his agent has sought to blacken the character of a prosecution witness, is a not unreasonable arrangement. (If it in fact exists; a lawyer I am not.) But in many instances the prosecution has far more ammunition to fire against the accused than *he* has against the opposing witnesses; and a shrewd or discreet silence prevents any of this from being brought out. Of course, if the defendant has the moral advantage then he will fire away good style and quite right too—but, is this a rule for helping us get at the truth?

Likewise, the convention that any previous, unconnected crimes committed by the accused are not to be brought out in court, or not until after the jury has reached its decision on the case before it, is based on the eminently admirable supposition that a person's past lapses ought not to unfairly influence the question of whether or not he is guilty of the specific offence he is actually being tried for. Revealing a past criminal record would or could lead to prejudice against the accused, and the present case would therefore not be tried fairly, on its own merits or demerits.

Of course, in reality this prejudice would often be singularly well-merited. Besides which, pattern and personal histories play a huge part in crime detection. And indeed—quite apart from the fact that it is frequently a matter requiring fine judgement as to whether two separate crimes are in fact wholly unconnected or not; or insufficiently so—there are numerous legal cases where the strongest evidence against the accused is precisely evidence of *pattern*. I think I have already mentioned that George Joseph Smith, who separately drowned his newest wife in a bath on three quite distinct occasions a full year or so apart. Had he been tried only for one particular murder, with the others kept out of it to prevent possible prejudice, he would very likely have been acquitted. For on any death considered on its own, the jury would most probably have decided that, whatever their suspicions might (or might not) be, the possibility of accident could hardly be said to be ruled out beyond all reasonable doubt.

However, this is not quite the same thing, for it was not a question of revealing a previous criminal record. So I think I'll try to execute a swift sidestep. Consider a jury hesitating over its verdict. It will assume, in the absence of any evidence to the contrary—and, I suppose, provided that the accused is of decent appearance—that this is the panel's first such serious encounter with the law, will it not? Some of them will, surely? Well, even if they don't we don't know that, do we? This seems to me to come rather close to misleading the jury, to say the least. Evidently juries may be trusted to come up with a verdict but may not be trusted to decide for themselves how much or how little weight to give to a previous criminal record. This may well be the safest and most pragmatic course to follow, I suppose. All the same, to believe that people who aren't up to doing the second are up to doing the first looks a bit optimistic to me. Why not just cast their votes for them and be done with it?

As things are, it is scarcely unknown for juries, after much wrestling with their consciences, to finally decide to acquit someone of a major charge; then have to listen while the court is told the criminal record of the accused before he is sentenced on some subsidiary misdemeanour. This record then itself induces gasps of horror and disbelief from the members of the jury. And why does it do this? Because it makes it suddenly very clear to them that this guy quite certainly did not deserve the benefit of the doubt they gave him. For, in their deliberations, they were assuming that they were dealing with someone who had never done anything like this before, and this assumption was wrong. So the laws of evidence might very well leave a jury believing (quite correctly) that they had, while inadequately briefed, effectively returned a murderer or a rapist or whatever back into the bosom of society, if such there be. Who is this fair to?

Take the Camb case, for instance. This is a celebrated personal disaster in which a ship steward was found guilty of assaulting a passenger in her cabin, and getting rid of the body through the port-hole. No corpse was ever recovered. Camb was, however, convicted of murdering Eileen Isabella Ronnie (eh?) Gibson— known as Gay Gibson: a twenty-one year-old actress. There were various telling circumstantial points—one of which was provided by a pathologist who appeared for the defence. He mentioned the presence of urine stains in the bed-wear, missed by everyone else. (I am told that a dead body evacuates its waste matter automatically when its muscles terminally relax. This quite possibly puts some potential sex murderers off doing all they at first intended to do—and many of the victims of whom it is said that any motive for killing them remains mysterious, since there were no signs of sexual assault, may have met with fates which ought to be interpreted with this offputting fact borne in mind.)

However, as one reads of the Camb case—and he was indeed convicted anyway—one is aware that, well, some strange things do happen; that coincidences occur which may with total honesty nonetheless be interpreted as resulting beyond reasonable doubt from someone else's criminal intention. But the legal system which habitually made room for extreme coincidences would presumably never convict anyone—making its utilitarian value somewhat limited.

So, one inevitably worries about the missingness of the body in the Camb case—even if the circumstances are such that there is next to no chance (which, be it noted, is not no chance at all) of the body marching in and apologizing for any unpleasantness which its previous absence might have caused. So that when one hears (as I presume the jury did not) that Camb had on three previous occasions assaulted other women on board that same ship—none of whom had reported him at the time—one feels that any possibility of judicial error has very definitely been decreased. Is this not so? In which case, can such information really be *irrelevant* to what went on at the trial?

Camb was not hanged. In fact, he was released after only eleven years, and he got a job as a waiter. However, after a few years, it was discovered that he was now molesting schoolgirls, and he was hauled back in again, his license revoked. It would obviously have been an atrocious thing had he not actually been guilty of this, but merely been convicted because of his criminal past. Yet, had a jury acquitted him, after some heart-searching, and then learned of this grim past of his, how are we to suppose they would feel about this? And what if, some time later, still at liberty, he had committed another murder? What then? However, that is enough speculation for the moment. It fair takes it out of you.

(2.12–28th August)

62

T he list of topics that I still want to broach seems if anything to be growing, rather than diminishing. It is now exactly thirty-one years ago, by the way, to the very day, that the De Kaplany atrocity took place. And, for that matter, it is exactly thirty years since the deaths in the Robles case, another American example for us all. On that day, a researcher for *Time* magazine, who shared a New York flat with two other girls—not, perhaps, the most neutral phrase in the language—came back after a day's work to find that both her flatmates had been brutally murdered by someone who had used three knives from their own kitchen. A few months later, a nineteen year-old illiterate negro was found guilty of attempted rape and given from five to ten years for the crime. This seems an amazingly lenient response under the circumstances—he had also confessed to the murders, evidently under extreme duress. However, slightly over a year later, the police were pointed towards the actual killer, a heroin addict, and the negro was exonerated. Fortunately he was still in a condition to benefit from this exoneration.

If I may make another half-turn here: I think my favourite example of grounds for quashing a verdict must be that which occurred in the Knowles case—in which a British district medical officer in Ghana in 1928 had been found guilty of shooting his wife. Well, nothing unusual so far. He was tried under Ashanti law, which, among other things, meant that there was no jury. A single judge decided the case for himself. He found Knowles guilty, and sentenced him to death. This was at once commuted to life imprisonment, and an appeal went forward. The result of this appeal was an acquittal—apparently on the unusual grounds that the judge had *misdirected himself*, in failing to consider manslaughter as a possible verdict. Well, perhaps it did just slip his mind and, had it occurred to him, he would have plumped for it with a cry of triumph. My own view is that it is overwhelmingly more likely that he realized from the outset that such a verdict was simply not applicable in this case. But no: it was necessary for him to tell himself that manslaughter was a possible verdict, before explicitly ruling it out; otherwise the trial was a fatally flawed one. So the good doctor was released. After all, what had he done wrong? Just a slight case of shooting dead his wife. It could happen to *anybody* who chanced to find himself pointing a gun at someone and fired it. A judge who misdirected himself would, I feel, be rather too crude a jest even in something like *Alice in Wonderland*.

The earliest striking example that I am aware of at present, touching this respect for technical nicety which I dare say lies at the basis of any legal system not dependent on inspired, fair-minded, incorruptible individuals, occurs in the case of John Pope and John Maycock, in Southwark, London, in 1806. (1806! Beethoven hard at work; Haydn still alive; Burns a decade dead; Napoleon in power; no photographs, no Schubert songs, no trains. And certainly no postcards of the famous Houses of Parliament across the river.)

A little old lady, or possibly a tall and strong one, by the name of Ann Maria Pooley in any case, is reputed to keep quite a tidy sum in savings hidden in her cottage in Cross Street. One labourer, John Maycock, persuades another, John Pope, to join with him in an attempt to remove it from her.

After dark, while a few pianos might be playing in the adjacent houses, I suppose—or, if that is too genteel for 1806 Southwark, a few songs are being raucously sung while glass ominously shatters—they make their way to her abode, perhaps indifferently, perhaps excitedly. Once there, quite unseen—or quite unobserved, at least—they take advantage of the rotting housing fabric typical of the area by removing a couple of bricks at the door, reaching in, and pulling back the bolt from inside, in a very early if somewhat crude solution to a locked room mystery. Once inside, they replace the bricks, and nobody is any the wiser. Except perhaps themselves.

One thing that they have learned, to their own disconcertment, is that they are now in—not the house itself—but a small scullery annexe. It leads to the house proper through a firm door which is at present immoveably locked. What can they do? They decide to wait there all night if need be, until someone (presumably the old lady) comes and re-opens the door. Which must happen eventually. So: this they do. Hour after hour after hour, whether there was food there or not. Probably not. At least there were no other housebreakers already there, awaiting a like opportunity—nor any who arrived, after a good thing, later that long night. Why, how terribly uncomfortable for them it must have been. Or perhaps it was pleasanter than their own homes or hovels, how should I know? While the little or large old lady slept on unconcerned, evidently wholly alone elsewhere in the building, dreaming her real dreams of who on earth can now know what.

Why was there a lock in the scullery door at all? So that she would be safer? Perhaps it did gain her a few more hours of life. In the morning, when she merely opened a familiar door yet again, she was instantly set upon. After a few seconds of bafflement and terror, not long enough for her to quite understand what was going on, far less to get used to the idea, she died of strangulation at the hands of one or other of a couple of ruffians whom she might well have never seen before in her entire life—as if that matters—and perhaps did not even quite see then. They hurried off and started to ransack a house still full of her existence.

Rather surprisingly, they did indeed find some sort of fortune. In these burglaries, it is almost a rule that nothing substantial is ever found. But this fine pair managed to unearth £90 in cash— with which you could in those days finance a trouble-free existence for quite a good few months. Had it been the labour of a now vanished lifetime, to piece that together? Perhaps from daily drudgery, so that she should have nothing to fear in her old age. Certainly there do not seem to have been concerned relatives and friends close at hand. Several further weeks passed, before 'puzzled acquaintances' forced their way into the house, to discover what, if anything, had been going on. Has she perhaps died? You never know. You never know indeed. So decomposed was the body that the cause of death could only be guessed at.

Yet someone seems at least to have been able to make a very shrewd guess—for Pope and Maycock, who had recently grown indiscreetly flush with money, were questioned by the authorities. The case came to trial—by which time I dare say Beethoven had managed to produce from somewhere a good few hundred bars which have probably been played more than once on every day of the past century and a half—and it emerged that the authorities had implied to one of the unwholesome duo, that, if he were to confess and incriminate the other, he would not be charged with the murder. (Which, of course, he nonetheless was.) This revelation caused the trial judge to instruct the jury forthwith that the man in question (who had only participated in the cold-blooded murder of an old woman in pursuit of a theft) must unquestionably be acquitted. So they acquitted one and had the other one hanged, for a crime which both took part in. Rather than, say, just discounting the confession as having been illegally procured—which I presume it was. For, if it wasn't discounted, then it must surely have gone some way to getting the other man hanged. (Which, of course, it will have done anyway—since it is simply not possible to 'dismiss something entirely from your mind' merely because a legal functionary asks you to; and then subsequently pretends that, since he has asked you to, you must therefore have been able to do it, and have done it.)

(4.01–28th August)

63

I often used to ask my mother whether or not she thought that any of the whodunnits I gave her were particularly good; for if so I thought I might even get round to reading them myself. Her most usual response was: well, they're undemanding reading. Of several she would say that she felt she could write a better one herself—not a reaction unique to her, of course. Only of one did she ever go so far as to hand it over to me just after she had finished it, saying that this was an ingenious one, and she suspected I might like it. Indeed, her exact words may have been, 'I expect even you might like it'. This was *Trial And Error*, by Anthony Berkeley. To my chagrin, I must confess that, even though this surely happened over a year ago, I have still not got round to reading more than the first few pages. It's not that it didn't look promising; it's just that I always felt I had other things to do or read. However, I do know enough about it to gather that it was based, in principle, on another significant English case from what is still, ever more precariously, the previous century.

This is the Mogni-Pelizzioni affair of 1865. (1865! Chekhov a lad; Ducasse just about to get started; still no Brahms symphonies; innumerable railways and photographs. Still no telephones, though. And the famous Houses of Parliament are across the river, but no one yet, I think, has any postcards of them.) There was a pub brawl in Holborn between a group of Italian immigrants and some locals—which led to one of the Englishmen being stabbed. One Serafino Pelizzioni was arrested, tried, and convicted—despite the testimony of other Italians that he had come hurrying in from another pub across the road, specifically to try to make peace between the mutually threatening factions.

This was no mere whitewash, for the Italians next saw to it that they turned up the man who was actually guilty—one Gregorio Mogni, himself no Englishman, 'who willingly gave himself up'. (I presume he had supposed that Pelizzioni would be acquitted. After all, he had what ought to be the best possible defence—he didn't do it.) However, the police had quite definitely closed the file on that particular death, and were not interested in re-opening it. They had other things to look to now. So the Italians themselves had to take out a private prosecution against Mogni, in order to make their point.

Of course, what ought to have happened now is that Mogni should have been acquitted—but I dare say he pled guilty, and Pelizzioni was subsequently released. However, I am only inferring all this from a rather laconic source. (21.11.93. In fact this case also appears in the book, *Hanged In Error*, that I alluded to earlier. I read the fuller treatment of it on my first night back from Aberdeen. Pelizzioni 'was told that he was freely pardoned for being innocent and was released'. One of the most striking details is a brief fillet of excerpts from the judge's address to Pelizzioni when giving sentence: 'The evidence was about the clearest and the most direct that, after a long course of experience of criminal justice I have ever known . . . I am as satisfied as I can be of anything . . . that you are the person who committed the crime . . . and that it was murder and not manslaughter.')

I may as well mention here before I forget it entirely, that one of Marshall Hall's most signal successes was the Lawrence case—when a man with a considerable record of violence (which included assaulting a police officer with his teeth) very much appeared to have shot his estranged wife.

It was much the usual story. First he had fired a shot in order to frighten her, wounding her in the arm; as one does. Later on there was a struggle, during which *she* was trying to kill him. And in the struggle the gun went off, with the usual result. He was acquitted, the judge expatiating in solemn tones about the possibilities of a better life yet remaining, if only he would learn from his unfortunate past errors, and so forth. Well, it may even have been true, I suppose. I wasn't there at the time. But, three days later, the acquitted worthy was in trouble again, for 'assaulting another man in a Wolverhampton inn'. Doubtless he was just swinging his arm to improve the circulation after his recent ordeal, and it accidentally hit the person beside him. It's so easily done.

(5.25–28th August)

64

I have finally managed to locate the case which an earlier one of these accounts brought to mind—the deserter hiding out for decades, and eventually being involved (in the most final way) in a murder. Astonishingly, the crucial date in this rediscovered one turns out to be August the 29th. It seems that August the 29th is a not insignificant date in the history of sudden death; so I think I'll just charge straight on to discuss this area, leaving for later any treatment arising from the 'John Lee of Babbacombe' reference in the case of Joseph Williams (66), which I wrote last night. (I write rather quickly, you may have observed. For the record: it's a Saturday now, and I began this whole thing two Saturdays ago. Now's the time for it, that's my motto.)

Firstly, the Walburger-Huberman affair. Like so many of the great crimes involving people with German names, this one occurred in the USA. On the 29th August 1922 neighbours of the Walburgers in Los Angeles heard shots and screaming. The police were called. They found themselves compelled by circumstance to break the front door down. Bert Walburger, tersely described in my source as 'an overweight cabinet-maker', lay dead on the floor. A small (.25) bullet from a lady's gun had been enough to account for him. (The idea that there is a specifically feminine way of pumping lead into somebody is a strangely intriguing one.)

The only other person they discovered in the locked house was the wife, Dotty; whom they eventually found locked inside a cupboard inside a locked bedroom. Such ostentatious innocence was almost too good to be true, and the police were not a little suspicious. It did not help that the house was absolutely full, ridiculously full, of the fingerprints of a third party. However, there was neither record nor suggestion from anyone as to the identity of this third party. So, although something was clearly going on here, the police were faced with a puzzle they could not crack. They reluctantly let go of Dotty, and filed this one under 'unsolved'.

So it remains for eight further years. During which time at least one child falls off a low wall outside Kelvingrove Art Gallery; wonders how a brother knows she had taken a bite out of his bar of chocolate (she hadn't been seen—but, alas, she had left teethmarks); and is terrified by a horse-drawn vehicle that has mounted the pavement beside her in Dalcross Street, Partick, on yet another ordinary morning when she is on her way to school. A police station is visited by an accountant whose conscience is troubling him. Not an everyday event, obviously. He says that, eight years ago, before they had released Mrs Walburger—and, perhaps, before she had known she was going to be released—Dotty had told him that her scapegrace younger brother was actually living in the attic of her home—which the police evidently never thought of inspecting. Would he (the accountant) terribly mind scratching on the wall to alert him, and then take him some food and water, because he couldn't actually get out of there under his own steam?

Well, other families are insoluble mysteries anyway, of course; but what on earth did he think was going on here? An untraced assailant, and a younger brother trapped in the attic! Perhaps he first of all wanted to find out whether it was true or not. So he went along, did as he had been bidden—apparently the police had not sealed off the house—and found that indeed it *was* true. He was soon facing a puny little feller with a receding chin, who admitted that he had been living in the Walburgers' various attics as they moved hither and yon for years. He was sick of it. He wanted out. And not only was he tired to death of the whole business, but it would do Mrs Walburger herself absolutely no good at all were he to be found there now. So the accountant, showing a flair, resilience and quixotic impulse not normally associated with those of his calling, intrepidly drove his new acquaintance to the San Francisco Highway, and thus Dotty lost her lover of the past fifteen years.

It had been as long ago as 1908, well on the other side of a World War, in the very year of the Marion Gilchrist murder no less, before even Dad had been born, that Bert Walburger, perhaps already an overweight cabinet-maker, had first suspected that his wife was carrying on with a most unlikely sixteen year-old Lothario called Gus Huberman, who worked for a paint and varnish company. Why anyone should be attracted to either was not obvious to many outsiders—which may well itself be some of the reason for it; although the fact that Gus was an orphan and Dotty had recently lost her eight-year-old son is also worth bearing in mind. They ran away together. And when Dotty returned, it was only to acknowledge her infidelity and to ask for a divorce. Bert refused, unwilling to pay out good money in order to nourish 'that shrimp'. In such a way, perhaps, does love express itself.

So things limped on, unresolved—until eventually, about 1911, Bert decided that he had seen off the menace to his home and could now sleep easy. In fact, by this time Gus was pretty well a permanent guest in his house. He had settled in the attic room, confident that his corpulent, unwitting host would never be able to make his way up the ladder and waddle disconcertingly through the trapdoor.

A complex new expertise had to be acquired: to move silently, *never* to sneeze freely or cough, to endure the hottest days unflinchingly, and not shiver too intensely on the cold ones. And, during the husband's working hours, he could always come down, help Dotty about the house, and no doubt jump into bed with her as Nature dictated. Dotty also gave him books to read, to while away the long hours of captivity and generally looked after and cared for him, under these hugely difficult conditions, lying night after night beside her vast, calmly snoring husband. Let us pray that the nights never worked him into a condition of raging jealousy up in the attic. Presumably, but for the eventual murder—perhaps, indeed, only because she panicked and talked to the accountant when she needn't have done—pretty well no one would ever have heard so much as a single word of all this. Which rather suggests that even so bizarre a situation might actually be by no means unique.

Anyway, Bert's business flourished, and they all moved from a good house to a better one several times. Each time, Gus would resettle in the new attic—for Dotty, of course, would never agree to any house which happened to lack such an essential feature. Gus could listen to the pair of them talking things over, and knew that his presence was wholly unsuspected by the hubby. Well, under the circumstances, a whiff of suspicion would probably be enough. What a permanent alert Dotty must have been on, forever deflecting conversations onto tracks that would be less painful or more acceptable to her invisible audience. Gus was also able, he thought, to pass on shrewd business tips via the wife which he claimed did a lot of good for Bert's financial position over the years. A sort of oblique rent, paid by an unseen agency above. If there is any truth in it at all.

When war came, it seems Gus rose to the occasion. At length he managed to fight his way out past the tearful, pleading Dotty. Perhaps still blinking uncertainly in the unaccustomed light and air, he tried to join up. Indeed, he *did* join up. However, an encounter with a crude, jeering sergeant soon led him to have second thoughts, and he sneaked or snuck back to Dotty's safe welcoming arms and attic. Now that he was also a deserter, he was more firmly kept in place than ever. (One rather wonders what address he must have given the military authorities as his own.)

But all went well enough, and eventually Bert decided to retire. They moved from the Mid-West—I bet you didn't know they were in the Mid-West, did you?—out to Los Angeles. Gus had gone on ahead. By now it was years since that dreadful moment when Bert had glanced up at a window while doing his gardening, and had glimpsed there something horribly like the face of his long vanquished rival. Who knows how often he had jocularly or triumphantly cast up to Dotty that ridiculous folly of hers of long ago—which she, obviously embarrassed to recall it, had sheepishly, good-naturedly hurried away from. Of course it wasn't him at the window. How could it have been? Surely you believe me rather than the evidence of your own eyes? You just love reminding me of that single past mistake, don't you? Why can't you ever just leave it alone? And after all: how *could* it have been him?

So they found a nice house with an attic, and Gus was installed in his fifth attic in fourteen years. And it was soon after that that the idyll came to an end. Forgetting all the earlier reports of a stolen diamond watch, a missing bank-roll, and so forth, the police gratefully followed up the accountant's lead. They traced Gus, who was now married—strangely, this comes over almost as an act of gross infidelity—and working as a caretaker of an apartment building. Something for which he was magnificently well-qualified, obviously. As for Dotty's former house (she had since moved, to a smaller, attic-free dwelling-place) it proved to have an attic which still bore clear signs of prolonged human habitation—spare us the details—and the police wanted to know why. So Gus told them what had happened.

On that night in August, years before, the Walburgers had returned from an evening out, which had also been a bit of a rest for Gus. He heard them quarrelling below. He then heard Bert slap his wife so hard that she fell. What else could he do? He hurried down the ladder, gun in hand.

Why this gun, which so suddenly enters the story? Well, the Walburgers, we are told, had recently been burgled, which made him very nervous. I mean, it was no fun to be alone in the house with burglars wandering about. What might they not have done if they had found him? Once they had got over the shock presumably.

So, he had slithered down, and found Bert standing over his prostrate wife. And also curious about the sudden activity happening on the loft-ladder, I should think. 'You little rat! What are you doing here?' he yelled. An entirely reasonable question under the circumstances one would have thought. It even sounds rather restrained—but that was probably just the total shock. But at least he still recognized him. Then there was a scuffle, and—yes—the gun had gone off accidentally, as is usual in murder cases. When the smoke cleared, it was found that Bert had fallen to the floor, never to rise. Dotty, meanwhile, had got up from it smartly. Then the brilliant, baffling inspiration of the plural locked doors. Remarkable presence of mind, that. If only the police didn't look in the attic, they might yet—except for Bert, of course—be able to get out of this alive.

This is not the most plausible story one is ever going to hear, is it? However, the implausible also happens; and the poor orphan boy was able to convince the jury at his trial that he had been guilty only of manslaughter. He was given three years—but since the killing had occurred eight years previously, according to my source, the statute of limitations (which, I take it, did not stretch to cover murder) meant that this was merely a technical expression, as he could not now be jailed for such a crime. So, Gus went back to his presumably mind-boggled wife and their apartment building and they probably had some very intriguing conversations in the following weeks.

Or perhaps he had already told her. Dot was also tried, but the jury failed to reach a decision. The public prosecutor decided to leave well alone while he still had his health and sanity. She too walked away free, back to her own smaller apartment, and went on living there until her death, peaceful and alone.

(9.28–28th August)

Quite literally within a week of the Saturday when I typed out what I thought were the very last words of this work (well, they still are), I made a minor but greatly disconcerting discovery. Suffering, I suppose, mild withdrawal symptoms, I picked a hitherto neglected book up off a shelf in a friend's house, which I am looking after in a somewhat intermittent and negligent manner while he is elsewhere. The volume bore the almost anonymous title, *Classics In Murder*. I had never paid it much attention before, having somehow got the idea that it was a reprint of various of Roughead's most obvious treatments, almost all of which I would probably have already read. When a closer inspection revealed that this was not the case here; that in fact it was a collection of essays by different hands, chosen for the quality of the writing, I decided to carry it home to see if it might yet be of any use to me.

It was. I already knew the articles by Roughead and Vulliamy. On that Wednesday evening I read a couple more—by H.B. Irving and Edmund Pearson, both of great interest. I also started an account of George Joseph Smith, often referred to as the 'Brides in the Bath' murderer, by William Bolitho, which is just about the best writing of this nature that I have ever read. By the time I finished it the next day, I very much regretted not having bought his book (*Murder For Profit*, 1926) when I saw it a while back in an Edinburgh secondhand book shop. I remember being tempted, since the cases looked so interesting—except for Smith, whose atrocities have almost become a music hall turn. (They included, I deduce or recollect, Landru, Haarmann and Troppmann—the last of whom is actually mentioned in the *Poésies* of Isidore Ducasse, the self-styled Comte de Lautréamont; who died aged twenty-four in 1870, and who is one of the few writers up òn the same floor as Shakespeare.) It may even have been the article on Smith which helped put me off. That and the rather serious price, which, since I didn't really have the money, I could not justify paying out for such an indulgence.

Anyway, after finishing the Bolitho article the next day, I eventually got round to inspecting something called 'The Case of the Man Who Came to Dinner, etc.', by Alan Hynd, of whom I had never previously heard. It was written in a lively style, and the build-up seemed promising. Gradually it began to remind me of the Walburger Case ('The Walburger Case' is the title which Colin Wilson gives it in his *World Famous Crimes of Passion*—the source of the previous section), and I once more quailed at the thought of how much similarly interesting material I must have missed. And then, after several hundred words, mention was made of an attic, and to my astonishment I realized that it actually *was* another discussion of this very case.

To the very obvious question, why did you not recognize the names, there is a surprising but, I think, fully exonerating answer. All the names were different. (Except, I think, for one of the defence lawyers. And Los Angeles.) It was vaguely disturbing that the first name of the woman in question was given as Walburga (here knowingly described, his italics, as 'an *over-sexed* nymphomaniac', rather than the mousy little female already famil- iar to us)—but since her surname was Oesterreich, and her hus- band was called Fred (not Bert), and their home town was Milwaukee (not Minneapolis), this was at best the mere whisper of a coincidence. Even when one Otto Sanhuber appears on the scene (curiously, the leading names are still all Germanic), a repairer of defective sewing machines, one suspects nothing. He has come to fix some defective machines in Fred's *apron* factory. And besides, he is seventeen, not sixteen. A wonderful age at which to repair sewing machines.

It is a fairly common experience, to start reading an account of some case or other which you think is a new one to you, and then for it to dawn on you that in fact you have already met it in another treatment—even though you have no idea of the where and when of the earlier version. It is also rare for two independent accounts to agree in every detail. But this is clearly something lying well beyond that. The disparity is so great and so unremitting that it even occurs to the bemused reader to wonder whether perhaps one of the reports might be a deliberate attempt to disguise the identities of those involved for some reason—perhaps to spare the blushes of living relatives. But how likely is this, given books published several decades after the fact, and that fact apparently one of the most celebrated American newspaper sensations of the 20s? ('Phantom Lover In The Attic' and so forth.) Why, for instance, change the youth's age from sixteen to seventeen? (Or from seventeen to sixteen?) Why change August 29, 1922 to August 22, 1922? (The latter date is Hynd's, but it does at least *look* more like an error.)

So one turns to the obvious remaining conclusion. That at least one of these writers (or both—but I have my favourite suspect) is presenting as fact what is only his own confused, erratic memory of the case, wholly unchecked—unless perhaps he is merely trustingly repeating the fatuity of some other source. (It happens to the best of us.) I suppose I could now do much to resolve this by going off and hunting out a reliable cross-section of contemporary newspapers. However, not only am I a bit tired of all this, for the moment at least, and congenitally lazy to boot—but there was a very heavy fall of snow late yesterday which, alas, would (I confidently predict) have prevented me from reaching the reference library anyway. Not to mention the fact that time is, as usual, short. Also, though I may of course be wrong, I have a feeling distinctly near to certainty that at least the weight of the errors lies with the version which I epitomized (not myself with 100% accuracy, I dare say) in the previous section. I have resisted the temptation to write in additional doubts about it, to add to those already there, as testimony to my uncanny prescience in the matter. The truth is, I suppose, that the author of it is some way off being a byword for factual reliability.

Divergencies in reported circumstance are so frequent that even to enumerate them would be a task lasting pages. Suffice it to say that very nearly all the new details in Hynd work towards making the set-up much more realistic and plausible. (Whether this is equivalent to making it truer is a debatable point—but I should say that, by and large, it clearly does.) Fred does occasionally hear inexplicable noises off and above (coughs and throat-clearings; usually at night), and notices unexplained losses from the kitchen and so forth. Otto does sometimes get let out at night for a wander. There is a two-year break after Fred happens upon Otto mooching around in the kitchen. There is no military interlude. (Nor for that matter is there a mention of any lost son.) Likewise, Fred sees only some sort of brief, clear movement at a dirt-encrusted attic window which Otto has disobeyed strict instructions to keep away from. Otto even has a reasonable way of passing the time. Not only does he read, he also writes adventure romances, usually set in the South Sea Islands. Apparently he even met with some success for his efforts in this field. If he can truly be said to be in a field. That he should himself be the central figure in so palpable a romance, even if a thoroughly *non*-escapist one, while churning it all out for magazines is a particularly nice touch. But what happened when he was taken ill? Was he never ill?

The story of the death itself (sounding something very like a murder) is not quite the same—and the story of the belated unraveling of the plot is radically different in some respects. It now features an attorney named Herman Shapiro in place of the accountant, Sol Shepherd. (Who, on one page, a straw in the wind perhaps, is credited as 'Shephard'. I forgot to add that there were no earlier burglars in the later version.) But I won't recount the details. Apart from anything else: what if I should stumble across yet another variant account tomorrow? It is noteworthy, however, that Sanhuber seems to have married a stenographer—or perhaps Huberman did—which is what Robert Willox snr had done on an earlier day, when, if Hynd's '1903' is correct (Wilson gives '1908'), Gus/Otto was already sitting up in an American attic, perhaps reading Mark Twain, a favourite of his. Very entertaining, Twain, of course: but sometimes a little far-fetched, no?

One advantage of the earlier version (i.e. the one I discovered earlier) is that it explicitly makes Bert obese, and therefore unable just to clamber up into the loft to investigate things for himself. We are never quite told why Fred doesn't do so—unless I missed that too. A mild inaccessibility in the trap-doors is about as far as it goes. (The wife here scratches on the trap-door; not on the wall.) However, on the whole, I am confident that any nice little winks and inferences in the previous section were directed at what was itself something of a phantom account. (In Hynd's version, one of the reasons why Fred moves is that he fears his present house is haunted. Hynd also tells us that Fred did not employ a maid, being too stingy to employ one.)

It is rather more proof than one ever expected to have, of the precariousness of one's reliance on other printed sources and on the research (if any) that lies behind them, to discover that a book produced for a mass-market might in a chapter entitled 'The Walburger Case' actually be discussing people who were really called Oesterreich; and that what you in fact have there is merely a sort of confused recollection of the leading lady's first name. Obviously she could not then be called Walburga Walburger—but, one wonders, why Dot? Could Walburga even be right? All most puzzling. I just don't know. One glimpses the wisdom of the legal requirement of two separate witnesses. Listen just to one and you could so easily end up naïvely trusting in a sincerely held but quite dramatically inaccurate belief.

(5.22–26th February)

66

That may well have been a murder, but somehow it doesn't feel as if it was. I very much hope it wasn't. Of course, one of the most interesting things about it is to ask where it would be, and what would we know of it, if the accountant had been able to keep his scruples to himself—or perhaps if he had died before he could ever quite get round to sharing them with the authorities.

Perhaps the least impressive example I know, of the police getting their hands on crucial evidence, occurred in a case in Middlesex in 1953. A couple of girls (Barbara Songhurst and Christine Reed) who had gone out cycling on the last day in May, were later found, assaulted, raped and murdered. (Mum will have been appallingly ill with hyperemesis at precisely this period. She was pregnant with my brother. Had she died, Dad might well have taken off back to Germany with his two older children—and for all I know I would right now be writing something else, in German; if that is how it works.) A local man with a relevant history was arrested in connection with the crime.

This adornment to society actually had in his possession at the time of his arrest the axe with which he had bludgeoned the two girls to death. Somehow he was able, unbeknown to the police—who, I presume did not observe that he had it with him—to slip it under the seat of the patrol car which was taking him to the local police station. The next day, another policeman, cleaning out the car, found the axe, and, apparently without a second thought, took it off home with him (I can only give the facts as I have them—this must surely mean: stole it); and used it to chop up wood. It took a month for it to be searched for and located—for all of which time it carried on its mundane, normal existence in a local house; despite having been lately used to end two young, promising lives. It was then taken away, presumably not without some harsh words spoken and was found to (still) fit the fatal injuries. Which is doubtless just as well.

It is, to say the least, a little odd that a copper finding an axe in a police-car should not pause to wonder just what on earth it might be doing there, and whether the find must not possibly be of some significance. I mean, do they regularly have axes under the seats? This killer, by the way, had an eyebrow-raising hobby. Knife-throwing. Any more volunteers? He was hanged three days prior to Christmas 1953—no false sentiment there, obviously. Of course, I'll have been given presents that Christmas too. But, even though they were certainly no secret, I don't see how anyone could ever succeed in finding out now what it is they were. Not by asking me, that's for sure. But I don't doubt they were given to me with love, all the same. I have never yet not been in the same house as Mum at Christmas. Not yet, anyway. Nor has Dad too, for that matter.

(12.23–29th August)

67

T hen, I suppose, there was some guy called Putt, in Memphis, Tennessee, who, on the 29th of August 1969, carried out his fourth murder. This must have been the last August of my life that was still fairly normal and under reasonable control. I was between first and second year at Glasgow University—and it was in the coming year that my life slipped off the rails a bit. I blame the local bus system. Alas, I have failed to get it back on them as yet; though, as the years pass, you get to care less and less about it. I remember I had just spent a couple of vacation weeks working as a barman at a hotel in Millport, on a wholly unknown island not far off Largs. It remains my sole visit there—but, at this very moment, I can see the northern ridge of this same island from the window near which I am standing, writing. I am using a tall loudspeaker as a sort of desk.

He was sentenced to 497 years in prison—a device, I take it, to rule out the possibility of his ever being released. So presumably he is still alive today somewhere; locked up; with no hope of ever getting out of a cell for all but the briefest period. He was twenty-three years old when he was apprehended. Repeated attempts to have him declared insane were not progressed with, apparently, after a Supreme Court ruling set aside the death penalty. Evidently the decision returned his sanity to him. I trust psychiatrists have been alerted to this promising if unconventional form of cure.

Which still leaves us with two crimes for this particular day; both of which, curiously enough, involve the clergy. The first is an Irish case from 1927, concerning a Father James McKeown and his two domestic servants: an eighteen year-old chauffeur/oddjobman named Gerard Toal, and the housekeeper, Mary Callan, who was twice the boy's age. One day the woman just disappeared. It was known that the two servants did not get on very well together but nothing further came to light to begin with, and no one particularly suspected anything. It was a complete puzzle. She had just disappeared.

A few months later, the new housekeeper, one Peggy Galagher found parts of a woman's bicycle hidden in Toal's room. What she had been doing there ('hidden', we notice), and why he had not got rid of this incriminating evidence, do not appear. Events seem to have proceeded with an odd casualness. The priest confronted Toal with this find—but the youth insisted he had only stolen the bike, and absolutely nothing more. Police searched his room, and questioned him—but the sole upshot was that Fr McKeown, not too happy with things, contented himself with ordering Toal to leave, whatever it was exactly the lad might have done. This he went along with, saying his plan was to travel to Canada.

Presumably, had he just gone ahead and done this, nothing more would ever have come of it. Instead, however, he went to Dundalk where, some ten days later, he was arrested on what I take to be a quite separate charge of stealing. And it seems to have been this which prompted the *Gardai* to make a more thorough search of Fr McKeown's house and garden. They found female clothing in an ash-pit, and yet more parts of a bicycle. (What parts, one wonders, did he decide to keep, and why?) Toal admitted that they had quarrelled. Then her badly decomposed body was found in a water-filled quarry at some distance from the house. He was tried in July 1928, while Mum was a very young schoolgirl, found guilty, and hanged on this day in that same year. I can't help feeling there must be more to it than that. But that is a feeling I have with almost all of these cases, and I have nothing more to go on than this.

My Dad has just told me, 'I don't think I will last long'. He does not feel like eating a meal just now. (I went in to ask him.) I must say, for an 81 year-old man, he looks all right to me. A few months ago, Mum made a similar sort of remark to me on a couple of occasions, under such vastly different circumstances. Do I want to describe them now? (I'll try one of them. 'I think my number's up,' she said to me once, very calmly, with overtones of sadness and resignation, after one of those midnights when I waited until she was settled for the night, on the couch which she then still preferred to lie on, before I too went off to my bed. There was nothing else I could do, since, through some oversight, I had not been given spare years to hand out to those who might deserve them. Dad was in his own room, from which he every so often emerged, more willing to help than helpful for much of the time, alas.)

I shall go on to the next case. In the early evening of the second day of 1894, in the parish of Entrammes, near Laval, the rector, Abbé Fricot, sits down to make up his accounts in the company of his curate, Abbé Albert Bruneau. The rector is never seen alive again. The curé goes off, plays the organ, and has his supper.

Next morning, suggesting that perhaps the good Abbé, evidently now missing, has killed himself, the curate leads a neighbour to a well in the garden. In very deep water, the body is discovered. He has clearly been battered to death. Bruneau tells a nun that the Abbé had killed himself; but that, since this is a mortal sin, he had faked it to look like murder, to avoid scandalizing the faithful.

A compelling line of argument. Alas, there is blood on the organ that Bruneau was the last to play; and in his desk is found 1300 francs which surely ought by rights to be located in the rector's strong-box. Alas, this is not the first such theft. For, shortly after Bruneau had arrived from his previous fief, 500 francs had disappeared from the same place. But who, I wonder, could prove that this wasn't a miracle?

Moreover, while at his previous cure, a bequest of 16,000 francs, intended for charity, had been rerouted by the curate for his own purposes. And the rectory had been burgled four times. Suspicion somehow fell on poor Bruneau; and, having fallen there, flourished an hundred-fold.

A notorious frequenter of the local brothels—though the brothel-keeper did at least say in his favour that he was not the only priest to turn up there in his clerical garb—Bruneau was unable to explain away some highly unfortunate details; including the cries and groans heard coming from the area of his final conclave with the rector. That he was known to have contracted gonorrhoea from a prostitute of course did little to win public opinion round to his side. For, though it is not illegal, it is not quite what people look for in their spiritual leaders, no matter how often it might be what they actually find. Bruneau was tried, found guilty, and sentenced to death. 16,000 people—one for each franc of the embezzled bequest as it happens—attended his execution on the 29th of August 1894. It is said that 'he died with dignity, declaring his innocence to the last'. So obviously the habits of a lifetime did not desert him at the end. He was 33 years old—or so I deduce. A particularly resonant age for a Catholic priest. Let he who has never purloined money intended for charity, caught gonorrhoea from prostitutes, and murdered at least one person, cast the first stone.

(5.52–29th August)

68

So taken was I by Bland's two-volume *True Crime Diary* that I bought a third book of his which I happened to notice in a secondhand-bookshop. This featured at some length three cases—two fairly interesting; but the third, the longest, an Australian saga of considerable tedium. However, the book concludes with a discussion of several people who have experienced what was meant to be the ultimate penalty of the law, and who yet survived.

The first of these, a hopeless recidivist who flourished in London circa 1760 under the flamboyant name of John Smith, is interesting for his account of what it felt like to be hanged until unconscious— and beyond, for all he knew to the contrary. Until he painfully came back to consciousness some time later. (His reprieve had been a little late in arriving.) Not that this most apocalyptic of experiences seems to have done him any good at all; far less turn him into some prodigy of wisdom rarely returned from the infinite beyond. Once fully recovered, he carried on his thieving exactly as before, just like any other common or garden miscreant who had never come back from the dead.

Though death, of course, is what one does not come back from. But anyway, soon after having been denied the simple support of his feet, 'he for some time' (says a contemporary report which Bland unearthed) 'was sensible of a very great Pain, occasioned by the Weight of his Body, and felt his spirits in a strange commotion, violently pressing forwards . . . to his Head, (when) he as it were saw a great Blaze or glaring Light, which seemed to go out at his Eyes as it were in a Flash, and then he lost all sense of Pain.'

So: it's as simple as that. Even this quite deliberate punishment is as simple as that. Only the extremely fortunate few will go through life without having had a worse physical experience—perhaps a much worse one—than that. Indeed, many good, unlucky, non-criminal people, before, during and after his own experience, will have died in a manner far more painful than that—with enduring, terrible pain. (Although most people, I suspect, die with about as much difficulty as they might turn over in bed.)

I remember once reading a fairly well-known actor giving an account of what his recent heart attack had felt like—from the inside, as it were. The most striking thing is that it all seemed to amount to practically nothing. He remembered suddenly becoming weak. Then, some time afterwards, he came back to consciousness. And if he hadn't done so, given that the interval had been a complete blank for him, then that too would have been that; without him even having quite realized that he was dying, that theoretically most significant of events. However, as has been remarked before, though the fear of death may be part of anyone's biography, death itself is part of no one's. Smith's experience, which sounds like a sort of grossly magnified version of a very bad passage during sleep; wanting to waken up, but for some reason being oppressed, not being able to break free, and then—either wakefulness, or presumably the complete opposite.

Of course, the long weeks and months spent waiting for the thing to happen, to get it over with at last, would not, you might say, do much to help your peace of mind—but that is a slightly different point.

(10.15–29th August)

69

To call 'John Lee of Babbacombe' 'the man they couldn't hang' is to invest a miserable killer with an aura of glamour which he cannot deserve. (I seem to remember noticing that some literary figure once wrote letters from Babbacombe. Was it Oscar Wilde?) Convicted for battering his elderly mistress—in the servant/master sense—to death, he was the beneficiary of some mysterious fault in the trap release mechanism of the gallows on which he was to be hanged. It failed to open on three consecutive attempts which the hangman made (though the hangman himself talked of only a double attempt) to despatch him according to the decision of the court. At which point, the chaplain decided that enough was enough and walked off; which led to proceedings being temporarily abandoned. It was hardly a case of being unhangable. A couple of hours with a decent carpenter and a later re-scheduling; and he would doubtless have found, if only for a split-second, that the laws of physics had recovered their equanimity.

However, the powers that be presumably decided that to try again would savour too much of vindictiveness, and so they commuted his sentence to life imprisonment, entirely because of a technical hitch. So Lee could more accurately, if less memorably, be termed, 'The Man They Decided Not to Hang After All'. He was actually kept inside for twenty-two years, far longer than the usual sane lifer—after which he vanished into merited and fortuitously provided obscurity. He himself claimed to have dreamt on the night before the attempted hanging, that such a thing would happen as did indeed happen; but whether this is true, a common fantasy of the condemned, or a self-dramatizing retrospective invention does not seem to me to be very much worth bothering about. But he certainly claimed that his salvation was due to divine intervention. 'It was the Lord's hand which would not let the law take away my life.' Instead, he let them incarcerate him for 22 years. It is only a pity that the Lord did not equally see fit to intervene just before Emma Keyse, the victim, had her throat cut and her head battered in.

I suddenly remember that Berry, the celebrated executioner, was so moved by the Jewish service which the officiating rabbi chanted, intoned and sang before the execution for murder of Israel Lipski— with the prisoner often joining in—that he there and then decided he would never be part of any other case involving a Jew. Lipski killed a woman called Miriam Angel, in Batty Street, London. One turning further west, in Berner Street (now Henriques Street), Elizabeth Stride, a Swede, was killed by the Whitechapel Murderer ('Jack the Ripper') in the yard leading to a Jewish club. Given that the killer was most probably Aaron Kosminski, it is perhaps just as well for Berry's peace of mind—not to mention that of all the law-abiding Jewish citizens of the locality—that he was never caught.

Assuming my topography is right, if we go two streets east rather than one west, we come to the top of what locals knew at the time as Grove Street. So much happened there that I am frightened to start on it. Have I already mentioned that it was here, in 1920— when it was still Grove Street—that one Mark Godmacher cut his daughter's throat when she and her husband refused to make up a quarrel with him on Atonement Day? I have a suspicion I must have done. Should I say more? Perhaps not. By a bizarre twist, the fourth street of this group is (still) called Christian Street.

(12.15am–30th August)

70

Hmm. I spent a very considerable amount of time on that last couple of paragraphs; rewriting them, worrying whether they might not sound (or, for that matter, *be*) anti-semitic; before deciding that enough was enough, and that an anti-semite would not be feeling all this stress. I remember much the same thing, *mutatis mutandis*, when I was doing other sections, earlier on, which involved members of other minority groups. But one continues anyway. Specifically, to Peter Kürten, the 'Monster of Düsseldorf'. (Not to be confused with Fritz Haarmann, the Monster of Hanover, who may well have been even worse—though both, obviously, are completely off the scale.) It was Kürten whose story is supposed to lie behind Fritz Lang's somewhat classic film, M, with Peter Lorre as the murderer, in his early German incarnation—although it would seem to lie a very long way behind it.

Kürten was a factory worker; a petty criminal, who graduated to major crimes at a comparatively late age, by his mid-forties. My own, limited understanding of the case is that a growing propensity for, among other things, child molesting, finally reached the stage (in 1929) of actually murdering a child. This tragically familiar sort of escalation may possibly have given him an intensity of release which he had begun to think was beyond him—

though I am not sorry to say that, actually, I have no idea whether it was more a question of him at last achieving his appalling heart's desire, or just, as it were, increasing the dosage to reproduce earlier effects. There were bouts of arson too, which also seem to have a sexual effect on him. I am told that it is all tied up with power and dominance. He was also a keen trade unionist. My tentative assumption here, however—though with a character like this, you can never quite be sure—is that this was for a different sort of reason entirely. And he was a married man; whose wife, it would seem, knew absolutely nothing about all this until just before the end.

Over the next few months, Kürten horrified the town (and far beyond) with a series of assaults which left at least nine people dead and seven more seriously injured. Animals were involved too, it appears. Indeed, he would assault pretty well any living being smaller than himself when the mood came over him; and would do so in a frenzied, repetitive way—whether with a knife or a blunt instrument (mind you, he did also strangle some victims; an unusual murderous versatility)—until the desired effect was reached. This I take, perhaps naïvely, to be nothing much more or much less than orgasm. But then I rather suspect that a lot of sexual crime has this extremely crude but sufficient motivation: that the assailant finds it is a way of overcoming his otherwise habitual state of pretty well hopeless impotence.

Anyway, setting such amateur speculation aside, on the 14th of May 1930, one Maria Budlick arrived in Düsseldorf from Cologne, looking for work. (All my four grandparents are alive, although they don't know that. I only ever met one of them.) At the station, she met a man who offered to show her the way to a hostel. Rather naïvely, she went with him. However, when he made to lead her through the Volksgarten Park, she refused to accompany him. This refusal led to something of an altercation in not the loveliest language in the world—which brought another man onto the scene: quiet, soft-spoken, gentlemanly, someone to be trusted. At this, the first man angrily left; and I do not know whether he too was some sort of pervert menacing on his own behalf, or was merely much irked at having his perfectly decent, citizenly motives so insultingly misconstrued.

Anyway, this second solicitous gent took her to a one-room flat of his in MettmännerStrasse—where he gave her a glass of milk and a bite to eat. I must say this all sounds very odd to me. Then they went out and got on a tram right to the edge of the city, alighting by the Grafenburg Woods, into which he then led his docile companion. She seems still to have supposed that she was being taken to a hostel; which shows either how plausible Kürten was or how *dumm* she was.

He stopped. He did not appear to be in one of his intenser moods. He turned and said to her, 'Do you know now where you are? I can tell you. You are alone with me in the middle of the woods. Now you scream as much as you like and nobody will hear you.' What a moment! Just time to think—what?—but is it me it seems to be happening to?—but how is that possible—; before he steps forward and seizes her by the throat. They struggle for a good while until she has almost lost consciousness. But, before she quite does so, even more strangely, or just as strangely, or whatever that should be, he suddenly releases his grip. I would hate to inject a note of crudity into the description of an aggravated sexual assault, but is it not likely that he had just, quite simply, ejaculated—insofar as ejaculation is a simple process—and was therefore no longer, for the moment at least, the slightest bit interested in the object still beside him? Or is this all too simple?

However, she might still be able to lead the police to him. To kill her now would, from his point of view, be unprofitable labour, more work for absolutely nothing—but, even so, it might have to be done. So, with considerable naïvety of his own, he asks the woman whether she could find her way back to his room unaided. Maria gives the correct answer—one not too hard to find, but utterly crucial. She says, no. How could I possibly do that? I don't know this place at all. At which the man wholly releases her, and even shows her where to go, in order to find the exit from the woods, back towards town. Making one wonder what sort of activity it was that he thought he had been engaging in. And off he walks into the night—presumably (as far as I can make out) thinking of himself as a reasonable kind of guy.

What an introduction to a new town! Perhaps she just assumed that everyone here must be a bit mad; but the fact is that Budlick *did not report* the incident to the police! Presumably it simply never occurred to her that it could have been the Beast of Düsseldorf she had been with. She can hardly not have known of his exis-tence, I take it. Some slightly deranged gentleman, with problems of his own, amateurishly attempting to imitate the monster who was on the loose? Who knows?

And here comes an astonishing coincidence now. When Maria next wrote to a friend back home—actually, just down the river— she did include a mention of this bizarre occurrence, as one might expect. I do not know in what terms she characterized it. And the friend told the police? No; not even that. The story runs, that when she sent off the letter to her friend, friend or not she put the wrong address on it, and it could not be delivered. Seeking to find out who the sender was, the authorities opened the letter; and, not content with noting the address therein, they evidently read the letter through, and arrived at a clearer estimate of what had really been happening to Maria than she herself had so far managed. (To be blunt, I suspect that, quite simply, the authorities were illegally opening and reading the mail on spec—though I would not voluntarily go to the stake for the accuracy of the source I am using.)

They got in touch with Maria, and she was indeed still able to lead them back to the flat in MettmännerStrasse. While they were inspecting the locus from the street, a man described by his wife as being a bit vain, but very fond of children, and a regular church-goer, walked into the building, looking over at them as he did so. A few minutes later, he came out again. He was neither questioned nor stopped, merely observed. This was not yet Hitler's Germany, and legality was still the norm.

A week later, Kürten's wife told police that her husband was the Beast of Düsseldorf. He had confessed to her, possibly so that she rather than Budlick would get the reward offered for information leading to his capture. Every cloud has a silver lining, I suppose. He was only now arrested. He admitted sixty-eight crimes and was clearly not barking mad; so he was sentenced to death by (I think) beheading.

He ate his final meal heartily and asked for a second helping. After all, you never know; something might still turn up. No point in being pessimistic. Things could always be worse. Some people have to put up with rheumatism. He said he was looking forward to hearing the blood gush out of his neck after his death. Well, he didn't, of course; and it did.

(2.59–30th August)

71

L et me move one more step down my list. Frederick Gosling, who lived over a shop he owned in Chertsey, Surrey, was found tied up and gagged in his bedroom, dead. 'A small sum was missing, but local rumour was that he had a fortune hidden somewhere in his house.' Identification of the culprits seems to have been helped by the fact that, on the previous day, an attack on him by two men in his shop was intercepted and deflected by the arrival of a group of schoolgirls. Then off the group goes, dispersing to their various Chertseyesque homes—oh hello, Belinda is back—having allowed someone another day of life. Or perhaps, since the world is that sort of place, their very intervention brought about an intenser attack the next day. I don't know. Certainly no one seems to have taken it quite seriously enough.

Two brothers called Brown and a man called Smith were charged—a suspiciously drably named trio; but, as it happens, such were indeed their real names. The case is noteworthy for the fact that one of the brothers was discharged, and gave testimony against the other two men. He had evidently been waiting in the car; and, when they returned, they had told him the old man was tied up but otherwise all right. Smith and the other brother were found guilty, and were hanged on April the 25th of the year I was born.

While on the subject of brothers, there is at least one example on record of a pair of them being involved in quite separate murder cases. In 1944, Thomas Jenkins and Ronald Hedley tried to carry out a smash and grab on a jeweller's in Central London. A retired naval commander, grasping what was going on, fatally obeyed his finer instincts by stepping out in front of their getaway car and trying to force it to a halt. Instead, they simply drove straight at him. He was dragged for nearly a mile beneath the car, right across the river to the south side of the Thames. A quick look back—through the sort of book that he can never for a moment have thought he himself would feature in, any more than (I presume) do you or I—reveals that his name was Ralph Binney. Ten minutes earlier, it must still have seemed like a perfectly ordinary day to him. Hedley was hanged; Jenkins was put in prison for a long while.

Three years later, a trio of aggravated robbers tried to do a smash and grab on another jeweller's shop in the vicinity. Since the trio included Charles Henry Jenkins, aged twenty-three, the younger brother of Thomas Jenkins, already in possession of a record for assault, one may suspect that the family had too intense a commitment to this sort of endeavour to be able to profit from the warning. Perhaps they assumed they couldn't be as unfortunate as the other two—scuppered by the irksome tomfoolery of some unnecessary member of the public. But, as it happens, they could be, and they were.

Not a thousandth as unfortunate, however, as Alex de Antiquis; a father of six, who, acting on the impulse of the moment, drove his motorcycle so as to obstruct the line of the getaway car. He was shot dead for it. One of the three—for they were caught and convicted—was too young to be hanged. The other two, including the younger Jenkins, were hanged in September 1947 while his brother was still in prison, perhaps trying to work out what made ordinary members of the public behave like that. A well-known photograph of the dying man lying by the side of the kerb conveys with immense power the sense of something uncanny and unintelligible having settled down on a perfectly normal street. It could just as soon have happened to any of those other casual occupants of that street at that time. The man squatting beside him; the man leaning over him; the two a little way behind, evidently complete strangers talking about it; or any from the small knot of people held in place, stationary, just beyond—though as yet no authority figure has turned up.

De Antiquis' last words were, 'I'm all right. Stop them. I did my best.' Not easily improved on, I think. He died soon afterwards, perhaps without even realizing that he could be dying. After all, how possible can it be that, one moment, you are just riding your bike down a familiar street for the umpteenth time, and the next moment some youth wholly unknown to you fires a bullet into you? These things obviously can't happen.

(8.03–30th August)

72

I note that people called Brown or Browne figure in at least half a dozen fairly prominent English murders, and more often as the killer than the victim. They include one of the rare parricides to be added to Bertie, who seems the soul of caution by comparison—in which, obviously, there was a Brown on both sides of the act.

On 23 July 1943—there was a war on—a nurse in Rayleigh, Essex, was taking her charge, a wheelchair-bound invalid, out on one of his favourite routes for a breath of fresh air. After a while they stopped, so that he could enjoy a cigarette while the nurse busied herself smoothing his blanket and so forth. Archibald Brown had been involved in—well, well—a motor cycling accident. Unlike De Antiquis, he came out of it alive; but he had as a result gradually developed paralysis of the spine. There was a sudden, violent explosion. The nurse was thrown sideways, but was left more or less unharmed. Brown, however, was blown to pieces.

As his son Eric, aged nineteen, a bank-clerk, had recently joined up and been taught all about mines, investigators did not have to look far for a convincing suspect. Interviewed, he eventually explained that his father had been making life next to intolerable for his two sons and their mother, and that he felt that this was the best solution for all concerned. He showed no contrition, evidently feeling there was nothing to be contrite about in any of this. Dad was now beyond the reach of suffering, and the family was now beyond the reach of Dad. I would love to have learned just what the mother made of all this.

Brown was found guilty but insane. I suspect he might well have elicited a harsher verdict if the nurse had been blown up too. Perhaps the Hawkins No. 75 Grenade Mine is a very direction-specific explosive. But, even so, how could he guarantee that it would kill only his father? (Only his father!) Was there a timer on it, or what?

It now occurs to me that this guy might well still be alive. After all, he was two or three years younger than my own mother. And at the time of all this, Dad, just turned thirty-one, and now in a nearby bedroom in a house on the west coast of Scotland, was serving in the Luftwaffe. He was helping to work the searchlights. It's all very odd.

(8.24–30th August)

73

As it happens, the 23rd of July—although, this time, the one in 1964—was a crucial moment in the dreadful saga of the man known as the 'Polish Ripper', and my first thought was to have a brief discussion of him now, then go next door to the more recent case of the so-called 'Russian Ripper'. This last, who was actually a Ukrainian, was not caught until November 1990— still under three years ago at the moment—even though he really ought to have been picked up after his first killing (in December 1978), as he so nearly was. Instead of just after his 55th.

However, not only did the police decide to charge someone else with the first crime (a man with a likely record, who lived locally)—their choice was found guilty, condemned to death, reprieved, and then, after an impassioned crusade by the grandmother of the nine year-old girl who had been abused and murdered, he had been, as it were, *unreprieved*, and executed by a bullet to the head. Presumably that woman is still alive, and, if she is, what sort of emotions is she having to deal with? No wonder that people sometimes refuse to admit the truth. She must surely have thought—little consolation though it must have been—that things could never get any worse. But it turns out that it could, even after losing a loved grandchild to a killer.

Incidentally, the mother of this man, Kravchenko, was visited by a very reluctant detective after the real killer had been apprehended; who had to tell her that her son had been posthumously rehabilitated. This is a club with, after Stalin, no shortage of ghostly members. As he manoeuvred his way towards trying to tell her this, the man realized to his horror, that the woman was worried only by the fact that her son had of late stopped writing to her from prison, and that she rather hoped nothing had happened to him. So, now that he had been found Not Guilty after all, when would she be seeing him again? She knew of the reprieve, of course; but no one had actually informed her that her son *had* been executed after all. While, next door, other people went about their lawful business.

Which is probably an even stronger argument against capital punishment than the actual murderer is an argument *for* it. But, as I said, I don't particularly want to discuss any of this now. I'll be going back to Glasgow later today for a short while; and, with any luck, I should be able to inspect at least some easy-to-locate accounts of Bertie's crime and his trial. Who knows: I may even be able to find out something of what happened afterwards—although I may decide that this is more trouble than it's worth.

(10.54 am 31st August)

74

W ell, it turns out I won't actually be leaving Largs for a few more hours, so I may as well see how far I can get with a treatment of the Polish case in question. I remember that when my elder sister was at secondary school, one of her classmates, presumably the daughter of a man who came over in the same Polish army as my father, was a girl called Danuta, known usually as Danka. I know nothing more about her; I dare say we hardly even met—though no doubt we were together for a few seconds in some room or other. It is not technically impossible, I suppose, that this may even have happened on that 23rd of July 1964 when another Danuta, Danuta Maciejowicz, was found dead in a park in Olsztyn, a town north of Warsaw—and, to go by the sound of it, once part of East Prussia, probably as Ollstein. She was only seventeen; a few years beyond us. The previous day had been a Polish national holiday, and she had gone out cheerfully to watch a parade.

(I take all this from Bland's *True Crime Diary 2*. Whereas most crimes that one reads of one will find discussed again and again in book after book, this is the only place where I have ever come across this one, staggering though it is. But for that one volume I would know absolutely nothing about it, and I would doubtless be writing something else at the moment. Something just as interesting, no doubt. Or perhaps I would just be out there enjoying the sun, as I suppose I ought to be—for these last two days of August have, without warning, proved to be a sweltering spell. I see that Dad has just sauntered out into our little front garden, to refresh a few of the flowers from a jug of water. No doubt he will soon be going in again for more. Still, it is always as if Mum is just about to come round any nearby corner.)

Back to this patiently waiting disaster. A letter in red ink, in spidery handwriting, then arrived at a newspaper office in Warsaw; the writer claiming to have 'plucked a rose in bloom in the gardens of Olsztyn', and purposing to do the same again shortly. A very similar letter, claiming that its writer would give cause for weeping, had arrived at another newspaper three weeks before. The report is a little unclear, but it is evident that this Danuta was not the weak-egoed homicidal maniac's first victim. Not for the first time I feel that, in a fairer universe, people so woeful in thought, intention and expression simply ought not to be physically able to have such a devastating effect on other people's lives.

Then, on the 17th of January 1965, much the same happened to a sixteen year-old Warsaw girl called Anna Kaliniak. This time the body was found only after the letter had arrived. Surprisingly little progress seems to have been made by November the first, All Souls Day, when an eighteen year-old hotel receptionist called Janina Popielska was attacked, chloroformed, raped repeatedly, stabbed to death, and posthumously mutilated, after she had set out on foot to her own village, just outside Poznan. (Posen in German. Looking at an atlas, I see that Olsztyn used to be Allenstein.) On Mayday the year following, a seventeen year-old student in Warsaw, Marysia Galazka, went out to look for the family cat. Soon after, presumably when someone else went out to see what was keeping her, her body was found, naked, raped and disembowelled, in the tool-shed behind the house.

And so it goes on. On Christmas Eve, a train pulled into Krakow late at night. Well, more than one did, no doubt. But on one of them was discovered another corpse: Janina Kozielska, a seventeen year-old Janina this time. She was now wearing only a leather mini-skirt, and both she and it had been repeatedly slashed. She too had been raped. The killer did not appear to be among the other passengers. However, in the mail-van, a note was discovered, in his own distinctive writing, saying, 'I have done it again'. How dreadful for him, if people had attributed his deed to someone else.

I am now trying to pick up the thread again, after a brief interlude when I went out and gave Dad's car a quick once-over with a sponge and warm water. It was a completely unexpected request—except that he usually finds some last task that can't wait, and has to be done just before I go away for a few days. I used to wash the car, or the van, regularly every Saturday afternoon while we were in West Princes Street, carrying the pails full of water up and down three flights of stairs. Actually, on reflection, I surely only ever carried the emptied pail back up. It must be literally decades now since last I washed the car. Cars must have come and gone since without me doing that.

But it was this last victim nonetheless which in some ways led to the breakthrough. For it turned out that she had a sister, called Aniela, who had been murdered, aged fourteen, while on a visit to see her grandmother in Warsaw in 1964. This had happened two years before, so Janina, obviously, was the older sister. Here too were people who must have supposed that, whatever else might happen to them now, things could not get worse. The worst had already happened. But even so much pain, it turns out, may be added to. Police did however learn that both girls had been connected with an academy of art in Krakow—the Artlovers' Club. Janina had been a part-time model; Aniela a part-time student.

This was of all the more interest in that the distinctive ink in which the boasting letters were written was not an ordinary commercial product, but a home-made solution containing artist's paint. I can't help thinking that this strong clue perhaps ought to have been successfully acted upon somewhat earlier than this. Police therefore carefully examined all 118 members of the club— one imagines inoffensive civil servants, housewives, public transport employees and so forth—and when they at last arrived at a male translator who had a preoccupation with red paint and a drawerful of knives, their deductive powers were fortunately strong enough for them to infer the rest.

It is thought-provoking that this information seems to have reached them at second hand—for they had to go to his home looking for him, intending to take him in. It was the last day of January 1967. He was not there—there being somewhere in

Katowice, which I seem to recall has some connection with the present Pope. (It is also rather near to Opole—Oppeln in German—the birthplace of Oscar Slater, né Leschziner.) He was arrested at dawn the next day.

This was just too late to help Bozena Raczkiewicz, an eighteen year-old student. She had been found murdered in a railway station shelter in Lodz, a town some way to the north. She too had been raped and the corpse had been mutilated. I don't know whether the timing of this was just a dreadful coincidence; or whether the killer had perhaps worked out that arrest must be immediately in the offing and thought, I'll show them what I can still do. But I feel I have better things to do with my time than try to work out what this man was thinking. What was the girl thinking, for instance, thirty seconds before she was attacked?

He had spent the rest of the night drinking. He confessed to twenty sex murders in under three years. He was charged, convicted, and sentenced to death. 'Later, however, the "Red Spider", as he had been popularly called, was declared insane and sent to an asylum in his home town.' Lucky Katowice. Where he presumably remains, an arty type in his fifties. I can't help wondering about this word 'popularly'. Popular with whom? I take it the name was started up by some journalist or hanger-on (like "Jack the Ripper" itself)—and was then used as a thrilling way of referring to the unknown maniac, glamourizing him as if he were some sort of brilliant but unreliable racehorse. But I suppose more accurate names like 'The Knife-Wielding Turd' would take up too much space.

(12.30–31st August)

I am now at long last able to appear in the proud guise of a diligent researcher. Yesterday afternoon, I spent a few hours in the reference library, ruining my eyes as I tried to decipher what the *Glasgow Herald* had had to say about the Willox case as it developed at the time. If that microfilm was at original size, as I suppose it was, then it amazes me that people used to put up with such near-unintelligibility for morning after morning. Nor were the rewards particularly great. But I suppose I shall have to persevere with this all the same.

The murder of Willox snr occurred late on the 4th of November 1929, and it was therefore, of course, not reported until the 5th. On the first of the month, there is an interesting report in the paper of 'the first all-colour talkie', which rather took me aback. Next day we hear of Arab unrest in Palestine, providing a reassuring note of permanence in a shifting world. On the third, we hear of a boy from 95 Bernard Street, who runs out from behind a bus on the Dalmarnock Road near Muslin Street, and was killed. He was seven. His name was Joseph Potter, and what has ever been written of the huge grief that that must have caused to all concerned? I have just looked up Bernard Street on a map of the city for the first and perhaps the only time in my life. Muslin Street, I am fairly sure, is where one of the greatest of Scottish artists was living only a few years before. But that is not what I am here for.

However, I'll add one more thing from the first anyway, if I may. (And I do rather think I may.) A Govan man, Henry Docherty (I am keeping on my toes in case I spot any relatives) was convicted of a break-in, after having left a letter in a shop which he had illegally entered. The message ran: 'I visit here tonight for the benefit of robbery. But there is no money in your desk. I get some some time. 121 Govan Street, South Side'—which last was indeed the man's actual address. The authorities were shrewd enough to spot the clue. His defence was, perhaps not surprisingly, that he was drunk at the time.

Oh, all right, I may as well add another report from 1 November, even though I'm not sure I have quite understood it correctly. A pair of twins had died at home, in Maryhill Road, No. 1422, at some point in the recent past, just an hour or so after they had been born. I can't work out whether the births or the deaths occurred at around 3.30 in the afternoon. But that was certainly when one of the central events of their paired lives happened—though these lives consisted of little more than their central events—and the point is so glaringly obvious to me that I have to point out that it was on or about 3.30 in the afternoon that Mum died, a bit over sixty-three years later. (Which involves over 23,000 afternoons, by the way.) We must have driven past that address together often enough.

Then, with alarming suddenness even to someone who was expecting it: BRUTAL MURDER/IN GLASGOW.//MYSTERY OF MAN'S/DEATH.//SON'S TRAGIC DISCOVERY. 'Complete mystery surrounds the death of a middle-aged Glasgow man who was found dead last night in his home with his head badly battered. The discovery was made by his son, and from the circumstances it would appear that a brutal murder had been committed.// So far the police have very little to work upon, as no weapon capable of inflicting the terrible injuries to which the man succumbed could be found in the house. An astonishing feature of the case is that, although the house is on the top flat of a three-storey tenement, no sounds were heard by the neighbours.'

I had rather thought it was decided pretty well at once that the hammer in the kitchen cupboard was the murder weapon—but evidently there was indeed uncertainty on that point for quite a while. The report continues that the dead man was fifty-five, and 'a commissionaire in a Glasgow shipyard'. He is understood 'to have been of a quiet and unassuming nature'. The son is called, not quite accurately, Robert *Smith* Willox. He left between 6.30 and 6.45; returned about 9.30—when, of course, he was horrified to discover what he did. Poor lad, poor lad, poor lad, runs a chorus from thousands of homes that morning, often even from inside some richer or poorer kitchens. What an awfy shock it must have been for him to come back and discover *that*. You never know the minute nor the hour. What time is it by the way?

The report rises to bold type for, 'It is evident that the man had been repeatedly and savagely beaten, as the greater part of his head was mutilated almost beyond recognition'. Then it reasonably points out that he must have let the assailant in himself—clearly no question yet of the latter having his own key, or already being inside the house, waiting for his unsuspecting victim.

The police are still labouring under great difficulties because of utter dearth of information, lack of knowledge of motive, and doubt as to the exact time of the assault. Much is made of the astonishing fact that no one else heard a sound. This is indeed a bit odd. Perhaps there is even a suggestion that the neighbours must know more than they were willing to say. Perhaps they did. But, with the whole thing left an almost intractable mystery, the report here comes to an abrupt end.

But the paper itself doesn't end there, of course. On the very next page, there is the rather staggering story of Richard Corbett, who shot his mother because she was in terrible pain from an incurable cancer. He then tried to kill himself, but failed. Presumably this would have been just like looking at Mum in her last illness, when, even with increasingly powerful medication, she still often had moments of great pain. Without the medication, I do not easily see how it would have been possible to endure it—either for the sufferer, or for those who could do little more than stand by and watch the suffering. Mention is also made there of another Pole, a young actress called Stanislawa Ominska, who a few years earlier (1924) had shot her lover from much the same motive, and had been acquitted. I'm afraid I was so involved in reading all this, that I neglected to copy out as much of it as perhaps I ought to have done.

Dad will have been a teenager in Poland when that happened,

so he may well have noticed it at the time. Or he may have heard his parents—whoever those strange people were—talking about it. But, even if he did, I can hardly expect him to remember it now, so long afterwards. Marshall Pilsudski, I note, seems to have been taking over the country round about then. I recall how Dad staggered us a couple of years ago when my sister brought him a paperback history of Poland, to see if it interested him. It didn't much. But one of the illustrations was a photo of the dead Pilsudski lying in state, and Dad electrified us by throwing into the talk the fact that he had been there at the time. It was during his Polish national service. The lying in state threatened to develop into some sort of demonstration, and, as far as I gathered, soldiers with bayonets fixed cleared the murmuring crowd from Warsaw Cathedral. That was the first any of us had heard of *that*.

And then, on the day after the Willox murder, Alexander Flint, recently headmaster of Woodside Secondary School, retired after fifty-two years of teaching. I remember that the first girl whom I ever looked at and thought 'Hello. Who is this?' used to go to that school, from West Princes Street. Since it was a Protestant school, I never went there myself. Instead I had a 15 or 20 minute bus journey every day, to and from Townhead, legendary for its beauty. However, in just over an hour's time, I am going to drop in at a friend's house for what he calls a spot of lunch—and he lives in precisely the small street which ends at that school. Ain't it all strange? Actually, I still have just over an hour. It is now 11.22 and I am due there at 12.30.

(11.22 am–1st September)

76

And what greeted the literate citizenry in the next day's newspaper? Poor, deprived people, to have had to stagger by as best they could over half a century before crucial eyes contemplated these columns. There was, did you know—and I am sorry to say that I expect you didn't—a 33.81% turn-out in the local election in Cowcaddens. (An electorate of 16,533—at least one of them [and almost certainly more] no longer able to vote even had he wished to. Or even if he had had time to do so.) Alas, John Kennedy, the Moderate, whose son routinely canvassed the Willoxes at so hair-raisingly inopportune a moment, lost; and lost by quite a margin. Alexander McLean (Labour), 3,672. John Kennedy (Moderate), 1,704. Majority: 1,968. (And what a year that was! I remember being in the big kitchen in Barra Street with Mum, at 1 o'clock of an afternoon, with a little yellow radio talking of the latest *évènements* in Paris, caused by revolting students. Mum shook her head in irritated amusement and said, they're all mad. I agreed with her then. After the passage of years, I find that I agree with her again, roughly speaking. And, had a few votes in Cowcaddens been different on that day—which she lived through as an eight year-old—I would certainly not just have recalled that now.)

What else? Jessie White of William Street, Anderston—presumably one of those tiny thoroughfares by Anderston Cross which no longer exist in any shape or form—was knocked down by a tramcar at the Cross and killed. A Scot who had confessed to being guilty of the murder that the actor Philip Drew was tried for (though only in the Coroner's Court) was quietly committed to a lunatic asylum. (A very interesting case. Coventry, 22 June 1929—Dad's 17th birthday. A quiet, inoffensive, happily-married tobacconist, sitting in his shop of an evening reading a brochure about his impending vacation—which I think was to start the very next day—was fatally assaulted in pursuance of a raid on his till. It is not completely clear that Drew didn't do it, as I remember.) A soldier charged with bigamy claimed to have been too drunk to notice, and so on, and so forth.

Then, on page 13, a startling development. GLASGOW MAN'S/DEATH//CHARGE OF MURDER/AGAINST SON//STARTLING DEVELOPMENT//. Bertie is still labelled Robert Smith Willox. Most interestingly, the father's age is given as sixty-six (i.e. born c. 1863), rather than the usual fifty-five (i.e. born c. 1874). Bertie is now said to have gone out on an errand 'shortly after 6 o'clock'.

'The murder caused a painful sensation in the neighbourhood, and all day yesterday little groups of people were gathered in the vicinity of the house where the tragedy took place.'

The father, we are told, was originally from Cruden, in Aberdeenshire and had been a commissionaire since 1919, after his demob presumably. 'It is understood that Willox was for a time a reporter on the staff of an Aberdeen newspaper during the early 1890's.' And one Robert Willox had indeed been a junior reporter there—but only for six months in 1891. Before the Lizzie Borden case. Was this the seventeen year-old future murder victim?

He is alleged to have been proficient in shorthand and typing—somewhat unexpected attributes, which he does not seem to have done much with—and was a quiet, rather reticent man with a kindly personality. 'He always had a genial greeting for his neighbours when he met them on the street or on the stairs to his home.' Still, he kept himself to himself, and he may perhaps have had good reason for it, quite apart from any innate shyness. (You'll understand, of course, that my researches, such as they are, are always running slightly ahead of that part of them which is being written up on the next morning.)

'An intimate friend of the dead man and his son, with whom the lad resided on Monday night,'—i.e. the Mrs Smith of Canal Street, who seems to have been almost the outsider closest to the Willox family—'has stated that the youth came to her in great distress and told her that his father had been murdered.'

This is interesting. It must have been picked up on the fifth, the day after the killing. Yet it appears, or shall appear, that when a policeman took Bertie along to Mrs Smith late on the Monday night, they were enjoined not to discuss recent events; leaving Mrs Smith with the definite impression that Willox *père* must have sustained some sort of serious injury at work. (As a Commissionaire? 'Member of the Corps of Commissionaires organized in London for employment as messengers etc.', *Concise Oxford Dictionary*. Well, he might have been knocked down crossing the road, I suppose. It seems to have happened to quite a few other people. I take it that this Corps is a sort of agency for employing ex-military men; reliable types, used to wearing a uniform, and amenable to being despatched to carry out orders.)

'It was also stated that the youth had said that he met a number of friends, and stood talking to them until about 9.30 pm.' Well, not quite. On the next day, the youth is bound over in custody. Very pale; looking younger than his twenty years. Alleged that he also stole £3. (Or is it £8—the finally agreed figure? The microfilm is dark, grainy, lined, near illegible; and a nearby group of Americans are pursuing their Scots ancestry very loudly, with the help of an equally uninhibited librarian.) There was little public interest. Remanded for a further forty-eight hours. Said not a word. He merely gave a slight nod of the head to indicate that he took in what had been decided upon.

Overleaf, page 8—the Woman's Page. Large heading: Are Maids Unreasonable? Meeting The Modern Problem.

Problems, problems, problems.

(10.25–2nd September)

77

Next day, Friday, the case still merited a mention. The police are now endeavouring to trace the movements of a £5 banknote—the one that Bertie was so set on denying possession of. It had been endorsed on the back with a full name and address: G. Hill, 6 Corporation Road, Darlington. Actually, just at that time, there is a lad called Harold Hill in motion somewhere, who, obviously unknown to himself, has already lived over half his life. In a distant November, in twelve years and eleven days time, he will kill two young girls in Penn, in Buckinghamshire—several years before the philosopher Karl Popper goes to live there. Actually, I have a letter from him (Popper), from that address, dated December 1978—the polite answer to a puzzled query. The soldier, for this other Hill, the one who never possessed the fatal five pound note, did indeed become a soldier, was executed in April 1942.

As for the weapon, Bertie's weapon: 'There is a belief' (what? floating free in the air?) 'that a small article, such as a hammer, was used.' It might perhaps, some think, or someone thinks, have been thrown into the canal—which comes to within a few minutes' walk to the north-east. Dragging, however, is not yet thought necessary.

A Mr Delisle Burns claims that we are ten years from the last war and that it will be ten years to the next. (1939. Very impressive.

Psychics have claimed arcane powers on the basis of far less.) And on page 19 we learn that Mrs Fox is to be exhumed. This is indeed Rosaline Fox, the victim in what is still perhaps the most famous English matricide case. She had died on the 23rd of October, twelve days before Willox senior. Perhaps there was something in the island air at the time, leading to the murder of sole surviving parents.

On Saturday the 9th, many thousands will have noticed the reference to 'joy-riding' on page 6; and some of them will no doubt have lingered over the latest news of 'The Glasgow Tragedy' on page 11. Bertie has been remanded until Tuesday the 12th. It is by now definitely £8 that someone has taken. Still no weapon. But Mr G. Hill has been revealed as a musician of Fleuchar Street, Dundee. I resist the temptation to share with you my few memories of Dundee. None of them are particularly pleasant. Mr Hill had been in Darlington two years before, when he was asked to endorse his funny Scottish banknote. The complex trajectory which led the note from Darlington to its more than walk-on role in a Glasgow domestic tragedy we do not know, and (I think we may safely claim) we never shall know now. Or then, for that matter: for I can't believe that anyone *ever* knew it. Nonetheless, we are now the proud owner of two of the addresses of Mr G. Hill, musician, towards the end of the 1920s.

Public interest is evidently growing. The benches are now filled. And an 'elderly woman' seated at the very front of them calls out 'Bertie! Bertie!' in a voice that trembles with emotion. Is this again the faithful Mrs Smith? But no name is given. The moment, of sorrow, or sympathy, or whatever compound of such emotions it might have been, is caught but not labelled. 'Willox looked in the direction of the woman and nodded.' After all he still could nod his head. And then, shortly afterwards, she went back to her home, whoever she was.

(11.02–2nd September)

78

On to next Wednesday, when we learn that Bertie has been bound over yet again—to no one's surprise by now, I should think. Mention is made of 'a hammer or other lethal weapon'. But public interest is still growing. Many were unable to get into the building, and had to mill around outside. Among the many topics available for them to discuss, had they so chosen, was the fact that (page 14) Thomas Mann has been awarded this year's Nobel Prize for Literature. A reasonable choice. After all, some people still read him.

Which nicely sets up an interlude involving another German. On Saturday the 16th, there is some horrible news: MANIAC'S NINTH MURDER/GERMAN POLICE BAFFLED/Panic in Düsseldorf/Ninth victim this week. This, of course, is a glimpse of Kürten before that name has ever emerged. He will not actually be caught until next May, and all that strange business about the misdirected letter. On Monday, the comparatively almost straightforward Bertie is remanded again. Three mummified babies have been found in a tin trunk in Glasgow. Three of them. On Tuesday, the Knowles appeal is described. (The African case, where the judge allegedly misdirected *himself*. The beneficiary had Glasgow connections.) On Wednesday, this appeal has been sustained. Thursday, Friday, Saturday, Sunday.

Monday the 25th. A theatre attendant who lives in Hathaway Street (under ten minutes north-west of here) was struck on the face by a couple of passing youths in Maryhill Road near Avenue-park Street. (Plus, you might say, ça change. Five minutes north-west of here.) He falls against a window. Clemenceau dies. Two days later, four men are injured in Sauchiehall Street when scaffolding collapses. And the next day we hear of the unfortunate Joseph Glancey, whose troubles began with a piece of great good luck. He was walking along the same street some time earlier (before the collapsing scaffolding, of course; but probably before the Willox murder too), when he found £50, two twenties and two fives—a very pleasant windfall even today, but at the time a dazzling sum. (It was more than Mrs Willox's life insurance pay-out, for instance.) A bank clerk had dropped it, but Joseph decided to take no steps to try to find the real owner. For this, theft by finding, he got three months. But I presume he had already had a good fifty quid's worth by then too.

Into December. Bertie is no doubt doing his best in Duke Street. Is Patrick McLaughlin also in the prison yet? Perhaps not. We shall hear of him shortly. However, there is a wonderfully intriguing story which comes to light, a dim mysterious light, on page 7 of the Monday Dec. 2 issue, concerning the sixty-four year-old Elizabeth Turnbull or Tannock. It is headlined: WOMAN'S DEATH/MYS-TERY//PECULIAR AFFAIR AT/HILLHEAD//FOUL PLAY SUSPECTED—but I dare not linger over it here or I'll never get through all this. Perhaps I'll return to it later, if only to give the basic facts in full. This must have been a particularly rewarding edition for the faithful audience. Three pages later, we hear of Andrew Caird of Alyth who, three hours after he had been supposed to be getting married, threw himself off a railway bridge in front of an oncoming train! A house in Dundee was already furnished and waiting for the happy couple. I forbear to make the obvious comment. Waiting for him too was his wedding-day suit, which he had not gone to collect.

So what was all that about, I wonder? Just understandable nerves and irresoluteness taken to a pathological extent? After all, people frequently back out of impending marriages, even after vast, lock-ing plans have been set into almost unstoppable motion—but without it ever quite occurring to them that they ought to kill themselves. Or was there something which was now going to have to be divulged, which he just couldn't face revealing? I don't know. I saw nothing else about it anywhere.

On page 13 comes the news that John Ogilvie, a religious enthusiast several centuries previous, has at last been beatified. Half a century or so later, he will earn a further promotion and be canonized, credited with affecting the physiology of an elderly Glasgow man in a wholly mysterious way, and bringing about a reversion in his far-gone cancerous condition. Two later cancerous growths in the same man also remitted—though opinions vary on whether this shows the wonderful resilience of the particular body in question, or a sequence of ghostly interventions by one or more long-dead saints. These wraiths, however, could apparently do nothing in the case of eighteen month-old Mary Jane Compton, reported on page 17 of the next day's paper. A table-top which had been left leaning against a wall had fallen on her as she was crawling about, and it killed her. Tuesday, Wednesday, Thursday, Friday, Saturday.

(12.35–3rd September)

79

Saturday, page 7. At last something relevant. GROVE STREET MURDER. ACCUSED SPECIAL PLEA OF INSANITY. Not only did Bertie's agents intend to plead not guilty to all charges anyway (murder, plus three of uttering—the pass-book frauds), but they were shaping to claim that he was insane into the bargain. This conjures up the bizarre theoretical possibility that their client might be found to be Not Guilty, but Insane too. So that perhaps, although innocent of the crimes, he might have to be locked up for his own good all the same? What a triumph of advocacy that would be!

But I can see that you couldn't very well plead both Not Guilty, and Guilty but Insane—so presumably this is the only method whereby you can indicate the desire to contest the charges while reserving the right to claim that your man was, in the end, not responsible for whatever might have happened anyway. But it's only a brief mention. On page 19, Patrick McLaughlin, of 183 Stevenson Street in the Calton, a fellow inmate on remand in Duke Street Prison on a charge of indecent practices, is found hanged in his cell.

On Monday, there is a razor attack in Garscube Road, not far from Bertie's former abode. Not far also, I suppose, from the spot

where, a few years ago, some unwitting German tourists decided to
rest overnight in their camper van (or could they even have gone
so far as to pitch a tent there?); being deluded—one trusts by fog
or darkness, or both—into thinking that this was a likely and safe
enough location for an untroubled night. They were, of course,
attacked, beaten and robbed by some of the indomitable and
high-spirited youths of the district. Actually it is only a few
minutes' walk away from here too. I mean, it's safe enough most of
the time—if never particularly inviting.

There is a list of eight or nine road accidents; superfluous real
fatalities. Fire Horror In American Talkie Studio. Nine Burned To
Death. 12 Dead In U.S. Prison Mutiny. 31 Women and three
children in Hungary are accused of mass poisoning over 20 years.
Sounds like quite a place. Willox's insanity plea is withdrawn—and
oh yes, Good Heavens, Tuesday the 17th of December, the beginning of the reports of the actual trial.

There he is, suddenly back in prominence. Unconcernedly
leaning to one side. Now and then exchanging a fleeting smile of
recognition with a witness. A pale, slight young man. *While admitting a friend*, the witness heard 'You won't get a penny from me,' or
something like that. (A rather more plausible version that, of
Florence Watt's strangely selective overhearing. Was Harrington
a friend of the house?)

James Turner, hotel porter, 110 Burnside Street. Just round two
corners; totally vanished now; rather surprising it reached 110,
considering its modest extent. Seems to have said nothing of much
interest. Jacovelli, 34 Abercrombie Street. So, he would seem to
have moved off to the East End of Glasgow since the night of the
murder. (Patrick McLaughlin's Stevenson Street finishes as a T-
junction halfway up Abercrombie Street—so Jacovelli might well
have known him too, by sight at least.)

Jacovelli had got married in October, just before the murder.
Bertie was his best man, no less. What, if anything, had he decided
by then? Did the excitement of being at the wedding give him any
particular cause for thought? Jacovelli said he had sometimes
given Bertie loans. (Two or three times, as far as I can gather.)
Presumably, opined the witness, 'he wanted money to take his girl
out'. (There is no evidence that an actual 'his girl' existed. (*Well;
I don't know about that now. See later.*) Possibly Bertie was putting
on a fairly normal young man's act for his friend. Or perhaps the

latter just wasn't really all that close after all.)

Bertie said he could not stay long as he was tired and wanted to get to bed. But they stayed together for a couple of hours all the same: Jacovelli, his wife, and Bertie, playing the gramophone. (From another source.) It was his first visit since the marriage. To leave early would be impolite—but perhaps Bertie found himself somewhat reluctant to go home as yet. Meanwhile the body cools, having ceased to leak any more blood.

Two men attack a draper in Dalhousie Street, round the corner from where my Granny will be staying (in Rose Street), with my Auntie Peggy, when first I become aware of them. That this was only after several decades of her actual life eluded me for long enough. Even working out now that she will already have been about forty-eight years old at the time of Willox's assault, older than I am at present, somehow disturbs me. Mum told me that I used to refer to their home in Rose Street as my other own house. 'I'm going now to my other own house.' I don't remember it myself, of course. It sounds faintly biblical, but I assume it was a remark that was really made. There was a large, impressive church just round the next corner. Well, as a matter of fact, at the moment it still is.

(10.04–3rd September)

80

The rest of the trial seems to hurtle by without revealing anything very much that I did not already know. The initial 'He could not have done it himself' from Bertie at the Police Station was in answer to the suggestion that it might perhaps have been suicide. On the second day of proceedings he 'betrays little emotion'. Isabella McKinney, 76 Grove Street—just across the road from Bertie's 79—says to him next morning, 'Sure, Bertie, you did not do it'; which is slightly better than the 'Are you sure, Bertie, you didn't do it?' of Roughead's account. The worrying thing is that it was said at all: although I suppose it could just about have passed as a statement rather than a tentative question.

The interesting suggestion is made, that he actually gave up work in order to look after the mother when she was ill. And that then, after she had died, he just sort of drifted into assuming her role. This is plausible; but every other mention of it I have seen suggests that the mother's death preceded his giving up his job, which I suppose is likelier. Two hammers and a bar of iron have been found in the house. Not found were a stone ring, a certain pair of trousers, two gold rings and some silver war medals—but pawn tickets for all of these were dug out of Bertie's pockets. (He had to keep them in his pockets. Anywhere else, and the father might have found them.) Official cause of death: shock. Also in that edition, a man from Jedburgh Gardens (go out this front door, turn left, it's the second turning on the left, three minutes away) dies in London, following an operation for a septic throat. A few more lives never the same again.

Harrington lives at 15 Windsor Street. It's pretty near Bertie's. One side of those old houses remains, just off Maryhill Road; though whether No.15 is among them I don't know. If odd numbers are down the left side (the west), then it certainly ain't. He arrived there, we now learn, at 6.37—on his first visit to the Watts. A flying visit, which no one ever seems to give an explicit reason for. Obviously, if Bertie didn't do it, this Harrington would be the Number One suspect. For one thing, he would be practically the *only* suspect available. At no point did the defence ever suggest who *else* might have done it. (They didn't *have* to do so, of course; but one can't help feeling that, in this case even more than most, some indication of an alternative to the glaringly obvious would not have gone amiss.)

Harrington said he asked a young girl at the very close-mouth if the Watts' house was in the building. She replied that she didn't know. She was a stranger to the district herself. Presumably that is the only time they ever exchanged words in their entire lives, no matter how long they may have stayed in the same city. Nothing more is ever heard of this small personage; who would, I take it, be the same age as my mother, and who therefore might very well still be alive. Well, actually, it might even have *been* my mother. Only microscopically possible, but you would have a hard time proving otherwise beyond all doubt whatever. Anyway, there she was— hanging around a close-mouth, as children do—or did, but I think they still do—without the least sense that adults are everywhere about them; far less any sense that an adult lies beaten to death somewhere not very far above your day-dreaming head, killed within the last few minutes.

At least, I trust we don't add *her* to the list of suspects. Had Willox left the house by then? I suppose so. He might have swept past the girl too: another adult come from nowhere, intent on going somewhere else, for some urgent but unimportant reason or other.

(10.33–3rd September)

81

J ust below Friday's report of the trial, there is another item from the courts. A man has been charged in the Messiter murder case. This is a story with a few interesting features caught in the callous gore: the dead man's body lay in a garage for months until the agent with whom the firm replaced him (evidently supposing he had absconded with the takings, as far as I recall) turned up to claim possession of the company car. I first read about this when I was up in Aberdeen in June. A used book shop in Rosemount Place, just round the corner from where my sister was staying (except that she was in Massachusetts, and I was staying there—Dad, quite unexpectedly and unasked, gave me half the fare), happened to have a copy of a motley collection called something like *Oh, I Do Like To Kill Beside The Seaside*. It was dirt cheap, and fairly well-written; and I have a vivid recollection of learning about the Messiter case for the first time while heating up a pot of soup in a large kitchen in a long quiet granite terrace. The book must be somewhere here in this room in Glasgow now, probably among the many columns of them on top of that heavy, dark wardrobe by the door, but I can't be bothered looking for it.

Saturday, 21st November. Rather surprisingly, nothing until page 9. SENTENCED TO DEATH/YOUTH FOUND GUILTY

OF MURDER/COLLAPSE IN DOCK. He rubbed his hand across his chin once or twice during the recording of the verdict. (How did I get into this? Am I really in this? Can I be about to be sentenced to death? Me? Don't they know it's me? Well might he have rubbed his chin once or twice.) He seems to have swooned just after sentencing—although some reports have him do so earlier. A woman had to be assisted from the court. One seems to know who this woman is. (Three women on the jury: ergo, twelve men.) It was noticed that the judge, in sentencing him to death, had a distinct tremor in his voice.

A week later, William Henry Podmore is remanded, on the charge of murdering Vivian Messiter in Southampton, for mere pecuniary gain. He will be hanged on the 22nd of April next year. He did not know it then, of course. And, come to that, he does not know it now either. But I did indeed cross the room a minute or two ago, to locate the book and find out the dead man's (I mean, the victim's) first name—and I am mighty glad I did so. For a different, quite astonishing fact leapt out at me. It makes me wonder what else I must have missed; and it reminds me that it was only in July, after I had returned from Aberdeen, that I first learned of the Willox case. For the address of the garage where the Messiter murder took place was: 42 Grove Street! (And, rather worryingly, I find that the book itself is called, simply, *The Seaside Murders*.)

(10.52–3rd September)

82

T his is a little unsettling. Messiter was murdered in *his* Grove Street, fortunately not *exactly* a year before Willox senior (one year and five days—the mother was still alive), by being beaten about the head. I suppose I have already mentioned that it was in Grove Street, Whitechapel/Stepney (also no longer existing) that George Gardstein died? I must check this. However, on the second-last day of 1929, entirely to my surprise, a further murderous Williams appeared. 'Father and son in double/tragedy.//Alleged attack while/shaving.' But this time it is a father who killed his son—before doing the same to himself.

It concerns one T.J. Williams, a fifty-six year-old butcher—who may also be about the same age as Willox senior, or possibly ten years younger than him—who, standing as an Independent, won a seat on the council last March from the sitting Socialist member. I take it that this is in Cymmer, South Wales, although no such place appears under that name in any of my guidebooks. He had gone thither from Abergavenny (surrounded by wooded hills; remains of an early Norman castle) some thirty-three years before; and since the son Wilfred was only twenty-five, *he* had presumably spent his entire life in this somewhat elusive place.

T.J. Williams was a church warden in Cymmer—had been so

for fifteen years—not to mention lay-reader and Sunday School superintendent. He had lately spent some months in Somerset, recuperating from a nervous breakdown. The recovery was evidently far from complete. On the morning of Sunday the 29th, while his niece, Mrs Oliver, was washing dishes, and Wilfred (who helped him in his business) was sitting at the breakfast table—a quiet familiar scene in one of the houses in the High Street—it is alleged that Williams, who was shaving, suddenly attacked his son, drawing his open razor across Wilfred's throat and killing him. He then did the same to himself. Both men fell to the ground, in a kitchen which must have looked so normal a minute before, with a few good devout folk preparing to go to church.

Mrs Oliver rushed out for assistance, but they were already dead before anyone else got there. One notices the total absence of the mother. Was she already dead? Perhaps all the better for her if she was. On the last day of the year, elsewhere, there is a report of a woman's alleged attempt to kill her four children by poisoning. And two men drop dead in Leeds, in quite separate incidents, apparently through exhaustion caused by having to battle their way through a high wind. A suitably macabre note with which to take leave of that year.

(12.41 am–4th September)

83

But what an unimaginably terrible way for a new year to begin. 'PAISLEY CINEMA HORROR./69 CHILDREN PERISH AT HOGMANAY MATINEE./Trampled to Death in Panic./59 others injured in struggle for life./Harrowing scenes at Infirmary.' Smoke had billowed out in some profusion from the projection room—although there seems to have been no fire as such. But someone had shouted 'Fire!' anyway, and there had developed a sort of children's stampede. This was ruthlessly halted by a locked door (which should *not* have been locked, of course), though those still pressing in panic from the back did not know this. The nearest window was immoveable too. As one small corpse after another was added to the line of them in the hospital, many of the nurses were simply unable to stand any more of it. There must, of course, have been many matinees throughout the country that day—and I would be staggered to learn that none of the others were taking place in breach of the fire regulations. There was a service in Paisley soon afterwards, where the officiating minister will no doubt have alluded to the mystery of the goodness of God—who obviously would not just have stood by and watched sixty-nine children suffocate to death without having a brilliant reason for it.

However, let me not get started on *that* one. A fortnight later, the Willox appeal hearings open. 'The actual commission of the crime would not take half a minute.' 'He might have laid the money on the table'—the father, that is: it's an attempted explanation of why the banknotes were not bloodstained, even though Bertie did the murder and then rifled them. Had they been folded together, presumably only the outermost one would have been at all affected—but might Willox senior's pay, if such it was, not still have been in some sort of pay-packet? Bertie Willox, who had been held for the interim somewhere else in the building while the appeal was argued, was removed in a taxi-cab at four o'clock. His departure was watched by a large crowd with nothing better to do, which had assembled in Parliament Square. There was no demonstration. I wonder if he had ever been to Edinburgh before in his whole life. The odds are probably against it.

On Saturday the 18th, we learn DEATH SENTENCE CONFIRMED. Lord Clyde alludes to the 9–6 decision on the murder charge—which I take to mean 9 Guilty vs 6 Not Proven, though no-one points this out explicitly hereabouts. 'Reasonable men might differ each with reason on his side.' (True; and insufficiently well-known.) He refers to the two newspapers as both being evening papers, which seems to be wrong. He wouldn't have called Not Proven unreasonable either, but the jury chose Guilty, so Guilty it is, sorry.

Sunday, Monday, Tuesday, Wednesday. A Memorial to the Secretary of State for Scotland. Signed by many Glasgow MPs and a large number of magistrates. (After all, unless I am missing something, he only murdered his father in cold blood.) And then, much earlier than expected, on the very next day: GLASGOW MURDER. REPRIEVE FOR WILLOX. Indeed, it sets a precedent. 'Hitherto the decision has not been made known until two days before the date fixed for the execution.'

So Bertie breathes again, and faces up to a life which neither he nor (after several days of desultory research) I know anything about. I more and more suspect I shall make no further efforts to find out what happened to him after this. Just let life go on. I hope he was not involved in anything spectacular later. One splash in the newspapers is surely enough. Next day, there are two collisions on his home patch, near St George's Cross. A bus and a motor lorry collide in Great Western Road. A tram and a milk lorry collide in

New City Road. No one is hurt. The streets are adequately full without Bertie. Life goes on.

On the 29th, there are two full columns on the Messiter case. Also, a bizarre story of how a man, in the dock on a charge of manslaughter (killing a woman in a car accident) suffers a terrible shock when he finds out that one of his defence witnesses had been killed the previous day in a car accident! Dangerous times, obviously. Have I already mentioned that, on the Monday and Tuesday of the very week after Mum died, I was interviewed for two quite separate Writer-in-Residence posts, at Dundee and Edinburgh? I got neither of them, but, at both, I again talked to a very likeable woman from the Scottish Arts Council whom I had met off and on for years, and whom I got along with very well. On, I think, the Friday of the same week, looking through a newspaper in Glasgow University Library, I was surprised to see a photograph of her. I then realized it was on the obituary page. Good God—it was an obituary! She had died in a car accident, the day after I had last seen her. I learned her age and much else about her only from her obituary.

(10.57 am–4th September)

84

W hat more? The soprano Emmy Destinn has died. We can still hear her, after a fashion. Three Murders in Chicago. Gangsters ambushed. Podmore/Messiter case continues. End of the scrutiny of this newspaper at the turn of 1929–1930. Not a single mention, as far as I noticed, of Stalin or Hitler, those deeply unimportant people. No doubt their names were, fleetingly, in there somewhere.

I've something of a feeling that this would make rather a good point at which to end. I have also just finished a classic and exhaustive programme of research involving five visits to a library each lasting from two to three hours, and I think on the whole I would prefer not to give up until I have managed to squeeze the most juice out of this almost inconceivable labour. Also, there are still one or two things in my notes which, if I don't do them here, I might otherwise never get round to putting to good use.

Oddly enough, one of the reports says that, after Willox junior had been sent off to the police station on the night of the murder, a neighbour then *phoned* for an ambulance—making one wonder why they hadn't just phoned for the police too. Is it likely that, in the excitement of the moment, no one thought of using the telephone? Or that people could not count on a single telephone thereabouts being available? It occurs to me that Bertie too must have been improvising here; and that he almost certainly had not expected to be sent off on a lengthy run so soon after events had begun to take their course. Was he somewhat caught out—a bit like a student who had been preparing the wrong material for the actual questions that came up in the exam? What *would* he have been prepared for? Anything?

The Northern Police Office was not in Stewart Street—where (I think) the modern police station is situated—but lay (I think) in Maitland Street, which cut perpendicularly across Stewart Street, from Dobbie's Loan down to Cowcaddens Street opposite the top of Hope Street. I presume though that it is all a question of a single building with different entrances. One of them must be where Bertie ran to that day, and it will be at the police court there that he was continually remanded in custody. The Y-shaped group of lanes behind the building, presumably meant for discretion in arrival and departure, has evidently been simplified when they built the motorways nearby, but I confess that I have never quite been able to work that pocket of Glasgow out. I suppose I should go along and try again some time, given that it's no more than twenty minutes' walk away.

85

Having had enough of the *Glasgow Herald*, I turned to another source mentioned by Roughead, to wit, the *Glasgow Weekly News*. Somewhat unexpectedly, I was brought what appeared to be an Irish edition—though this seems to have been individuated only on the sports pages, where the exploits of Irish teams were given a prominence which at first baffled me. I then deduced that the *Glasgow Weekly News* was presumably only a somewhat localized version of a London weekly paper, rather than the local Glasgow paper which, in my complete ignorance, I had hitherto taken it for. I've never looked at it before, although I am almost sure it is still about.

Issue No. 1855, for Saturday November the 9th, 1929, five days after the killing, suddenly appeared from the ruck, sporting on its front page a small picture of the relevant doorway in Grove Street. It was just beside an off-license, which does not figure at all in the case. (There is no mention whatever of either Willox ever drinking alcohol, which is striking almost to the level of prodigy.)

Dad is given as being age sixty-six, which I must say does seem to be the more likely estimate. 'An army veteran, and a popular member of the Corps of Commissionaires.' His picture (acquired from Bertie, of course), so schematic that one is not entirely sure it is a photograph rather than a drawing, shows a thin-faced, moustached man, with youthful dark hair. He is in uniform, and one feels that the image—presumably the most recent of him in existence—is probably older than his son himself is.

He was a most methodical man, we hear, and army ways were engrained into him. (A slightly threatening remark.) After his tea, he would polish his buttons and then read the papers. Since he had to be out at Pointhouse for 5 o'clock, he habitually went to bed early. Having arrived home, he rarely strayed from his own fireside. If he was an elderly man who worked a twelve-hour day this is far from surprising—but I must say: I don't know what effect this monotonous, impoverished, grinding, limited life had on him and the very few people around him, but the mere description of it practically has me howling with frustration. And I am rather far from being a social lion myself.

The paper also nonchalantly notes the contradictory information that Robert Willox snr joined the army in 1898 at the age of twenty-four. If he really was sixty-six in 1929, then obviously he must in fact have been something like thirty-five then. Of Mrs Willox we learn only that she died suddenly. 'After the death of his mother recently, it is disclosed, Robert practically took over a woman's place in the house, cleaning and tidying, making the meals, and devotedly tending his father's every want.' Eh? That's one way of putting it, I suppose. But some of his father's non-wants seem to have crept in too.

The table that evening had a cup, saucer, bread plates and marmalade on it. No suspicious character had been seen in the vicinity. Mind you, a neighbour, Mr McKenzie, did say that not too long ago someone had knocked at his door, but when he had gone to answer it there was nobody there! A close call, obviously. I remember as children we used to knock doors ourselves and then run away. Not all that often, since it was a curiously boring game for something so ostensibly risk-taking. I don't suppose it can have been us? No, no; of course not. That evening there were hundreds of people standing in Grove Street, uncomfortable drizzle or not. And when Robert Swift Willox appeared at the Police Court, now wearing a dark blue suit, though before he had had only a brown one and a black one (is this right?), it got to the point of there being 2,000 people milling around Maitland Street and the adjacent lanes. And all Bertie had thought he was doing was trying to force his way through an intractable, local and purely personal problem! Strange how nosy other people can be.

(10.22 am–5th September)

86

The next issue of the *Weekly News* mentions a 'Clyde Steamer Thrill'. 'Thrill' was definitely a buzz-word of the time. (Well, it still is, I suppose; but it is rarely over-used quite so blatantly. 'Bullock jumps overboard. Clyde Steamer Thrill.') And how peculiar it was to see, in page 3 of some 4 issues later, an article about Landru—already safely ensconced in history, no threat to anyone real, a decade in the past. A long line of small pictures marches right across the page. His victims. Can such a parade of foggy, cropped, routine images, smiling in their scattered groups and occasions throughout France, really be one small, tireless criminal's victims? Though they are beginning their drift back into a sort of wraith-like posthumous existence in the entertainment industry, they seem so out-of-place in the outmoded day-to-day quaintness of defunct old newspapers.

By the next week, the 21st of December, the trial was over. Having paid Willox £3 for pictures right at the start—more than the father earned for a whole week's work—this paper only narrowly avoided being dragged into the case itself.

Their reporter has obviously made a bit of an effort all round. For who should the front page article turn out to be devoted to, but Mrs Smith of Canal Street! She was evidently looking after him while he was—'temporarily, she was sure'—in prison. 'When he is free, he need not worry about where he is to go. He will make his home with us, and I can assure you he will be welcomed with open arms.' An impressive display of basic human decency, I would say. She had been his first visitor (one wonders how many of them there were in all), and brought him cigarettes, papers, and the odd luxury—not that she could easily afford it. (There is a whole way of life in those last few words.) He termed her his 'new Ma', and he asked after Chrissie and Willie (whom I take to be the younger Smiths) and Mrs McKenzie next door—she whose husband endured the mysterious knocking. The other neighbours do not seem to have been remembered in his thoughts.

Inside, page 15 is devoted to the trial itself. Here, after an intriguing alteration to '78 Grove Street' on the front page, the address is correctly given. A few scraps fall to be rescued. This time it is once again, 'You will not get a penny piece from me'. 'There was a bang at the door. It was a terrible bang.' (A wonderful title for a book: *It Was A Terrible Bang*. They get the time wrong, though. At 'twenty to nine'.) Margaret Duffy lent him fifty shillings to let him get Da's medals out of hock, saying that she had to have the money back by rent-day: hardly the traditional demeanour of a money-lender. And, incidentally, why did the father give Bertie 'from 2/6 to 4/6'? Did it merely depend on what he had to spare? If Bertie were to be expecting 4/6, but received only 2/6, this itself could obviously lead him very easily into difficulties.

Jacovelli was surprised when Bertie, on arriving, said he could stay only a short while as he was feeling tired and wanted to go to bed. But evidently the effort to be social was not beyond his powers after all. Was this perhaps a subtle piece of preparation for some later suggestion that he had been perfectly prepared to go home earlier than he did? Obviously, the longer he stayed out, the more scope he gave for the arrival of some phantom murderous caller. Given that *someone* would have had to be suspected of doing it, and that his father's extremely terse lifestyle would mean that likely culprits would be rare, he seems to have made no attempt whatever to suggest the existence of some assailant other than himself.

When Jacovelli stepped down from the witness-box, he and Bertie smiled at each other. Did they ever do so again? 'Are you sure, Bertie, you did not do it?' 'He went into a fit.' (Testimony of the officer on duty at the police station.) Was called to the police station at 5 on the evening of the Tuesday; not free since. And—an unexpected touch, recorded, I think, nowhere else—Willox senior, on the day of the murder, 'gave his son a cup of tea in bed before he left for work.'

The trial judge, Lord Hunter, on hearing of the pawntickets (which he did for the first time during the actual trial, of course; unlike, say, in France, the judge is not expected to know in advance the case he is about to try), softly remarked 'Dear, dear'. Clearly, this evidence made rather a difference. Though whether a judge ought to be quite so public about it (if such he was) is another matter. Mrs Dreyer of 63 South Seventh Street, Newark, New Jersey, has become Mrs Drain, of the same address, Newark, New Zealand. Not a detail to encourage confidence in the accuracy of the source. But the Editor wishes all his readers a Merry Christmas anyway. What: *all* of them?

(5.59–5th September)

87

By the next week, having evidently made a few more pertinent enquiries, and judging the Willoxes still to be a matter of sufficient public concern, the *Weekly News* had delved further into the human interest aspect of the matter in a way which seems to have been its forte. 'For over thirty years an Aberdeen couple puzzled over the fate of their uncle, who had mysteriously disappeared from the city without leaving any hint of his intentions.' Then one day they picked up their newspaper, read a gruesome tale featuring a certain Robert Willox who had Aberdonian connections, made a discreet enquiry or two and discovered that this was indeed their Uncle Bob. Given that Glasgow and Aberdeen are something less than a continent apart, this is striking testimony to the capacity for anonymity offered by the modern city. The son himself seems to have known absolutely nothing about the Aberdonian side of his family. One wonders what he was told. Still: to learn the whereabouts of a missing relative from an account of his murder by his son! I anticipate a little, true: but how soon their realization that they had a Glaswegian cousin must have been superseded by the realization that he was probably a murderer. Truly, no gain but is attended with some overtone of loss. We do not hear of them ever courting further acquaintance with this sudden new relative of theirs, who arrived so inopportunely at another's departure.

Indeed, it is never even quite made clear who it is they are; though, if they have indeed been wondering about 'their uncle' for 'over thirty years', they are presumably the offspring of some brother or sister of Willox senior—and there is an exclusive ring to all this which suggests that all older Willoxes have already died. Thus they will have missed out on witnessing this astonishing episode in the history of the family. No doubt they thought the *first* Robert Willox was bad enough.

He had left Aberdeen 'about thirty-five years ago' (i.e. circa 1894: aged either twenty or thirty-one, depending on who you believe). These relatives are said to be living in 'the King Street district of Aberdeen'—which is a fairly clueless way of designating an Aberdeen district, given how long and varied King Street actually is. However, one of the afferents of King Street is Helen Priestly's Urquhart Road, and the irrational conviction grows on me that it is here that any Willoxes must inevitably live.

His mother died long after he had left. 'All these years she had hoped and prayed that her son would return to her. She was ailing and badly in need of assistance.' This makes him sound rather like the only son. In which case, of course, any nephews and nieces would have to descend from a daughter, and so almost certainly would no longer be called Willox themselves. However, it dents my confidence in the accuracy of these deductions to learn that 'one relative had nothing good to say of him'. How many relatives, in all, lie behind this report? Despite Willox's later impressive military career, 'that did not atone for his life at home'. In short, no wonder that Willox kept himself to himself so much, and was ultra-discreet about his past. I wonder if his late wife knew anything at all about this. I very much suspect not. One almost gets a whiff of Nemesis deciding that enough was enough, and now at last is the time to close in.

Nothing is said of any career as a reporter. But he apparently opened a stationer's cum newsagents in the King's Gate district. (A fine road out to the west, quite different from King Street. Indeed, I wonder whether the second might not have been a journalist's slip for the first.) This, however, did not prosper, and he sought to recoup his losses by gambling, with the usual results. At which point he borrowed £10 from someone—presumably a family member: enough at the time to keep you going for some weeks—then upped and ran. One assumes that, even if his creditors did not turn to the family for payment, whether successfully or not, there would at the very least have been a very keen sense of shame and abandonment among those left behind. One also assumes that no twenty year-old would be starting up a business like this—despite what his twenty year-old son will eventually get up to—and that this is itself strong evidence, if true, for his having already been over thirty when he left the city.

And of course, it is certainly not everyone who is even in a position to try to start up a newsagent's business. He sounds more and more like someone who messed up his life, and had to pull out all the stops to get it back into any sort of harmony. Having done so, he wanted nothing more, I take it, than to be left in peace. Suspicion hardens further when we learn that he then joined the army even though he was too old for service—by lying about his age. He fought in the Boer War. And when he joined up for the Great War too, he must, it seems, have lied about his age again. Perhaps the army at least relieved him from worrying about the practicalities of living. But what he might have done between leaving Aberdeen and first joining up is unknown, and 'it is unlikely that the mystery will ever be solved'.

(10.19am–6th September)

88

At which point Mrs Smith of Canal Street, whom the capricious Muse of Local History seems to have fallen in love with, steps forward yet again. Her given name, we learn, is Christina, and she 'knew his mother before Bertie was born'. We do not quite discover how they met, but she is able to give *some* information on the considerably under-represented Margaret Swift or Willox.

'Mrs Willox, when a child,' to whom the names Willox and Mrs Willox as yet meant nothing, 'went to America with her parents,'—one recalls Mrs Dreyer of 63 South Seventh Street, Newark, who begins to sound very like a sister—'but after their deaths she returned to Scotland and when I made her acquaintance she was employed as a stenographer at the Corps of Commissionaires in Glasgow.' So Kismet played its never quite convincing little old trick. How much remains only to be guessed at. Did these parents die at fairly normal ages? Together? Not together? Why on earth did she return? Might she too even have been fleeing from something? If not, what if anything was she, as it were, fleeing *to*? What age was she?

The Willoxes met in 1907. He was probably about forty-three years old. Willox was a Commissionaire for the Stock Exchange (which sounds a cut above his later post), but I presume they met at the Corps office where Margaret Swift was a stenographer. So she had had training in shorthand. (Just like him. Presumably he had tried to work in newspapers on, you might say, the production side, before deciding that retail might suit him better.) They must have been married very soon afterwards, in time to have two children. Their first child, who died at the age of two, was a girl called Beatrice. A name with some pretensions, I would say. The mother herself was presumably under sixty when she died. Bertie was the only other child.

This is the only mention of Beatrice that I have ever found; although clearly her death must have been an event which devastated the lives of her parents. Bertie too had been born in the interim, of course.

But there is something profoundly elusive about them. Your typical working-class family, if there is such a thing, is not one in which both parents can take shorthand. Mrs Smith says they were both well-educated, and I see no reason to doubt her. They had obviously both been given the opportunity to do well for themselves, to better themselves, to get on in life. And it looks, somehow, as if they never quite made it. Well, Willox sounds to me to have been something like an undischarged bankrupt from his early years—something approaching the status of a shady businessman. What he might have told his wife about all this, God only knows. But the parents seem to have had only one real functioning parent between them—a predicament which they may almost be said to have transmitted—so presumably it wasn't too difficult to have this one discreetly and prematurely buried among the other three. They seem to have been the sort of people to whom life happened, with a vengeance.

(10.57 am–6th September)

89

Absolutely none of which would probably have survived, if it has survived, but for a single brutally violent assault. What, for instance, do we know of their early neighbours in Cambridge Street—where they lived till about 1921? Nothing, I suppose. This was a distinctly better address than Grove Street. It was a street full of character, though now it exists only in a truncated wreck of its former self. It was once much more clearly the main thoroughfare through the district, linking Sauchiehall Street to New City Road with the aplomb of a social equal. We were often there in the last years of its existence, since my grandmother and aunt lived barely three minutes away from it, near the bottom of Buccleuch Street— which for some aberrant reason I called Rose Street not long ago; which in fact was (and still is) the only road you have to cross between their house and Cambridge Street. As I compare what it was with what it is now I experience an emotion which 'rage' does not seem an adequate word to cover. It had a very strong sense of local character—a most distinctive street indeed, with a sloping curve in the middle of it. Most of it has become a motorway: a major barrier to pedestrians, who are generously allowed to risk their lives crossing it at a couple of points. But I was forgetting: a sort of tunnel for them has also been thoughtfully provided.

One feels almost that the rest of it should be mercifully put out of its misery—like a terminally wounded animal still managing to cling on to a terrible imitation of life. Anyway, the Willoxes used to live here, along with many hundreds of others. Father, we learn from Mrs Smith, was very strict. From a friend of the family this is particularly eloquent. Bertie was asked by his father to remain at home, after his mother's death—which leads one to suspect that, left to himself, Bertie would much rather *not* have done so. (This 'asking', I take it, was something more than a request.) However, we are also told that the son 'had done so before' (i.e. help out at home) 'off and on since his youth'. This is a somewhat intriguing remark. Was he just helping out? But with only three people in a small house, what exactly needed to be done? I presume the Cambridge Street flat was no palace. Was Mrs Willox, whom one would have expected to run the home, somehow incapacitated? Perhaps, bearing in mind her sudden early death, she had poor health—although if so one might have expected her friend to mention this. Perhaps there was some other physical or psychological (or even alcoholic) one—which her friend might well want to keep a discreet silence about. But this is all the sheerest guesswork.

Anyway, they lived in Cambridge Street for a dozen or so years, before taking something of a step downwards to Grove Street.

Even so, if Bertie had only ever had two addresses before the murder, it's hard to see why he should have attended four schools in all, as Roughhead says he did. (I've never seen any other mention of this myself.) Two Catholic and two Protestants: were the parents of different religions? Is there anyone in the real world (or the unreal world) who knows this; or who knows why Margaret Swift came back to Glasgow? Well, if there is, it isn't me, whatever world I'm in. One thing I do know, however, is that, while we were still in West Princes Street, it was in Cambridge Street our family doctor had his surgery. We went there very rarely, it being the opinion of both my parents that the man was something of an idiot. (They were right. And, indeed, one parent is still able to tell me so.)

(11.50 am—6th September)

90

It might be as well to clear up just what remains of
this eventful issue of the *Weekly News*. After a detective had
brought the bereaved son to Mrs Smith's house (we never at any
point hear mention of a Mr Smith), in her own words as given,
'Bertie seemed to be quite himself but I got him to go to bed, and
at seven o'clock the next morning, when I called him, he was
sleeping soundly. He seemed to have had a good night's rest.'

Well, he needed it, obviously. Actually, I am not sure that these
were quite her *ipsissima verba*. It might well be that that first phrase
should run more along the lines of, 'Bertie seemed to be not quite
himself, but I got him to go to bed etc'. A good example of how
crucial is one's dependence on the words of others. As it stands, it
is testimony to the man's astonishing calmness.

But what of Roughead's 'Miss McKinney stated that the morning after the murder young Willox came into Haddow's shop at
seven o'clock, "very flustered and upset-looking" '? (The occasion,
of course, either of 'Are you sure, Bertie, you didn't do it?' or 'Sure,
Bertie, you didn't do it'.) Here we have him, at the same 7 o'clock,
sound asleep in Canal Street, a good ten minutes' walk away; and
not looking as if he intends to make his way to a Grove Street shop
'to buy cakes for his breakfast'. A useful reminder either that I can

misread my sources or that when people retrospectively estimate times of day they are particularly prone to error.

It is rather a relief to learn that Mrs Smith, after the trial, still believes wholeheartedly in Bertie's innocence. She is doing all she can and 'another friend is giving him breakfast and dinner'. Sending it into prison, presumably. It's a considerable pity that we don't learn who this other friend is—beyond that, according to Mrs Smith, neither of them has very much to spare. She prefers to dwell on the happier times: when Bertie and three pals, 'his jazz band' (he was the drummer—though what he made do with for drums is not given) used to come round to Canal Street and entertain her. They were often (!) in demand at parties (!) and other gatherings. This I take to be, broadly, the truth, for Mrs Smith sounds like someone you could trust, but as far as I can see absolutely none of this ever surfaced anywhere else.

'I know also,' continues Christina, 'that he did not go about with girls to any great extent.' (Apparently there had been rumours that it was the necessity for money to finance his career as a ladies' man which led to the debacle.) 'There was one girl about whom he sometimes spoke to me.' (And to Jacovelli, apparently.) 'She was a girl he saw now and again, but they had never been out together.' Which rather makes one wonder where they saw each other.

It turns out that Bertie even sent regards to this girl from prison. A rather ambiguous remembrance, I should think. Indeed, this reporter actually managed to catch up with her, or track her down, or whatever was necessary to be done. He elicited from her the distinctly cool response that he was 'a nice polite sort of chap'— once again the hint of aristocracy choosing to dwell in the Cowcaddens; not one of your roughs—but that she knew very little about him! (*All extremely piquant; but since I did not at that point go right on to the next volume of the* Weekly News, *which dealt with January 1930, that is where I must leave it for the moment.*)

His good friend Jacovelli also comes out with a very cool quote, and one which leaves little doubt that, whatever Mrs Smith might think, Alfonso has had his eyes opened by the trial. 'I cannot understand what can have caused Willox to commit such a crime.' ("Willox", notice.) 'In all the years I knew him to be a quiet, gentlemanly fellow, and not in the least quarrelsome.' Whether this comes from a fellow member of the (presumably now defunct) jazz band, I do not know.

Nor do I quite know what the 'Snap. 2 ambulance men.' with which I concluded that section of notes precisely refers to. Is it that two neighbours separately phoned for an ambulance, and that two separate vehicles arrived? I think I recall that they arrived before the (pedestrian) policemen reached the scene, with Bertie—and that, under such circumstances, they would know better than to touch the body. Of course, in principle, I suppose anyone waiting there could have done anything to the body while Bertie was off to the police station, and no official presence had as yet intruded. However, since there is absolutely no reason to suppose that any such thing is the case, we shall not linger at this point.

(12.57–6th September)

91

On to a diligent perusal of selected microfilms of the *Daily Record*, the leading popular Scottish daily paper. I'll be as brief as I can. November 2. Fighting in/Warsaw.//Police with swords/charge crowds.//Dictator's Coup.//Author's Father/Working in Tax Office. (Or so I have always been led to believe.) Mr Drew mobbed. Four Encores from Rachmaninov at the Albert Hall. The *Canary Murder Case*, with the face of the century (Louise Brooks) and William Powell. Established 1847. No. 25,830. One penny. Tuesday November 5, 1929. Brutal Murder in/Glasgow.//Commissionaire's body in/lobby.//Son's terrible discovery/behind door.

Grove Street, a respectable working-class thoroughfare (i.e. no gangs). HEAD BATTERED TO PULP. Fifty-five year-old. And someone did call an ambulance. Found he'd been dead for some time. It is believed that the crime was an act of revenge. Presumably the assailant closed the door at once, an indication of his coolness, and went downstairs into the street so quietly that he did not attract the attention of the neighbours. (True enough, I suppose. None of the neighbours would have been surprised to see him. It is sheer chance that no one did.) Superintendent Murray (Northern Division). Det-Supt Forbes (Central).

At which point a wholly new point of view is introduced. At least, I trust he hasn't appeared before, even though he too, like the next-door neighbour, is called Mackenzie. This is Sergeant-Major MacKenzie, at the Corps of Commissionaires HQ. He was, not surprisingly, horror-stricken. (I presume he knew nothing about it until an enterprising reporter rang him up.) 'Poor Willox; he was one of our most popular members.' 'A quiet, exceptionally well-educated man,' (that note again). 'He was a general favourite.' He first joined them on April the 17th, 1906. There is a hint that, since he would have met his wife more or less at once if she too worked at that HQ, the fact that (according to Mrs S.) they did not meet until 1907 indicates that she did not join the Corps as a stenographer until that later date—but clearly, this takes a variety of imponderables for granted.

The Sgt-Major, of course, believes that Willox is a decade younger than he really is. (Indeed, perhaps Willox would no longer have been being kept on if they were aware of his true age.)

'I was speaking to his son earlier in the evening,' continues Mackenzie, 'for I knew them both well.' This can refer only to the Monday evening surely, which makes it more than a little odd. *Was* Mackenzie a neighbour? With, like Watt, job connections with Willox? (What a startlingly beautiful sentence.) If not, when on Monday evening would he have had occasion to speak to the younger Willox? Not at the billiard hall, I trust? And where had they ever met? In the Willox flat? Another intriguing mysterylet.

However, when our intrepid reporter goes on to enquire of the dead man's colleagues at Pointhouse (more or less where the Kelvin flows into the Clyde), a rather different story threatens to emerge. 'A strict disciplinarian; extremely reticent about personal affairs.' 'We were very friendly but he said nothing about himself,' said the night commissionaire, taken by surprise in the middle of a normal night's commissioning. Presumably he just happened to be the one who picked up the phone. 'We know no more about him now than we did when he came to us.' The ease and immediateness with which 'a strict disciplinarian' broke the surface here (and in Mrs Smith's account) is not a little thought-provoking. What does it actually mean? It would certainly not seem to indicate someone whom it was a particular pleasure to live with, whatever else it might signify.

He walked to work. He lost his wife in January. Bertie was offered shelter overnight in the house adjoining. (First I've heard of it.) Corbett is acquitted in France after shooting his terminally ill mother. Forty-five people on a bus designed to hold only twenty-six. An irritating interruption to yet another clutch of people on a shared journey. And a story from another Cambridge Street. This one is in Coventry. A boy dies from a jag from a pen-nib in a playground. A trivial interruption to a game. Blood-poisoning set in; then pneumonia. Herbert Pollard, aged twelve. What a world, Herbert, eh? And I drift on to the next issue anyway.

(1.59–6th September)

92

And there is more of the same on the next day. A banner headline proclaims: NEW SENSATION IN GLASGOW MURDER MYSTERY. What: you mean they don't already know? It's not as if I haven't told them often enough. Robert Smith Willox (20). Under 5'6"; medium build; attractive. (To whom?) Robert Willox (66). 'Whose age the police the police now know to have been 66, and not 55. As was at first supposed.' (Well, that sounds definite enough. Did Bertie know how old his father really was?) 'A widower for some little time.' 'Junior reporter to an Aberdeen paper in youth.' Secretary to an officer at Fort Matilda, Greenock, where he used his shorthand. 'Not known to have a single enemy.' (Or friend, for that matter.)

There is also a fairly large diagram of the locus of the crime, inaccurate in some important respects. The door opens the wrong way, not towards the wall. No bed recess; fireplace wrongly sited, etc. Presumably it is part made up out of verbal descriptions, and part from sheer guesswork.

But enough of that. What about the Booth family instead? A double killing caused by a wasp. By a creature which does not even know that life and death exist in the universe.

A family outing in the car. The father, George Booth, a policeman, driving. The wife, Maud, holding the baby daughter, Doreen. A wasp flies in the open window, and where does it land? Why, on the baby, of course. Nowhere else in the world would do. The driver leans over and flicks it off as lightly as possible. It then lands on his small son. (Who I take it, though I may be wrong, is seated in the front of the car, between Mummy and Daddy.) The son, scared by the insect, jumps sideways against the steering wheel. The husband remembers nothing more until he wakens up in hospital, now without either wife or daughter. A transit of barely ten seconds from normal success and happiness to a shattering and irrecoverable disaster.

Mrs Booth was discovered lying over the side of the car. The baby was hanging (from foliage, I take it) midway between the car and the grassy bank. The car was lying sideways in a ditch. The two males seem to have survived—one of them no doubt too young to grasp or remember much of what had happened, and the other not. The wasp, I dare say, was by this time untroubled elsewhere, after a moment or two of minor vexation. Perhaps in an hour or so, someone shall clobber it with a newspaper, taking it for just one more moderately irritating insect, better removed lest it might do some damage; though one always feels a bit guilty about crumpling them—particularly if they don't die at once. Then you unfold the newspaper, and read on again, round the small stain.

(3.02–6th September)

93

I'll never get through my notes at this rate. 'Well set-up, attractive face crowned by fair hair; hung his head on entering.' Occasionally blinked or pursed his lips, we learn—at his first appearance in the Police Court. Though since he was there for barely two minutes, this 'occasionally' hardly had time to establish itself. 'Not fewer than a dozen wounds.'

An eighty-two year-old and his seventy year-old sister die in a gas mishap. Out together, not knowing a single thing about it (I hope). A man who earns his living by farting in public this time overdoes it and dies. I'm sorry—that never happened. Not that I know of. I was seduced by the ability of a single-letter substitution to change things utterly, whether or not it causes a terrible beauty to be born. A man who earns his living by fasting in public this time overdoes it and dies. Still, we can joke about it. He was in an amusement arcade, surrounded by monkeys, birds, cats and so forth. ('They have killed me this time.') John Sommerville dies at Straven, aged ninety-two—for seventy-two of which years he was a Freemason. On Saturday, a photograph of Lusette, 'the brilliant young dancer, who is appearing in a Glasgow dance club with her partner, Leon.' (This last, which is among other things the Polish version of Leo, was the name by which my mother always addressed my father. He was pretending to be an ordinary Polish soldier when she met him.)

In the next column to this picture: Dramatic Scene In Court. Call to Prisoner. Woman's tears in Court. Glasgow murder. Dundee man and note mystery. Needless to repeat the details. This paper is, however, particularly rich in striking irrelevancies. Father of ten to hang, for instance. John Maguire (43) of Liverpool. Killed his wife. He seems to have had a staggeringly easy attitude all round to some of the most complex phenomena in the universe. About my age too. All distinctly worrying.

Then there is the husband from 26 Crichton Street, Springburn, who has been missing for over a fortnight; since Friday, October 25. When I check the city map-book this evening, I find it is still there. I also find—to my astonishment—that it is off Keppochill Road. The first time I ever became aware of my father as a worker—it was a quite specific moment; he had not yet graduated to having his own shop—he had a job either in Keppochill Road or in Pinkston Road, just off it. I remember a journey out there late one afternoon, perhaps to meet him. What did he do there? Have I forgotten that, or did I simply never learn it? I have lived nearby in the same city all my life, held in place I suppose by a mixture of poverty, naïvety and an interesting combination of failures, but I don't distinctly recollect *ever* having been out there again since my very early childhood. I could walk there in under half an hour. I must ask him about it when I next get back to Largs. I suppose he'll say little about it, as no longer being of much interest. (*I reach this point in my typing-out on the 10th of February 1994. Another tenth of the month. Since no comment seems adequate, I shall pass on without comment—except to say that someone upstairs is making a quite appalling racket with beating and hammering and so forth. I think new neighbours are moving in.*)

Burns' grandparents. Tombstone in neglected condition in Glenbervie churchyard. Then the 11th Remembrance Day. This is the first that Willox senior ever missed of course; the first, it turns out, of very many. A prize-winning picture in New York is found to have been hung upside down. A new group of 'pygmies' has been discovered on the Colombia/Venezuela border. A woman in Eglinton Street is attacked by a 'shawlie' (impoverished woman dressed in a shawl), 30/35, wielding a hatchet. Hullo: a piece about a smithy 'just off the Main Street in Largs'—the street where I buy my father his herring. It has been in the possession of the Mackie family since 1608. 321 years. (It's not there now, unless I have somehow missed it too.)

And have we time enough for a couple more deaths? Samuel Young (15) of 135 Stobcross Street—another street massacred by the new road system. One of my mother's first jobs was as a message-girl in that district. She once told me how much she dreaded having to go to some of the ill-lit tenements in that area, which were four to a landing (like Bertie's), and full of dark, evil-smelling corridors and recesses, where, as she put it, 'you never knew what you might be standing in next.'

Anyway, young Samuel evidently thought it would be something of a giggle to stand on the handle bracket of a crane while other boys pushed it round. He lost his balance and fell off—a distance to the ground of precisely four feet. Even so, he was found to be dead on arrival at the Western Infirmary. Nobody's lost grandpa, obviously. And, on the next page, another John Smith— this one a sixty-nine year-old of Nelson Street in Ayr. He ran for the train home from Troon and caught it; but the exertion caused him to collapse in the compartment. He was dead by the time the train pulled into Newton-on-Ayr—a town which Mum once took us down to by bus, to visit relatives who were living there. In my head, I can still see and hear how we were laughing as, near the end of the journey, the bus turned a corner to the right, beside some sort of field in the middle of a town.

(7.10–6th September)

94

On Wednesday, the 13th of November, nine days after the unexpectedly sudden demise, the funeral of Robert Willox snr took place at Lambhill Cemetery, Glasgow, at 2.30 in the afternoon. Lambhill is a vast burial ground towards the extreme north of Glasgow, opposite Possil Loch—and it has only at this moment occurred to me that this is surely where his wife is buried too. I suppose a more assiduous researcher would follow up this hunch to see what other information it might unearth. If so, I wish him luck.

On that day, Baillie Sedding dealt with his very first charge-sheet at the Police Court—the first of hundreds, I dare say—which involved him in again remanding Willox for the slaying of his father; his third remit so far. Actually, on second thoughts, this must have happened the day before. The paper reports on the court scene, but anticipates the burial. It also tells us of yet another Smith—Philip Smith who owned a secondhand-goods shop in the Canongate. (A street in Edinburgh, m'lud.) He was crossing the road opposite his shop when he saw a bus approaching at a fair rate. Convinced that it was about to hit him, he threw up his hands in self-defence, and collapsed in the roadway. (Who observed or deduced this?) He was then found to be dead. The bus was actually about to stop to pick up more passengers anyway. Another exciting interruption of a normal journey. And might the phantom murderer of Düsseldorf perhaps be a woman? A possibility worth bearing in mind? How strangely ignorant these people are of matters of general knowledge. Why don't they just go off to Mettmännerstrasse and ask for a guy named Kürten? Look: I've given you the name and address. What more do you want?

I see that that nice Lord Blythswood died suddenly while he was attending a Masonic meeting. Keeled over while rolling up a trouserleg, presumably. And we are given a charming picture of Miss Evelyn Spillsbury (19), daughter of the celebrated pathologist, Sir Bernard—who will suffer one blow after another before killing himself when his daughter is not yet forty. (His last important case was the De Antiquis murder.) She has just made her film debut at Elstree Studios. And then, towards the end of the same issue (November 15, Friday), there occurs a truly bizarre trio of connected headlines: Black Boys/Barred//Parson's Knickers/Bequest//Will disputed. I should say so.

The film actress Pola Negri gives her thoughts while awaiting divorce: 'Men are nearly all intensely selfish. Generally they take everything and give nothing.' Another reference to the three mummified children. And then the first mention of *Goodbye To All That*, Robert Graves' memoirs of his youth and the war years. Over the coming weeks, the *Record* will work itself up into a fine old lather over certain uncomplimentary remarks made about the Scottish troops—I recall a phrase something like 'You can always rely on the Jocks to leg it at the first sign of trouble'—until Graves is finally prevailed upon to make a statement which can be taken as an abject apology for this gross slur.

And, while we are on the subject of literary gents, we welcome the return of an old favourite. Sir Arthur Conan Doyle's action against Oscar Slater (for reimbursement for his own expenses in the matter, now that Slater has received his £6,000 compensation) has been settled amicably. Slater's present address, most unusually (and for him surely rather embarrassingly) is here given in full: 435 Sauchiehall Street. This still exists, very near the great canyon of the new motorway. Appropriately enough, it is right opposite a couple of present-day casinos.

Why doesn't the Prince of Wales marry? (Of course, when he eventually did, some eight full years later, it led to the abdication crisis.) A piece by C.M. Grieve, whoever he might be. And Robert Boothby MP, giving a radio talk on 'Scotland's Way to Prosperity'. This was sent down the line from a London studio. All too perfectly symbolic. This chap, whose main claim to fame previously had been, if I remember rightly, setting aside his *réclame* as an early media pundit, that he was the secret great love of the wife of Harold Macmillan (British Prime Minister 1957–1963), now apparently turns out to have been a predatory homosexual who was a close friend of the celebrated psychotic twin and gangster, Ronnie Kray. (He also once won a large sum in a libel action, against someone who had suggested that he had links with gangland.)

Do you want to hear more of A Glasgow Parson on Paganism? Alas, I noted down only the title. But I can give you the whole of A LETTER BOX TALK, from the 29th of November. *Mr Oscar Slater's Denial./No Romance.* 'Mr Oscar Slater denies the story which appeared in an English newspaper that he intends getting married./When a *Daily Record* reporter called on him at his address in Glasgow last night, Mr Slater spoke to him through the letter-box aperture.//On being asked whether it was the case that he contemplated getting married he replied: "It is only a rumour. I know nothing about it." '

Not much of a conversation, perhaps; but an interesting vignette. It is odd, and strangely powerful, this unexpected glimpse of Slater after he has, as it were, outlived his narrative usefulness. He is living under five minutes' walk away from the building in St George's Road where he stayed for only a few weeks in late 1908, twenty-one years before. I would guess it is a walk that he must take fairly often; and the uninsistent routine sameness of the route must make it seem like a dream to him, that he has spent all but a year or two of these decades locked up in prison for a murder which he certainly did not commit. He is in his late fifties by now. Five more minutes' walk would take him on to the actual scene of the crime. The real culprit was never apprehended. (*The latest discussion of the case, a fine one by Thomas Toughill, basing itself on contemporary letters, names Wingate Birrell, a nephew of the deceased, as the killer; working with two sons of, bear with me, the second marriage of the widow of the brother of the deceased. No likelier solution is known to me, and something like this, if not exactly this, must be what did indeed happen.*)

Perhaps he tried to dismiss it all from his mind. Perhaps he wandered around, vaguely wondering where he ought to go to get his lost years back. Does he yet know that he will eventually end up, to all appearances quietly retired, in a house on the coast, in Ayr? Perhaps not. However, as the man said: you will, Oscar. You will.

(10.39 am–7th September)

Apart from anything else, it would be quite interesting to see just what the dates on Willox snr's tombstone were. Always assuming there *is* such a tombstone there at all. And let me repeat the fact, since I was so struck by it and it is after all my book—that, even though we tend to think of the thirties as being preponderantly the decade of Hitler, there was absolutely no mention of the man's name that I could see in any of these 1929/30 newspapers that I looked through. (Nor, again, any of Stalin that I happened to notice.) Thus, it seems to me to be far from unlikely that neither of Willox's parents, both of whom died in 1929, never so much as heard of Hitler in their entire lives. I find this rather an attractive and comforting thought, I must say. Nor, I suppose, ought it to be so surprising. I would imagine that many an avid reader of newspapers who died, say, three years before the current Prime Minister (John Major, for the record) took office, would never have so much as heard of him.

On the 30th of the month, just over a fortnight after Willox was buried, there was a major affray in Saracen Street—which is by no means the present tourist heart of the city. The road to Lambhill Cemetery (the Balmore Road) leads off it to the north-west. As I check this on the map, I realize that it was exactly at this southernmost curve of Balmore Road, right there between Sunnylaw Street and Stronend Street, that a unique occurrence happened while I was helping my Dad with his heavy tv sets. I took one out of the dull-grey almost windowless van (*a very old model now, of course—but I saw one exactly like it, in olive-green, in Great Western Road about two weeks ago, in January 1994*) and carried it into the home of the owner, an old lady living there. She was so glad to see it safely returned to its habitual corner near the window that, as I turned to leave, she actually pressed a coin into my hand. It was not an insignificant coin either. This is the only time in all my numerous visits of this kind that anyone ever gave me a tip. I suppose she might even still be alive, just about. But your kindness, madam, has not been forgotten. Nor has the lubricious look of frightening ferocity which a woman who was younger than I am now, once threw at me when my father introduced his set-carrier with, 'And this is my son'. We were on the street in Maryhill Road at the time. (*I passed the place again a few days ago, on my way to take a writing class. The number of the close was, I am quite sure, 1422, just where the twins had died decades before. I checked up and thought, no one will believe this. So perhaps I should soften the claim to, one of the doorways in that very distinctive little group of tenements.*)

Anyway, eight youths were involved in a sort of gang-fight. Three of them had their alibis given the benefit of the doubt—reluctantly, as the judge or magistrate said. (At this point, just before noon, my father phoned me up. Well, to be exact, it is now 11.28 on Tuesday the seventh of September 1993. He wants me to come back to Largs on Friday, which I'll do.) The five others, members of the 'High High' gang, were each given two months in jail. One woman cries out 'My boy! My boy!' and faints. Presumably she thought he would never hurt a fly. (He was always such a quiet lad at home.) She may even have been right, I dare say.

Then more about that woman who was found dying on the stairs outside her house. I must return to this some time. And then an item about construction work at Barrfields Pavilion, a well-known building facing the sea in Largs, set back from the main, coast road, behind a putting green. I've been on the putting green often enough, but I don't think I've ever been inside the building itself. This may even refer to its actual original construction, I suppose. 1929? Extremely probable, I would say. Anyway, John Davidson, aged forty-five, of 683 Pollokshaws Road, Glasgow, (which I must have passed every time I took the bus to visit my Auntie in Pollok in the 1970s—assuming the building survived, of course), while fixing up an internal scaffolding, fell seventeen feet to the ground, and was killed. His fifteen year-old nephew was also seriously injured. They were temporarily residing in Brisbane Road, Largs; which is the street where my aunt spent the last years of her life.

Onwards. More about the Smith Street stairway death. (There is no Smith Street in Hillhead today, and I have no idea what this street is now called.) (*More astonishment! Smith Street was the old name for the greater part of what is now Otago Street. At that time the first block, at the top of Great Western Road monopolised the current name. The two sections are clearly somewhat misaligned. So, it is in a lane off a secret Smith Street that I have bought many books—among them, to give but one,* The Day They Shook the Plum Tree.) Then the Largs man is buried—in Glasgow, I think it was. But there is also a service in St Columba's, Largs—which I take to be that large church on the front, just across Nelson Street (another Nelson Street) from Nardini's famous restaurant. I have walked past that so often. Well, we all have. On my last visit but one, there were some steeplejacks working very near the peak of the steeple. Even to glance at them was to risk vertigo.

Just below that announcement, we learn that James Myles, aged seven, of (yet again) Hathaway Street, Maryhill, was found yesterday afternoon lying unconscious on Maryhill Road. Not unknown, but comparatively rare for one so young. Had he perhaps leapt from a moving tram, fallen and struck his head? Who knows? He was taken to the Sick Children's Hospital. It's a very busy street, that one, but no one saw a thing? Most odd. And here's another thing. Eight days later, we learn that C.M. Grieve is recovering from a bus accident in London, after having been unconscious for two full days. (He fell from the top of an open-topped, double-decker bus onto the hard stone far below. I have never quite managed to find out whether it was accident, drink, or attempted suicide. Or, indeed, attempted murder.)

Not so lucky is Susan Jane Todd (66) who is mentioned just opposite. She lived at No. 63 Chancellor Street—the street where, as I remember, the tallest lad in my class in the earlier years of secondary school used to live. She was knocked down and killed by a bus in Dumbarton Road, perhaps very near to that very cafe where I once sat beside unquestionably the most beautiful woman in the world. Glaister was called in here too. To what effect I do not know; but the driver was held to be at fault for this one.

A few days later, a trial opens. She asked her husband to answer the huge noise at the door. He in turn asked her to go. So she went. Only after the murder did the husband learn that they were working for the same firm. In short, pure coincidence. It was him, William Watt, who sent Bertie for the police. And for a doctor, apparently. (If so, the doctor gets very quickly lost sight of.)

Margaret Maguire, of 68 Grove Street, testifies that, at around 6.35 that evening, the accused came in to ask for any theatre pass that might be going free. Presumably this cannot mean, for that very night—after all, he had already arranged to go along to the Jacovellis. Anyway, she had none to give. Did he just wish to establish a time by which he was out of the house? Perhaps also, by implication, that he had no money of his own to spare for such luxuries? (Yet, he went along to the Billiards Hall, and he paid for the game there.)

She saw him again the following morning, when he came in 'for some cakes for breakfast'. He breakfasted on cakes? Was this, rather extravagant-sounding procedure, his normal practice? Hadn't Mrs Smith given him anything? Maguire told the court that Willox had said he wanted to return home (why? not for sentimental reasons, one trusts), but that 'reporters were after him'. (At least one of whom, of course, got to him. It sounds as if Bertie did not realize that, reporters or no, the *police* would certainly not allow him to wander at liberty that morning through his old home.)

Then Turner gives his evidence, denying that he had asked for change of a £1 note. Perhaps he had his own private reasons for doing so—having, for (a purely speculative) instance, stolen it from his mother's purse and not wanting it to be shown that he had had money. Or perhaps someone is just remembering things which, like so many things, didn't happen. Or didn't happen like that. He met Willox entirely by chance that evening, he said; when Bertie came out of a shop with a packet of cigarettes in his hand.

And once when Bertie had got £2.10.0 from 'a money-lender' (i.e. Mrs Duffy), Bertie had bought cigarettes, treated the pair of them to the cinema, and bought fish and chips on the way back. Which looks as if Bertie at this point was on a live now, pay later spree. He was normally a poor billiards player, but 'he played a good

game that night'. Relief? Adrenalin? The consciousness of innocence? (*This £2.10.0 must surely be the money which he was supposed
to be using to redeem his father's medals. Incidentally, before I forget,
with regard to the not particularly common name of Harrington—two
quite distinct Harringtons appear in the Lizzie Borden case; and one of
them, Uncle Hiram I think it was, is apparently the only person whom
she ever at all tried to incriminate for her own murder of her parents. I
learn this from Victoria Lincoln's A* Private Disgrace, *which I read only
this month, and which is perhaps the only book about crime which has
made me think, while I was reading it: yes, this author is something of
a kindred spirit.*)

The maligned Margaret Duffy (70) testifies to having given
Bertie £1 after she had met him in the street—unless I have
misinterpreted my abbreviated note on this. Jacovelli testifies to
having given him a loan 'two or three times', and that Bertie's visit
that night was the first since Jacovelli's marriage. Apart from
anything else, he could hardly risk arriving back too soon. Da might
still be alive.

(2.00–7th September)

96

Courage! We are already well over halfway through the notes. 'Does Scotland Really Want Composers?' asks Erik Chisholm. Sure, Erik: anyone particularly in mind? 'Sure, Bertie, you didn't do it?' Went to billiards ('Come, let's to billiards,') at 6.45, on his own reckoning. Sat with Jacvollei (sic) and his wife, playing the gramophone. Evidently Alfonso did not object to the presence of this strange man. Inspector Cook admitted that a piece of wallpaper which had been cut from the Willox kitchen had gone missing. Shades of the policeman who chopped wood at home with the crucial exhibit in the case. I trust that at least no other policeman used it to paper his kitchen with.

The reporter that I talked about long ago, evidently inaccurately, under the name of Christie, here appears under the impressively circumstantial name of John Richard MacLeod Ritchie. When the Judge took the black cap off, the accused stared straight at him in an unseeing way; then suddenly his eyes closed and he fell sideways, apparently heavily. Fortunately he did not hurt himself. The Judge's voice, in pronouncing sentence, was husky and somewhat unsteady. He, however, did manage to keep more of a grip on himself. It would hardly have done much for the solemnity of the occasion had both of them collapsed at the same time.

William Power writes about 'A Neglected Masterpiece in Scottish Literature'. (Scottish Literature sometimes seems to consist of little else.) He was discussing Hogg's *Confessions of a Justified Sinner*. I read Power's autobiography on either side of my latest visit to Aberdeen. I found it rather boring. Perhaps it's a deservedly neglected masterpiece. The Pope surprises his court at dawn. Which conjures up one or two fairly entertaining images. An appeal is to be made. Mr Graves apologizes for his libel. Pipes skirl in the Vatican.

This is not the early morning surprise mentioned earlier: that the Pope had been secretly mastering the pipes, if that is possible. It has to do, rather, with the Blessed John Ogilvie as he then was yet again, as far as I remember. But then, what doesn't? And that's enough of the *Daily Record*. What next?

(2.29–7th September)

97

At that time there were three Glasgow evening newspapers. By the time we were in West Princes Street, there were only two: the *Evening Citizen* and the *Evening Times*. (The *Evening News* had folded by then.) The *Citizen* was the one we used to get. It was a broadsheet, and I liked it rather a lot. However, it too folded, a few years after I had left West Princes Street. So now there is only one, and in all the years since then, it has always seemed to me to be the wrong shape, the wrong size, and (not to mince words) the wrong paper for the sort of thing you would want to buy of an evening. So, for old times sake, I decided at least to scour the *Citizen* as closely as I had done the other papers. ('Francis, nip out and get a *Citizen*, will you?' must have been said to me by Mum very many times. And I always did; and there was nearly always one waiting; and it seemed at the time that there always would be.)

Possibly the *Daily Record* is the morning paper which the elder Willox had in his pocket—though, even here, given the insistence on how well-educated he appeared to be, it may be that he was seen to favour something more solid. But what the evening paper was is anybody's guess. None of the papers saw fit to report these particular facts, as far as I could see. We learn instead that Only Two of Trotsky's Followers Remain Faithful to Him. Garden

Tragedy: City Stockbroker Found Shot Dead. Refused to Leave House: Govan Beggar Sent to Prison. King's Return to London. Trial at Dundee. Sequel to Camp Shooting Tragedy.

In Springburn, a boy is knocked down by a man fleeing on foot from the police. However, since the man is caught and the boy recovers, let us go on to: Suffocated by Bedrail. 'Falling, while in an epileptic fit, Jennie Jordan (43), 7 Cranbourne Terrace, Regent Street, Hull, caught her chin on the rail at the foot of the bed, and was suffocated in that position. At the inquest on Saturday a verdict of "Death by misadventure" was recorded.'

There is more. 'Whilst Charles Taylor, of Sidmouth, was discussing the use of a humane cattle killer with Harold Head (25?—or possibly 23—perhaps even 29), of Exeter, in the slaughterhouse at Sidmouth today, the weapon went off. The bullet entered Head's chest and he died within a few minutes.'

I don't suppose you want to hear about the gent who was fined 10/6, or five days, for marching through the municipal streets 'beating a drum and shouting "—— the Irish" ', which must require a certain technique, I suppose. Was he drunk? No; not particularly. Or how about another vignette of troubled domestic circumstances? James Dick of Kinning Street (another quick look at the map—no associations this time), arriving home, gave his mother £1 for board and lodgings. She, evidently risking a showdown, said it should really be more. Her husband backed her up. Faced with so much unreasonable behaviour, young James lost his temper and hit his father with a chair. So they had him taken to court, son or no son. £5, or 30 days. And no invitation back, one assumes.

And thus we pass on to yet another Tuesday. Issue No. 20,417. One penny. (I think the price had tripled by our day—requiring, when the transaction was at its neatest, the relinquishing of the charming, chunky twelve-sided coin that one would not be sorry to see resuscitated in some new, improved denomination.) What's this? BAFFLING CRIME. SON'S TERRIBLE DISCOVERY. NO ROBBERY AND NO SIGN OF STRUGGLE. 'One of the most baffling murder mysteries with which they have been confronted.' Exceptionally well-educated. 'Almost prostrate with grief and the shock of the discovery, the son was given shelter for the night by a neighbour.'

Later, a *Citizen* reporter visited the scene of the murder. Little groups were 'displaying considerable interest in every motor-car and person that came near the house'. 'The police who were on duty stated that the case was most baffling.' Every little helps, I suppose. How an investigator works. Ask the policeman at the door exactly what is going on.

'A woman who lived in the flat below said she did not hear a sound. "I would have heard," she said, "if there had been any fight or disturbance, because my room is directly underneath, but I did not hear anything" '. I have still not worked out what to make of this. Does a body crumpling to the floor just not, or not necessarily, make as much noise as you might expect? Possibly the fact that it, as it were, happened half in the lobby and half in the kitchen meant that the tumult, such as it was, was divided between spheres of influence. Perhaps the fact that he apparently fell against the door, pushing it across to the wall, disguised what was going on as nothing more than a loud or clumsy opening of a door, or shutting of it. But beyond these sheer speculations, nothing. 'At the Northern Police Headquarters it was said that they were mystified, and no arrest had been made or clue obtained.'

Ah well; there is always tomorrow. Here's a penny. Nip out and get us a paper, will you? How can I refuse?

(7.13–7th September)

98

Yes, yes, yes—sensational developments. Fewer than fifty people there. 'Something strangely casual in the atmosphere.' The lights were switched on, and Bailie Swan came in. Not a mention the next day. Another penny. WOMAN'S OUT-BURST IN COURT. 'No sign of recognition passed.' HUSBAND JUMPS OUT CUPBOARD. Man's amazing story of scene in house. Alleged blackmail. Crowds of men and women now in Maitland Lane. The Rise and Fall of Tripe. Not the title of the article by Dean Inge on Bertrand Russell's *Marriage and Morals*.

Also: what lies behind the mystery door to the left of the main entrance to the Central Station? A Japanese tearoom opens in Glasgow, and Arnold Bennett wonders whether biographies are too long. Papal Railway Collapses. No long-dead fanatic holding it up from Heaven, evidently. REUNITED AFTER 20 YEARS. GLASGOW GIRL AND HER THREE BROTHERS. Thought they had been killed in the War. Talking of which—Annie Hammersley, a 36 year-old woman who had *twice* been widowed in the War had her throat cut by her mentally unstable 33 year-old husband, Samuel.

One is horrified to learn that there was an affray in the Imperial Dance Hall, St George's Road. John Roy Tutton, the culprit, of 74

Buccleuch Street. The hall is just round the corner from where I used to stay; the accused comes from just a bit further up the hill from where my granny used to live. ('The accused commenced toying with Thompson's chin'—the dance instructor—'and telling him what a fine fellow he was.' Rather refined, I would think.) I don't know how many other houses granny lived in before that one—though I do know they were not few in number. There was only one more to come.

Oscar Slater's proposed marriage, we learn (they learned), is 'with a negress whom he met in Paris before his conviction for the murder of Miss Marion Gilchrist twenty years ago.' I take it that by now he had at least managed to shake off his legitimate wife—a serious pre-War complication. And, finally, wouldn't it be nice to live in Edinburgh and reach the age of eighty-four? (Granny just failed in the second, by a year or two. (She totally failed in the first.)) And, with any luck, one would die naturally the day before one might have dropped a lit oil-lamp—like Mrs Jane Craik—and (probably) have fainted across the bed, with the result that one was burned to death. I hope she did faint. A brief moment of confusion and shock, perhaps.

(4.03 am–8th September)

99

A medium in Liverpool, one Thomas James Quinn, forcefully recommended a young woman during a seance that she really ought to go to Australia. She went. However, on arriving there, she received a cable from a friend of such a nature that she took the first boat back forthwith. Soon, she was demanding the return of £100 and various valuables from the man who had received messages from beyond, and who had, so conveniently to himself, advised her to quit the country. An interesting story, but I mention it here chiefly because his surname was also the maiden name of my mother's oldest friend. They first met when she was six. They remained in touch for comfortably over six decades, and they last met on the very day before my mother died. In a small back bedroom in one of a row of very similar houses in one of the slightly more important roads in a small coastal town. A room which, I suppose, must have been waiting there for every day of their lives, right from that moment when they first met, not knowing for how unimaginably long their closeness would last; and on most days it will surely have been occupied.

I ignore line after line of notes. We learn that Florence Watt opened the front door for Harrington at 6.40—and that it was *as she was doing that* (when numerous other witnesses already have

Bertie well out of the building) that she heard 'You won't get a penny from me'. She had heard angry conversations on three previous occasions. Then, from her husband, William Watt (sixty-nine—but still working): on the evening of November the fourth, I saw Willox on the subway train. This is the father, of course. They had both got on at Partick Cross. (Now called Kelvinhall.) Just another trip home among the crowds of an evening. A bit lonely; a bit tired; a bit sad; but nothing special, and nothing much to expect. At St George's Cross, where Watt alighted, he did not see Willox—who, he presumed, must have got off and out ahead of him. Evidently in quite a mob, if his neighbour could not distinguish him. 'I thought the panel'—of the door—'was caving in.' So he sent his wife to investigate. Bertie could obviously be forceful when he needed to be. Sheffield Sensation. Twenty-four Policemen Suspended.

'I told him to control himself,' said Inspector Cook, 'and bear up, as this was a serious matter'. Sometimes he got cigarettes on credit, said McKinney. He could be irregular in payment. (Did his father ever get anything on credit? Not at this period of his life, apparently.) At seven the next morning, when not still sleeping in Canal Street, he was flurried and upset-looking. He told her his father had bought him an overcoat a fortnight ago. He was waiting for some 'Heid Yin'; he wanted to go up to the house to change his trousers.

His Lordship duly intervened to ask what she made of the term 'Heid Yin'. Presumably the actual phrase Willox used. Barely articulate grunts and groans, M'Lord. The hairdresser, Thomas Duff, is living at 33 Agnes Street—which is five minutes' walk away, perhaps six, from exactly this room where I am at present sitting on the edge of a bed, writing, at 4.35 in the morning. It has been largely redeveloped recently. I used to pass it whenever I got the tram or the bus to primary school (the same primary school whose ringing bell and clamorous yard-full of children I hear on most mornings in this very room, often taken as a signal that it's about time (8.57 a.m.) that I got out of bed), just after climbing the steep stairs of the very appropriately named Stair Street— which I must have done many dozens of times. Accused came into his shop just after eight.

Two newspapers. One, a morning paper, had been opened and read. The other, an evening paper, had not yet been disturbed. Did he buy it before or after his trip back home—which turns out not to have been on foot, as I had always for some unremembered reason supposed, but by underground. An extremely minor point—though it was probably the dead man's last purchase of the unnumbered thousands which he must have made in his life, and involved a real penny really handed over to someone or other. Of course, change may have been involved.

One naturally assumed at the outset that the 'two papers' would, sensibly enough, be a morning one and an evening one. Then one read an account of, I think, the Appeal that December, when one of the judges talked so precisely of two evening papers that one took it that that, though somewhat surprising, must have been how things were. Then, out of sync, one comes across this apparently unique mention of the truth in a discussion of the trial in November. This rather disappointed me, as it more than halved my feeling of conviction that, in poring over the *Citizen* I was at one point surely reading a copy of one of the very newspapers which Willox snr was carrying in his pocket on that fatal evening. It is also a little disconcerting to reflect that even the judges on such a solemn and critical occasion might be making rather blatant errors when it came to grasping the details of the case they were considering. Hmm. 4.44. That's enough for now. With any luck I'll drop back off to sleep again soon.

(4.45 am–8th September)

100

Alarming incident in tenement. Landing collapses. Sorry: I can't hang around at this one. 'A shoemaker named David Lee spoke to seeing the accused in Grove Street at half past three on November the fourth.' (Dad still off, unsuspecting and comparatively innocent, at work.) 'He asked Willox if he was going to play a game of billiards, and Willox replied that he would go if witness would stand the game as he had no money.'

One is a little surprised to have seen this mentioned nowhere else. I may just have missed it, I suppose. What, one wonders for a moment, was Bertie doing, back out on the street like this? And then you think: well, what else was there for him to do? How could he occupy his time at home all day? We never hear of him reading books. His domestic chores might take up an hour or two at most. Then what? Presumably he put in his day, for the most part, by hanging around the immediate neighbourhood on the off-chance of meeting someone he knew, practising his jazz somewhere or other, looking in shop windows, and, we have reason to suspect, visiting the licensed bookmakers. (*Actually, I don't remember anything about bookmakers in the background. I suspect this was just a crass way of introducing the next paragraph.*)

Perhaps the bookmaker he patronized was even Queen's, who I

remember had a shop in the general area when we were there; even though I can't recall exactly where it was. But I do recall how Mum—and I am sure this happened more than once over the years—when at some point she mentioned Queen's the Bookmakers, altered her tone in an, of course, riveting 'not in front of the children' sort of way; and said sympathetically to whoever she was talking to, probably her sister, 'Wasn't that terrible what happened', before tailing off short of any too explicit a detail. But at the time I never quite found out what was behind this.

It can only have been years afterwards that I discovered what it was all about. Almost exactly two years after Bertie's disaster—and his father's doubtless even greater disaster—in November 1931— the female alcoholic that the bookmaker's son lived with was found strangled in her bed (in Dumbarton Road, as it happens). Two famous pathologists, Spillsbury and Sir Sydney Smith, agreed at the trial that it might well have been suicide. This sounds pretty weird to me, and the jury, quite understandably, chose to differ. Queen was sentenced to hang, respited to life imprisonment, and released after a decent interval. I see that he died in 1958, about the same age as the century. So it may actually have been the recent news of his death that had made my mother be particularly aware of him: a suggestion which occurs to me only now, $3\frac{1}{2}$ decades later, just too late to ask questions.

Something else comes back to mind. Dad never bet on horses (or anything else), except on the Saturday of the Grand National—on which day he would also put two shillings on my own selection. This was a rare chance of a windfall for me, since it cost me nothing. I remember one year I picked a horse called, I am fairly sure, O'Malley Point. We watched on television (Dad was as usual away in his shop working, Saturday or no)—and the horse came in third! This won me, even at a shilling each way, a mighty sum; quite a few shillings. I seem to recall the price was either 100/8 or 100/6—and of course I also got back part of 'my' stake. Dad, who had been watching (he repaired television sets, after all) phoned up soon afterwards; and I remember hearing Mum telling him that 'Francis is running about here as excited as if he had ridden the horse himself'—a remark which I did not particularly approve of. I think I must have felt it failed to do justice to my dignity in success.

All the winnings were duly made over to me, no questions asked, just as if I had backed it with my own money. And it may well have been because of this that I subsequently tried to get Dad to put another bet on. I'm not sure whose money would have been involved, but I suspect it was his. Dad seemed to be interested, but Mum was having none of this—as she let us know in fairly succinct terms. My feeling is that, but for Mum, Dad would have bet more freely: he used to go to the dog-racing before the two of them met. (But never since.) Thus it is, I suppose, that I have never actually so much as set foot in a betting-shop in my entire life—though I always gaze in through any opened door to one with mild interest. I suppose the name of the t horse that I wanted Dad to back wasn't really Blue Parrot—but the name is brought forward so enthusiastically by whatever part of the brain has charge of such things that I feel I really ought to record it anyway. I do remember that it did actually win the race. So Mum, I suppose, will not have had much immediate thanks for that particular good turn of hers.

(10.11–8th September)

101

But, if Bertie had had the good fortune to find in this suddenly appearing Lee someone who was indeed willing to stand him a game of billiards, what then would he have done in the evening? I suppose he might just have gone back there anyway. Or perhaps he knew that Lee wouldn't want to or be able to pay—though this is all getting a bit too intricate. We may even reasonably doubt whether it was already definitely in Bertie's mind to go on to the Billiards Hall when he was coming calmly downstairs at about 6.30—after, one suspects, having exited his house and closed his door with extreme caution.

After all, he had established an alibi for 7.30, at Jacovelli's; and it is unlikely that he would know in advance how much time he would need in order to do what he felt had to be done. Having done the minor amount of washing up that was in fact required, he found himself able to leave at about half six; when the most important thing was to get a witness as soon as possible to his no longer being in the house. This could be achieved easily enough in the neighbouring shops.

In any case, he still had to have sufficient time left for him to make the rounds, paying off the debts. At least he managed to escape before Florence Watt heard the father's raised voice, while both in the w.c. and while letting Harrington into the flat. (There never seems to be any suggestion that the visitor himself heard anything similar while at the door.) Faced with the need to make a choice between this isolated, somewhat confused report from an elderly neighbour, and a concerted weight of testimony which contradicts it, there is surely only one decision that may reasonably be taken, troubling though it may be to have to take it at all. Besides which, immediate reports all seem to talk of *no one* hearing anything. I have not noticed any appearance of Mrs Watt's version of this episode prior to the trial itself, weeks later.

Well, someone must have done it, and the body must have fallen to the ground, I suppose, whether anyone else heard it or not. There doesn't even seem to be an identified second suspect after the son, and the son does make such a *convincing* suspect. The whole thing is utterly consistent with a sudden, wholly unexpected attack on someone who, as far as he was concerned, was simply embarking one more time on a safe, familiar routine. A shattering blow to the head, almost too sudden and decisive even to be a surprise. An arm thrown up in sheer mechanical reflex. Further blows, some of which also hit the hand thus raised automatically for protection. What was his last conscious thought? (*What?*, perhaps.) What was his last conscious act? Did he even *decide* to walk into the kitchen?

(11.38–8th September)

102

And still novelties about the case are appearing. Now, something quite unexpected about the actual paying-off of the debts. Willox had periodically told Daly that he would be coming up to his house to square things up—the latest suggestion having been October 30. But he did not in fact appear there until 7.15 pm on November the 4th. This is from Daly's evidence at the trial. If Bertie finished playing billiards at 7.05, it would take him ten minutes to get from the hall to Hopehill Road—whether No. 89 (*Herald*) or No. 91 (*Record*).

Now, here is the thing: it was of course Bertie's denial that he had paid Daly with a fiver (which the police knew he had done) that led straight to his arrest. I still can't work out why he did this but it may have some significance that, according to Daly, he (Daly) had since discovered that, at the time of paying off the debt, he had charged Bertie £1.2.6d too much! Apparently relying on memory, perhaps caught out by the unexpected visit, he had thought that the Willoxes owed him £2.14.11—when in fact all they owed was £1.12.5. This may explain why Bertie was so taken aback: 'first of all, he took £2 out of his pocket and laid that in his cap, then he took some silver; and when I told him it was £2.14.11'—which he did not seem to be already aware of—'he said

"Can you change me a fiver?" and I said "Certainly" '.

Perhaps he had expected that the £2 would be sufficient to clear it—as indeed it was, had Daly been better informed. But is this much help? Why did he claim that his father had given him six single pound notes (plus odds) to pay the debts? If he stole £8, which included a fiver, he was going to have to use the fiver anyway; whether at Daly's or Mrs Duffy's hardly mattered. I simply cannot see why he persisted in this crucial, and surely wholly unnecessary, lie. Did he just wish to dissociate himself from an item which he knew had been stolen from his dead Da, and fail to think straight? Then, having retailed his story to the police on the night of the murder, in the heat of battle, he may have decided that he had no better choice than to stick with it, trusting, if need be, to face any contrary evidence out. This is very weak, but I can think of nothing better. I rather suspect I must be missing something here; but, obviously, I can't quite work out what it is.

(12.24am–9th September)

103

Only a little more, to clear us entirely of the *Evening Citizen*; for I find I gave up on it after the end of the trial, not even bothering to read its reports of the appeal. I mean, one can take this research business too far. Then we are onto the broad sunlit uplands of a few occasional bits and pieces.

As to how he dealt with the fact that his falsifications of the insurance passbooks would be instantly obvious to the man from the Hearts Of Oak—a Mr J.S. Gunn—that is simplicity itself. Bertie told him the passbook had been mislaid. 'I offered to give him another book, but he said he'd try to find the old one.' Very wise, under the circumstances. Mr Gunn did actually receive a payment when he called on the 28th of October. And the total owing was only £1.11.0—which Bertie could easily have cleared after the unfortunate event, if he had been allowed to. (One rather wonders whether the inadvertent surplus which he had paid to Daly was ever returned to him.)

'Who put those (false) entries there?' the Judge sternly asked during his summing up to the jury. There is obviously only one feasible answer to that. And the answer to that takes us a long way towards the answer to the other questions in this case. Unless, perhaps, we are to believe that, by a truly amazing coincidence, just as Bertie's final depredations were about to leap out of their state of secrecy, some other, wholly unknown person providentially happened along and eliminated the awkward parent. Not impossible, of course; but the mightily more probable has to be enough for any practical system of law; and people will always be at the mercy, very very rarely, of truly ludicrous injurious coincidences.

The very last snippet of all from this paper is a largely unrelated one—except that death comes here from a blow to the head too and in the same season of the year. Even the location, although it is to be found in exhaustive maps of Glasgow, is miles away from the city centre, right at the edge of the book, halfway to Dumbarton. Isabella Ross, aged thirteen, daughter of John Ross, an engineer, of 20 Scott Street, Dalmuir (apparently a small dead-end backing onto a railway line—like its neighbour, Burns Street) was playing with some other girls, this is the life, in nearby Duntocher Road, when a boy, who presumably was also playing, accidentally ran into her, knocking her to the pavement. She hit her head when she fell. She was helped up and taken home. Her condition worsened. The doctor was called in, and he had her removed to hospital, where she died very soon afterwards. The girls who stood beside her may well, for all I know, be grandmothers now. Cars will be passing Scott Street this very morning.

(10.20 am–9th September)

104

Ⅰt was at this point in my researches, late in the evening, tired of poring over unwelcoming microfilm, that I thought I might as well use up the brief period before the library shut by inspecting the January 1930 editions of the *Glasgow Weekly News*, which are kept in bound yearly volumes, before dragging my weary way homewards. What I discovered was little enough, I suppose; but it still gave a great shock to someone expecting nothing.

The fourth front page. Jan 25th. No. 3895. Sweetheart's Joy Over Bert Willox reprieve. Told by herself (in an interview). As far as I can see, this female 'Cathie Niven, his former sweetheart' (complete with photograph: pleasant and sensible-looking) appears nowhere else. I presume that, like Bertie, she was paid for her appearance in this tenacious organ. What I can't tell is, to what extent any desire to earn the payment might have encouraged her to exaggerate or invent her own intrusions into the story. But, if it is sheer fantasy, it is certainly a very circumstantial fantasy.

'For over a year we were the best of friends, and our friendship was marred by only one little quarrel, which, however, we patched up just before the crime was committed.' That her dear friend had just been convicted of battering his father to death—something which she does not appear to refuse belief to—is nowhere directly mentioned. Probably that would all be in rather bad taste.

'I can remember very clearly the night I first met him. He was on the way home from a New Year party,'—evidently not that last New Year; but his mother was still alive, whatever Hogmanay it was—'with some friends of mine and was in a very happy frame of mind.' Ah; this here might well be a discreet allusion to drink taken. 'He laughed and joked for a while, then in the course of the conversation that ensued,' ('the course of the conversation that ensued'—evidently they speak a very literary patois in the Cowcaddens), 'we struck up quite a warm friendship and agreed to meet again'.

So well did they click, that they apparently met 'about three times a week during the twelve months before his father's death'. If true, this means there was easily more than a hundred such meetings of the pair. Which would indicate rather a steady and lasting commitment; and a possible explanation of why Bertie was always rather strapped for cash. But what are we to make of Mrs Smith's contention that there was only this one girl whom he 'saw now and again, but they have never been out together'? I *suppose* this may just have been the line he peddled to her.

However, the 'many enjoyable evening walks' she attested to do not sound too expensive. Nor too blood-stirringly exciting either. But about a fortnight before 'the death' Bertie got a bit jealous when Chrissie went out with another girl. What? Does that mean, rather than going out with *him*? It's possible, I suppose. Daft, but not excessively daft for love's young dream. (Is this the 'Chrissie' of the 'Chrissie and Willie' that he asked after to Mrs Smith? If so, they must surely have directly known each other. Indeed, it was perhaps Mrs Smith who led the reporter to her.)

Then, on 'the eve of the tragedy' she was standing outside a cinema. (Deep in thought? Looking at the placards?) Willox, who by now must have had other thoughts heavily on his mind came up to her out of nowhere (whether to her surprise or not) and asked, 'Are you trying to jilt me?'. No less. 'Certainly not,' she replied. If this really happened, it does suggest that their relationship was a rather serious business. Jilting requires real emotions for it to work—even if they are to some extent only adolescent impulses towards self-dramatisation.

They arranged to meet later. She did not say when. She then

left him, to go over to a shop for a message—which is to say, to make a purchase. Since this was a Sunday and most of the shops would have been shut, one rather wonders what this message, so belatedly remembered, might have been. But at this rate I'll end up doubting everything, like Pyrrho. What this casual discovery of source material does, more than anything else, is make one rather nervous as to what else might not be lying out there in publicly-available material, totally unobserved by me. Or, indeed, by any-one else.

One other thing, however, that I did manage to pick up, was in the March the 8th issue of that same year. It said that a seventy-one year-old woman, a recluse, who lived in the East End of Glasgow in no great affluence, even though her two highly successful brothers in America had often entreated her to join them, had recently died, alone in her small, spare dwelling-place. It's just that this too was in Stevenson Street, Calton. No. 177 of the very street which the man hailed from who hanged himself in Duke Street Prison while on an indecency charge. She too was right next to Jacovelli's Abercrombie Street. Same age as my mother, whoever she was. No one's mother, I suppose.

(5.49–9th September)

105

N ext, with (I must confess) a certain air of weariness, I turned to the briefest possible exploration of a second evening newspaper, the *Evening Times*, the only one which is still being published. Though I often see it, and occasionally even glance through it (well—what else can you do?), I am even now often aware that I am the product of a *Citizen* domicile. I shall confine myself entirely to reports of the murder and the trial.

Incidentally, there was an item in a newspaper I bought today which much interested me. A woman from London, who apparently had a rare brain disorder ('rare' is putting it mildly, I should think) did not know that alcohol changed her personality until, after drinking, she wounded her boyfriend by stabbing, and killed his sister, who was also 'her best friend'.

It's only a brief report, and doubtless no more accurate than most; but there are some intriguing points to it as it stands. Had the woman, by sheer chance (or what?), never drunk alcohol before? Or had the brain disorder perhaps only recently gone critical? 'She could not remember the incident and has not touched alcohol since.' I should think not. But what if, for whatever reason, she should drink alcohol again? and does she remember where the knife came from? (It appears right out of nothing in the report.)

She was placed on probation for three years—by someone who, of course, will have known far more about the facts of the case than this.

But, back to the case in hand. Florence Watt here claims to hear voices, one of them probably Bertie's, just after Willox senior had gone into the house, at six or so. She seems to have had a rare facility in hearing neighbouring voices, at the very least. Perhaps the body fell as she shut her own door? (We still don't quite know why it was open at all.) Isabella McKinney testifies that Bertie's credit was wholly stopped as early as *April*. 'If he could not purchase cigarettes and these things,' a dark phrase, nowhere explicated, 'he could do without.' He used to buy various papers, often to do with racing. (*Ah. So there is a racing connection after all. I did myself an injustice.*) He tendered a two-shilling piece, but she could no longer remember what he had bought. (Cigarettes, apparently, to go by James Turner's evidence.)

34 Grove Street is presumably the location of the hairdresser's shop of Thomas Duff, whose home was in Agnes Street—a good fifteen minutes' walk; far enough away to be definitely not local. I wonder how many of his customers knew this. I have seen the Grove Street Institute—a religious gathering-place of evidently considerable respectability, across the road from the Willoxes and doubtless visible from their front window—mentioned in the posthumous autobiography of Catherine Carswell, who is best known perhaps as a biographer of Robert Burns. That will have been before Bertie's abode there, but perhaps he heard the hymn-singing of congregation after congregation. One imagines that innumerable arriving and departing congregations must have seen *him*.

'Are you,' (to Inspector Stewart, from Bertie's Counsel), 'in the habit of losing things which you recognise as important evidence?' (The piece of removed wallpaper.) 'It is the first I have ever lost in my life.' (Rather a desperate, 'try anything, you never know' question. What did he expect: 'Oh yes. It happens all the time with us.') There were light stains inside each pocket of the dead man's trousers, suggesting that a bleeding hand had reached into each of them. Is it not then likely (continues Counsel) that such a person would have blood *all over him*? 'A chance,' replies the Inspector— and is not even asked 'A good chance?' Too risky.

Would the deceased have taken his uniform off, have polished his buttons (Bertie said he left his father cleaning his buttons), and then have put it back on again? (The corpse was still in uniform. This trivial detail is in fact a strongish point against the son's story.) He opens the door, lets the keys drop from a chain in one of his uniform pockets (in his trousers, one presumes; since the chain is attached to a trouser button), takes his coat off, turns to go into the kitchen. Where is Bertie? Behind him, obviously. (Apart from Roughead, I have seen absolutely no suggestion anywhere of this strange 'completely empty room'. Where did he get this from? Is he right?) 'He appeared to have no friends at all.' And less even of a family than most.

He swayed before sentencing, and fell only afterwards. The foreman's voice shook slightly. The summing up lasted over an hour. A line right through that column. Enough for today, I think. Off back down to Largs tomorrow.

(6.32–9th September)

106

It is late in the next evening now. I came down to Largs from Glasgow by the 11.45 train this morning, and got into the house yet again about 1 o'clock. I was loaded down with my own luggage (chiefly of books) and a bagful of Marks and Spencer's groceries, specially brought for Dad. I went through into the kitchen, and loaded all the stuff into the fridge and freezer. Only then, since the noise I was making still hadn't brought him in, did I go through to his room, formerly my parents' bedroom, to see how he was.

The room was empty. As were all the other rooms. But his car was still by the side of the house. (It still is.) I rang my sister's home, which is only round the corner and down at the end of the road. There was no reply. So I just busied myself in a fairly low-key way, content to let what felt like a very minor mystery solve itself in its own time, as doubtless it would. I made myself an omelette; I went across the road to buy a few things we seemed to be short of. I sat and read the newspaper; and even had a look at a book which I had to review. So it went routinely on; until about 2.30, when the phone rang. It was my sister calling from the hospital, a large ominous building on a hill, quite a good distance away. She said that Dad was here in hospital; that he had been taken a bit badly early that morning, and could I possibly make my way there?

So, I quickly prepared myself, took the ten minutes' walk down to the appropriate bus-stop on the sea-front, and waited. The last time I did that (indeed, the only other time I did that) was just over six months ago. Mum had phoned up from the hospital, where she was being held for a few days. She sounded a bit woozy and sedated, but she clearly enough asked me to bring her a little hand-held fan that she had in a drawer somewhere. I agreed. I then rang up the hospital, and discovered that this was the first they had heard of any such wish of hers. They arranged to put a fan beside her. Mum may not have wanted to put them to more work; or perhaps that option simply never occurred to her. However, thinking that no doubt she would welcome an extra visit anyway—which may even have been the motive in the back of her mind—I decided to take the little hand-held fan up to her anyway. I was glad I did. The fan is at present still in a drawer in my own room.

I had to wait on the sea-front for about twenty minutes, until a bus came along. It was just after 3 o'clock. It took some twenty-five minutes to get to the hospital. I caught a lift, got up to Ward J Centre, and at last announced my arrival to the nurse at the desk. She asked me whether my sister had told me much about my father's condition. I said I knew absolutely nothing of what was going on. She then led me to a small room, with the words *Relatives' Room* (I think) on a plaque on the door; and there she left me. It had drawn curtains, and there was only a subdued light from two or three table-lamps.

Very soon afterwards, my elder sister, who works in that building as a theatre nurse, came in. She was silent and in tears. She sat beside me, clearly very deeply upset. Thinking to make things a little easier, I asked, is he dead? Even as I did so, I think I still more expected her to reply 'No' than 'Yes'. She nodded her head: yes. It would not in the least have surprised me to find him sitting up and joking. So: my father is now dead. And I was not there. I was sitting nonchalantly in his house. (*No. He died about 3.10. I was on the bus.*)

We went into the room where he lay. Soon I was left alone there. Only his head and the very top of his shoulders were visible beneath the bedclothes. He rang me up on Tuesday, asking me when he was going to see me again, and asked me to bring him his favourite herrings. I kissed his head, which had a look of such nobility in it.

What else can you do? What else can I do now? It is nearly midnight; getting on for the first midnight which he will not have lived through since before the First World War. And for eighty years afterwards, including all sorts of upheavals: landing in a strange country becoming the father of a son, various financial crises, and at least managing to enjoy fifteen years of fairly contented retirement before his wife died.

Soon I shall switch off the small night-light in the hall, as he certainly did two days ago, and so many hundreds of times (with Mum) before. The clock in the next room should be striking soon enough. On this day last year, they will both have been alive and talking to each other. It's unlikely, but I suppose I may even have been here too, in this very room. I just don't know how this leaves me—whether with regard to this, which almost seems like a bad joke to me, something I should have thought about and known better than to start; and with regard to other things too. I had assumed he would be waiting for me, as usual. The very possibility never really occurred to me.

(11.45–10th September)

107

At five in the morning, I got up and walked through some of the rooms. I found his watch lying beside the clock. It is one of those ones which has to be wound up every night if it is to keep going. I suppose it was his habitual last act before going to bed. It had stopped at some point between ten and five to one in the earlier morning.

Strangely enough, one of the things we discovered today was Mum's exact place of birth. She was born, as I think I once mentioned, during her family's anomalous, brief stay in Airdrie. I asked her once, during her final illness, whether she had ever been back to the place at all. She hadn't been. I very much suspect that she herself may not have known what the full address actually was. I suppose I may as well add, it was 6 Mill Lane. I have not the slightest idea whether it is still standing or not. I should try to find out reasonably soon. I have no maps available of that locality. And, obviously, it never meant much to her. She will have had no memories of the place—though her eyes must have swept it innumerable times all the same.

I also found out that I was born in West Princes Street at 9 o'clock in the morning. Mum had been born at forty minutes past midnight, August the 15th 1921. She was the youngest of six children, five of whom survived infancy. And Dad too was the youngest of six children, so my hold on life is more precarious than I had thought. Father: Joseph Michael Kupczyk, born 18 March 1873 in Schönfeld (West Prussia, I assume). Died 30th of November 1936. So: only sixty-three. He had been a farmer—but in desperation he gave it up for a secure job on the railways as a driver. Dad said next to nothing about him, ever; and that little was not particularly warm. I think he said he died of some sort of blockage in the bowel. Whether that or not, a pretty unpleasant death anyway.

His mother, Gertrud Hellwig, was born in Görsdorf, on the 20th of November 1870; over two years before her future husband. Dear God, who were these people? She died on the 28th of August 1945, at the end of a disastrous war, not knowing which of her sons were alive, and which were dead. (Her only daughter, Anna, was at home with her.) Dad was pretty well content to call her 'an angel', and leave it at that. We have found the letters which Anna wrote to him not long after the war, when she learned that her youngest brother was, after all that upheaval, astonishingly still alive. So, Dad kept them. They are written in the old German handscript which makes them extremely difficult for me to decipher, quite apart from the language difficulties themselves of course. Looking over them, I feel almost as if I am somehow half an extraterrestrial and half a very close relative.

The brothers, Albert and Joseph, were also still alive. Another brother, August, was certified as having died in battle on the 30th of June 1917. He was seventeen. His date of birth was August 28, 1899. So his mother actually died on what would have been exactly his 46th birthday. And what might she not have been thinking, when her eyes last closed? My German grandmother. (The father was the only one who could speak Polish as well as German—except, through a quirk of history, for Dad himself.)

My baptismal first names are Francis Joseph—shared with Haydn and the Austrian Emperor (1830–1916). But they are also, I am sure, crucially affected by the fact that Dad had a brother Franz and a brother Joseph. Joseph lived 1905–77; when Dad came back from his funeral, I remember him saying that he had never realized before that Joseph's middle name was Georg. Franz was born on September 20, 1907. He went missing while on active service during the war. God knows where he was buried, if anywhere. He was officially held to have died, obviously as a matter of administrative convenience, at midnight on December 31, 1945. Sometimes I think of myself as being one of the ones that Europe threw back.

It all fits together just like a jigsaw, Dad said to me one afternoon a couple of weeks ago. It was really only a couple of weeks ago. If I had not done my ankle, I would never have been brought over here. I would have stayed there (in Germany, on the Mosel), and I would probably have soon died. But they left all the injured behind in a hospital by the river, where the Americans found them. And so now I am standing at this window. I hesitate, looking for something to pin down the moment with. If only the traffic outside were not so nondescript.

(5.46–11th September)

108

And it was also today on which I saw Mum's gravestone for the first time. It has been in place for only a few days. My younger sister had bought some flowers to take there, and I walked up with her. Dad himself saw it for the first time, and I think for the only time, on Tuesday—the day when he last phoned me. It seems he approved of it. I liked it too. But more has happened than I am able to trace. I suppose, in a few days, it will be taken away and a few more details, ordinary unremarkable details for that place, will be added to it. If that is how these things work.

(*I have cut out a couple of longish paragraphs here which are just too much.*)

The more complex my mother's life in retrospect becomes to me—which is to say, the more I learn about it; and of course this goes for my father too, though I suppose to a slightly lesser extent—the more, what can I say, the more I love her, and the more I identify with her. And I am so gratified that I was able to say to her some of the things which I did manage to say to her in the last few weeks before her death. It becomes clearer and clearer to me, how much more or less the same thing must have happened in the other direction too. To care for those whom our care can help, in this real world: that is the main thing. But if I don't stop now I suppose I'll start sliding into the easy defensiveness of irony.

(9.02–11th September)

109

An utterly dazzling Sunday morning. How many Sunday mornings have there been since the middle of 1912? How many dazzlingly sunny ones? Actually, when you start working it out: in Northern Europe there might only have been a thousand or so.

We walked back up to the cemetery again and put some flowers there. Strangely enough, we bought them, a bunch each, at a garage. As she pointed out, they will probably start digging the earth up again tomorrow. Afterwards, we walked down what was almost a delightful side-street to the sea-front. I have never been down that road before in my entire life. Yet they had lived in this fairly small town for some seventeen or eighteen years, and I often visited them.

The last time I hung out washing to dry, as I did today, he was still alive, and somewhere in the house. And this evening I made a salad for myself, using up some of the things I had specifically, and not without a tinge of resentment, brought down here for him to enjoy. It was not easy to do, and it took me some time to finish it.

His clothes fit me too. I wore one of his lightest jackets while I was out, since I had only a heavy coat and a heavy anorak of my own here. I had not expected such brilliant weather. But there is so much I did not expect.

One of my book reviews appeared in the newspaper yesterday morning. I had written it here, and had phoned it in from here, while Dad was alive. Indeed, I read the whole book here, all but a couple of pages—I picked it up in the front office the day after Dad went into hospital for observation. What good did *that* do him, I wonder? I suppose they did all that could reasonably have been done.

I also found an old watch of Mum's, broken and stopped, the expandable bracelet also broken where it joins the top of the small face, in the drawer at the side of Dad's bed (a double bed). I remember it well. It surprised me to realize that she had stopped wearing it. There was much else there too, of course.

It is strange, trying to decipher those letters, scratched out with a miserable post-War German pen, ink and paper, to my father, somewhere in this country here, well before I was born. Perhaps even before he met my mother. Strange how we tend to assume that we are the reason for our parents' existence. I will just have to try to acquire mastery of the script, and then perhaps use that fine, thick dictionary which Dad bought for his two eldest children when they were doing their best to learn German. In fact, he paid for many lessons out of his own pocket. He never spoke German to us himself. My own suspicion is that he felt we would eventually somehow pick up the language naturally anyway. After all, we were his children. Well, we still are, for the moment.

110

We were going through some of Dad's heaps of papers earlier tonight, looking for the addresses of one or two people who will have to be informed as soon as possible. I suddenly noticed that one of the mute succession of envelopes, in which he had stuffed sundry material about car insurance, was addressed to him in my own handwriting. It gave me such a peculiar shock. Except for cards at Christmas or on birthdays, I very rarely wrote either to Dad or to Mum. There never seemed to be any need to. It was like a sudden, unexpected reminder that I really was his son.

I retrieved the envelope, and stuffed the contents into a near empty one. Actually, as I found out later, a thin and trivial slip of paper nonetheless remained within it, but I'll just let this stay where it is. There is a beautifully clear postmark: Glasgow/7.45pm/17 Feb/1987. I have a far less clear idea of what I sent him in it. Possibly it was something I had typed out for him—perhaps to do with his long and unavailing attempts to get a retirement pension from Germany. (He never lived in the post-war Federal Republic. Apparently, had he done so, he would have been given the pension to which he was entitled. This seemed unfair to him, and periodically he tried to discover whether anything had changed. But the crucial part always remained the same. He never got that pension.)

I see that, though it was February, I used a Christmas stamp on it. Evidently I had over-estimated the number of Christmas cards I was going to send out the previous year. (Dad kept all the birthday cards we sent him. We found them all together in a box, in little strata of years.) He has written something on the outside—I think, to do with an insurance policy. Only right now, as I stare at it, do I recognize it as the phone number of Dot (whose name he has also written there), the insurance woman in Largs. Last year, perhaps on her birthday, she sent my mother a bouquet of very attractive flowers. I had sellotaped the flap of the envelope down with a thin type of tape, the roll of which I have still not come to the end of, over six years later. Dad duly slit the envelope open at the other end, the bottom end. So, this hand wrote those quick letters on that sturdy brownish paper, much as it now runs over this cheap, lined white A4 paper beside it now—and my memory of the second incident is only marginally better, I would say, than my memory of the first.

But the main thing was an old passbook of Dad's from the Ministry of Labour and National Insurance (E.P. No.12296) from the time when he had to go to Northern Ireland to find work. I had no idea that he had spent a full year there. Practically the only detail I can remember Mum telling me of it (Dad, typically, said absolutely nothing) was that in one of his letters he had mentioned 'kitchen soup'—and it had taken her a while to work out that this must have been meant for 'chicken soup'. This suggests a still fairly basic level of language acquisition on Dad's part. (He always spoke English with a very strong accent. Specifically, with a very strong German accent—not to mention the typically Germanic formulations which he never abandoned: things like 'all what matters is', 'as when' for 'as if', and 'What is here going on?'—which last was pretty well adopted by the whole family.)

So, he was there, or registered as being there, for two 6-month periods, in Bay Road, Larne. I've never been to Ireland yet myself. Mum was never there, I don't believe. A Radio Mechanic at Carran Works Ltd (or Carron?) of Larne Harbour. From 27 April 1949 to 26 April 1950. So, he was actually in Ireland, or had work there, when his eldest child was born! Indeed, I can only now deduce that I was born precisely nine months after his permit to work there ran out. One surprise after another. Perhaps, under such circumstances, everyone has surprises.

I only now fully realize too that Dad's car is still parked by the side of the house, through this wall here that I could reach out and touch—there—and yet, though I know the initial letters of its registration number (RCN—the usual abbreviation of the Royal College of Nursing; I can't remember who it was I heard commenting on that some months ago), I haven't the least idea what the numbers on it are, or what the final letter is. Yet those were the number-plates I washed, or at least ran a sponge over, barely a couple of weeks ago.

(11.35–12th September)

111

A thought vaguely relevant to all this struck me at last early on Monday afternoon. There is quite a modern car-atlas in a bookcase in this very room. I have often used it as a reference book when I was here. I suppose Mum or Dad must have ordered it by mail (it is one of these *Reader's Digest* productions) a couple of years back. It contains small maps of the general lay-out of many towns in the British Isles. I wasn't sure whether Larne would be big enough to figure; but it suddenly occurred to me a few minutes ago to look and see.

It was there: on the very last page of the map section of the book, an insert in a corner which would otherwise be largely sea. Almost the last street-name I observed was (I presume) exactly this Bay Road, where Dad was staying the year or two before I was born. Just north of the ferry terminal from Scotland, leading from the sea-front to a clearly major road.

When I went through, just there, in that space between paragraphs where so much can happen, or so little, to tell my sister this, she replied by handing over to me a Trustee Savings Bank book which she had just found. Mum opened it in my name on January 7th 1957, just before my sixth birthday, paying in ten shillings to an account at the branch in 101 New City Road. The building survives. (*The new motorway has made rather an island of it—but a sort of Chinatown has recently opened up just across a road.*) So now, immediately after investigating an object which must exist in millions of copies (the atlas), I am inspecting a small, unique booklet, saved from the fire, I suppose, for sentimental reasons.

What next? Bear with me a moment. 22 shillings (a peculiar sum) was paid in on May the 28th. Well over a year passes. Ten shillings on October the 6th 1958. Ten shillings on June 15th 1959. None of these dates says a thing to me: it must simply have been an intermittent determination to keep the project from foundering completely, despite the scarcity of available cash. Ten shillings more on my ninth birthday: Jan 19, 1960. And then she seems finally to have admitted defeat, at least for a long while. Then, seven years and seven days later, on the 26th of January 1967, when I have pretty well grown to be another person, £2 is paid in. I find all these small sums, willingly but with some difficulty paid over inside that very distinguished, wood-lined banking interior at the gushet of Shamrock Street and New City Road, by a woman slowly changing over the decade with her family, profoundly moving, and rather humbling too. Five months later, on the 19th of June, comes the first withdrawal made in the decade-long existence of this account. £4 was taken out—and I very much suspect that it was me who did it. Dad's 55th birthday was just coming up, though that may have had little enough to do with it. Nothing at all the next year; then two separate fivers put in in 1969—by the time of the second of which, even after so few transactions, the five-year-old whom the book had been taken out for was now at university. Mum was probably trying to reactivate it for me. Even though they never had much in the way of money—or because of that—Mum was in principle a great one for savings and insurance.

The action culminates in 1970, which I still rather think of as the year when my life must have slipped out of its proper phase. I assumed it was some sort of temporary hiccup, but it turned out to be a hiccup which spanned decades. I think I assumed that a year or two would see me able to write brilliantly; and I would then merely hand over my deathless work (*in this context, the most inappropriate adjective I could conceivably have chosen*) to the smoothly functioning artistic infrastructure, who, in some wholly taken for granted way, would then do the rest of what needed to be done. This is not a particularly accurate description of what actually happened.

£5 more on the 16th Jan, doubtless for my birthday. On the 17th of April, £10! Sheer, over-worked generosity, I take it. (Total: £28/18/1. My first serious old currency calculation since decimalization suggests that it accrued some £1/6/1 in interest overall.) The catastrophe came quickly. £15 withdrawn on the 13th of May; £11 on the 30th of July. I'm sure I was the beneficiary of these too, although the £4 is the only one I can more or less remember. The eighteen old shillings and one old penny remain in the book, never realized. It all adds to the general profitability, I suppose. It makes thirteen transactions *in toto* in over thirteen years. They did not have it very easy in material terms. Not that it ever occurred to me we were anything like poor. I would appear to be carrying on the tradition in this too. I still think of myself of having, in financial terms, struck a doubtless temporary bad patch; which is proving a little difficult to get out of, that is all. I prefer to think of it as optimism.

(2.09–13th September)

112

My sisters variously remember scattered talk of going back to Germany (my elder sister), or of emigrating to Canada (my younger one)—but I remember not a word of any of this. Where was I while these things were being said? What was I doing? Did I notice or absorb nothing? Meanwhile, I must force myself to press on from time to time with a book about the secret life of Howard Hughes, for God's sake, which I have to phone in a review of by next Sunday.

Earlier, I went to the house of a neighbour, who lives a few buildings away down the street. I'm not sure I had ever seen her before, although she had been a good friend to Mum, and exchanged the time of day happily enough with Dad whenever she happened to meet him. I was invited into the house, and I sat there in a pleasant room which I would otherwise never have seen, looking out at a strangely distorted view of a very familiar stretch of road, and scratching the back of a persistent and enthusiastic small dog.

And that strange dream I can still remember wisps of. Bizarrely, it involved my Uncle James, the eldest on my mother's side, whom I met only when he was staying at my aunt's house in the late 1970s, on a visit from Australia to his native land. In the dream, he was somewhat the worse for drink. (I have absolutely no idea whether in real life he drank or not. I never heard any suggestion that he did.) And he decided to lie across the bed in Dad's old room, a double bed, on the side where Mum used to sleep, nearer the door, where he lay snoring, I told someone indignantly, for over an hour in all. I suspect it may well have been me who was really snoring.

(We live in the real world alongside real people. I suppose I'll have to take out this paragraph too.)

But what does still exist is a strange profusion of documents. Most of them can be gathered together in two hands. In the debris of Dad's bedside drawer, I found a tiny identity photograph of him—obviously from his Polish army days. Whether from his conscript years around 1936 (three years, apparently), or near the start of the Second World War, I do not know. 92794 AP, it says—the AP possibly indicating a variant of Polish Army, with the adjective after the noun. He looks more like my brother in this than I have ever otherwise seen him. It is also easily the youngest image of him that I have ever seen—younger even than that gaunt uniformed figure from near the war's end. Childhood snaps, if any, must have been immolated long ago. A sudden glimpse of my father (sudden to me) looking much younger than myself. A fragment of a stamp adorns the bottom left corner, showing that it has been cut from a larger document.

I have just been holding it up to the light, and I can make out quite a bit of the stamp. ZUPE . . . IEW on an outer curve. On an inner curve, rather worryingly, . . . AND RECORD OF . . . Then part of a Polish eagle (only a head). The outer curve is in Polish, obviously; but the inner looks extremely like English. But 'Poland Record Office' sounds more than a little improbable.

Here too I have a new photograph of the grave as it is today. Soon, more details will have to be added. Flowers still beside it, that we bought in a garage forecourt last Sunday—which, now I come to think about it, is in fact only yesterday. I'll keep all these things together. And I also have a photograph of Mum in her final illness, on my sister's birthday at the start of February this year. I used to shy away from this picture, and wish it had never been taken, because it catches a momentary sad, desperately-ill look which was so untypical of her even then. Her granddaughter is in front of her. I am behind her, somewhat inanely holding a toy badger that we had been playing about with. Mum looks so astonishingly like what her own mother had looked like when I got to know her. (She was about sixty-seven when I was born. Almost all my memories of her, therefore, will have been of a woman older than Mum.)

Someone who knew nothing else of that afternoon would probably see only an old woman, evidently very ill, whose eyes, cast towards the camera, but looking lower, showed her to be off lost in a sad world of her own. But if that had been how she was then, we would obviously not have taken the photograph at all. Such, however, are the risks. The camera catches transitions, archness, moments of self-consciousness, and offers them up as a permanent and typical record. This one seemed to me for a while to be a callous piece of misrepresentation. What would it have cost to catch her courage and her good humour? Why not just show her spirit?

However, last night I forced myself to stare at those ravaged, treasured features for a long while; and to my joy I was able to see that, to those who knew, there was still something there in the configuration of the eyes, the mouth, and the cheek lines; something subtle, which with so little alteration would, a moment afterwards in that real time, have become a smile (she smiled warmly at us almost to the last—even when talking was difficult) or a remark which still had humour and what I can only call life in it. Just shoot me if I start losing my mind, she said. It won't be me you are shooting. However, she was herself right to the end.

(8.34–13th September)

113

T uesday morning. I open the curtains in my parents' bedroom. I have done that perhaps five or six times. They must have done it thousands of times each, I suppose. There is a rainbow out there; a full arc stretching from the wooded ridge at the north end of the Island of Greater Cumbrae, to a gap between roofs in that street off to the right. By the time I come through here to write this down, since otherwise I would probably just forget all about it, it is still there, although it has faded a little.

Few things show just how unnatural nature can be, than a rainbow does. It is so starkly artificial. The world of fridges, televisions, satellites and so forth is suddenly very obviously the same place as the world of cloud and rain. It is, in short, all one world, and only one world.

My God!—half an hour later, there is the arcing base of another rainbow, coming out of the rightmost of the clump of trees at the foot of that other street off to the left.

I can remember only two or three seconds (as it felt) of a dream I had last night. Mum was beginning to tolerantly explain to me how silly I had been in supposing that she was really dead. No doubt the belief in survival derives from this sort of thing. Then there was the onset of a sort of burst of golden emotion, before some other part of the brain cooled things down with some sort of fairly direct reference to the true state of the situation. Odd, that it was not Dad who spoke.

At eleven, I went with my sisters to the undertaker's in West Kilbride, to take a last farewell of my father before the body was sealed up forever in his coffin. Or if not forever, no doubt for long enough. I'm glad I went there. Not only did he retain the calm, noble appearance which I saw in the hospital, when I arrived there less than half an hour after he had died—but it turned out that the actual location, entirely to my surprise, held certain associations for me.

A few years ago, at a couple of successive Christmases, my parents drove out to a church in West Kilbride just before midnight, for the midnight Christmas Mass. They did not much favour their own local incumbent at that time. I went with them, for there was no point in giving offence by flagrantly refusing to play the game. It got it all over with fairly painlessly and quickly, and, besides, it was actually itself a distinctly pleasurable experience.

(After watching a bit on tv about the World Chess Championship, live—Kasparov is pondering his reply to Short's 13.Sd1—I went back through to my parents' room. These are, as far as I can remember, the only sentences I have ever written there.)

It is just that this church is in the same street as the undertaker's, a little bit further up the hill. Where Dad parked then, and where my sister parked today, must be only a few paces apart. I dare say the three of us took those steps. When we drove away years ago, we, in fact, must have passed that small, cramped place at the end of the street where, a few years in the future, within six months of each other, each body would eventually lie. If life lasted forever, what would it be worth? Well, perhaps, it might have been nice to find out by direct experience. But what good is it, what sense does it make to ask: if we were all utterly different, what would we be like? It would be a different sort of universe, unimaginable in the way it was propelled forward, and it is only here, in the actual one, that we are to find our answers, or not at all.

From West Prussia to West Kilbride. Is that a sort of progress? I touched his head a few times and said good-bye. I am still in their room. In a couple of hours, at seven, he will be brought to the church by the edge of the sea here, as Mum was on a strange, windy dark night six months ago. When I was beside him, I had a few of his things in my pocket—in the inside pocket of one of the anoraks which he himself had lately been wearing. They included the tiny photograph of him, and the late one of Mum. At the top of the hill, there was a school, with many children playing in it. Of course. There always are. And I found something else too, not many minutes ago.

When I was last here, Dad asked me if I had seen a throat-spray lying about anywhere. He had misplaced it. Of course I hadn't. But it was not an emergency. At the very least, he had another one. I thought no more about it. Time without number he used to ask Mum if she knew where something was—even when there was not the least likelihood that anyone but him could possibly know it.

But, a while back, I was sitting in his chair, writing. When I got up to talk to someone who had just come in, I dropped the pencil I was holding. Searching for it later, I eventually thought to look down the side of the cushion of the chair I was sitting in—Dad's armchair, the only chair in the room. I found it there. I also found the missing spray. For a terrible moment, I wondered whether the loss of this might have had some serious significance; but I am sure he had another, not to mention all the various different pills and medicaments. So, the loss was presumably as casual as the rediscovery.

(4.43–14th September)

114

Wednesday morning. The body was brought into the church last evening. There were four other people there whom I talked to. One whom I had not seen for years, a German nun; and three whom I had not seen since Mum's funeral in March. Dad's funeral starts later this morning, at 10 o'clock. Last night, I slept downstairs in their bed, for the first time in my life. It worries me that I slept so well.

Another of these endless, free mail-shots arrived for Mum yesterday, trying to sell her something. Six of the novels of Thomas Hardy, no less—in exquisite illustrated volumes. It's more or less the sort of thing he used to write about himself. And an offer along with it, to have your name put forward for a prize draw.

'Would you like £10,000 to spend on travel, books or the time of your life?' A complex and interesting question; rarely likely to be answered 'No'. £10,000 on books? What books exactly were you thinking of buying? And couldn't you manage to have travel, books *and* the time of your life for that sort of money? 'Think what you could do with £10,000.' The Folio Society takes great pleasure in inviting Mrs M. Kuppner to accept, absolutely *FREE*, etc. Your prize draw number: 00255934. Space for signature is provided. She had very distinctive handwriting, instantly recognizable; the letters were well-formed but extremely small. Dear Reader: I very much look forward to hearing from you.

I think I know the feeling.

In the mid-afternoon, after it was all over, I went for a walk along the shore, with a choice of islands off in the middle distance. I had the further extent of the promenade pretty well entirely to myself. Going back on an arc, I passed the bus-stop where I had stood those few months ago, with a small, battery-driven fan in my pocket, waiting for the bus which would take me to see my mother, still alive. It was the stop one up from where I had waited when going to see Dad. Then I turned and walked along a street which I discovered—it has a curiously inconspicuous opening onto the coast road—just after Mum had died. I have now walked up that street only twice in my life. A schoolgirl passed me, intent on her very precise way to somewhere, and a couple of distinct and separate old ladies.

I passed the football pitch which some of the family visited, once, while a match was in progress. I forget many of the details entirely. But all this time, I was reliving those ordinary days, those mornings and afternoons, so difficult to remember because what filled them was an ordinary happiness, almost absent of distinguishing characteristics—or other emotions which in retrospect turn into an ordinary happiness. This, I trust, shall always be mine. (*The rest is not worth it.*)

115

Thursday morning. So. That is it then. This time last week, Dad was still laughing and joking. And complaining too, of course. Well, actually, at exactly this time of day, he will probably still have been in bed, snoozing or thinking or sleeping. In the late evening, he felt rather bad, and a doctor was called out to visit him. He was still joking then—about someone who had unexpectedly died while recently in hospital, so far as I can quite decipher what my elder sister told me about it. He had been eating pickled herring, and so the heart condition was confused by the possibility of mere indigestion. The day before that, on the Wednesday, a week before he was buried, he had been talking to his other daughter on the phone. He had said that he thought he might have another year left. Which means, mainly, that he did not expect to die quite yet, thanks very much. He also said that, after what happened to May next door (the neighbour who died only three or so weeks ago: Dad was on the phone when her sister called to tell us this), he was just going to spend his money as he needed to, and let the future look after itself.

As everyone was leaving, I turned and went back to the still open grave, which now has two virtually identical coffins in it, and dropped in one or two utterly trivial things. I wish I could have thought of something better or more fitting. Maybe even the cassette which is playing in this room right now. (Mum bought it many years ago, when collecting cassettes was a thing just starting up. It's Schubert's 4th Symphony; with the 5th on the other side. I last played it not long after her own death.)

Not long before last Christmas, Mum gave me £40—it's more than the return train fare from Glasgow to Aberdeen, for instance—for me to get myself something worthwhile. I got a very good pair of shoes at a sale for half that price, durable black ones, and the rest of the money drifted away in general living costs. These shoes, of course, I wore at her funeral. And then at Dad's too, for I just happened to be wearing them again when I came down here last Friday.

The inadequacy of the gesture comes close to making me feel ashamed now; but I could think of nothing better than to cut off the end of one of the shoe-laces. And it was planned too; I did it in advance. After all, it was a part of her gift, which she had looked at and approved. For some reason, I liked the idea of that fragment being in there with them, while the rest of the shoes were continuing to be dragged purposively about in the world above. I also took a couple of nails from a wall in their bedroom; small nails, on which pictures which were familiar to them from almost every day of their lives used to hang, and I dropped them in too. Actually, a third nail is still in the pocket of the suit I was wearing—a black suit which I had also worn in March. Only now did I learn that it had once belonged to my late Uncle Joseph—the music ends—who died about 1977, and whom I never met, although I wore a blue trench-coat which I know had been his on numerous occasions in the late 70s and early 80s. In 1978 I was very ill for a while, the illest I have ever been I suppose (I assume it was just some sort of genuine, virulent flu—a dreadful experience which lasted for weeks; my Auntie Peggy, then still in Glasgow, looked after me well; the doctor could not even put a half reasonable name to it), and at some point near the start of that, when I was still hoping it would go away, I somehow got a red paint-mark, fortunately not too bright, on one of the sleeves. So: a life of endless drama, obviously.

I suppose I just have to run the risk of sounding like some sort of sentimental litter-lout emptying his pockets wholesale and at random into the grave, but there was something else too. I dropped

in a black pen which ran out of ink a day or two ago. I had found
it a while back, I suppose since Mum's death, in Queen's Crescent,
a leisurely walk of a couple of minutes from the house where I was
born, and where I lived for nearly the first seventeen years of my
life. I wrote much of this very work with it. And though death has
a terrible capacity for—no. Death has a terrible capacity for sim-
plifying people. I mean, that memory can make them so much
simpler than what they really were.

(9.36 am–16th September)

116

I remember, when we were still in West Princes Street—I must have been about fifteen, I suppose—my brother telling me that Beethoven's Fifth Symphony was on the radio that evening. So we must already have known about it and known something about music—in my own case chiefly perhaps from the twenty or thirty records that Mum and Dad had somehow managed to purchase in those particularly straitened years. Even now, the Hungarian/Slavonic Dances take me instantly back to that time, to that atmosphere: the white fireplace, the fringed cushions inset into the suite of furniture, the cluster of spires seen from the kitchen window.

We listened to it, and were highly enthusiastic. This must have led us on to his other symphonies, including the Ninth, the Choral. Not long ago my mother told me that I sometimes used to come down from my room in Barra Street (where we lived from 1967 to 1975) singing something like the opening chorus of the finale of the Ninth; and she just assumed that it was something I must have made up out of my own exuberance. (Few have thought it staggeringly accomplished, from a melodic point of view.)

But I don't see how this can quite be right. For I remember that, when I was still in West Princes Street (well, we *all* were), my Uncle

Stephen (whose widow broke down and cried against me as she
was about to leave yesterday) (*I shouldn't really just have slung that
between a couple of brackets like that*) brought an already rather
elderly L.P. which he claimed (and I don't doubt his veracity) had
been immensely prestigious on its first appearance. It was Jascha
Horenstein conducting the Ninth Symphony. Did he leave it
behind when he departed from a holiday with us? (He usually spent
a few weeks with us every year.) Did he send it by post? I just don't
remember.

But I do remember being utterly entranced by the record. I
listened to it at least once a day for two or three weeks. And I have
just looked in the cabinet below the cassette-player one pace to my
right—and the old record is still there! While Mum, in the last
year of her life, was sitting here, which she so often did, listening
to tapes of music, it must always have been docilely lying there, not
worrying that time seemed to have totally forgotten it. Vox PL 10
000. Wilma Lipp; Elisabeth Hoengen; Julius Patzak; Otto Wiener.
Singverein der Gesellschaft der Musikfreunde, Vienna. Pro Musica
Symphony, Vienna. Copyright 1956. My first year at school. I
didn't realize it had just been copyrighted. I carefully replace the
record; while just above it Schubert's Fifth is being played—this
ecstasy of over twenty-five years ago, when Dad was in his fifties,
and Mum was only slightly older than I am now.

As to Vienna: Mum went there a few years ago. She had long
wanted to visit the city. She brought back a couple of similarly
framed pictures, one of which (of the Opera House) she gave me,
and it is at present hanging in my room. The other one, rather by
chance, was hanging in the room where she died, up on the wall
just to her right. It too is hanging in my room now, rejoining its
colleague of a few years back.

But I meant to say that once we gathered in the living room in
Barra Street—certainly Mum, Dad, and the two boys—and we
listened to a broadcast one evening of the Ninth, direct from
somewhere in Germany. This was very unusual. In fact, it was a
unique occasion for us. I think we must have been going to listen
to it upstairs, and they asked us to bring the set down. It was a fairly
heavy valve radio—a Ferguson, I think—which lit up memorably.
However, I have just put on my shoes, since I mean to go out for a
newspaper. The abbreviated lace makes tying it up a little more
awkward than before. That the other bit of it is now beside their

remains, in the impacted earth, is also rather difficult to grasp. Should I be thinking up brilliant puns at just this juncture? We went back yesterday evening, to see how things were. It was, to a degree, very peaceful and beautiful. Nearby lay another opened grave, waiting. (Except, of course, that graves don't wait.)

When I came back from buying the newspaper, I picked up another cassette—this one also of Beethoven's Ninth Symphony. This is an ultra-cheap reissue of a performance which seems to date from 1958—long before, or so I would imagine, I had ever discovered our little stack of records. I bought a couple of them and left one down here. One March afternoon I was playing it—for the first time, I suspect; although it has been here for some years—always vaguely looking forward to reaching the third movement, the *Adagio*; and at one point during the scherzo (176 revs from the end of the side, I notice on the counter of this Hitachi) Dad suddenly came hurrying into the room and said, 'You had better stop playing that. I think she has stopped breathing'.

In disbelief, I went quickly through to the small bedroom. It took a good minute or two, misled by the sounds which her throat was still making, and by attempts to find her pulse or feel the continued expulsion of her breath, before we realized in amazement that he was right. She had stopped breathing. I had left the room about half an hour earlier, after being in and out of it fairly regularly since about five that morning. My sister had taken over, and had left only a couple of minutes before, since Dad had asked the priest to come round, and he had said he would be there at half past three. None of the rest of us was ever to be there when the priest came. (This was his third visit, all arranged by Dad, in a week or so.) He eventually showed up at about five to four, and the whole thing was fairly obviously all part of a day's work for him, which is understandable enough, I suppose.

That cassette lay untouched until last Friday evening, which was the day when Dad himself had died. (He never, strangely enough, got the priest to visit himself; no matter how bad a turn he might have taken.) Late that evening, I put the tape on again. It played on from the very point it had reached on that afternoon six months before. So, later than I had intended to, I heard that slow movement again.

Perhaps I should add, while someone hoovers the hall carpet just beyond, that there was another reason for me putting that pen into the grave too. But it may be impossible for me to give it exactly. On one of the last nights of her life, when Mum had some difficulty falling asleep and used to talk in an at times unpredictable manner (she was sedated, and she did not have the energy needed for long complex sentences anyway) one of the things which she very clearly did manage to say to me was, 'and to write books that people might want to read, that must be interesting'. I noted down pretty well all the remarks of her that I could hear and which I was free to write. I can't really repeat what I said to her then, although I did tell her that as far as I was concerned none of this was ever going to be lost; and part of the reason why I am writing this at all, though I suppose only part of it, is what I said to her then. She looked as if she believed me, and smiled at me in a reassured way.

(11.21 am–16th September)

117

Friday. After a long circuitous walk, chiefly along the seafront, two of us stood at the grave again, somewhere about half past one—exactly a week after I had been wandering through the house, wondering where Dad had got to. Three tributes of flowers to mark his life. There were flowers opposite too, for a mother who had died on the same day. I had noticed that she had been commemorated in the local paper, next to his own intimation. Little empty verbal events to others. Much of the food I brought for him is still in the freezer.

Earlier, on a shaded part of the path by the sea, we had met a woman taking her dog for a walk. The dog was, of all things, an elkhound—still rather a rare breed to see anywhere. But when my parents came down to Largs from Glasgow in 1975, the family dog of course went with them, and that too was an elkhound. Many of these dogs look virtually identical; and this one looked exactly like our old Kuss. It was very old itself. Had it too been in this locality for all those years, without our ever seeing it?

Reluctantly, I am forced to assume that it can't have been some direct descendant of Kuss, the eventual product of some illicit nocturnal ramble. When he got too arthritic and pained, he was taken to the vet. I remember Mum once sadly saying, 'They are so

trusting', as she described to me on my next visit how nonchalantly
he had got down out of the car for the final time just beside the
vet's. All I could have said was that it happened a few years
ago—except that, a few days ago, when looking for some addresses,
I was given Mum's old address book, and there, at the top of the
last page, put there on its own presumably because of its importance, there is the single line of words: '8th October 1980. Kuss put
to sleep.'

So: thirteen years ago next month. That must surely be longer
than his actual life was. About three years before I had my first
book accepted. Not that that made a colossal amount of difference.
Mum was fifty-nine; Dad, sixty-eight. Well: people die at those
ages. But we had a bit beyond twelve years further of them—as
indeed did they, I suppose. If I had been a bit more successful—and
there was room enough for that, I should say—I could have helped
them more. So: as far as I am to blame for the first thing, I am to
blame for the second too. But enough of this—before I say something I might regret about some of the intellectual giants I have
had to deal with. Oops; too late.

(*Since, on second thoughts, this is probably not the right moment for
a virtuoso display of personal spite and rampant small-mindedness, I
have decided, as some sort of mark of confused filial respect, to cut out
a paragraph here. But I shall very likely substantially repeat the contents
somewhere else. Perhaps when I feel less inhibited.*)

I slept in their bed on Tuesday night and Wednesday night. And
what else? I did learn one thing from a German document which
I found and translated with the help of the trusty Langenscheidt
dictionary that Dad insisted we should get during our initial
struggles with the language in the early 60s. I seem to have
temporarily misplaced it somewhere among all the mementoes—
but the most salient detail I can still recall: from 1930 until 1941
(with a break for National Service, I assume) he worked permanently at the Tax Office in Konitz (Chojnice). Then the War
intervened, and threw his life off on a ridiculous tangent, which
produces me writing this at 8.19 of an evening (according to the
watch which they brought me back from Germany about a decade
ago), under a flowery lampshade within the hearing of a ludicrously
heavy but unseen lorry passing by just outside. No: it's me who
hears the lorry, not the other way about. Dad had his *Abitur*,
apparently—according to the German nun who came to the Tues-

day evening service—which I take it entitled him to go to study at a university. Presumably he was forced by family stringencies to pass up the chance. So it was me who went to university instead. But now I am definitely going to say nothing about that.

(8.22–17th September)

(The letter—or rather, my copy of it—was actually secreted among my photocopies concerning the Willox case. It runs:
    'Wegberg, den 20.6.1977.
    Bescheinigung.
    As former Bürgermeister of Hennigsdorf (Krs. Konitz—Westpreussen) I hereby certify that Leo Kuppner, born in Hennigsdorf, was at the Gymnasium in Konitz until June 15.6.1930; and worked as a permanent employee at the Finanzamt in Konitz until his call-up on 8.10.1941. He was enlisted into the German Luftwaffe.

Signed, Josef Grote, etc.' (17.2.1994))

118

Saturday. Dull; overcast. This will be my last full day here for a while. I don't know for how long. My elder sister will drive two of us into Glasgow tomorrow morning—me to my shack; my other sister to the station for the train to Aberdeen.

I happened to have brought with me out of Glasgow University Library a recent book of essays and talks by Karl Popper—*In Search Of A Better World*—which is exactly and blessedly the right thing for present circumstances. I remember first taking an interest in this extremely considerable thinker when we still all of us were living in Barra Street, and an article about him, triggered by a forthcoming paperback book, came out in, of all places, a Sunday colour supplement. I kept it for several years, before giving it to a young woman I loved in (I think) 1979. God knows where it is at the moment, if anywhere. God knows where she is at the moment. During all that time since, I must have visited my parents here in Largs, on what, on over a hundred separate occasions—for usually at least three days per visit. Usually I arrived on a Tuesday, and departed on a Friday—that was certainly the pattern it eventually settled into—for time after time after time. It was only very recently that it started to seem precarious and threatened.

In the afternoon, I was up at the cemetery for the first time by myself since Dad was buried there. I stood at the graveside, reading a few pages of a book (*I still haven't finished it*) that Mum owned. It was by one of her favourite newish authors; who wrote detective novels, the hero of which was a medieval monk. Actually, Dad threw out most of them, along with many other whodunnits that I had brought down for Mum over the years, the fruit of my dredging through a few local Glaswegian secondhand-book shops. But I managed to save a few of them.

A minor bonus of the book I had with me was that its cover was patterned on a religious illumination, so that one vaguely felt that one was handling an appropriately religious text. It probably looked better too, than some lurid, gore-dripping picture would have done. I also had a couple of photographs that I had kept in it for months. One of my younger sister standing beside my mother, who is wearing the PhD gown that her daughter has just earned. In this, taken in the garden, her smile looks staggeringly like the one which I had always remembered as being the unique property of her brother Stephen—to a degree which I failed to observe in life. In the other picture, it is now Dad who is wearing the gown—which he does with the magnificent aplomb with which he always carried off formal attire. Doubtless he it was who took the earlier (or later) shot; as it was obviously my sister who took the later (or earlier) one. Mum stands beside Dad, holding one of the branches of the tree which still grows there, identical branch included, near the living-room window. It has grown quite a way in those ten or so years.

I've been looking at various books today, including a fascinating one about a Japanese inn. I bought this last October, for £1, in King Street, Aberdeen, in easily the dirtiest-looking used-book shop I've ever seen. (It had vanished when next I went looking for it.) I started reading it when Mum was still alive; read quite a few more chapters (I always leave it in Largs) while Dad was still here; and I still have about a third to a quarter of it left to read.

When I bought it, Mum did not yet know that the pain in her back was the result of the spreading cancer. Neither did we, of course. If any doctors knew, they weren't telling. When I next came to Largs after Aberdeen, she mentioned a fairly new pain in her back, which she thought might have been caused by the uncomfortable seats in the car which regularly took her off to hospital for (as it turned out, wholly unavailing) treatment. Within five months she was dead. Another six months brings us to now; those of us who got here. I go back to Glasgow tomorrow, the city where they first met (at the moment) just under half a century ago.

(7.14–18th September)

When I mentioned Catherine Carswell a while back, I think I forgot to add that a strange sort of mausoleum right up in a high back corner of Largs Cemetery, perhaps the single most striking feature there, is inscribed with the name Carswell. Since it's not all that common a name, I suspect there may well be a family connection there (principally with the husband, obviously). Indeed, for all I know, she may well even lie buried within it.

And how could my parents have guessed, fifty years ago, that they would be buried in Largs? Dad would never have heard of the place, off at almost the other end of Europe. Mum would, obviously, have heard of it, and may even have been here by then (though I rather doubt it)—but she would as yet have no important associations with it. We visited here a few times, during day-trips to the coast, when we were children.

(7.43.)

119

So: back in the city where I have mis-spent almost all my over-optimistic existence so far—which I last left, carrying a black pen in my pocket, while my father was still alive. In my room, I ate the last chocolate biscuit from a packet of seven that I must have bought about ten days ago. There was a note on my door, asking me to phone my younger sister when I got back. But that was an old note, stuck to the door for day after day, recording a phone-call from her made less than an hour after I had left for Largs. I am even wearing a brand-new shirt of his; which he liked so little that he had left it lying, entirely unwrapped, in a drawer, possibly for months.

A typically magnificent total of two letters awaited me. One of them was from an editor of a publishing-house, to whom I had written a few days before I left. Did I mention this? I wrote to her about this very work here, even though it wasn't quite here yet, saying that it was more or less finished. Such innocence. I suppose I had better just go on and finish it broadly as I had intended to—if I can remember what that was.

After an hour or so, a sudden thought struck me, and I inspected the letter again. I wanted to see when it was that she had written it. What I saw drew from me a cry of some emotion or other—I am not exactly sure what. The date on the letter is—I almost feel like adding, *of course*—the 10th of September 1993. This is the day when my father died.

That my father should have died while I was writing this of all works is, I suppose, wonderful enough as coincidences go. Now that it has happened, it will be obvious that it was always going to happen; and it will seem, perhaps, that I should have seen that it was just about to happen. But whatever I should or should not have done, and I don't for a moment doubt that there is much I should have done that I neglected to do, this turn of events was almost entirely unanticipated, and utterly uninvited, however inevitable it might seem to the better informed now. I assumed, as usual, that things were just going to go on like this for an ill-defined while longer.

(7.02–19th September)

120

I typed out the first two sections of this very work today, on the same old Adler typewriter that Dad got for me from somewhere—I don't even know that: where he got this typewriter from—over two decades ago. Have I hit these keys a million times yet? Several millions? I want to alter it as little as possible as I type it up; for it is to some extent a diary, and to revise a diary is usually pretty much the same as to pervert it. Still, I noticed little accretions and would-be improvements going in. (Well! It would have been something if I *hadn't* noticed them.) But now, late in the evening, I am rather tired; and it strikes me that this might be as good an opportunity as I can ever reasonably expect for clearing away some of my remaining unprocessed research.

Vamos. The *Evening Times* of 5 November 1929 has on its front page a very striking picture of the external facade of the tenement where the homicidal attack took place. There is a seller of spirituous liquors just beside its close-mouth. I shall here insert a thought which, oddly, occurred to me only today. Although it was then the Fifth of November, now a celebrated occasion for firework displays (well: *the* celebrated occasion, Guy Fawkes Night—I saw a sign in a shop-window today, September the 20th, over six weeks premature, advising the lieges that they now had fireworks in stock),

I don't remember seeing so much as a whisper of this in any of the newspapers of the time. If they were at all numerous, I would surely have noticed *some* of them.

'As nice and quiet a man as you could wish to meet in a lifetime.'

'The last man in the world one would think could be treated in this horrible manner.'

I've forgotten who said this. Presumably the neighbours.

'A comb out of lodging houses throughout the city was carried out by the police in every division,'—three 'out's in one clause: well done that journalist there—'but so far there have been no results.' Which perhaps is just as well. The phrase 'colossally misapplied effort' springs to mind. I suppose you have to do *something*.

Once again, the unnamed woman in the flat below the Willoxes is interviewed. This must have been just about the dramatic high-point, surely, of her entire life. 'As it was, I heard absolutely nothing out of the usual. I cannot understand it.'

Well, neither can I, really. Perhaps the father lay down quietly on the floor of his own accord, as was his normal practice of an evening. Mind you, now that I come to think of it, I don't recall that we are ever told the dead man's height and weight in any source.

'There are usually a few stragglers about the stairs at night, but they are usually young people larking.' One gets a hint that extraneous noises may have been so common that one more or less might very well have got lost in the general melee.

'Poor Mr Willox's son is completely knocked out with grief.' A rare sensitivity in the choice of words there. 'He was very fond of his father.'

Every neighbour was interrogated. All his co-workers at the shipyards too. And, next day, 'Apparently few people in the vicinity were aware of the sudden dramatic development.' The arrest, of course.

And there, perhaps through sheer oversight at the end of a previous long evening, I seem to have completely given up the *Evening Times*. There was another diagram somewhere of the fatal room, this time with the fireplace sited at the exterior wall.

I now turned, unrewardingly, to the *Bulletin And Scots Pictorial*. Could I possibly have looked through the *Evening Times*'s accounts of the trial, and have found absolutely nothing new there worth recording? It does not sound very likely. But, if not, I must quite simply have lost sight of the fact that I still had some work to do on that publication on the following day, whenever that was. Another valuable insight into the working methods of the creative artist, I dare say. Certainly something of a lucky break.

(8.33–20th September)

121

The *Bulletin* need not detain us for long. Let me gallop through my sparse notes from it. The police sometimes had to move the gawping crowd on. The mother of Dr Knowles (the man who killed his wife in Africa, I think) lives in Holborn Street, Aberdeen. ('There's not much to Aberdeen,' my own mother said to me some time last year. 'Union Street; Holborn Street—that's about it.' Terribly unfair, but it means I remember Holborn Street in particular rather fondly.)

Eugene Meechan (31); surfaceman, aged 31. ('Keeping permanent way of railway in order.') Wife keeps a confectioner's/fruiterer's opposite. A shop that sells fruit! Clearly Grove Street was not quite at the bottom rung of the societal ladder.

James Turner said he accompanied Willox when the latter went to get the £2.10.0 from Margaret Duffy. Also, 'His father had given him some money to pay some debtors.'

Unusual generosity. Most people have sufficient trouble in paying their creditors.

Alexander McLeod (30), Caledonia Loan Company, New City Road. Assistant pawnbroker. Had not seen the accused from January 29 to September. Which strongly suggests that he had already seen him before 1929. But it would seem then to have been in September that the precarious financial balance finally tipped over.

Nonchalance fails when the judge passes the death sentence. (The first clear suggestion I remember that he was putting on some sort of act.) Dark-complexioned young man of twenty-two . (Who? Bertie?)

Father left £1. The accumulated riches of a lifetime.

The Advocate-Depute: Willox 'took special pains to prevent two collectors from calling to see his father on the 4th.'

The summing-up lasted seventy minutes, and someone is playing rock music irritatingly loudly in the distance, so that practically all that survives is the monotonous thumpthumpthump of the beat.

And that's the *Bulletin*. I did return to the library on the Saturday for a last bout of research, however; so I'll go on now to the *Evening News*. That of course, though no one yet knew it, was the last Saturday of my father's life. But I will still talk to him on the phone the next Tuesday.

(8.47–20th September)

122

Right. Let's get on with it. The *Evening News*.
Friday, 20 September 1929—exactly sixty-four years ago today.
'Greenock Woman Married as a Man in a Roman Catholic
Church.' Always the same old story. I believe Inverclyde Hospital
is just outside the Greenock city boundary.

'Warder felled by sledgehammer in Barlinnie.'

'Airman's head cut off. (It's dark—but I can hear a plane right
now.) Extraordinary mid-air accident.'

October 3rd. 'BBC accused. Is television being held up? Baird's
limited facilities.'

October 29th. 'Billions lost. Fortunes go in Wall Street Panic.
Wall Street's Dark Day.' Now you come to mention it—I suppose
you wouldn't expect the Wall Street Crash to impinge very keenly
on Grove Street, but there seems to have been very little mention
of it in any of the papers I looked through. I must have skipped
more than I thought I was doing.

'Mysterious Murder of Commissionaire in Glasgow. Police all-
night search for assailant. And I can still hear that plane. Is it a
helicopter, perhaps?'

'Where Mr Willox has lived for a period of eight years.'

'Shortly before 10 o'clock.' A neighbour at the same time

phoned for an ambulance. The house was noted for its calm. We never heard a sound, not us. So I took all these notes, and covered all these pages, and I had seen Dad alive for the last time, even though he was still living as I added line to line. If he had asked me to go back sooner, I would have gone back sooner. Would that have made a difference? I don't know. Everything makes some difference. Proceed.

'It is a coincidence that the constable on duty at the door of the house was the officer summoned there in January last when Mrs Willox died with tragic suddenness of a heart attack.' Heart problems. Here, there, and everywhere. But particularly here. (*Beats me.*)

It's not quite clear to me why they summoned a police officer in January at all. What could he do? Or was it just the hopeless confusion of the moment? One minute, everything fairly normal; and the next, the mother attacked from where, from within, why, by something which she bafflingly could not cope with? But I do also seem to recall some talk of a more extended ailment. Was it really one sudden event, completely altering the surviving lives for the worse?

A woman in Edinburgh is celebrating her 101st birthday.

6 Germans have died in an air-crash in Croydon.

I feel I have had enough of this for today.

(9.06–20th September)

123

T his morning, a rather heavily pregnant young woman was standing talking to another woman of about the same age just outside my front door. Some people have a really dreadful sense of timing. However, back to the mopping-up operation.

'Did not indicate that he fully realized the gravity of the charges.' Willox at the committal proceedings. He had gone to the Northern Police Office that very evening at 4 o'clock. Three hours later, he was charged.

'Young Willox is described as an apprentice marine engineer, but has been unemployed for over a year.' Of course, if literally true, this would go back to some months before the mother's death.

On the next day, a photograph of the celebrated £5 note. Royal Bank of Scotland. And on the next day, her tears were audible as she went down the stairway into the street. ('Oh Bertie!') The fiver had been in the possession of a man employed to play the clarinet at the Darlington Music Hall. For such is life.

On the 20th, a bizarre cartoon. Trotsky is looking into a crystal ball, and he says, 'I see a dark and deadly shock lying ahead of you'. Behind him, an energetic youth, blithely labelled 'Common Sense', is about to smash him over the head I forget what with—it may even have been a sledgehammer. I didn't take a precise note, but it's obviously just the sort of thing that common sense is forever doing: battering people's heads in. Common Sense is saying, 'I see a dark and deadly shock lying behind you—and anybody like you'. Given how Trotsky eventually died, over a decade later—and I feel I should say that I have not the slightest admiration for the man myself—this shows, whatever it also shows, remarkable powers of clairvoyance. 34 people lost in a tidal wave.

'A fairly large piece of meat with a bone in the centre.'

McKinney had been owed 22 shillings (*22 shillings! The mysterious* second payment *in my bankbook*!) when she stopped credit in April 1929. She was paid in full in June. Willox jnr bought a newspaper devoted to racing every day. This was not likely to be a money-saving venture. 'Did he ever say anything as to why he bought that particular paper?'—'No. I had a good idea what he bought it for.' Isabella is a rather unfriendly witness; but I'm surprised that remark was allowed through unimpeded. 'And when she left at 6.25 pm, he was at the counter, with his arms folded, waiting to be served.' A slightly unnatural attitude, perhaps?

Onto the very last full sheet of notes. The heart leaps.

Detective Stewart was in the box for almost six hours. He assumed that the father had just been hanging up his coat, the kitchen door then being shut. Then a plea from the heart of the cross-examined Dr Campbell: 'Please let me answer in my own way; I am letting you put your questions in your own way.' (As if a witness could stop him!) Later, when Mr Black, KC, says to him, 'I am asking you to make a hypothesis,'—this has to do with the degree of blood-staining found on Willox's clothes, if I remember rightly—the Doctor replies, 'They are dangerous things in a murder trial'.

'With folded arms and head thrown back.' 'One of the most engrossing murder trials in the history of Glasgow High Court.' And beneath this, at the bottom of column 1, an advert for Skerry's College. This was a private college in Bath Street, very close to Buchanan Street, and it was still going in the 1960s, although it closed soon afterwards. It was there that Dad sent his eldest son and daughter, in the early-mid 60s, to try to get them to learn German. It was not taught in our schools, and he would never speak German to us himself. Indeed, even when we stumblingly tried out on him what we had learned, he would as often as not lose patience with our ineptnesses, and would sometimes even resort to ridicule.

Still, he paid out some of his hard-earned cash in fees for us at
that college. We went there for two or three years, I think—twice
a week. Our teacher was an attractive young woman with very long
red fingernails (almost certainly her own natural ones) and I used
to fantasize wonderfully about her on very many adolescent mornings. We never quite got to the end of our set textbooks before we
left. And Dad was fairly scathing when he discovered that we had
not been taught the 'Ihr' forms of verbs—the plurals of the informal
'du'. What will it have amounted to? One hour, from 5 to 6, on a
good few dozen evenings? Ah well. At least I can now directly tell
what most of Schubert's songs are about.

'And then steps into the kitchen for his evening meal.' One
more evening meal. Whereabout is he?

It seems the speech for the defence was not entirely audible from
the press seats. This may explain rather a lot about the coverage it
got. Perhaps people just couldn't hear for much of the time.

'The amazingly calm demeanour.' He folded his arms for the first
time on hearing the verdict. 'In a voice shaking with emotion.'

(5.20–21st September)

124

On to the Appeal. 'He (the Lord Advocate) was not quite sure in his own mind what the actual objections to the judge's charge really were.' 'For six months prior to the 4th of November 1929, the accused was guilty of gross dishonesty in connection with the money affairs of his father.'

Well: that takes care of the Appeal. No point in overdoing it. And then, in a fit of diligence, I thought it would be as well to round things off by inspecting one of the Sunday newspapers. So I sent a librarian off to collect the *Sunday Post* of that era. She returned with the news that that production did not commence publication until the 1940s—which surprised me, for I rather supposed it had been a part of Scottish life for ever—but she brought along with her the *Sunday Mail*, in case I might want to look at that instead. So, quite contrary to my expectations, I found myself scrutinizing the *Sunday Mail*.

'In conversation with several public men and women, and with officials connected with the case, the *Sunday Mail* representative found a unanimous feeling of sympathy towards the accused.' Unanimous! This is from Dec 22, after the trial and verdict, and the surprise continues.

'It is stated that the lad's home life was not of the happiest, and that as a boy he was subjected to considerable neglect, not knowing the parental care and affection which is every child's birthright.' (And, in the absence of which, it becomes a reasonable response to bump off your father?) 'His father, of course, was absent on war service for some years.'

The treacherous passive! By whom was this stated? By someone who knew what he was talking about? What might or might not lie behind these tight-lipped forays into criticism? It might be just about anything. Anything from the more or less formal special pleadings of defence agents trying to get a death sentence commuted, to a coded allusion to some considerable, unrevealed domestic scandal. Or anything in between. But one does get a very discernible suggestion that Mrs Willox did not look after Robert jnr quite as she ought to have done, while Dad was away fighting.

'Domestic life not of the happiest'? 'Subjected to considerable neglect'? Deprived of parental care and affection? What exactly is this? Mere callousness? Hard-heartedness? Some form of abuse? Who can tell now? Anyway, on the 29th of December a Leith man, William Mitchell, who was 52, awoke his son one morning by the faint sounds of his groaning. He had just cut his throat. His wife had died very recently, obviously far too young.

Then on January the 19th, which my parents again lived through separately, not yet knowing it was their elder son's birthday, we return to the same charge: 'It has been pointed out too that the boyhood of Willox was not a happy one, and that his life, especially during the war, when his father was in the army, was of a sordid nature.'

Sordid? And pointed out by whom? Or, for that matter, *to* whom? Was the *Sunday Mail* reporter the sole recipient of these disclosures? But here there is at least a tiny step forward towards explicitness. Life was sordid, especially when alone with Mum. It looks as if, in some way, she was incapable of acting as a good parent. Perhaps, on a moral level, this was to some extent a marriage of like with like.

And one which produced like? 'Willox has lately taken to grumbling and displaying bad temper. He objects to nearly every meal that is served him, stating that the food provided is not good enough. On one occasion he deliberately upset his dinner, demanding in a loud voice to know, "What's meant by giving trash like that to a fellow who's going to be hanged"?'

On the other hand, it would be understandable if your nerves were a little on edge. And the fellow was not hanged anyway. I wonder what ever happened to him? Too young, apparently; with a hint that the father only got what was coming to him. I am not particularly eager to spend any more time here with this rare collection. But there is one ponderable final detail. The wrongly convicted, it is often said, are noteworthy for the vociferousness and unremitting nature of their protests that they are innocent. It's not a sufficient condition, but it is usually held to be a necessary one. Of Willox, however, we learn that 'for a few days' after the trial, he professed innocence. But this did not last, as such. 'Now, however, he does not have anything to say about it.'

(6.07–21st September)

125

I now have something of the same feeling, believe me. I can just about recall that there were other things I had certainly intended to do, and other things that I was once fairly eager to discuss. But that was in another world at another time.

I think I'll keep back the strange affair of Mrs Tannock, which I discovered in the background of the present case. I'm pretty sure I promised to end this work with a discussion of this bizarre episode; but to investigate adequately such mysterious events might well turn out to require a commitment which at the moment is simply not there for me to give. Some other time, perhaps. My plans have been rather scattered by the intervention of real life.

I do recall once sort of intending to discuss the recent appalling case of the Ukrainian mass-murderer, Andrei Chikatilo—which I read with what I suppose may be called a nervous serenity, in Largs a few weeks ago, while looking after my father; which I had certainly assumed I would still be doing well beyond now. This Chikatilo murdered over forty people—usually female. The book about him which I was reading then didn't have time or space even for the briefest mention of many of the murders, which at times were waved by in crowds. It shows once again that human beings can get used to just about anything. By the end, he was going out to kill any likely candidate that he might next meet, to put a real human being to death, pretty well as others might go out to hear an exciting concert, or collect rare train numbers. One of his own preferred pastimes—and I suppose the question 'Why couldn't you bring yourself to say it?' must worry me more than the question 'Why did you say it?'—was to walk away from the scene of the crime, nibbling on a ripped-out uterus. 'They're so springy,' was, I think, the remark he made, and I doubt if I am mis-remembering it. I don't think I'll bother with the other details, if it's all the same to you. Take a left turn, and you go home to familiar faces. Take a right turn, and you meet a diffident, inoffensive-looking man who strikes up a casual conversation with you. But a single movement can take you out of normality.

He was in fact a leading suspect for the very first of his murders; and it is difficult to see how any even half-competent investigation would not have brought the charge to his door—which, I seem to recall, is where a trail of blood actually led. But a likelier candidate came painlessly to hand, so they nabbed him instead and over fifty other people were now no longer safely walking about. Eventually, the team of supposedly top-level, razor-sharp detectives who were gathered together and assigned to this case, which they pursued literally for years, got to the stage of just waiting for another murder to turn up, in the hope that it might be the one that furnished them with a fresh and vital clue. Finally, this did happen—but not before other lives had been ended.

This is not quite how one envisages the best detective work as being conducted. Perhaps in one's naïvety one supposes that the main point is to *prevent* any further such incidents—in the time-worn tag, to catch them before they strike again. All in all, this was a rather weird book, in that about half of it was written from the standpoint of the detective leading the hunt, presented as being an almost unique genius. At first one docilely took the author's word for this—until at last it dawned on one that, good man though he clearly was, and surrounded though he was by corruption and incompetence, he was not exactly covering himself in glory as regards tracking down a killer who was actually number nine (I think it was that) on the list of suspects long before the final stages. Had he chosen to go through this list comprehensively, he would surely have unearthed the giveaway documentation which linked their man so shriekingly with the very first murder of all—and much trouble and bloodshed might well have been avoided. Or perhaps not—but this obvious piece of procedure was not even tried, as far as I could see. However, I have quite possibly forgotten many of the most salient details.

It does remind me, however, of what I thought was a prize-winning example of official obtuseness that I once read of in a casually acquired cheap (50p) paperback of modern continental European crimes a couple of years ago. As I can best recall, but the actual book must still be in this room somewhere, probably up there. I'll try to search it out tonight, and perhaps write about it in more assured detail tomorrow. 'If,' as my aunt so often used to say, 'I'm spared.'

(8.32–21st September)

126

The new phone book was delivered today. I wonder how long it'll be before someone makes off with it. The last time I saw Dad, one of the things he asked me to do was to see if I could bring a more up-to-date Glasgow city telephone directory with me next time. Next time. His own copy was from 1982, I think. There are one or two distinctly more recent copies lying about in our hall, and I very nearly did end up carrying one of them down with me—but I had just too much to carry already, so I thought, in all my innocence, well, that one will have to wait, that's all.

Still, sometimes when I pass a call-box in the evening, and it is rarely and invitingly empty, I have the occasional, familiar impulse, not yet drained out of me, to go in and ring Mum up, to find out how things are with her, what things are happening at home, whether she feels she is improving. But then I remember: no number in the known world will be of any use to you for that here, son. And this evening there was a call at the flat, and for an instant I thought—oh, that may well be Dad, wanting to know when I will next be coming back down there, to help him out. But instead it was only (my 'only') the wife of the man in room 5, who works in Glasgow but has a house of his own in Edinburgh as far as I have ever been able to gather, to which he disappears on holidays, weekends and so forth. That, to me, rather peculiar arrangement has been going on for years now—but it's really none of my business, is it?

But then, what is? I found that book I was talking about yesterday evening, and I've re-read the particular account in question. It was of a series of murderous attacks in Amiens in the early 1980s. 1983, in fact; more recent than Dad's telephone book. What happened? First of all a girl was attacked by a knife-wielding maniac next to her home, which was near the main railway station. The blade struck a holy medal round her neck, and the knife broke. She was remarkably little hurt by what could just as easily have been a lethal attack. She was wearing jeans and tennis shoes, and her hair was in a short blonde cut.

A few days later, much the same happened to another girl. Well, one could almost say, to much the same girl. She was wearing jeans, a short jacket, and tennis shoes; and her hair was blonde and cropped. She was attacked near the main railway-station by a knife-wielding maniac. She was also, as things turned out, a black-belt judoka! So, when the berserk assailant lunged at her, she automatically responded in judo mode, just as she had been trained to—and he landed painfully on his face on the paving-stones. All right so far.

At this point, she reacted in a way that is so endearing that one again feels it should just not even be physically possible for maniacs to torment such people. Horrorstruck by what had happened and by what she had done, she stood rooted to the root, staring open-mouthed at the prone figure who had just tried to murder her. He, of course, was very soon on his feet again, and back on the right tracks in no time. She too was stabbed—but, mercifully, some passers-by came onto the scene at this crucial point, and the assailant fled.

Five days later, a woman, who was standing right at her own door beside her latest shopping, fumbling for an elusive key, suddenly felt herself consumed with pain. He was stabbing her. Not even afraid yet, she thought 'Why, but he's killing me!' and faded into unconsciousness. Her husband, investigating the noise, opened the door and found her. She too survived. They lived near the train station. She was wearing jeans and trainers, and she had short blonde hair.

Can you, by any chance, spot any sort of pattern emerging in all this? No; of course you can't. It's all a complete mystery, isn't it? Perhaps I have been meanly highlighting the crucial details, so much more easily identified in calm, unhurried hindsight—but I would have thought that anyone trained to look for patterns should certainly have figured something out by now. Then, shortly afterwards, a schoolgirl who had missed her train—a set of circumstances not designed for any great security—was also attacked by a knife-wielding maniac. Alas, the bizarre resilience which the previous victims showed, which threatened to divert the real horror into some sort of allegory or farce, at last broke down here. This girl died.

Now, however, there was a breakthrough in the case. And not before time, unless perhaps you were expecting to hear that the fourth victim was a redhead in high heels and a ballgown. In fact, her hair was short and blonde, and she was wearing jeans and trainers. And some laser-like mind with the rank of Inspector sniffed out the beginnings of a clue here. A public appeal was launched; a restaurateur near the station knew of a man who had used to go there with just such a female, but who was now doing so alone; and the whole thing was cleared up before you could say pigtails.

I hope it is not just wisdom after the event to point out that that appeal could well have been made at least one attack earlier, without preternatural powers of detection having been required. In which case, there would probably be one more woman in her twenties—by all means extend to suit—in the world today, who instead is nowhere. Except that even 'to be nowhere' is more than she can hope for now. By the way, the very next case in the book in question features one of the most astonishing slices of sheer good luck in detection that I have ever heard of.

In it figures a young man who preyed on old women's modest home savings, and who had developed a staggeringly simple but ingenious way of getting into their flats, even when the city (Berlin) had been worked up into a state of very jumpy alert. (He used, latterly at least, a novelty American tin badge which said 'New York. FBI. Special Agent', claimed to be an FBI agent sent over specially to help with tracking down the fiendishly clever 'Doorbell Killer'—perhaps a fair description of himself—and was habitually let into the flat. Of course, all sorts of unexpected agencies were working in post-War West Berlin.)

A sales receipt was found in the house of the most recent victim. She herself was known to the staff of the shop in question, who were able to say that she definitely had not been there on the date given on the slip. Furthermore, an assistant was able to remember who it was that had made the purchase there receipted. And, as if that wasn't enough, she was even able to give the police his name! For, when he had taken out his wallet, to pay, there had by sheer accident dropped onto the counter his personal identity card. The assistant, not necessarily from motives of mere politeness, picked it up and handed it back to him. As she did so, she just happened to notice his name, which she might easily have missed; and, since it was an unusual name, she could still remember it. For the record, it was Waldemar Stepinski.

Rather surprisingly, there were no fewer than *nine* Waldemar Stepinskis listed as being resident in West Berlin. They managed to pick their way through to the right one. I would imagine that the other eight must have felt rather aggrieved by such an unwelcome coincidence. Also, perhaps, by the discovery that so many other impostors were masquerading under their name. Such little pockets of discrete resentment scattered loosely across Berlin.

(8.46–22nd September)

At which point I am suddenly brought face to face with the fact that my writing of this work is virtually complete—or, if not that, then at least virtually over. I would surely be better off writing about my own family and friends than about this pretty dreadful lot. Did I ever even ask, for instance, what was happening on November the 4th 1929 to a seventeen year-old who had recently entered his final year at Konitz *Gymnasium*? Or to an eight year-old who, I presume, was sitting down to tea again with her family just across the road from the biggest Museum in Glasgow? I don't think so.

How could I have foreseen it? I have written hundreds of things. I thought perhaps there was *already*, right at the outset, a bit too much father–son resonance about it all. I never thought there would get to be more. I was buying food for him a fortnight ago. He never once discussed his own father's character with me; although from others I have heard the phrase 'a bit of a bastard' offered as a fair summary of his views on that subject.

Of his mother, he said only—as far as I could gather, for, again, he never once talked of her character to me—that she was an angel. I suppose this means she was a decent, good woman, after the fashion of decent, good women. It would be appalling cupidity to ask for more. But angels are not real things—*pace* the many hundreds of millions of human beings who think otherwise. What is more interesting is real goodness rather than the idealization of virtues. When my mother was dying, I saw so many fine qualities in her which I fear I had at best only glimpsed before. I was not imagining them: they were real qualities, real responses called out by an extreme situation. I saw very clearly what I hoped I could claim had produced my own character. We all have our hopes, I dare say.

A few days before she died, I was keeping her company late at night, sitting reading in the armchair in the corner while she dozed on the sofa. It was very late—almost certainly after midnight. 'Now, don't feel you have to go' she would say when she first settled down to try to sleep—an indirect request, meaning, I would like you to stay. Often she slept very fitfully; and this time she soon woke up again, and seemed to want to take off the crocheted woollen shawl that she used to protect herself with against the chill of the night. She had stitched it herself, years before, the routine labour of a succession of ordinary days. It used up the spare wool, and doubtless the vague future would find something worthwhile to do with the finished product. It is here in this room with me now.

I tried to stop her, believing she had no coherent and useful plan in mind, but she was insistent that I take the covering off her. Then she instructed me—with some difficulty, but we worked it out—to put the shawl on the floor and fold it over diagonally. Then she asked me to put it up round her shoulders, and to help her sit up straight. This I did. Then she said, with a wonderful attempt at normal animation, 'Right. Let's hear some music now.' So I switched on the cassette recorder which stood on the ledge in an alcove at my left shoulder, and it continued to play from where it had left off some considerable time ago.

As it happened, it contained a cassette of Schubert piano music. It played a full movement. (D960. The third movement.) She faded a little, but tried very hard to stay alert. Then, when the piece was over, I stopped the tape. Pleased to have managed something so normal, she said: 'Right—now let's try to get to sleep', and she settled back for the night. I still have the tape too, of course. I thought I would play it over and over again, but the truth is I have never been able to touch it since. It's as if I don't deserve to move it; or it's too important and precious to be moved; or that only some other astonishing or virtually transcendent moment will deserve to have that music playing in it again. I want it to stay exactly as it was then. (*No. I have listened to it again recently.*) Anything that I can keep the same, I will keep the same. The rest will just have to do its best, I suppose.

Well; that's that. I'm not going to try to add to this.

(7.07–23rd September)